Unconditional LOVE

A JOURNEY OF *love* NOVEL

NEW YORK TIMES & *USA TODAY* BESTSELLING AUTHOR

KELLY ELLIOTT

Unconditional LOVE

A JOURNEY OF *love* NOVEL

PREQUEL
Michael/Clark

I WATCHED AS NIKKI drove away in her red Mustang convertible with her two best friends. As she lifted her hand and waved, I shook my head and tried to smile. I was still a bit upset she chose to go to the coast with her friends rather than my parents' place in New Mexico with me. I stood there until the red car was no longer in my sight.

I turned and made my way back into the frat house. "Damn Williams, I can't believe you're letting your girl go to the coast with her hotter-than-hell friends. Three blonde hot chicks at the beach like that—I don't know," said Rob, the resident man-whore, as he raised his eyebrows. "You want to go get some ass tonight now that you're girlfriend-free for a bit?"

I shook my head and laughed. "Damn, Rob. You ever get tired of sleeping with a different girl all the time? Don't you want to just settle down with one?"

He looked at me like I was nuts. "You're kidding, right? Dude, you've got money, you've got the looks…you could be hooking up night after night."

I raised my hands as I started to walk by him and head to the staircase. "Thanks, but no thanks. I'm perfectly happy with Nikki."

I heard him utter something about never being with just one girl as I made my way upstairs. I opened the door that led to my bedroom. I was going to be getting a new roommate next semester. His name was Scott and we met once. Seemed like a nice guy and someone I would for sure get along with. Country boy and liked to shoot.

I collapsed onto the bed and let out a sigh. I couldn't shake the uneasy feeling I had in the pit of my stomach. Was I jealous about Nikki leaving for a week and hanging with her friends? Nah, I trusted her just like she trusted me. I would never think of even looking at another girl. I loved her and planned on asking her to marry me this Christmas. She was the perfect girl to marry. My parents liked her. She had a good head on her shoulders and I knew I could trust her. It was a perfect match.

The next few days passed by and I somehow managed to keep myself busy and not think about Nikki. I had gone for a run and was exhausted, so I headed up to my room.

As I closed my eyes to drift off to sleep, I dreamed of a brunette with shoulder-length hair, walking along the beach. As I walked up to her, she turned around. Just as I was about to see her face, I woke up.

"Michael, dude…wake up. Come on man, you've been holed up in this room for the last week. Come play volleyball with us. Nikki's coming back tomorrow, so snap the hell out of it."

I looked up and saw my older brother Tristan standing over me, throwing a volleyball up in the air. I looked around for a second and ran my hand through my hair. *What in the hell? Why am I dreaming about a brunette girl?* I smiled and said, "Tell me again why I pledged to the same frat house as you?"

He smiled and said, "'Cause I promised Mom I'd look after your pansy ass."

I jumped up and snatched the ball out of his hands and took off running. I was surprised I hadn't busted my ass running down the stairs I was moving so fast.

"Bastard!" Tristan called out from behind me.

After four games, all of which my team won, Tristan walked up to me while nodding his head. "I think you need to be on my team, little brother."

I threw my head back and laughed. "You had your chance and you picked poorly."

I was about to start yelling out for the next game to start when I got a glimpse of Mr. and Mrs. Russell. *Why are Nikki's parents here?*

I smiled as I walked up to them and held out my hand to shake Nikki's father's hand. One look at Nikki's mother and I knew she had been crying. When I turned and looked at Mr. Russell my heart started pounding in my chest.

"Michael, may we please go inside and talk to you?" Mr. Russell asked.

"What's wrong? Is Nikki okay? Did she get hurt down at the coast? I haven't heard from her all day but I figured they were just having fun before they left tomorrow."

"Michael, let's head on inside so we can talk in private," Nikki's father said again. Tristan walked up next to me and said, "Mr. and Mrs. Russell, is everything okay?"

I balled up my fists and the first thing I thought of was that some asshole hurt my girl. I was going to kill whoever it was.

"Please, just tell me what's going on?" I pleaded.

Mr. Russell looked over at Tristan and said, "Tristan, I really think we need to move this inside."

"Tell me!" I screamed out.

Mrs. Russell jumped and then began crying. My heart was beating faster and harder. I could hear it pounding in my ears.

Mr. Russell shook his head and said, "Okay, Michael. Nikki was in a car accident today about fifty miles outside of Austin."

I shook my head. "No, that's impossible, she's not coming back until tomorrow."

Mr. Russell cleared his throat and swallowed hard. "She called us last night and said she was coming home a day early to surprise you. They left early this morning so that she could be here by noon."

I grabbed my cell out of my back pocket and looked at the time. It was almost six.

"What? She's coming home early?" I asked. I felt Tristan put his hand on my shoulder.

Mrs. Russell began crying harder.

"What in the hell is going on? Where is Nikki?" I shouted.

Mr. Russell looked down and then looked back up. His eyes met mine and I felt as if I couldn't get air in when I saw the tears in his eyes.

"Nikki was in a car accident earlier today, Michael. A drunk driver hit her car going over ninety miles an hour and all three girls...they all..." his voice trailed off and I felt sick to my stomach.

Please don't say she died. Please God no. Please don't say she died.

Mr. Russell wiped the tears from his face and took a deep breath as he looked me in the eyes again.

"Our Nikki is gone, Michael. She and the girls all died instantly."

I started to take a few steps backward.

"No." I shook my head. "No. She can't...she would never leave me...no. God, please no!" I screamed out. I felt my legs give out and my knees hit the ground.

Tristan was next to me trying to help me stand up. All I could hear was Mrs. Russell crying and Nikki's father attempting to comfort her. I looked at Tristan. "No...she's my whole world, Tristan...she's my whole world." I broke down crying as my brother quickly ushered me back inside and up to his room, the whole time telling me everything was going to be okay.

Nothing would ever again be okay. I sat down on my brother's bed and looked up at him. "I lost the one thing I lived for. I have nothing left to live for. Nothing."

* * *

I walked out of the restroom and ran my hand through my hair as I smiled. The blonde I'd just fucked walked out right behind me. "Lark, please tell me we can make that a daily thing."

I smiled as I kept walking toward the bar. It was still hard for me to get used to people calling me Lark instead of Michael. After Nikki's death I vowed to never let another woman say my name when I fucked them. So I started going by my middle name. "Sorry darling. I'm not interested in a relationship."

She grabbed my arm and pulled me to a stop. She looked around and then looked back at me and licked her lips. "I've never been fucked that hard and good before. I just want a fuck buddy. That's all."

I smiled and looked her perfect body up and down. "A fuck buddy? That's it. No strings attached?"

She smiled back and nodded her head. She handed me her business card and when I looked down I smiled.

"So, Sherry, you're a lawyer?" I asked.

She winked and said, "My first year. And, might I add, I'm pretty good at it."

I nodded my head. "I'm heading into the Marines, so I won't be around a lot."

She bit down on her lip. "No problem. When you're in town, just give me a call."

I had to fight the urge to make plans to meet up with her again.

Guarda mi corazón siempre. Guard my heart always.

I slipped her card into my pocket and winked at her before turning around and heading to the bar. I grabbed a beer and made my way over to my best friend Scott, who was still talking to the same damn girl he'd been talking to all night.

I walked up to the table and Scott looked up at me and smiled. "Where did you disappear to?"

I shrugged my shoulders and sat down. It wasn't lost on me how she was eye fucking the hell out of me. "Went and had a quick fuck in the bathroom."

Scott sat back and sighed. "Jesus, Lark."

I smiled at him and took a drink of my beer as I watched the girl sitting across from me lick her lips and raise her eyebrows.

Women are all the same. I will never fall in love with one of them again. All they are good for is a good hard fuck.

I stood up and slapped Scott on the back. "I'm leaving in the morning. We better get out of here."

Scott nodded and looked at the girl and said, "It was a pleasure talking to you, Lorie. See ya around."

As Scott began heading out of the bar, I held back a second before I walked up to Lorie. She looked up at me and her blue eyes were begging for a good fucking.

She handed me a piece of paper and winked before turning and walking off. I laughed and made my way out of the bar. I glanced down at the paper and saw she had written down her number.

Yep. They're all the same. There would never be another Nikki. Ever.

CHAPTER 1
Lark

AS I STOOD THERE and listened to yet another girl ramble on and on about how much she loved my eyes, I glanced over to Azurdee. She looked beautiful. Her long dark hair was pulled up and piled on top of her head with just the right amount of curls hanging down and framing her face.

"So, you and Scott have known each other since college, huh?" the girl asked. I'd been trying to shake this girl the whole reception. I was the best man at my best friend's wedding. Scott and I had known each other since our sophomore year of college and I'd been spending more and more time out at his ranch in Mason, Texas. It had been almost a year since he'd called me asking for my help in finding Jessie, who was now his wife.

Of course, seeing Scott wasn't the only reason I had been coming to the ranch to visit. Azurdee Emerson was the other reason. Jessie's best friend from college had been the only girl since Nikki to make me feel something I had buried deep down inside of me long ago. One mention of her in Mason and I was on my motorcycle busting my ass to get a chance to be around her.

Azurdee Emerson. She filled my thoughts almost daily, except when I was on a mission. That was the only place she hadn't invaded my world.

The young girl touched my arm, pulling me out of my thoughts.

I glanced down at her and smiled. "So, are you busy later tonight?"

I gave her a smile and wink and said, "Yes, ma'am, I have plans." Her smile faded and she looked away but then quickly looked back at me.

"That's a shame. I was hoping to show you around Mason, and other places." She ran her tongue along her bottom lip and I rolled my eyes before I looked back at Azurdee. She was talking to the dick she brought as a date. I was hoping she was telling him to take a hike.

She turned and looked directly at me and gave me a weak smile. I was instantly brought back to the day I met Azurdee right here at Scott and Jessie's house.

***

"Skip, don't worry. I'll take care of it when I get back to Austin. Just let me enjoy my leave, please. Yep. I know it's back to work on January fourth. Yes, I know our work doesn't take a vacation. January fourth, we are heading to Columbia at oh-five-hundred. I'll make sure everything is ready to go."

I heard the buzzer for Scott's gate go off.

"Listen, Skip, I've got to run. If anything comes up, I'm just a few hours away from Austin, and I can get things up within a matter of hours."

The gate buzzed again.

"Have to run. Stop stressing. Fuck, in our line of work, how have you not had a heart attack yet? Talk to ya later."

I walked up to the intercom and pushed a button. "Talk to me."

"Hey, Scott! It's Azurdee. I'm so sorry that I'm a day early."

I smiled and shook my head. I glanced at the clock. It was nearly nine, and I was pretty sure that Scott and Jessie were go-

ing to be home soon.

"Come on up. I'll meet you on the front porch."

"Okay!"

I quickly walked to the front door and out onto the porch. I perched myself up against the post and waited to lay my sights on the P.U.R.E. Azurdee. Jessie made sure to let me know Azurdee was off-limits. She made the mistake of telling me that her best friend was a virgin and I'd give anything to be the one to strip her of her P.U.R.E. title.

How in the hell does a girl in her early twenties stay a virgin these days?

As I saw her Toyota Camry pull up and park, I couldn't help but smile when I saw it was a hybrid. The moment she stepped out of the car, she stretched, and my knees about buckled. I grabbed on to the railing.

Holy fucking shit. That hasn't happened in a long time. Get a grip, for Christ's sake, Williams. She's just another pussy. You've seen one; you've seen them all.

I watched her as she took her hair down from her ponytail. She had long, wavy dark brown hair that went down to the middle of her back. She pulled it back up into a ponytail as she turned and saw me standing there. I followed her eyes as they moved up and down my body. When her eyes caught mine, she smiled.

Jesus Christ.

"You most certainly are not Scott," she said with a smile.

It took me all of thirty seconds to get my wits about me. "No, ma'am, I am not. You must be Azurdee," I said as I made my way down to her car.

I put my hand out, and she shook it. I was pretty damn sure she felt the same thing I did when we touched.

She looked away quickly before glancing back at me and focusing in on my lips. "You have an advantage on me, it seems. Mister…"

"Lark Williams, old college friend of Scott's. Going to be staying for a few days."

I purposely licked my lips and bit down on my bottom lip. She sucked in a small breath as her caramel eyes darkened. They were breathtaking, and I swore they sparkled.

Those are the most beautiful brown eyes I've ever seen. I wonder what they would look like when fucking her.

"It's a pleasure to meet you, Mr. Williams," she said with the cutest damn smile I'd ever seen.

"Lark, please call me Lark."

She nodded and looked around. "Azurdee Emerson. Are Jessie and Scott here?"

She seemed nervous as hell, and I couldn't help but let out a laugh.

"I promise I won't bite, sweetheart," I said with a wink.

"Azurdee."

I tilted my head at her. Feisty. "You don't like the word sweetheart?" I asked.

Now, it was her turn to lick her lips before biting down on her bottom lip. She tilted her head back as she said, "Oh, I love the word sweetheart. I just don't like it coming from a guy who probably bags at least two girls a week."

My mouth dropped open as she pushed past me. She opened her trunk and started to pull out her suitcase. Then, she stopped and looked at me.

Pure, my fucking ass.

I walked over and took the suitcase from her. I made my way into the house and up the stairs as she pulled out her cell phone and called Jessie. From the sound of it, Jessie was freaking out that Azurdee was here alone with me.

"Honestly, Jess, I'm fine. It was my fault for coming in a day early. I finished up work, and I was so excited to see you that I didn't even think of calling."

I made a beeline straight to the bedroom next to mine. Before I walked into the room, she cleared her throat. I stopped and turned around to see her standing outside the bedroom at the end of the hall. She smiled and pointed into the room.

Fuckin' A.

"Yep, and Lark is being such a gentleman by carrying my suitcase."

She let out a laugh, and when I walked by, my arm brushed up against hers.

Shit! What in the hell is with the weird feelings every time I touch this girl?

I put her suitcase down on the bed, turned, and ran my hand through my hair. I didn't like the way I felt when I was around her, and I'd only been around her for about ten minutes. When I looked up, I saw she was staring at me.

"Oh, um...what did you say, Jessie?" She quickly looked away. "Okay, I probably will because I am starving. Okay, see y'all soon." She hung up and looked at me again. She gave me the sweetest smile. "They're, um...they're going to be heading back soon. Have you eaten dinner?"

My heart dropped to my stomach, and I was starting to get pissed off at how my body was betraying me. I just needed to either fuck this girl or completely ignore her.

"Nope," I said, cursing myself the moment the word came out

of my mouth.

She nodded as she set down the two bags she'd carried up with her. Then, she turned and walked out of the bedroom. I followed her out and down the stairs to the kitchen. I sat down as I watched her open the refrigerator. She took a quick look, and then she went to the pantry and looked around. She pulled out powdered sugar, cinnamon, vanilla, and the bread. She walked back over to the refrigerator and pulled out some eggs.

"Do you like French toast? I've been craving it so bad the last few days." She pulled out a bowl and began cracking eggs into it.

I had to swallow the lump in my throat before I could talk. "I love French toast." Nikki used to make me French toast all the time.

"Hey, are you okay?" Azurdee asked as she placed her hand on top of mine.

I instantly pulled it away. "Yeah. Why the fuck wouldn't I be?" I snapped.

The hurt in her eyes made me instantly regret snapping at her. She took a deep breath and went back to mixing everything in the bowl. She got out a frying pan and put some butter in it.

"Jesus, you sure do know where everything is. Do you come here often?" I asked, trying to make up for being short with her.

She gave me a weak smile and began dipping the bread into the egg mixture.

"I've only been here a couple of times. I made Scott and Jessie dinner a few times. I love to cook, and I've been told I make a pretty damn good fettuccine alfredo," she said as she wiggled her eyebrows. "All from scratch, I might add."

I let out a small laugh as I shook my head. "I think maybe I need to be the judge of that."

She flipped the toast in the pan. "You got it. I'll make it while we're here. When are you leaving? I'm staying until the third and then heading back to Austin."

The feeling of disappointment washed over me. I wanted both of us to stay longer. I wanted to leave my world behind just for a few days more, so I could get to know this girl better.

"I'll probably leave on the third." I got up and took out two glasses from the cabinet. I grabbed the orange juice and poured us each a glass. I glanced over and noticed her watching me.

Yeah, I just need to stay away from her as much as possible.

I sat down and watched her whip out the French toast in record time.

"Will you get out some plates, please?" she asked without even looking at me. She reached and stretched to put the syrup in the microwave.

I stood up, took out two plates, and set them on the island. She put French toast on each plate, and then she took a spoonful of powdered sugar and sprinkled it on top.

She turned and stood on her tippy toes to get the syrup out of the microwave.

I smiled as I looked down at her tight-ass jeans. Motherfucker, she has a nice body. No way is this girl still a virgin.

I made my way over toward her. I leaned against her as I reached up and grabbed the syrup. When I pushed myself into her, she turned around quickly.

"I never understood why they placed that microwave so damn high," she said as a flush spread across her cheeks.

I couldn't help myself. I reached up and pushed a piece of hair that had fallen out of her ponytail behind her ear. She quickly touched the side of her face.

"You're just short," I said with a wink.

I backed away when I noticed her chest was heaving up and down quickly.

Yep, she felt it, too.

She let out an awkward laugh. "I guess so. Anyway, um…dig in!"

We sat down on the bar stools and ate at the kitchen island.

"Damn girl, this is the best French toast I've ever had." I shoved another bite into my mouth.

She giggled. "Thank you. I've always loved to cook. I get to do a lot of baking with my business," she said before taking a bite.

"What do you do for a living?"

She smiled, and my breath was taken away when her beautiful eyes lit up.

"I own a coffee shop called Rise and Grind. It's right outside of Austin in Wimberley."

I laughed. "I like it. Cute name."

She smiled. "Thank you. It's been a dream come true…well, at least for me it has. My father, on the other hand, is still upset with me for not coming and working for him. He keeps telling me that my degree was a waste of his money—even though the coffee shop has done so well this last year. This is the first time I've left it. My mother has a business degree, so she has been helping me out with it."

For a moment, she almost looked sad.

What is it about this girl that is getting to me?

"What is your degree in?" I asked.

"Ocean engineering," she said with a weak smile. "My father is a petroleum engineer, and he owns his own company."

I let out a small laugh. "Well, hell, why open a coffee shop when you could be building dikes and flood control systems? If you worked for your dad though, I guess you would be exploring offshore gas and oil fields," I said.

Her mouth dropped open.

"What's wrong?" I asked with a smirk.

"No one ever knows what an ocean engineer does. I always have to tell them," she said with a small smile.

I smiled and gave her a wink. "Well, you've finally met someone who knows."

I heard Jessie and Scott come in, and I turned to see Jessie barreling through the door.

She stopped the moment she saw us. She smiled when she saw Azurdee, and Jessie immediately walked over to her. She took Azurdee in her arms and hugged her.

Jessie turned to me and gave me a look. She put her two fingers up to her eyes and then pointed at me as if to say that she'd be watching me. I was just about to take a bite, but I stopped my fork right at my mouth. I couldn't help but laugh. I shook my head and winked at her.

Scott walked up, hit me on the back, and sat down. "You behaving, Lark?" he asked with a cocky smile.

"Yes, I am. Isn't that right, Azurdee? I've asked her to sleep with me only three times."

"What?" Jessie yelled out.

Azurdee laughed and shook her head. "He has not. He's really been a gentleman."

She looked at me, and I gave her my signature smile that I knew drove all the girls crazy—except it didn't seem to faze Azurdee at all. Her smile dropped, and then she turned away as Jessie held up her ring finger. They both started screaming and jumping up and down. I threw my hands up to my ears and looked at Scott, who was laughing.

Holy hell, why must girls scream when they're happy? The only time I want a woman screaming is when I'm giving her an orgasm.

"Jesus, make them stop, Scott," I said.

I peeked over at Azurdee. She was talking a mile a minute as she kept bouncing up and down. Fuck, she has nice breasts. Ugh, I need to get the fuck out of here.

I got up, walked over to the sink, washed off my plate, and put it in the dishwasher. I leaned against the sink and looked at Scott. "Is the Wild Coyote Bar still open?"

He nodded, and I noticed Azurdee look over at me.

I pushed off the counter and started to walk out of the kitchen but not before I said,

"Good. I need to get laid."

"Oh, really nice, Lark. Do not bring a girl back here!" Jessie called after me.

I took the steps two at a time and quickly changed before heading back downstairs. Jessie and Azurdee were engaged in a conversation as they sat together on the sofa. I looked over at Scott, and he shook his head. He must have known I was going to ask if he wanted to come.

I shrugged and said, "Well, thank you, Azurdee, for dinner. Y'all have fun tonight."

Scott stood and walked me to the door. "Dude, are you sure you want to go out? Why don't you stay here? We'll grab a few beers, head down to the barn, and catch up."

I smiled and put my hand on his shoulder. "Dude, I haven't had a piece of ass since Belize. Don't wait up for me," I said with a wink.

I glanced over his shoulder and saw Azurdee looking at me. Our eyes caught, and then she rolled her eyes and looked away.

He slapped my back and laughed. "Yeah, 'cause Belize was so long ago."

As I walked out, I made a vow that I would not let this girl get under my skin. I sat down in my truck and threw my head back against the seat. I hadn't felt this way since Nikki. One good fuck and I knew I'd get over it.

***

"Lark? Hello? You're a million miles away."

I shook my head and looked back down and smiled. *Shit, I'm just ready for this reception to be over.* I glanced back over toward Azurdee and her body language changed. She seemed nervous. She glanced back over at me and then quickly back at her date.

"Listen sweetheart, enjoy the rest of the reception, I think we are going to be wrapping it up soon." Her smile faded as she shook her head and walked away.

I decided it was taking too long for this dickhead to leave. The sooner he left, and the quicker we got these people out of here, the sooner I would finally get to make Azurdee mine.

CHAPTER 2

Azurdee

THE FIRST TIME I ever laid my eyes on Lark Williams I knew I was in trouble. No guy had ever caused me to lose my normally calm train of thought like he did. His piercing green eyes looked right into my soul and seemed to know every dark secret.

Dark secret. Who was I kidding? I was a 26-year-old woman who had yet to lose her virginity because of some silly idea that I had to wait for the one guy who made me feel…different.

I glanced over toward the back door and saw Lark standing there talking to some girl who looked like she was about nineteen. Lark was the only man who ever made me feel different. He made my body ache to feel his touch almost from the first moment he spoke to me.

"Azurdee? Are you even listening to me?" Paul asked. I pulled my eyes away from Lark and tried to smile at Paul. "Um…I'm sorry, I just keep thinking about all the clean up and everything."

Paul smiled and said, "Are you sure you don't want me to stay? I don't mind at all."

Oh for the love of all things good. This guy is not getting the hint that I want him to leave. "No, really, it's taken care of. Thank you so much though. I guess now it's just trying to get everyone to head on home so we can start cleaning up," I said, hoping he would get the hint.

"I think I should stay. I could crash on the sofa after I help clean up, if you'd like," Paul said as he wiggled his eyebrows up and down. *Ugh. What did I ever see in this guy?*

"We've got it covered. You can head on back to Austin now. I'll be sure Azurdee is well taken care of."

I immediately felt the goose bumps cover my body when I felt Lark behind me and heard his authoritative voice. I was pretty sure my cheeks flushed when I thought of how Lark would be taking care of me.

Paul looked at Lark and then me before laughing and looking at Lark again. "And who might you be?"

Oh shit. Lark laughed and said, "The guy who isn't a pussy and afraid to say he most certainly will not be sleeping on the sofa tonight but will be sharing a bed with…"

I quickly grabbed Paul's arm and lead him away from Lark. "Okay well, Paul, let me walk you to your car," I said as I turned and looked at Lark, who was standing there with a huge smile on his face. As much as I wanted to be pissed off, I couldn't be. Something about his smile has always been my weakness.

As I walked Paul to his car, he stopped right before he got in and spun around and looked at me.

"Azurdee, are you going to be okay tonight? I mean…"

I smiled and nodded my head, "Yes, I'm going to perfectly fine. Thank you so much, Paul."

He nodded and got into his car, shut the door and started the engine. He rolled down the window and asked, "May I call you? Maybe we can meet for dinner this week?"

Damn it how do I get out of this?

"Azurdee? Honey, we have a slight problem and need you right away!" Ari yelled from the front porch.

I gave Paul a weak smile and said, "I have to run but maybe I'll talk to you soon." I quickly turned and headed toward Ari, who was standing there giving me a shit-eating grin.

Ari was one of Jessie's closest friends here in Mason, along with Ellie, Heather, and Amanda. They were all friends but acted more like sisters. I stopped right in front of her and asked, "How did you know I needed rescuing?"

She gave me a Cheshire cat grin and said, "Please, bitch, I saw the way you and Lark were dancing earlier. Too bad your date didn't notice the hotness between the two of you on the dance floor. I knew you were trying to ditch the date and I was pretty sure when I saw him roll down that window he was asking if you would like to meet for coffee sometime?"

I chuckled and said, "It was dinner."

Ari rolled her eyes and said, "Stupid bastard must have been the only one to not see you and Lark practically humping on the dance floor."

"Oh my God, Ari! It wasn't that bad...was it?"

She gave me an evil smile and said, "Let's just say I'm wishing I would have started a bet among the girls because I have a feeling someone is going to be coming over to the..." Ari looked around and then looked back at me and whispered, "My-cherry-was-popped side."

My mouth dropped open and I stood there frozen. "I just don't even know what to say to that, Ari."

"I get that a lot. Okay, just make sure the bastard gives you an orgasm before he sticks his..."

I held up my hands and said, "Please stop! Really, I think I'm going to be okay without your...tips."

Ari laughed and said, "Okay, seriously though, it does help you relax. Are you on the pill? Please tell me you are at least on the pill."

My heart started pounding and my hands started sweating. "Um...yeah, since college. Just to be safe. I dated a guy in college for a while and thought he might be the one but turns out he was far from the one."

Ari's mouth dropped open. "You haven't had a boyfriend since college? My God Azurdee, do you just not like men?"

I laughed and pushed her back some. "Yes, bitch, I like men. I just haven't met a guy who did it for me. One that made me want to give myself completely to him until..."

Ari wiggled her eyebrows up and down and said, "Mysterious and handsome Lark Williams has though, hasn't he?"

I let out a sigh and walked over to the porch swing and sat down.

"Oh my God, Ari. I don't know what it is, but when I'm around him my body just goes into overdrive and I have to do everything in my power to keep from jumping him. It's been like this from the beginning. I've dreamt about him, I've thought about him while driving, working, out on other dates. I cannot get him out of my head. He is my weakness."

Ari sat down and gave me a weak smile. "Is it just a sexual thing? I mean...do you have other feelings for him?"

I nodded my head. "No, it's not just sexual. I mean, a big part of it is of course, and the fact that I pretty much threw myself at him tonight has my stomach dropping. But there's more to it. When he enters a room, I swear I have to take a deep breath. He brushes by me or touches me in the slightest way and my stomach flips around like I'm on a damn thrill ride. His eyes…oh my God. I get totally lost in them. I swear—if he had told me to strip down and let him make love to me on the dance floor, I would have done it."

I threw my head back onto the swing and thought about earlier when Lark and I danced.

***

I walked back outside and looked around. Lark was sitting at a table, and two of my college friends were talking to him. He looked bored out of his mind, and I didn't think he was even listening to them.

Billy Currington's "Must Be Doin' Something Right" started playing, so I walked up to the table. I smiled at the girls and looked at Lark. "I think the best man and maid of honor should dance to-gether at least once, don't you?"

He looked up at me and smiled. "Yep, I think so." He set his beer down, grabbed my hand, and practically dragged me to the dance floor.

As he pulled me close to him, he said, "Thank God you showed up when you did."

I giggled as we started to two-step. "Why? You aren't enjoying yourself?"

"Sorry, but the girls you went to college with are either bitches or boring as hell."

I placed my head on his chest and closed my eyes. When I felt his chin rest on top of my head, the butterflies in my stomach went crazy.

I looked up at him. "So, what type of girl are you looking for anyway?"

The left corner of his mouth moved up just a bit further when he smiled. It almost felt like my knees might have wobbled for one quick second.

"What do you mean?"

I hit him in the stomach. "You know what I mean, Lark. What kind of girl is it going to take to get you to settle down? You know, for you to stop your man-whoring ways?" I asked with a wink.

"Why do you want to know? What makes you think I even want to settle down with someone?"

He instantly took the offensive approach. I shrugged my shoulders, wishing I hadn't even brought it up. I looked away and tried to act like his response hadn't bothered me.

"Are you wanting to apply for the position?" he asked as he pulled me closer to him.

"Um...I thought you just said you weren't looking for someone," I said, my voice sounding so small. I was kicking myself for letting him catch me off guard like that.

"If I was, you'd be my type, Azurdee. Your innocence just pours off of you, and it's sexy as hell," he said in almost a whisper.

I smiled even though I tried desperately not to. "Oh yeah?" I said, trying to be calm, even though my heart was racing a hundred miles an hour.

He looked down at me as he gave me a slight smile, and then he looked away. "But I'm no good for you, Azurdee."

My smile faded. The anger started to build up inside me. "Don't you think I should be the judge of that?" I asked in an angry tone.

He looked back down at me and laughed. "You have no idea what you are saying. You know nothing about me, Azurdee. Why would you want to be involved with someone you know nothing about? I have secrets, and I've done things I'm not proud of."

I saw the hurt in his eyes, and all I wanted to do was make it go away. "*I know everything I need to know about you. Everyone has secrets and has made mistakes in life.*"

"*Is that so?*" *he asked, in such a seductive way.*

"*Ah...yep. Isn't that what it's all about though? Getting to know each other. I would think that would be the best part of a relationship.*"

He threw his head back and laughed. "*That is one of the best parts. Sex is the other.*"

I felt my face blush. If he ever knew I was a virgin, he would probably run away as fast as he could. He looked at me, and the look in his eyes caused goose bumps to pop up all over my body.

"*Trust me, Azurdee, you need to just stay away from me. I'm no good for you.*"

I pushed him back. "*I think you just say that because you're afraid of being in a relationship with someone.*"

He tightened his eyes as he glared at me. The hurt in his eyes was replaced by something else, but I couldn't figure out what it was.

Anger? Lust maybe?

He pulled me back into him. The song had changed at some point, but we were still dancing slowly.

"*Do you want to be with me, Azurdee?*"

Oh God. He just came out and asked it. What do I say? Do I tell him the truth?

I looked into his eyes and whispered, "*Yes.*"

He closed his eyes and shook his head. "*Azurdee, no, you don't.*"

"*Yes. Yes, I do. I want to be with you, Lark. I want you to make love to me.*"

He opened his eyes, and the look in them caused me to suck in a breath of air.

He placed his hand on my face and whispered, "You don't know what you're saying, baby."

I put my hand on top of his. "Yes, I do. I want you, Lark. I want to get to know you...please let me."

He looked into my eyes for what seemed like forever before he finally gave me a small smile.

"If I do this, Azurdee, you need to know what you're getting into. I'm...I'm not sure if I can be what you want me to be."

I swallowed and nodded my head. "I understand." He's just scared. That's all. He needs someone to love him.

He pushed his hand into my hair and grabbed it. "Once you're mine, you're mine though, Azurdee. I won't share you with anyone."

I smiled. "I won't share either, just so you know."

He shook his head. "This is a dangerous game you're playing with me."

It felt like my heart dropped to my stomach. What does he mean by that?

"I'm not playing any games, Lark," I whispered.

Right then, Katy Perry's "Dark Horse" started playing. The smile that spread across his face shocked me. I wasn't sure if I should be turned on or if I should turn around and run. He pulled my hair, making my head tilt back some, exposing my neck to him.

He leaned down and put his lips against my neck, and right before Katy started singing, he whispered, "Do you want me to make you mine, Azurdee?" Chills ran up and down my body instantly.

The moment the beat started, he pulled me to him and started dancing with me so seductively that I could feel my face blushing yet again. I didn't know if it was the way he was dancing with me or the song itself, but I felt like I was falling deeper and deeper into a trance, and he was in total control of every single one of my emotions.

I'd never danced like this before, and I had never felt so incredibly turned on like I was. The way his body was grinding into mine had me going insane. If he were to tell me to strip down for him and make love to him right here in front of everyone, I would do it.

His hand was moving up and down my body, and I was quickly falling faster and faster for him. I wanted him more than ever. He let go of my hair and moved both his hands over my body. Everywhere he touched I felt like I had been zapped by tiny bolts of electricity. He placed both of his hands on my face and tilted my head up to him.

Then, he just stopped moving. I had to hold on to something to keep my legs from going out underneath me. I grabbed on to his arms and stared into his eyes. He brought his lips barely up to mine and stopped just short of kissing me. I could feel his hot breath, and I was trying like hell not to seem desperate for his kiss.

"Who's the guy you're with?" he asked.

I shook my head to clear my thoughts. He had me pressed up against his hard-on, and I was going insane with lust.

"Um...just a friend. He's just a friend."

He smiled as he tilted his head and looked down at my lips. Then, he looked back up into my eyes and said, "What's your answer?"

"My answer?" I asked, confused as hell.

He lightly brushed his lips against mine, and I let out a moan. I was inwardly cursing myself for seeming so needy. He dropped his hands and took a few steps back from me.

No! I wanted to call out and reach for him to pull him back against my body. I needed to feel him close to me. I needed to feel his heat.

The farther he moved away, the colder I felt.

"If it's a yes, Azurdee, tell him he can leave anytime, and the sooner the better, because I really want to make love to you. Now."

He turned and started toward the house. I stood there, just watching him walk away from me, as I tried to catch my breath. He turned back around and smiled at me right before he walked into the house.

Oh dear God. This is the moment I've been waiting for, dreaming about since the first time he ever looked into my eyes. *He had been the one I was saving myself for.*

I looked around to see if anyone had been watching us. I could feel the heat burning my cheeks. I took a deep breath in and slowly let it out. I looked around and found Paul, my date for the wedding.

As I walked over to tell Paul good-bye and to thank him for coming, I had the strangest feeling that I was about to give my heart and soul to someone who could possibly take it and crush it into a million pieces. I knew one thing for sure though. I was about to walk into something that both excited and scared me.

***

"Azurdee? What in the world are you thinking about?" Ari asked as she bumped my arm and I jumped. I shook my head and smiled.

"Earlier, dancing with Lark. Just something he said to me," I barely said.

Ari's smile faded and she looked down and then back up at me. "Do you think he knows that...um...that you're a virgin?"

I shrugged my shoulders. "I'm not sure. I wouldn't be surprised if Jessie told him to keep him away from me." I turned and looked at Ari. "Do you think that would turn him off? I mean…if I tell him, do you think he will change his mind?"

Ari threw her head back and laughed. "Please. Show me a man who doesn't want to be the first to journey down that valley. I would guess he knows but you're going to have to tell him, Sweets, just in case."

I nodded my head. The screen door opened and Jeff, Ari's husband, came walking out.

"Hey baby, everyone is pretty much leaving. You about ready to say good-bye?" Jeff asked as he reached his hand down for Ari.

Before she stood up, she smiled. She gave me a hug and whispered, "It's going to hurt and feel good at the same time. Call me tomorrow morning."

She pulled back and smiled at me as I smiled at her. *Was I really going to do this? Give Lark the one thing I'd guarded so strongly? Yes.* I was and my clenching stomach couldn't wait another minute. I'd waited almost a year to feel his lips on mine. I've dreamed about his hands moving gently over my body. Yes. I was more than ready for Lark to make love to me.

We both stood up and I followed them back into the house. As I made my way around thanking everyone for coming, I couldn't help but look over at Lark doing the same. I swear every girl either asked him out tonight or gave him her phone number. I rolled my eyes as one of my college friends attempted to get Lark to come back to Austin with them and show them around all the dance clubs.

After the last person walked out the door, I walked upstairs and got out of that damn dress I'd been in for hours. I left my lace bra and panties on, but put jeans and a T-shirt on over them and made my way back downstairs.

I wasn't sure if Lark's brother Tristan was still here or not. He had been the last person talking to Lark. Their conversation seemed to be a serious one, so I was hesitant to even go outside.

When I stepped outside and made my way down the steps I looked over at Lark and Tristan sitting down talking. Lark looked up at me, and the look on his face when he saw me was one of disappointment. I stopped in my tracks.

He's regretting what he said earlier. He doesn't really want to be with me.

I swallowed hard and wished I hadn't even come back out. Tristan turned and saw me and smiled. "Well, it looks like you decided to get comfortable." I smiled and nodded my head. When I looked back at Lark he seemed…angry. He was regretting what he said. He was probably pissed at himself for saying he wanted to make love to me.

I looked around and quickly walked over to a table and began cleaning it off. I tried desperately to hold back the tears that were threatening to spill over.

Oh God. How stupid could I be? He had so many girls asking him out tonight and here I was stupid enough to think he wanted to be with me.

I began piling everything up and was about to pick it all up and toss it when I felt a shock run up my arm. It didn't take me long to figure out Lark had grabbed my arm. He pulled me to him and said, "What are you doing?"

I still had been fighting the tears in my eyes, so I didn't want to look at him. I kept my head turned. "Cleaning," I said as my voice cracked. *Damn it, why he had such a hold over me was beyond me. I hated how weak I felt when I was around him.*

"Look at me, Azurdee," he whispered.

I turned and looked at him and he sucked in a breath. "What's wrong?" he asked.

I shook my head and said, "Nothing." I pulled my arm out and picked up the trash and quickly headed to the trashcan.

"Azurdee, put that stuff down and just let this go. Y'all can clean up in the morning," Tristan said.

"The wild animals might make a mess of things if we don't get…" I looked around and saw all the food was gone. That's when I noticed the only table that had any trash on it was the table I just cleared off.

"Who? When did this all get taken care of?" I asked as I looked over at Lark. He smiled and said, "I hired someone to come in and take care of it. They were cleaning up as we were trying to get everyone the hell out of here. It ran over later than I thought, so they said they would be back tomorrow."

I wanted to run over and kiss him I was so relieved. But instead I smiled and said, "Thank God. I'm exhausted." I looked at Tristan, who was looking back and forth between Lark and me. When Lark looked at him they exchanged a look and the next thing I knew Tristan was saying good-bye.

No! No, don't leave me alone with Lark.

"Um…are you sure you don't want to stay the night, Tristan. I mean, it's a long drive back to Austin and it's so late and all." I peeked over at Lark, and now he really did seemed pissed. He walked up to Tristan and slapped him on the back.

"He has a hotel in Fredericksburg," Lark said as he looked back at me.

Tristan laughed and shook his head. "I better get going, I'll be back tomorrow to help with anything that's left to do."

I wanted to scream out for him to stop, but I just stood there for a second before I followed both men into the house. Tristan headed to the stairs as he called back over his shoulder, "Give me two seconds, I need to grab my stuff."

I watched as Tristan took the stairs two at a time. My eyes wandered over to Lark, who turned and stared at me. The way he was looking at me had me confused. He began walking over to me, and I instinctively began backing up until I backed right into the wall.

He stopped just short of me and put his hand on the wall, then looked down into my eyes. They weren't filled with lust like earlier. My heart began pounding and I wished like hell we weren't staying here together in this house.

"Why did you take your dress off, Azurdee?" he hissed.

What? He's upset that I took off my dress?

My eyes quickly moved around his face before I looked back into his eyes. I slowly took in a deep breath and said, "I, um…I was uncomfortable and wanted to take it off. Lark, are you upset with me about something? I mean, if you've changed your mind about wanting to be with…um…with me, then…"

Something about his eyes changed and he looked down at my lips. He slammed his lips to mine and I was quickly lost in his kiss. *Oh my.* The way he tasted…the way his tongue danced with mine had me feeling light-headed. He slowly pulled away and I wanted to tell him not to stop.

He smiled and said, "Azurdee, I haven't changed my mind. I wanted to peel that dress off of your body myself and I'm pissed I won't get the chance to now."

All I could say was, "Oh."

Tristan cleared his throat and Lark took a few steps away from me before he turned around and said, "Well, big brother, not to rush you out the door or anything…"

Tristan looked over at me and his smile faded for a brief second. I'm sure I looked a mess. The emotions playing in my heart right now had me more confused than ever. I smiled and began walking toward them both.

As they both made their way out to the front porch they talked about heading to their family ranch for Christmas. I tried to listen, but I kept thinking of what Lark said.

I wanted to peel that dress off of your body myself and I'm pissed I won't get the chance to now.

I stood on the porch as I watched Lark talk to his brother. Tristan turned and waved to me and yelled, "It was a pleasure meeting you, Azurdee. See ya tomorrow."

I waved back. "The pleasure was all mine."

Lark took a step back and we both watched Tristan's BMW retreat down the driveway.

Lark turned and looked at me, and my heart began pounding in my chest. He walked up to me and when he started up the steps, the left corner of his mouth began moving up into that damn crooked-ass smile of his that caused the throbbing between my legs to grow stronger.

What do I do? What do I say? So, hey, are you going to take me to bed now and rob me of my virginity? Oh, I didn't mention I was a virgin? Surprise!

Lark walked up to me and reached down and scooped me up. I let out a small scream as I wrapped my hands around his neck. He quickly walked through the house and up the stairs.

Wow…he certainly isn't wasting time. Not even any romance? Foreplay? I guess I shouldn't expect much more from him.

My heart dropped in my stomach just a bit as I thought about how Lark was probably going to just fuck me, and that would be the end of it.

He pushed open my bedroom door, walked us through and

then kicked it shut. He slowly put me down as he began to push me back against the bedroom door.

I bit down on my lower lip as I looked up into his eyes. They were filled with passion and something else. I couldn't really put my finger on it but it almost seemed like he was just as nervous as I was.

He pushed a stray piece of my hair back and smiled at me. "Are you scared, Azurdee?"

I swallowed hard and whispered, "Yes."

He leaned down and brushed his lips against mine and whispered, "*Te adoro,* Azurdee. I'd never do anything to hurt you."

I closed my eyes and when I opened them again I fought to hold back my tears.

"I'm going to make love to you for your first time, Azurdee. I wish I could make it more special for you but I'm going to take it slow and easy. But after I make you mine, I'm going to fuck you hard and fast. I've been dreaming of this night for months."

I sucked in a breath of air and felt my stomach drop. *Oh. My. God.* I didn't know if I was more shocked he knew I was a virgin or by what he said to me.

He licked his lips as he ran his hand up my neck and into my hair. He grabbed a fist full of hair and pulled my head back and placed his lips on my neck.

"Are you sure you want this, Azurdee?" he whispered against my skin.

I couldn't even form words in my mouth, so I attempted to nod my head.

"Tell me what you want, *mi amor.* I want to hear it from your lips," Lark whispered.

I swallowed hard as he pulled back and looked into my eyes. I knew there was nothing else I wanted more than for Lark to make love to me.

I ran my tongue along my top lip as Lark let out a small moan. "I want you, Lark. I want you to make love to me and…"

His eyes lit up with passion as he slowly smiled and said, "And what, Azurdee?"

He placed his lips on my neck again and began kissing me softly along my neck and up to my ear. "Ohh…I want you to make me…ahh…" He was driving me insane and all I wanted was for his lips to be on my body. *Everywhere* on my body. I had fantasies of Lark giving me an orgasm through oral sex. My core clenched at just the thought and my betraying body let out another moan.

"Azurdee, those little noises you're making are driving me crazy. I really want to take it slow your first time but if you don't tell me what you want soon I'm going to fuck you against this door."

I let out a breath and whispered, "Oh God."

He pulled my hair harder and the pain that raced through my body both turned me on and scared me.

"You! I want you and I want you to make me yours." I yelled out in a shaky voice. "I need to feel you inside me, Lark. *Please.*"

The smile that spread across his face caused chills to run up and down my body.

"Take off your clothes, Azurdee. Slowly."

CHAPTER 3

Lark

A ZURDEE'S EYES LIT UP with fire when I told her to undress. I took a step back and watched her shaky hands reach up and pull her T-shirt up and over her head. I sucked in a breath of air when I saw her white lace bra. Her nipples were begging to be sucked on and now it was my turn to let out a moan.

She smiled slightly as she hooked her thumbs on her pants and slowly began sliding them down, never taking her eyes off of me. The second I saw her matching lace panties I felt my knees shake.

It had been years since a girl had this kind of an effect on me, but then again, Azurdee was no ordinary girl. She was different. She was the first person since Nikki to wake something up that I had buried so deep down that I almost forgot it even existed.

I licked my lips as she stripped her pants off and gently kicked them off to the side. She stood there in nothing but her bra and panties as she began ringing her hands and biting the hell out of her lower lip. She couldn't have stood any taller than five feet five inches. You could tell she ran with how toned her muscles where on her perfect hourglass shaped body. But it was those caramel eyes that got me.

I wanted nothing more than to take her right there and have

my way with her, but I had to take it slow. I ran my hand through my hair and watched as her mouth opened slightly. *She must like when I do that.*

"Don't be scared, *mi amor*," I whispered.

She closed her eyes and said, "What if...I don't know what I'm doing, Lark. I've never..."

I quickly walked up to her and picked her up. She buried her face into my chest and something crazy happened inside of me. My heart dropped and my stomach did a wild flip. She trusted me to not hurt her and take this slow and that was exactly what I was going to do. I cared too much about this girl not to take my time.

My heart started pounding as she placed her hand on my chest and whispered, "I've waited so long for this."

I stopped at the bed and closed my eyes.

Recuerde guarder mi corazón.

I gently laid her down on the bed and watched as her chest heaved up and down. I moved my eyes down her perfect body as she began rubbing her legs together.

"Do you need to come, *mi amor*?" I asked as I watched her hand move down toward her panties. I didn't think my dick could get any harder than it was.

Her eyes snapped open and she quickly brought her hand back up. I slowly began getting undressed. I unbuttoned each button slower than I probably should have as I watched her eyes light up with excitement and she continued to chew on her lower lip. I wanted those lips wrapped around my dick so badly.

I wonder if Azurdee has ever given a blow job before? I secretly hoped she hadn't.

I let my dress shirt hang open as I began taking off my belt and unzipped my pants. I leaned down and began taking off my shoes as Azurdee let out a frustrated moan.

"Are you trying to kill me slowly, Lark?"

I smiled and raised my eyebrow at her. "I want to take this slow, Azurdee."

She smiled back slightly and said, "My grandfather undresses faster than you."

I stood up straight and kicked my shoes and socks out of the way. I took my shirt off and tossed it on the chair that was sitting next to the side table.

I couldn't help but smile as I watched her look at me. I was glad I made the decision to go commando today as I pushed my pants down and my erection sprung free, causing Azurdee to let out a gasp.

The way her eyes moved straight to my dick and her legs began rubbing together I knew she was working herself up big time. It wouldn't take long to give her the first of many orgasms tonight.

"Make yourself come, Azurdee," I said as I took a step away from the bed.

She quickly shook her head and whispered, "Excuse me?"

I tilted my head and looked at her as I said slowly, "Make. Yourself. Come."

She swallowed hard and looked away from me. "Azurdee, I know you're a virgin but I refuse to believe you have gone this long without giving yourself an orgasm. Pleasure yourself, now."

Her mouth dropped open again slightly and she looked like she was about to say something but she slowly moved her hand down and slipped it into her panties. The moment she touched herself her hips bucked and she let out a moan. She moved her hand slowly as she closed her eyes.

I walked up to the bed and reached over and quickly pulled her panties off.

"Spread your legs wider, I want to see you touch yourself."

She looked at me and said, "Lark…I'm not sure…"

I reached over and spread her legs wider and watched as her hand moved back down and began rubbing her clit. *Oh fucking hell.* I wasn't going to last a minute inside her.

"Put your fingers inside, Azurdee, and don't be so gentle."

She turned her head away from me and did as I asked. She slipped two fingers inside herself and began moving them in and out faster. I reached down and began stroking my rock-hard dick.

"I've never seen anything so sexy in my life," I whispered as I watched her withdraw her fingers and begin her assault on her clit. Within seconds she was calling out in pleasure.

I waited until she finally settled down, and then I picked up her foot and began kissing along its edge.

"Oh God…" she whispered. I slowly began moving my lips up her leg.

I glanced up and saw she was gripping the sheets and biting down on her damn lower lip again. The way her body responded to me was amazing. I was betting I could make her come without even touching her.

I slid my hand up her thigh and placed it on her stomach. Her breathing began to turn to almost a heavy pant.

As I moved further up her leg she began moaning. "Oh… God…what is happening to me?" she whispered. I placed gentle kisses on the inside of her thigh as she sucked in a breath of air.

I wasn't sure how Azurdee would react to me kissing her pussy, but I was about to find out. Without giving her a chance to tell me no, I buried my face between her legs, eager to finally see what she would taste like.

Azurdee called out, "Lark! Oh God…oh my…oh…God!"

It didn't take long before she had her hands in my hair and was pushing my face deeper into her. *Oh yeah, she likes this.*

"Lark, oh God…not again…it's…oh God! Yes! Feels…oh…" When I pushed two fingers inside her she began calling out even more and I could feel her squeezing my fingers. I spread her open just a bit to stretch her and she about jumped off the bed.

Fuck. She was so tight. I wasn't going to last long.

I quickly jumped up and grabbed my pants and reached for the condom inside my pocket.

I crawled back onto the bed and looked into her eyes as she came down from her high.

"Baby, I'm going to make love to you now." Her eyes widened as she watched me open the condom packet.

She quickly sat up and said, "Wait. Stop."

Oh dear God, please don't let her change her mind.

"Have you always used a condom when you've had sex?"

What? I can't believe she's asking me this.

"Always, even with Nik…" My voice trailed off and she tilted her head slightly and gave me a strange look.

Fuck. What in the hell made me almost bring up Nikki?

I quickly shook the feeling I had deep in the pit of my stomach and said, "I've never had sex before without wearing a condom."

She smiled and said, "Never?"

I shook my head and said, "Never. I get tested a few times a year and I'm clean."

She looked down and then back up to my eyes. "I've never been with anyone, so obviously I'm clean and I'm on the pill. I don't want anything to be between us."

My heart slammed in my chest. I'd never in my life felt this way. For the first time in my life, I didn't want a barrier between a girl and me. "Azurdee…" I whispered.

Her face dropped and she quickly said, "It's okay. I'm sorry I even suggested it."

Everything was spinning around in my head. I wanted nothing more than to make love to her and feel her completely, but I had to guard my heart.

Guarda mi corazón.

This was my barrier. No condom would make the emotions too raw. Too real. Every girl I'd been with since Nikki had always been just about the sex. Nothing more.

I looked down into her beautiful eyes and saw how confused and scared she was. This girl was doing things to me that had me so damn confused. I closed my eyes and felt her lay back down.

"I'm sorry, I shouldn't have even asked such a thing…I just…" Her voice trailed off.

"Maybe we should just stop," she said as she began to move away from me. I snapped my eyes open and whispered, "Don't. Please don't leave."

She froze in place and slowly took in a deep breath. I took the condom and dropped it to the floor.

"I want to feel you completely, *mi amor*. I need to feel you. If you're sure." I couldn't even believe what I was saying. My head was screaming for me to stop but my heart…my heart was screaming for her. "Lay back, Azurdee. Please."

She slowly laid back and her beautiful brown hair spread across the pillow.

I placed my hand on her leg and she jumped slightly. I moved in between her and pushed her legs open as I reached over and in one swift move unclasped her bra in the front, allowing her breasts to spring free.

"Motherfucker. You're perfect in every way," I said as she smiled, a slight pink flush moving across her cheeks. She sat up a little and I removed her bra and tossed it on the floor. I leaned down and took one of her nipples into my mouth as she let out a soft low moan that moved through my body like a warm sensation.

"Oh God, Lark," she said as her hands moved through my hair. When she grabbed a handful of my hair and pulled it I almost moved and slammed my dick in her.

Slow. Must go slow.

I gently bit down on her nipple as she softly said my name. I moved over to her other nipple and gave it equal time.

I looked up at her and she had her eyes closed and was moving her head back and forth, letting out sweet moan after sweet moan. I couldn't wait a minute longer. I began kissing up her chest and along her neck. She opened her eyes and gave me that smile that had been haunting my dreams for months.

"Azurdee, I'm going to make love to you now," I said as I stared into her eyes.

She smiled bigger and said, "Okay."

I wanted to laugh at how innocent she was. I knew she was scared, but she tried so hard to seem like she wasn't.

I brushed my lips against her lips and was shocked when she sucked in my lower lip and gently bit down on it. *Shit.* I couldn't wait to fuck her and fuck her hard. I had a feeling she would like it rough.

I reached down and slipped two fingers inside of her and began moving my fingers in and out.

"Jesus…you're so wet, Azurdee. Do you want me?"

Her eyes flashed with nothing but pure lust. "Yes. More than you know."

I pulled my fingers out and put them in my mouth and sucked on them as Azurdee let out a gasp. "You taste like heaven."

I placed my hand on the side of her face and gently kissed her as I slowly began to push myself into her a little bit at a time.

I felt her tense up so I pulled out some. "*Mi amor*, you need to relax."

She nodded her head, and as I pushed in a little more, she let out a whimper so I stopped. "Don't stop. Please don't stop," she whispered.

I ran my thumb across her cheek and pushed in a little more. Her eyes locked onto mine. "I'm almost all the way. Relax, Azurdee."

I literally felt her whole body relax as I pushed in all the way. I dropped my head and let out a moan. I'd never felt something so amazing in my life. I wasn't sure if it was just because I was having sex for the first time with no condom or if it was because I was making love to Azurdee.

I slowly began moving in and out of her body. I wasn't going to last long but I needed to give her an orgasm, and I would hold off as long as I could to make her feel good.

"Lark..." she whispered, and my heart dropped at hearing her say *Lark*. I wanted to hear her say *Michael* so damn bad. I closed my eyes and continued to move in and out, pushing those feelings deep down inside. I pushed a little deeper and she let out a gasp and I snapped my eyes open. "Did I hurt you, *mi amor*?"

The moment I saw the tear slide down her face my whole world stopped. If I had hurt her I would never forgive myself.

She slowly shook her head and whispered, "No. I've never felt...something so amazing in my life. Please don't stop."

I used my thumb to wipe away her tear as I leaned down and kissed her. The way her fingers were moving up and down my back was causing my mind to go insane. No girl's touch ever affected me like this. I don't even remember it feeling like this with Nikki. *It must be from not wearing a condom. It had to be.*

Guarda mi corazón.

When she began moving her hips in perfect rhythm to mine I about lost it. We fit together perfectly.

She wrapped her legs around me and looked into my eyes. "Can you go faster?"

Oh holy shit. "You have to tell me if I hurt you though?"

She nodded her head and said, "I promise."

I began moving faster as she reached out and grabbed onto the sheets. Fuck. Watching her was driving me insane. I'm not going to last much longer.

"Oh God. Lark…deeper…please…harder," she said, in between pants.

I've died and gone to heaven.

"*Mi amor,* you are killing me," I whispered as I pulled out some and pushed back into her harder and deeper. She looked into my eyes and cried out, "Oh God, Lark! I'm coming. Faster."

I gave her just what she asked for but tried to keep it gentle also. I wanted her again and the last thing I was going to do is make her so sore she couldn't have sex again tonight.

"Oh my God. Yes. Ahh…" I tried to hold off but the feel of her squeezing down on my dick had me letting go. I leaned down and pushed in harder as I placed my lips next to her ear and whispered, "I'm coming. Oh God, Azurdee, you feel so good."

She squeezed her legs around me tighter as I felt myself pouring into her body. It was probably the most intense moment of my life…and it was scaring the fuck out of me.

When I finally stopped moving she wrapped her arms around me and held onto me, almost as if she was afraid I was getting ready to leave her.

I was frozen. Unable to move. The thought of just making love to Azurdee had my head spinning and my heart pounding so loud in my chest I was sure she could hear it. I pulled my body weight off of her and looked into her eyes. She smiled and I was immediately lost in her beautiful eyes.

I placed my hand on the side of her face as she leaned into it. Something inside me was forever changed by what just happened between us. I wasn't sure what was happening or how I felt about it, but for the time being I was going to just lose myself in it.

"Lark, that was the most…" I held my breath as I watched the tear slide down her cheek.

"Did I hurt you, Azurdee?" I asked as my voice cracked.

She began shaking her head. "No! No, that was the most amazing moment of my life. It was everything I ever dreamed it would be."

And there went my heart again. It slammed so hard in my chest and my first instinct was to get up and leave. This was all too much. I was giving her too much of me.

She tilted her head and her smile faded slightly. "Do you…do you regret what just happened?"

I pulled my head back in shock. "Of course not. That was just as amazing for me as it was for you, Azurdee. I'm just glad I didn't hurt you."

I could feel my dick twitching inside her and she raised her eyebrow. "Um…when can…I mean…" she looked away and I could swear the beautiful rose color that was sweeping over her cheeks was making my dick hard again.

"Talk to me, Azurdee."

She glanced back at me and bit down on her lower lip. "When can we do that again?"

I let out a chortle and whispered, "*Mi amor.*"

CHAPTER 4

Azurdee

EVERY TIME LARK CALLED me *mi amor, his love,* my heart beat ten times faster and the butterflies in my stomach went crazy.

When he finally pulled out of me, I instantly missed his warmth, but also felt a sense of relief. He placed his lips on my neck and whispered, "That was amazing."

I closed my eyes and smiled. *Oh. My. God. That couldn't have been more perfect.* It was everything I had dreamed of and more. Having it be Lark who shared in this moment with me made it all the sweeter.

I heard him in the bathroom that joined my room and the next room. He was filling up the bathtub. I stretched and could feel every muscle in my body, especially in my core. I opened my eyes and watched as Lark came walking back into the room with a towel wrapped around his waist.

"Are you taking a bath?" I asked, as I realized I was sprawled out naked on the bed. I grabbed the blanket and pulled it around me. The left corner of his mouth slowly started to move up into a smile and my desire for him bloomed again. *What is wrong with me? Now that I've had sex, am I going to want it all the time?*

As Lark moved toward me, my eyes were drawn to the tattoo on his chest. *Guarda mi corazón.*

I hadn't meant to read it out loud, but when I heard my lips speaking it I wanted to kick myself. "Guard my heart?"

Lark stopped dead in his tracks as he looked down at his chest, and quickly back up to me. "*¿Hablas español?*"

I let out a giggle and nodded my head. "My father is from Spain. I speak Spanish fluently. I'm going to guess so do you with how you kept calling me *mi amor.*"

His smile faded and he ran his hand through his hair. "I'm sorry if that makes you feel uncomfortable…"

I sat up and practically yelled out, "No! I love it."

He smiled and walked up to the side of the bed. I could feel the heat coming from his body and it caused a chill to run down my back. "To answer your question. *We're* taking a bath."

Oh my. I do believe my heart just landed in my stomach. He reached down, grabbed me by the arms and pulled me up quickly. "After you soak in a hot bath, I'm going to bring you back in here, Azurdee."

My mouth dropped open and I whispered, "And make love to me again?" God, I was praying this wasn't a one-time thing. I hadn't wanted to let go of him after we had finished. I was afraid if I did he would leave and never look back.

He gave me a wicked smile that made my core clench tightly with need. "No, *mi amor.* I'm going to fuck you. Hard and fast."

I swallowed hard and licked my lips. I never would have thought I would like for a man to talk to me that way, but when Lark talked like that my insides throbbed and I needed immediate relief.

"Oh…I um…" I quickly looked away as I felt his hand move

down my arm and grab my hand as he walked us into the bathroom. I went to grab the blanket but Lark stopped and looked at me. "Don't be ashamed of your body, Azurdee. It is amazing and I could stare at it all damn night."

I couldn't form words in my head to even speak. As we walked into the bathroom, I looked down at the garden tub and let out a moan.

Lark dropped his towel and I quickly looked back at him and let out another moan. *Jesus Christ. What is wrong with me?* I was sore as hell and all I wanted was to feel him inside me again.

He stepped into the bath and held my hand as I followed. I slowly sank down into the hot water and let out a long sigh.

"Oh God…that feels so good," I whispered as I sank down into the water and put my head back. After the long day with the wedding and the most amazing sex of my life…well, hell…the only sex in my life…I was exhausted and my body was beginning to feel it.

Lark grabbed my right foot and began massaging it. I kept my eyes closed and let out another moan. *I wonder how many times he will make me moan tonight?*

"Tell me about your life, Azurdee," he said as he massaged my foot. I wasn't sure if it was his hands on my body or the massage itself, but I was quickly becoming a loose noodle.

"What do you want to know? You pretty much know everything about me," I said with a giggle.

"How is the coffee shop doing?"

I lifted my head and smiled. I had just toured the new building the day before yesterday and construction for my new restaurant was set to begin any day now.

He let out a chuckle and said, "I'm going to guess by that smile on your face the coffee business is going well?"

I laughed and nodded my head. "I'm expanding. I'm opening a restaurant."

He smiled bigger. "No shit?"

"Yep," as I popped my *p* loudly. "Nothing big. Just a small place along Cypress Creek in Wimberley. It will be mostly sandwiches, soups and dessert. Of course some of the best coffee in Wimberley still."

"Azurdee, that is wonderful. I'm proud of you for following your dreams. Your parents must be so happy for you."

My smile faded and I looked down. "Yeah, well. My mother's been helping me a lot with things."

He reached over and placed his finger on my chin and lifted my eyes to his. "Your father still isn't happy about your career choice?"

I sucked in a breath. "You remember that?"

He chuckled and said, "Yes. I do."

I sighed as I dropped my head back and relaxed as I closed my eyes. "I don't think I'll ever make my father happy."

Lark moved onto my left foot and began his sensual massage on this foot now. Oh dear Lord…the feeling was somehow moving up and going right between my legs. I had to fight the urge to touch myself.

"Nonsense. Your father is proud of you. He just has a hard time showing it is all," Lark said as he began to move his hand up my leg. I slowly lifted my head. His eyes captured mine and it felt like he was looking into my soul.

Something changed and his eyes turned to lust. "Turn around and lean against me, Azurdee."

I didn't even have to think about it. I had never moved so quickly in my life. Before I knew it I was between his legs and resting my head on his chest. He moved his hands up my stomach and my whole body was covered in goose bumps, even in the hot water. When he cupped both breasts I let out a moan. He began twisting each of my nipples and I'd never felt pleasure like I was feeling. He slowly moved his right hand down and began rubbing my clit.

"Oh God, Lark," I whispered as I pushed my hips into his hand. What was he doing to me? Was it always going to be like this now that I had a taste of this pleasure? I needed it more and more.

"Does that feel good, Azurdee?" he asked with his lips against my ear.

"Oh…God…feels…so good." I called out as he slipped two fingers inside of me and kept up the endless torture on my left nipple. His fingers began moving in and out faster as I felt his erection pushing against my back.

I wanted him again. I needed him. I was so close to having an orgasm but I wanted to have it with him inside me. I quickly moved away and turned around as I positioned myself on top of him while he made room for my legs to wrap around him.

"Azurdee, I don't want you…" His voice trailed off as I lowered myself onto him. The way he stretched me open even further was pure hell and pure heaven at the same time. The stinging only lasted a few seconds as my body quickly melted into one with Lark's. I wasn't even sure if I was doing this right, all I knew was it felt amazing.

I dropped my head back as Lark took one of my nipples in his mouth and began sucking on it. I let out a long moan and Lark grabbed my hips and forced me to stop.

I snapped my head forward and looked at him. "I don't want to come yet," he panted. I couldn't help but smile. I was doing this. This time I was in control and I loved that I had such an effect on him. I leaned down and slammed my lips against his as our kiss became almost frantic. I wanted to crawl inside his body and stay there forever. I wanted to tell him that but was too afraid I would push him away. I could feel his dick getting harder inside me and I began rocking on him.

"Fuck," he hissed as he pulled away from my lips. He grabbed me tighter to force my hips to stop moving. He didn't like me being in control and I wasn't sure if I should push him or not.

I decided not to push my luck. "Lark…please…I need to feel what it is like when you fuck me."

I'd never seen anyone move so fast in my life. Before I even knew what was happening, I was out of the tub and a towel wrapped around my body as Lark picked me up and carried me back out to the bedroom.

When we walked up to the bed I let out a gasp. "Oh my God," I whispered as I looked down at the blood.

Lark slowly put me down and turned me to face him as he placed his hands on my face and looked into my eyes. "That's me claiming you as mine. You're always going to be mine, *mi amor*."

I swallowed hard and wanted to ask what he meant by that. I wanted to be his and for him to be mine. The idea of Lark being with anyone else had my stomach twisting in knots.

"I told you Azurdee, if we did this, I wasn't sharing you with anyone. I meant it."

His voice sent chills down my body. "I'm yours, Lark," was all I could manage to say.

The look in his eyes changed and he almost seemed scared. "I'm…I'm yours, Azurdee."

As soon as I smiled he slammed his lips to mine and we continued on with the frantic kissing we had started in the bathtub. I wasn't sure how long we stood there and kissed but our hands moved just as frantically on each other's bodies.

I pulled away and panted…. "Lark. I need to make the ache go away. Please."

He quickly pushed me onto the bed and at first I moved away from the blood but once I felt him get on the bed with me I no longer cared. All I cared about was feeling him inside me.

I went to move onto my back and he stopped me. "Get on your hands and knees, Azurdee." I did as he said, my heart pounding in my chest faster and harder than it ever had in my life.

"You have to tell me if I'm hurting you. Promise me."

I looked over my shoulder and nodded my head.

"Say it."

My breathing was erratic and all I wanted was to feel him moving in and out of me. *Oh God. What have I turned into?*

"I promise. Lark…please, I need you inside of me." He grabbed onto my hip as he pushed his fingers inside and primed my body to receive him.

My mind thought back to his words. I'm going to fuck you hard and fast.

I was scared and excited at the same time. Then his other hand grabbed my hip and I took a deep breath. "Promise me, Azurdee."

"Yes! Yes! I promise." I couldn't believe how needy my voice sounded. He was like a drug I just couldn't get enough of.

I felt him at my entrance and my whole body quivered. He slowly pushed inside of me as I sucked in a breath of air. This way was going to feel different. He pulled out slowly and then slammed back into me. "Ah!" I cried out as I felt him go deeper inside of me than before.

"Fuck," Lark whispered. "Am I hurting you?"

I quickly shook my head and felt him grip my hips harder. "No. I'm fine, it was just so much deeper and…"

I hadn't even finished talking when he pulled out and slammed back into me. *Oh God.* The feeling was both pleasure and pain. I needed more. I pushed my ass back into him and he leaned over my back and began kissing it. "I love the way your body reacts to mine. I love that you want this as much as I do."

I looked over my shoulder at him and whispered, "Yes. Oh God, yes."

And with that Lark began taking me to somewhere I'd never imagined. I was beyond aroused and with each hard stroke he began building my orgasm up more and more. When he reached his hand down and began touching my clit, that was all it took. I began calling out his name. I couldn't believe how hard this orgasm was hitting me. I could feel myself pulsating around his dick.

"Jesus, Azurdee. I'm going to come." Lark began calling out my name as he gave me every ounce of himself. My legs and arms were shaking and it was taking everything I had to hold myself up.

When he finally pulled out of me, I collapsed onto the bed. *I'm not going to be able to walk.*

Lark lay down next to me and pulled me to him. "Every time you move for the next few days you're going to feel me with you still."

I let out a small whimper as he turned my body to face him and captured my lips with his. I could very easily have him again with no complaints. I *wanted* to feel sore. I *wanted* to remember this night forever.

He slowly pulled his lips from mine and I wanted to cry out *no*. I instantly missed the connection. "Are you sore, *mi amor*?" Lark asked as he pushed a strand of hair away from my face. My heart melted every time he called me that. I slowly shook my head.

"Tell me what you're thinking," he whispered.

I swallowed hard and said, "How amazing you make me feel. How that was beyond my wildest dreams. And how long we have to wait to do it again."

He smiled and there went my stomach, flipping and turning like I was a teenager in love.

His smile slowly faded a bit and he looked into my eyes. "Azurdee, you're everything I've ever wanted, and everything I've ever feared."

Everything I've ever wanted. Everything I've ever feared.

My heart dropped slightly as I thought about the night Scott had told me about Nikki, Lark's girlfriend who passed away in college. I closed my eyes and fought to hold back my tears. *Why would I be something he feared? Was he thinking of her? Did he compare me to her?* A million thoughts started running through my head.

I felt his hot breath against my lips. I snapped my eyes open and looked into his eyes as he whispered, "I never want to hurt you, ever. Please know that."

It was almost like he was expecting to hurt me, and that caused an uneasy feeling in my stomach. I tried to smile as I said, "I never want to hurt you either, Lark."

Something in his eyes changed and he pulled away. He got off the bed and said, "I'm going to take a shower. I'll run another hot bath for you to soak in."

I sat up and wanted to argue with him and say I wanted to shower with him, but something had changed. He seemed distant all of a sudden. All I could do was whisper, "Okay."

I watched as he walked into the bathroom. I was all of a sudden overcome with a sense of being completely alone. I had just given my virginity away to the one man I probably should have guarded it from the most.

The one who had the power to destroy my heart and soul.

CHAPTER 5

Lark

AFTER I STARTED A bath for Azurdee, I tried to calm my beating heart. What in the hell just happened to me? Making love to Azurdee had changed everything. I was feeling things I hadn't felt in years. Things I'd never felt before, even with Nikki.

I stood there staring down at the water in the tub. She was like a drug. I needed to feel her body up against mine. I needed to taste her lips against mine. I needed to make her understand how I felt about her. That scared the shit out of me. When I walked away from her just now I felt empty.

I slowly turned around and saw her standing there with a shirt on. *Holy fuck. She's the most beautiful woman I've ever seen.* I wanted to take her again but I knew after what I just did she had to be sore.

"Um…it might be a little hot, but soak in it for awhile. It will help with the soreness."

The look on her face was pure disappointment. She walked over to the tub and slipped the shirt off her shoulders and climbed in.

"Oh wow. That is hot!" she said with a nervous chuckle. I tried to smile, but it felt like the room was closing in on me. She slowly sank down and leaned her head back against the tub. "That feels amazing."

She opened her eyes and looked up at me. "You sure you want to take a shower?" She winked and my heart dropped.

I just stood there. Frozen. I needed to get away.

"Yes. I'm going to head to my bathroom while you soak." I quickly turned away and made my way out of the bathroom and to my room. I was staying in the bedroom that had a private bath.

"Lark?" Azurdee called out. I knew I was making a dick out of myself by walking away from her, but I needed space. I wasn't sure what was happening to me and I needed to get away.

As soon as I got to my room I shut the door and ran my hands down my face. "What in the fuck is happening? Keep it together, Williams. You don't lose control. Ever."

I walked into the bathroom and turned on the shower. I walked in and let the scalding hot water run down my face and body. *What was this girl doing to me?* I needed to stay focused. I've always been focused. *Always.* I closed my eyes and thought back to the day I first met Skip.

***

I sat in the small office looking around at all the pictures. I wasn't sure why I was called in; I did my job and I did it damn well. The door opened and I looked up. I stood up and was immediately told to sit down.

"Sit down, Lieutenant Williams. Don't bother with all the formalities."

I slowly sat back down and said, "Yes sir."

He looked down at me and said, "Call me Skip."

I nodded my head.

He pulled out a file and read over it for a few minutes before looking up at Colonel Walker. "Colonel, may I speak to the lieutenant in private please?"

Colonel Walker nodded and looked at me and gave me a nod. He and I had become rather close. He'd told me on more than one occasion I was the best shot in the Marine Corps and I liked that he didn't question anything I did.

The door shut and Skip tossed my file on the desk.

"I want to pull you out of MSOR and have you come work for me."

I moved slightly in my chair and looked at him. "What exactly would I be doing, sir?"

The smile that spread across his face caused me to smile.

"I hear you like to live on the dangerous side. Tell me why?"

I shrugged my shoulders. "I don't know what you mean, sir, by living on the dangerous side."

He let out a sigh. "I'm going to cut to the chase, Williams. I've read your file. I probably know more about you than you do. Your girlfriend in college died and since then you live life like you could care less if you die or not. You fuck everything with a pussy if given the chance and have no desire to settle down. You're good at what you do. Very good. I don't think I've ever seen anyone with as accurate a shot as you in my life. You fly helicopters and planes, you know your way around when they drop your ass off in the middle of nowhere and you have a sixth sense about things. You speak Spanish, Italian, and German. You're an overachiever who doesn't give a fuck about anything but serving his country. I want to use that to my advantage. I want you to come work under me. CIA."

I looked at him, confused. "How in the hell did you know about

Nikki?"

He smiled and said, "I've talked to almost every person I could find who has had some sort of contact with you."

"Why?"

"Because I want you to come work for me. Some things would change in your life though. I need your life to appear somewhat normal."

I laughed and shook my head. "I'm sorry sir, but my life has been far from normal for some years now."

"You'd have to tell your family you were discharged from the Marine Corps. Medically, as far as they need to know."

"I don't want to leave the Marine Corps, sir. It's my life," I said as I began to feel the anger build up inside of me. Being in the Marines had helped me forget about Nikki. I loved the Marines.

"Listen to me for a minute, Lieutenant, before you keep interrupting me. You would still be in the Marines. You would just be telling your family and friends you're not. You'd be living in Austin, Texas because I'm based out of there. I like the night life there," he said with a wink. "When we have a mission I call you, you get all the shit ready, and we head out. Some missions only take a couple days, some a few weeks, some a few months. You finish your mission and come back to Austin and resume your normal life appearance."

I leaned back and took it all in. "What type of missions?"

The smile that spread across his face almost gave me chills. "The secret kind, son."

I sat there for a good two minutes not saying a word. "So let me see if I have this right, sir. You want me to tell my family and friends I've gotten hurt and will be medically discharged from the Marines, but actually I'll still be in the Marines but assigned under you at the CIA? I'll move to Austin, appear to live a normal life, but when you call, which I'm guessing could be at any given moment, I would be heading out on a secret mission? Is it danger-ous?"

"Yes son, it is. I'm asking you to be dropped off in remote loca-tions with a partner, or sometimes alone."

"What would I be doing, sir?" I asked, and he let out a laugh.

"What you do best, son. Shoot."

I already knew what was next, so why I asked I had no idea.

"Shoot what, sir?"

He stood up and looked down at me. "The enemy."

The element of danger rushed through my veins. This is what I lived for. Putting myself out there on the edge. "I'll give you twenty-four hours to think about it."

I stood up and said, "I don't need twenty-four hours. I'll do it, sir."

He threw his head back and laughed. As he looked back at me he shook his head. "I knew you were the perfect guy for this. No commitments, no fucking woman to hold you down or mess with your head. The perfect shot. You're a dream come true for me."

As he put his arm around me and led me out of the room, he said, "Lark Williams, your whole life is about to change."

***

I opened my eyes when I felt her hands run down my back. I slow-ly turned around and looked into her eyes. I had to suck in a breath as she looked at me with nothing but passion in her eyes.

"I missed your touch," she whispered.

Recuerde guardar mi corazón. I have to remember to guard my heart. I can't let her in.

I pulled her to me and lifted her up as she wrapped her legs around me. I turned and pushed her against the cold tile shower and brought her down onto my rock-hard dick. This girl was going to drive me insane.

She moved her hips in perfect rhythm with me and before long we were both whispering each other's names as I poured myself into her for the third time tonight. The feeling of being without a condom made it all the more incredible.

I slowly set her down and reached for the washcloth and soap, and then began cleaning her body. When I cleaned between her legs I slowly massaged her clit, causing her to call out in another orgasm. I glanced up to see her smiling down at me. I closed my eyes and pushed the feelings I had deep down inside.

When I stood up, she was about to do the same for me, but I turned the shower off. I saw the hurt move across her face and I hated myself but there was no way I could let her touch me like that. I would never let her do what all the other women have done to me. Thinking of Azurdee getting me off or giving me a blow job about turned my stomach.

I stepped out of the shower and wrapped a towel around my waist as I took another towel and wrapped it around her. I was about to start drying her off when she smiled and quickly began drying herself off. I had to admit it hurt like hell, but I knew she was only doing what I had just done to her by not allowing her to take care of me.

She yawned and I couldn't help but smile. She was so damn beautiful and looked adorable trying to hide her yawn. I walked up to her and picked her up.

"Come on *mi amor*, let's get some sleep."

She settled her head into my chest and let out a small contented sigh. I knew she had to be exhausted, not to mention sore as shit.

I walked up to my bed and gently set her down. I pulled the

sheets back and watched as she dropped her towel and climbed into the bed. I followed her and as I lay down I pulled her close to me. I needed to feel her against me for some reason. I had a feeling our night was going to come to an end sooner than I wanted.

I listened to her breathing settle out and knew the moment she had fallen into a deep sleep when her entire body relaxed into mine. I wasn't sure how long I lay there taking in the fact that I had the most amazing and beautiful girl in my arms. And it had been the first time I'd slept in a bed with another girl since Nikki.

As I drifted off to sleep, I began dreaming of Azurdee and me walking along a beach holding hands. We both turned and looked at each other and I was overcome with how much I was in love with her.

I quickly sat up and tried to control my breathing. I looked over at Azurdee, who was fast asleep. I quickly pushed my dream aside. There was no way I was in love with her. *None.*

I was about to lie back down when my phone went off. I reached for it and looked at Skip's message.

Skip: Heading to Venezuela. Get back to Austin ASAP, Lieutenant.

I quickly typed back.

Me: Leaving in twenty.

I set my cell down and turned to look at my sleeping beauty. *Mi amor.* I couldn't bear the thought of calling her sweetheart. That's what I called the girls I hooked up with so I wouldn't have to remember their names.

I slowly got up and cursed myself for bringing her to my bed. I grabbed my bag and pushed everything into it as I slipped on a pair of jeans and a T-shirt. I grabbed my phone and put it in my pocket. I looked down at Azurdee and smiled. I dropped my bag and headed out of the room, but not before I went into her room and grabbed her sheets and carried them down to the laundry room. I quickly put them in the wash and started it as I made my way out back and over to the garden. I walked up to a rose bush and broke off a rose. I brought it up to my nose and took in a long deep smell. I wasn't sure why red roses reminded me of Azurdee, but they did.

I made my way back into the house and up to my room. I leaned down and gently kissed her on the lips. She barely smiled and whispered, "Lark."

I pulled away quickly and set the rose down on my pillow. I picked up the pen and pad of paper on the end table and wrote her out a note.

I slipped it under the rose and looked at her one more time. A feeling I'd never experienced before washed over my body. My hands began shaking and I quickly turned and walked away as I pushed the feeling away and started thinking about what I had to do to get ready for the mission.

CHAPTER 6

Azurdee

ISLOWLY OPENED MY eyes to see the bedroom was filled with daylight. I stretched and smiled as I felt muscles ache that I didn't even know I had. I closed my eyes and thought back to last night.

Lark had made love to me.

As I moved my legs I could feel how sore I was. *Oh shit.* I instantly worried I wouldn't be able to do anything today with Lark, and that caused my stomach to drop. I sat up and looked to my right. The bed was empty and my heart began pounding in my chest. I looked and saw the rose on the pillow with a note under it.

I picked up the rose and smelled it as I let a smile play across my face. I reached for the note and opened it.

Azurdee,

I am so sorry I had to leave. My boss called and I have to meet him in Austin to leave for a few days. I'll call you as soon as I am back in town.

Thank you for such an amazing night last night. I could never put it down in words what it meant to me. I hope you're not too sore, mi amor, but sore enough to think of me every time you move.

Until next time,

Lark

I held the note to my chest and let out a sigh. I swung my legs over the edge of the bed and stood up. The moment I walked I felt it. *Oh yeah, Lark had nothing to worry about. Every step I took I would think of him.* I giggled as I made my way to the bathroom.

After taking a quick shower, I headed to my bedroom. I was walking on air I was so happy. Even though Lark had to leave I was filled with a sense of excitement. I stopped when I walked into the bedroom and saw he had taken the sheets off my bed. I smiled and shook my head.

I quickly threw on some yoga pants and a T-shirt. I made my way over to my purse and grabbed my cell phone. I couldn't wait to text Jessie and tell her I had finally done it.

I swiped my finger and saw I had three text messages. Two from Jess and one from...Lark. My heart did a silly little flutter as I opened his text.

Lark: Good morning, beautiful. I hope that you aren't too sore this morning. I should be back in four days, five at the most. Last night was amazing, Azurdee. Thank you for giving me such a special gift.

I smiled as I wrote back.

Me: Good morning. I missed you this morning, but honestly if you had been here I think I'd be even more sore than I am right now. It's the most amazing sore I've ever experienced though. Please be safe. See you when you get back.

Then I opened Jessie's messages.

Jessie: Hey girl! So I'm dying to know...after the way Lark was looking at you all afternoon, I have to know. Did it happen finally?

Jessie: Bitch. Why are you ignoring me?

I grinned as I hit reply.

Me: You're on your honeymoon. Why are you texting me? Shouldn't you be having hot sex right now on the beach?

Jessie: Hot sex in the ocean baby...and let me tell you it was H.O.T. Anyway, Scott fell asleep so I'm sitting by the pool. Call me!

I hit Jessie's number and got ready for the inquisition. "Hey girly! So...tell me everything!"

I laughed and said, "There's nothing to tell, really."

I heard her sigh. "No! No no no. I saw the way Lark couldn't keep his eyes off of you. Ari texted me and told me you and Lark practically had sex on the dance floor."

I rolled my eyes and was going to kill Ari the next time I saw her. "Lark left for work," I busted out.

"What? Oh Azurdee, I'm so sorry."

I closed my eyes and could almost feel his breath on my neck. "Don't be sorry, he left earlier this morning," I said in a husky voice. I snapped my eyes open and let out a sigh. "Were you super sore after your first time?"

Silence.

"Hello? Jessie?"

"What did you just ask me?" she said.

I chuckled. "After your first time. Were you sore?"

Then she screamed. Right in my ear. "Azurdee! You and Lark? Oh. My. God. Was it good? I mean, I know it hurts at first, but after that? How many times did y'all? Was he sweet to you? That bastard better have been sweet to you! Was it hot? Oh my God, tell me everything!"

I laughed as I made my way downstairs. I saw about a half dozen people out back cleaning up the rest of the reception. Tables and chairs were being taken down and placed into a trailer.

"Azurdee!"

"Oh, sorry. I was watching them take down the rest of the things from the reception."

She let out a long sigh and said, "Azurdee, spill it."

I moved into the living room and sat down on the sofa. "Oh Jessie, it was amazing. He was amazing. He kept calling me *mi amor*! It melted my heart every time he said it. He was sweet, passionate, and so gentle. It was beyond anything I had ever dreamed."

She let out the silliest little yelp. "I knew Lark Williams had it in him. He just needed to find the right girl."

My stomach dipped a little and my smile faded a bit. "Well, I'm not sure if I'm the right girl or even *the girl*."

"Wait. Was this a one-time thing? Please tell me you didn't agree to him taking your virginity and walking away!"

"No. We both agreed that we would be exclusive, but I have a feeling this is the first time he has been exclusive since…well since…" *Why couldn't I say her name?*

"Nikki?" Jessie asked.

"Yes. Jessie, why do I feel like I'm in competition with someone who passed away years ago? I can't shake this feeling that he was comparing me to her."

She let out a breath and said, "Pesh. Nonsense, Azurdee. He would never do that. I'm sure it was probably just very powerful for him. I mean, by his own admission he has said he has no intentions of ever…"

Her voice trailed off and I knew she was regretting what she had just said. "Jessie, I knew how Lark was and how he thought when I got into this. I know he could walk away at any given moment."

I silently prayed that would never happen, but deep down inside I knew it was a strong possibility.

"He won't walk away, sweetie. I see the way he looks at you. I think you are the game changer he's been waiting for."

I bit down on my fingernail and began chewing it. "Maybe. I don't want to get my hopes up, ya know?"

"So tell me…are you sore?" she asked with a giggle.

I felt like a teenager in high school. "Let's just say he told me he was going to make it so I would think about him every time I moved…for a few days."

Jessie let out a gasp and began laughing. "Oh my."

I dropped my head back onto the sofa and said, "Jessie…he is amazing. I mean…the way he can be so sweet and then so dirty. *Oh God*. He had me going insane with lust for him."

"The sweet part surprises me, but not the dirty," she said with a laugh.

I laughed in return and said, "Four times."

"Four times! Look at the stamina Mr. Williams has!"

We both lost it in a laughing fit. "Jesus, Azurdee. No wonder you're sore."

"Bed twice, bathtub once, and then the shower," I said in an almost whisper.

"Well damn. I'm a bit jealous. I think I'm going to have to run a hot bath," Jessie said with a giggle. "When will he be back?"

The strangest feeling moved over me and I wasn't really sure what to think of it. I almost felt scared. Like Lark might be in some kind of danger.

"Azurdee?"

Jessie's voice pulled me out of my daydream. "He um…he said he'd be back in five days at the most."

"He mention where he was going?" Jessie asked. I could see her now all perked up. I let out a weak laugh and said, "Nope."

"Damn it. What does that boy do for a living? One of these days I'm gonna find out."

Right then my cell phone buzzed and I pulled it away. A text message from Lark scrolled across the top.

"Oh my God!" I screamed.

"What? Is everything okay? What's wrong?" Jessie screamed back.

"He just sent me a text. I gotta go!"

"No! Wait. Don't hang up you bitch—put me on speaker and read it," Jessie said in a panicked voice.

I hit speaker and opened up his text message.

Lark: I can't stop thinking about you. I hope your morning is going good.

Even with Jessie on the phone, I had to reply right away.

Me: I can't stop thinking about you either. My morning has been...uneventful so far.

He quickly replied back.

Lark: Have to take off again but just wanted to say hey. See ya in a few.

Me: Be careful and have a safe trip.

Lark: Always.

Jessie cleared her throat. "Hello! I'm still here, ya know. What did he say?"

I sighed and said, "He said he was thinking about me and that he hoped I had a good morning. He said he had to take off again and would see me in a few days."

Jessie and I both let out sighs and then began laughing. "Well,

I mean it's not very romantic considering he just popped your cherry and all."

"Jessie! Oh. My. God. Really?"

"Hey, I have to run. I see my handsome husband walking my way. Take it easy and stay at the house as long as you want, sweets. I'll see ya when we get back."

"Hey, Jessie?"

"Yeah?"

I took a deep breath and slowly let it out. "Do you think Lark is…well, do you think he is capable of just being with one person? You don't think I just made a mistake, do you?"

"Azurdee, I know I've never seen Lark look at someone like he does you. I know he never talks about bagging girls, as he so lovingly puts it, anymore. Yes, I think he is very capable of being with just one person. Do you think you made a mistake?"

I chewed on my lip and said, "No. Either way, I wanted it to be him."

"Don't worry, babe. I have a feeling Mr. Williams is officially off the market."

I gave a weak smile even though I knew she couldn't see me. "One more thing, Jess. Bathtub sex is amazing."

She let out a laugh and said, "Oh hell yeah it is!"

I hung up and tossed my phone to the side of me. I held out my hand and it was shaking. I dropped my head back and let out the breath I had been holding. I looked up and glanced over to the buffet table and saw a picture of Scott and Lark when they went fly fishing a few months back. I got up and walked over to it. I reached down and picked it up and ran my finger across his face.

I closed my eyes and whispered, "Lord, please keep him safe and please let me shake this uneasy feeling I have."

I set the picture back down and decided I needed to go for a run and clear my head.

I headed into the laundry room and put the sheets in the dryer and then bolted upstairs to change.

By the time I was running on the dirt road that ran around Scott and Jessie's place, I was finally feeling better. I began running a little faster as I thought about all the things I wanted Lark to do to me when he got home.

I attempted to push Lark from my thoughts and began planning things for the restaurant. Another half a mile and I stopped. I put my hands on my hips and let my head drop.

"Shit. Shit. Shit," I yelled out. I shook my head and took in a few deep breaths and totally pushed Lark Williams out of my mind as I began running and started laying out the table locations in my head.

When my cell phone buzzed, I stopped and pulled it out, shocked I even had a signal. One look at who it was and I rolled my eyes. I hit reject and started running back toward the house.

The last thing I wanted to do was talk to Paul right now.

CHAPTER 7

Lark

I SAT ON THE HOOD of the jeep and watched the sunset as I wondered what Azurdee was doing. I felt someone slap me on the back and I glanced over to my left and saw Skip standing there smiling.

"You're deep in thought, Lieutenant. What's going on? I don't think you've ever been this quiet."

I shrugged my shoulders and said, "Probably just tired from all the wedding bullshit."

Skip laughed and said, "Don't even be thinking of settling down like that crazy-ass friend of yours. I need your head clear."

I gave him a weak smile and nodded my head. "Roger that, sir."

Skip and I always addressed each other properly when on a mission. We never went by first names. Away from this madness and he was probably one of my best friends.

"Damn, I swear the sunsets in Venezuela are some of the most beautiful I've seen."

I nodded my head and the ache in my heart grew ten times worse. *What in the hell was wrong with me?* I couldn't get Azurdee out of my head. I hated that I had to leave her and hoped like hell she understood.

Skip gave me a good slap on the back and said, "Come on. Get some sleep. Y'all head out at oh-five-hundred."

Once I got to my quarters, I pulled up Azurdee's text message.

I took a deep breath and hit reply.

Me: Just wanted to say I won't be able to text ya for a few days but know I'm thinking of you. I'll text you when I'm able to.

Azurdee: Okay. No worries. I've decided to head back to Austin tomorrow and check on things at the new restaurant.

I took in a breath.

Me: I'm really sorry I had to leave you like that, Azurdee. I hope you know I had no choice.

Azurdee: I understand, so please don't worry. I'll be thinking of you, Lark.

I took a deep breath and decided to just be honest with her... and myself.

Me: I miss you, Azurdee. I just got you and I had to let you go. It's killing me inside because I want to feel your body next to mine. I want to breathe in your smell and get lost in your kiss.

Azurdee: I miss you too, Lark. I feel the same way. I've been trying to shake this feeling all day. I've just missed your touch. The sound of your voice and what you feel like inside of me. But just think how nice it will be when you get back!

Me: I've got to run. I'll talk to you in a few days.

Azurdee: Okay. See ya in a few days.

I tossed my phone aside and put my head in my hands. "Fuck!" I called out. The second I read her response back to me I had to stop talking to her. I can't let this girl affect me like this. I didn't want to care about Azurdee, but I did. More than I wanted to admit. I cared enough to be exclusive with her and just like that, she was missing me today. Missing my touch and what I felt like inside of her.

Son of a bitch. I needed to forget about her for just a few days. My phone beeped and I was afraid it was Azurdee. I picked it up to see I had a text message from Sherry.

Sherry: You in town? I need to release some stress and I need a good hard fuck right now.

Sherry had been my fuck buddy since before I joined the Marines. Neither one of us wanted a relationship with each other. It was purely sex and a way for both of us to release stress.

I clenched my jaw as I wrote back.

Me: Sorry. Out of town working.

Sherry: Can you Face Time, baby? Come on…I need you.

Me: I can't. People are around. Go find that guy Mark you've been fucking.

Sherry: Lark. I don't want Mark. I want you. Please baby…I have my dildo right here and I know how you like to watch me use it. I want to hear you get off to me getting off.

I rolled my eyes and let out a sigh. Now that Azurdee was in the picture, I wasn't sure how to handle the whole Sherry thing.

Me: Sorry sweetheart. I've got to run. Have fun!

I turned off my phone and set it on the side table. I needed to get my head clear. I lay down and slowly began concentrating on my breathing to relax myself. Before I knew it my head was completely clear and I was drifting off to sleep.

***

We had begun our hike up Pico Bolivar early this morning. I had Jason Philips with me, and a new guy, Ricker. I've worked with

Jason many times, but never with and Ricker. I stopped and looked back at them. They might be expert riflemen but they sucked at physical endurance.

"Come on ladies, my mother could move up this mountain faster than you pansy asses."

"Fuck off, Lieutenant," Sergeant Philips said. I smiled as I made my way up to our check-in point.

I sat down and began glassing the area we were headed. "Sergeant, call in our location," I said in a low voice.

"Yes sir, calling in our location."

We sat there for a few minutes so they could both drink and get rested up for the rest of the hike up. I could have kept going but these two pussies needed a break. I let out a deep breath and wished they would give me a Navy SEAL to partner up with. Those bastards are in-shape motherfuckers.

I stood up and grabbed my shit and kicked Sergeant Philips. "Let's go."

***

One of the things I liked about my job was the fact that I could sit for hours in silence and not think about anything but what I was set to do. We'd spent the night up here and that was exactly what I needed to clear my head. I glanced down at my watch. The target should be showing up soon. I looked through my scope at the small village below. Things seemed to be normal and nothing looked out of place. The target was supposed to show up with limited bodyguards and in an open jeep. That made my job a hell of a lot easier. I put my headphones on and hit play on my iPod. I listened to the same song every time, "Gotta Be Tonight" by Lifehouse.

I looked back and gave them the signal to the countdown. Five minutes later, my target was pulling up in a jeep. I settled into position, looked into my scope, and let out the breath I was holding as I squeezed the trigger.

Two minutes later we were humping back out as fast as we could, making our way to the extraction site.

As we made our way down, the new guy, Sergeant Ricker said, "Shit. If my girlfriend ever found out what I did for a living, she'd probably leave me."

I stopped dead in my tracks and looked at him. "What?"

He held up his hands and said, "Oh no sir, I don't talk to her about what I do. She just knows I'm in the Marines."

I shook my head and said, "No, why would she leave you?"

He shrugged his shoulders and said, "I don't know. To me, killing someone like that douchebag is no big deal, but I'm not sure how she would feel. Ya know?"

"Lieutenant, we have to get a move on to make it to the extraction site on time," Sergeant Philips said.

I couldn't shake the uneasy feeling I had as we made our way down the mountain. *If Azurdee ever found out what I did, would she leave me?* I was so lost in thought I wasn't paying attention and slipped on a rock and tumbled forward, hitting the side of my face on a rock as I made my way to a stop.

"Fuck, Lieutenant Williams, are you okay?" Ricker asked.

"Shit, Lark, what the fuck?" Jason said.

I wiped the blood away and kept moving. "I'm fine. Let's just get the fuck out of here. I'm ready to get home."

As we sat in the helicopter and made our way back to the base, Ricker leaned over and said, "Lieutenant, I just wanted to say I'd never in my life seen anyone shoot so damn accurate at that far of a distance. No wonder they say you're the best."

I smiled and nodded my head and closed my eyes, giving him

a sign I wasn't in the mood to talk to him. My head was killing me and I knew I was going to end up with a black eye all from a stupid-ass mistake. I couldn't afford to make mistakes in what I do. I knew Skip would give me hell about this and ask a million questions. To him I was perfect and never made a mistake. Bad enough I was a Marine, but I was a Marine working for the CIA.

As I jumped off the helicopter and made my way over to the medic, Skip grabbed my arm and pulled me off to the side.

"What in the fuck happened?" he asked, with a cigar hanging out of his mouth. Skip was five years older than me and was a built motherfucker. He stood about two inches shorter than me, with brown hair and blue eyes. The girls went crazy for him.

I pulled my arm from his grip and asked, "What do you mean? I did the job. Target is dead and we extracted with no problems. I'm ready to get the fuck home."

He looked up to the cut above my eye. He reached for my chin and grabbed it and turned my head as he pointed to my right eye. "This. What the fuck happened to you? You never called in that you were hurt."

I pulled my head back and took a step away. "Jesus Christ, Skip. It's just a cut."

"It's Agent Martin, Lieutenant Williams."

I let out a sigh and shook my head. "I tripped and fell. It's nothing."

He just looked at me. "Something hasn't been right with you since I first saw you a few days ago. You want to tell me what's going on?"

All I could see was Azurdee's eyes as I made love to her for the first time. I shook my head and cleared the image from my thoughts. "I just need to get laid, sir."

A smile slowly spread across his face. "That's it? I was think-

78

ing that wedding was messing with your goddamn mind. Making you think you might want what your friend has."

I laughed and said, "Fuck no. Marriage is the last thing on my mind."

He put his hand on my shoulder and gave me a small shake. "Good. Lark, you can't afford to be having some girl get in the way of what we do. Trust me. It fucks with your head and before you know it you're fucking up left and right. I picked you for a reason, son. Your time is almost up in the Corps and I want you with us in the CIA. That means money and more action."

I nodded my head and he winked as he said, "Go get your head checked out. That bitch looks bad."

As I walked over to the medic, I let out a chuckle. Fuck, I didn't care about the money. Tristan and I had inherited more money than we would ever need from our grandparents. Plus with the trust fund from my other grandparents, I had more money than I knew what to do with. It was never about the money. It was always about the job and the thrill I got from the danger of it all.

Something was slowly starting to shift ever since the day a beautiful brown-haired beauty smiled at me and woke something up deep down inside me.

***

I stood and looked at myself in the mirror. Fuck. How was I going to explain this to Azurdee?

I didn't need stitches, but my eye was swollen and starting to turn black and blue. I flopped down on my bunk and let out a sigh. There was a knock on my door and I yelled, "Come in."

Skip poked his head in and said, "We leave at oh-six-hundred. Make sure everything is ready to go. We're heading into town. If you want that pussy, I bet we could find you a sweet little *puta* to help ya out."

"Nah, I'm exhausted. I think everything from the wedding is catching up to me. I'll make up for it when I get home. Besides, Sherry wants a FaceTime fuck session." I had no plans on FaceTiming Sherry, but Skip didn't need to know that. I'd told Skip about Sherry a while back, so it wasn't something he would question. I'd turned down going out before to FaceTime with her.

"All right, but I bet a real woman with her lips wrapped around your dick is just what you need." He laughed and shut the door. I let out a sigh and got up and walked to the shower and turned it on hot. I turned my cell phone on and then stripped out of my clothes and got into the shower.

Damn, it felt so good to have the hot water run over my body. My eye stung like a son of a bitch, but I quickly got over it. I closed my eyes and pictured myself fucking Azurdee against the wall in the shower. I let out a moan as I could practically feel her body against mine. I moved my hand down to my dick and began stroking it as I thought about Azurdee. The look in her eyes when I came inside her for the first time. The sweet little noises she made while I fucked her hard from behind.

I began stroking myself faster and could feel the build up. Fuck I was getting close. My damn phone rang and for some crazy reason I thought it might be Azurdee. I quickly jumped out of the shower and about busted my ass as I swiped my finger across the screen without paying attention to who was calling.

"Hello!" I said, as I panted hard and fast.

"Michael? Are you okay? Oh God, am I interrupting you having sex?"

Wait. What in the hell?

"Mom?"

"Hello, darling. Am I interrupting anything? Do you have a

girl with you?" she asked in the most nonchalant way.

"Um…I was um…" I couldn't even think straight. *What in the hell is wrong with me?* I was whacking myself off in the shower and now I'm talking to my mother. I reached for a towel and quickly dried off.

"Michael, if you're with a girl, just call me back."

I quickly shook my head and wanted out of this conversation. "Mom! For shit's sake, I'm not with a girl. I was in the shower and I thought you were Azurdee and I didn't want to miss her call and…"

Oh shit. Fuck me. I've just opened up Pandora's box.

I heard her let out a little squeal and I was pretty sure she clapped her hands. "My oh my. What a beautiful name. Now who is this Azurdee girl? Michael, did you meet her at the wedding yesterday? What does she look like? What does she do for a living? Oh please tell me she doesn't know you have money, sweetheart. You know how women can be."

"Mom. Please just stop with the questions," I said as I ran my hand through my wet hair. I looked down at my poor dick and sighed.

"Well, I'm sorry but that is the first time you've mentioned a girl's name in years. I'm just curious. Can a mother be curious about what is going on in her son's life?"

"Sure you can, Mom, as long as that son is Tristan and not me. Hey, speaking of, did you know he is dating someone?" I said as I sat down on the bed and let out a small laugh.

"Don't even try that with me, young man. Come on. Spill it."

I let out a loud groan and said, "Fine, Mom. If I tell you a little bit about her, will you drop it?"

"Yes."

I could picture her now with her fingers crossed and a wide smile on her face.

"Azurdee is Jessie's best friend from college. I met her last year right after Christmas. No, she has no idea how much money I have, nor does she care. She owns a coffee shop in Wimberley, Texas and is fixin' to open a small restaurant. Her father is filthy rich but she won't take a dime from her parents. She's beautiful, with long dark hair and caramel eyes that sparkle in the daylight, she speaks Spanish and we just started…" I trailed off. What did we just start? Fucking? Dating? Could you call it dating when all we've done is had sex?

"Michael Lark Williams. You like this girl," my mother said, with shock pouring out of her voice.

"Well of course I like her, Mother, I've…"

"You've what?"

"Um…well I've um. I've ah…it doesn't matter. There. I told you about her. Now can we drop it?"

She let out a laugh. "You have to bring her down to the ranch. What about Christmas? Tristan is bringing his *friend.* It would be wonderful to have you bring a friend home, Michael. Please say yes."

"Wait. Tristan is bringing a girl home?" I asked as I quickly put my mother on speakerphone and sent a text to Tristan:

Me: What in the fuck? You're bringing a girl home for Christmas? Are you out of your damn mind?

Tristan: Yes I am. I'm bringing Ryn home. She's fun and not looking for anything. Plus it buys me time with mom.

My mother was going on and on about Tristan's girlfriend. She had no idea that Tristan had been fucking two different girls at once since he couldn't decide which one he liked better.

Me: What about Liberty? I thought you liked Liberty.

Tristan: I do like Liberty but she keeps talking commitment. Ryn is more of the type who just goes with the flow.

Me: She won't be once you bring her home to meet the ma and pop. Jesus dude, nothing spells commitment like bringing the girl home to meet the parents. Are you out of your mind?

Tristan: Fuck off Lark and go back to doing what it is you do best, avoiding feelings altogether. At least I'm happy.

I stared at my brother's last text. "Michael, are you even listening to me?"

"Yeah, sorry, Mom. So Tristan is bringing home Ryn, huh?"

"Yes. And oh, honey, it would be amazing if you brought Azurdee home, too."

I rolled my eyes and said, "Sorry, Mom. That's not going to happen. I just started um…we're just taking it one day at a time, so don't be going and getting your hopes up. I'm perfectly happy with the way my life is going."

I heard my mother let out a sigh. "Well, if you happen to change your mind."

"I won't. Listen, Mom, I need to get dressed. I'll talk to you soon, okay? Tell Dad I said hi and I'll see y'all a few days before Christmas."

"Okay darling. Please call me if you need anything, Michael. You know I just want you to be happy. I want you to find love, honey. You deserve it. We will see you soon."

I dropped my head and barely said, "I know you do, Mom, and I wish I believed that. I've got to run, Mom. I love you."

"I love you too."

I hung up and sat there staring down at my phone. I saw that I had four text messages and two voicemails. My heart began beating in my chest as I opened up the text messages.

Not one was from Azurdee. I didn't know why I felt so disappointed by that. I told her I would call her when I could.

I scrolled through them and they were all Sherry begging for a FaceTime fuck session.

I deleted them all and then went to my voicemail. One from Sherry and one from Scott. I listened to Sherry's first.

Lark. I need you desperately. Come on baby, call me back and the next time I see you I promise you can fuck my ass and screw me until your dick doesn't work anymore. I just need you this one time. Baby, please.

My dick jumped at the idea of fucking Sherry in the ass. She had been hinting at it for the last year. I've used her vibrator to fuck her ass but she never would let me do it. I went to push the call back button when I stopped. Azurdee's beautiful face popped into my head. I backed out and hit Scott's message.

Dude, call me as soon as you can. It's important.

My heart began beating faster. *Azurdee.* What if something happened to her, and here I was, the asshole almost about to call Sherry.

I panicked and before I knew it, I was dialing Azurdee's number.

"Hello?"

I let out the breath I was holding when I heard her sweet soft voice.

"Lark? Are you there?" she asked. I could hear noise in the background and wondered where she was. *Was she out with someone?*

"Hello? Lark, can you hear me?"

I cleared my throat and said, "Hey, sorry about that. Bad connection I think," I barely said.

"Is everything okay? You sound like something is wrong."

"Nah, I'm just really tired," I said as I slipped on a pair of sweats.

I heard her talking to someone else. "Will you please excuse me, I have to take this call."

That's when I heard a male's voice reply with, "Of course."

I balled up my fists and instantly wished I hadn't called her.

The noise slowly faded away as I heard a door open and then shut.

"I'm sorry, I'm at a fundraiser for my father's company and wouldn't normally answer the phone but when I saw it was you I…well…I…"

I instantly relaxed and smiled. "You what, *mi amor*? Talk to me."

She let out a giggle and said, "I feel so foolish, like a high school girl with a massive crush."

I fell back onto my pillow and pictured the flush covering her cheeks. "Tell me, Azurdee."

She sucked in a breath and said, "I missed hearing your voice. I can't tell you how many times I wanted to call to just hear your voicemail but I thought that might make me seem like a stalker, so…"

I let out a laugh and said, "Maybe just a little."

"Is your work done? Are you going to be heading home soon?"

My smile faded and I closed my eyes. She can never find out what it is I do. *Never.*

I heard someone talking in the background. "Mom, I'll be right in, just give me a few more minutes."

I opened my eyes and asked. "What are you wearing?"

She giggled and said, "What?"

"What. Are. You. Wearing?"

"Um…a black skirt with a white blouse. Why?" Her voice changed and I knew she was already turned on.

I reached down into my sweat pants and began stroking my dick again.

"Is there somewhere you can go and sit down outside?" I asked, and my breathing increased a little.

"There is a little bench next to an oak tree, but…"

"Go sit down, Azurdee."

I heard her walking. "I'm ah…I'm at the bench."

"Are you sitting down?" I asked as I slowed down my pace. Just the sound of her voice could push me over the edge.

"I'm standing and leaning against the tree because my heart is pounding."

I smiled and asked, "Why is your heart pounding?"

She barely whispered, "I'm not sure."

"Lift up your skirt and slip your hand in your panties, Azurdee, and tell me if you're wet."

"Lark…" she whispered.

"Do it for me, *mi amor*."

She sucked in a breath of air and moaned as she whispered, "Yes."

"Yes, what? Yes you're wet, or yes it feels good to touch your-self?"

"Both. Lark, what are you doing to me?"

I began stroking my dick faster. "Azurdee, I want you to make yourself come, baby, while I make myself come. Put your leg on the bench and let me hear how it feels."

She whispered something I couldn't understand. "Azurdee?"

"Lark, I'm at a fundraiser, anyone could walk out here at any time."

"I miss you, Azurdee…I want to hear you come," I whispered as I slowed down my pace.

I heard her let out a gasp and I knew she had begun touching herself. "Talk to me, Azurdee."

"Oh God…I feel so…oh…it feels so good."

I stroked my dick faster as I asked, "What are you doing to yourself, Azurdee?"

Her breathing was beginning to pick up and I knew she was close. "I'm rubbing my …my…I'm touching my clit. Are you… oh God."

"I'm stroking my dick and the sounds of your moans are pushing me to the edge, Azurdee…I'm so close."

Then I heard her whimper. "Oh God…Lark…I'm coming. Oh God, I'm coming…"

Two fast pumps and I was coming right along with her. "Fuck," I hissed through my teeth. "I'm coming, baby…ahh… God I want to be inside you so damn bad."

"I can't breathe…oh God. I can't believe I just did that!" she whispered as I grabbed my towel and wiped myself off. I shook my head and couldn't believe how incredible that was.

"Jesus, Azurdee. You're my weakness, I swear," I said as I tried to get my breathing back under control.

She let out a giggle and whispered, "Um, excuse me, Mr. Williams, I do believe you are my weakness. I can't stop thinking about you. Dreaming of you making love to me again. I woke up this morning and was touching myself because you were taking me to heaven and back in my dreams."

I let out a long breath and rolled my eyes into the back of my head. "Azurdee, you can't say things like that to me or I'm going to make you go home and do this again."

"Lark…please tell me you're coming back soon," she whispered.

"Tomorrow, I'll be back late tomorrow night."

She let out a little whimper and said, "Will I be able to see you as soon as you get back?"

Don't do this, Lark. "Yes," I whispered before I could stop myself from saying it.

Guarda mi corazón.

"I mean, if I can make it happen. I'm not sure yet, though," I closed my eyes and felt like a dick instantly. I wanted to see her more than anything, but I didn't want her to know that.

Silence. "I see…um…I have to go. I'll talk to you later."

"Azurdee, wait."

The line went dead and I slammed my hand onto the bed and yelled out, "Son of a bitch." I jumped up and ran my hand through my wet hair. I couldn't believe I just did that to her.

I hit dial and her phone rang twice and went to voicemail. "Fuck!" I yelled out.

I redialed and again, two rings and then to voicemail again. "Come on, Azurdee, answer your damn phone."

I called her back again and this time it went straight to voicemail. She must have turned off her phone. I sank down onto the bed and all of a sudden I was so damn tired.

I texted Scott and told him I'd call him tomorrow.

I lay there in bed and stared at the ceiling for what seemed like forever. This is exactly why I needed to guard my damn heart. I couldn't afford to get all tied up emotionally with someone.

Not only could my heart not take it, but also my life depended on it. I slowly gave myself over to sleep.

Guard your heart…always.

CHAPTER 8

Azurdee

I PICKED UP MY phone only to see another missed call from Lark. He had texted me late last night to let me know he was home. I knew it was shitty of me to ignore his calls today, but I couldn't shake the hurt feeling I had when he blew me off the night before last. I had felt so used after he just brushed me off.

I closed my eyes and thought back to the dance we had together at the wedding.

I'm not sure if I can be what you want me to be.

I felt a tear run down my cheek. I knew what I was getting myself into with Lark. The idea of him meeting up with another girl had my stomach turning. I knew he said he wouldn't do that, but I couldn't shake the feeling that he was hiding something from me.

I thought back to my conversation with Jessie earlier this morning.

***

"Azurdee, I think it's because you know he is so secretive about his job. You're reading too much into it. Just take a step back. It's Lark we're talking about. The boy did not do commitment ever, so don't push him."

"I'm not pushing him. At least I don't think I am. What do I do?" I asked as a sob escaped my lips.

"Sweetheart, just take it a day at a time and don't expect too much from him all at once. I think with Lark it's going to have to be baby steps."

***

I slammed my hands down on my sofa and let out a not-so-lady-like sound. I needed to go for a run or something to clear my head. I made my way into my room and changed into a pair of sweats and a T-shirt.

My phone began ringing again and I looked to see it was Lark calling again. I hit reject and decided I would call him after my run when my head was clearer.

I walked into the kitchen and set my phone on the counter and then grabbed a cold water bottle out of the fridge.

I stuck my keys in my pocket and made my way to the door. I opened the door and let out a small scream. Lark was standing there.

How? When?

I sucked in a breath of air and asked, "How did you know where I lived? I mean…what are you doing here?"

"Why are you ignoring my calls?" he asked as he stood there with sunglasses on looking hot as hell. The heat from his body was making it hard for me to think straight.

What did Jessie say? One day at a time.

"Well, after your reaction to me on the phone the other day, I thought maybe you needed some time."

He tilted his head and looked at me. "Time for what?"

I looked down at his lips as he licked them. *Oh God. I want his lips on my body.* I wanted them to give me another mind-blowing orgasm.

"I don't know. Time to think. I thought maybe you were having second thoughts about us… I mean…this."

He took a step closer to me, causing me to take a few steps back into my house. "I've been calling you all day and you haven't answered. It seems to me you're the one who needed time."

I swallowed hard and took in a long slow breath. I slowly shook my head and said, "No. I just…I don't want to push you or make you think that…that…" My mouth dropped open slightly as I watched him pull his T-shirt up and over his head as he walked in and shut my front door. I kept walking backwards until I hit the sofa, my eyes fixed on his massive built chest.

"You have no idea how much I missed you. How much I've been dreaming about being inside you. Yes, Azurdee, that scares the shit out of me, but I don't want to end what we've started. I want you so damn much it almost hurts."

Lark removed his sunglasses and began unbuttoning his pants as I smiled and looked up into his eyes, and that's when I noticed it. I put my hand up to my mouth and said, "Oh my God. Your eye!"

He stopped and didn't move. I looked at his eye, which had a huge cut above it. The entire area around his right eye was black and blue. My heart instantly hurt knowing that he had hurt himself.

"What in the world happened?"

He smiled again and said, "I was hiking and slipped on some rocks and fell." He continued to take off his pants. The daylight streaming into my front windows allowed me to see his body perfectly. I noticed he had a small round scar on his right side. *Why didn't I notice that the other night?*

When he dropped his pants, his erection sprung free and my

stomach dropped. I began licking my lips.

"Do you like what you see, Azurdee?" he whispered.

I swallowed hard and nodded my head. Unable to talk, I just kept staring at him. I couldn't believe that thing was inside me. He was now standing in front of me completely naked.

He placed his hands on the sides of my face and lifted my face so that I was looking directly into his beautiful green eyes. "I'm so sorry I hurt you the other night. I didn't mean to, I just…I got spooked. I'm not used to feeling like this, and it scares the shit out of me. The last thing I ever want to do is hurt you. When you weren't answering your phone, I was scared to death I had pushed you away. I can't lose you, *mi amor*. I won't lose you."

I bit down on my lower lip, trying to keep my tears at bay. His voice was almost pleading.

I said in almost a whisper, "I'm sorry I wasn't answering my phone."

He leaned down and brushed his lips against mine as he let out a low growl. "God you drive me insane with want, Azurdee. I need to be inside you so badly. Please let me make love to you."

Oh. My. God. I think I've died and gone to heaven.

I wanted to quickly strip out of my clothes and tell him to have his way with me, but I had a feeling he needed this to be slow, intimate, and sweet.

I reached for the bottom of my T-shirt and began to pull it over my head. Lark dropped his hands from my face and took a step back. I pulled my sports bra over my head next, and watched as Lark licked his lips. His eyes were moving over my body quickly and I knew he was trying like hell to keep his hands off of me. I decided to use it to my advantage.

I removed both my sneakers and then slowly slid my pants down. I removed them and kicked them off to the side. The only thing I had on now was a pair of light pink lace panties. When I looked up at his face, his mouth was open slightly and I could see his breathing was increasing. I loved that my body could pull such a reaction out of him. Especially since I knew Lark had been with many women before me, but I was pretty sure I was the only one who could evoke this type of passion from him.

At least I hoped so.

"You're so damn beautiful. I've never seen anyone so beautiful before in my life."

The butterflies went off in my stomach and I wanted to throw myself at him and beg him to fuck me fast and hard, but I took a deep breath and decided I was going to be brave. Something about Lark brought out the naughty in me and I was really beginning to like it.

I slowly slipped my hand into my panties as Lark whispered, "Oh God."

I smiled slightly and then let out a gasp as I brushed against my clit and slipped two fingers into my still sore body. I was soaking wet. *What would he do if I said how wet I was?*

"Oh God...I'm so wet..."

The next thing I knew my hand was being pulled out of panties and they were ripped off my body. Lark grabbed me and set me down onto the sofa as he pushed my legs apart and one quick lick of his tongue across my clit had me pushing my hands through his hair and whispering to him how good it felt.

"Lark...oh God...that feels...ahh..."

He pushed two fingers inside of me and I bucked off the sofa and began calling out his name as he massaged out the orgasm. *That has to be one of my favorite ways to come now.*

He pulled his face back and smiled. "I love the taste of you. There is nothing sweeter in this world."

I bit down on my lower lip as he stood up and quickly grabbed himself and stroked his dick a few times. I was shocked at how much it turned me on to see him touch himself like that. I wanted to watch him make himself come so badly.

He reached down and pulled me up into a standing position and then picked me up. He looked around and said, "Where is your bedroom, *mi amor*?"

"Turn right down the hall, last door on the left," I said with a raspy voice. I couldn't believe how much I wanted him. Even after he had just given me such an amazing orgasm, I needed to feel him inside me. I wanted to feel him moving in and out of me and be completely and utterly lost in him.

Lark walked me into my bedroom and I noticed he looked around quickly. I loved my bedroom. The walls were a light silver blue and my wrought iron king-sized bed looked amazing against the color.

I had a small reading nook in one corner and a fireplace in the other. It had been my dream bedroom and when I had the house remodeled, the fireplace was the first thing I had put in. It was cozy and romantic.

Lark walked over to my bed and gently laid me down. "Move up and put your hands above your head, Azurdee."

Something about the tone of his voice when he talked to me like this pushed me almost over the edge. I swore sometimes I could come just from the way he talked to me.

I put my hands above my head and took a deep breath in. "Hold onto the bed frame and don't let it go, or I'll stop making love to you."

I nodded my head. "Okay."

He smiled that smile that wreaked havoc on my heart. When I felt his tip teasing my entrance I instinctively put my hands on him and he stopped.

"Azurdee, your hands." I quickly grabbed onto the wrought iron bed again and let out a moan as he placed two fingers inside of me and massaged me almost to the brink of an orgasm.

"How sore are you?" he asked as he looked into my eyes.

"I was more sore yesterday but all I feel now is a pulsing need for you."

The way the left corner of his mouth lifted in a smile caused me to smile. I loved his smile and would do anything to make him smile every single moment of my life.

"I like that answer." He pulled his fingers out and placed himself right at my entrance.

"Your pussy is always so ready for me," he whispered against my lips.

"Yes," I whispered. The way he talked so dirty to me drove me beyond insane.

"Do not let go of the bed frame. Do you understand?"

I nodded my head frantically. I just needed to feel him inside me. I pushed my hips up some just to feel him.

He pulled back some and said, "Repeat it, Azurdee."

I shook my head, I could hardly think straight. Not being able to touch him and the way he talked to me had me practically panting with need. "I...I won't...let go. Lark, please!"

He smiled at me as he slowly pushed himself into me. I could feel my body stretching to accommodate him. The burning was mixed with pleasure and I let out a long moan at the same time Lark did.

"Fuck, I've missed you," he hissed between his teeth as he pulled out some and slowly pushed back into me.

I let go of the bed frame before grabbing it again. I wanted to touch him. I wanted to pull his body closer to mine. If I could crawl into his body to be closer to him I would.

He began moving in and out a bit faster and every time he pushed in it felt like he would push in deeper. He kept hitting a spot that would push me right to the edge.

He took one of my nipples into his mouth and I reached down and ran my hand through his hair and he stopped moving.

"Azurdee, if you touch me one more time, I'm going to tie your hands to the bed frame."

I let out a gasp and the idea both scared me and thrilled me at the same time. "I think I would like that." Oh my God. Where did that come from? What would my mother think if she knew I was behaving like this wanton creature?

Lark's eyes lit up with something I'd never seen before. He began moving again and the pressure was building up again.

"You have no idea the things I'm going to do to you, Azurdee, now that you shared that, but right now, *mi amor*, is not the time for fucking. I want to make love to you."

My whole body was covered in goose bumps and I shuddered. Lark grinned and put his lips against my neck as he began covering my body with gentle kisses. "I love how your body reacts to me, Azurdee."

"Me. Too," I panted out as Lark let out a chuckle.

He began moving faster, and I felt the build up in my toes slowly moving up my legs. "Oh God."

With each thrust into me, Lark spoke. "You're mine."

"Yes…" I whispered.

"I'm yours," he panted next to my ear.

When he said I was his, it pushed me to the very edge. "Lark, oh God, I'm so close."

He began moving faster as he panted out, "I. Will. Forever. Be. Only. Yours."

That was my undoing. I began screaming out his name as one of the most intense orgasms pulsed through my body. I couldn't believe how fast and hard it hit me. It was still pulsing through my body as Lark bit down on my shoulder and let out a moan as he poured himself into my body.

Lark was hovering over my body as he tried to get his breathing under control. I went to tell him I loved him, but quickly stopped. "Lark, I…"

I closed my eyes and tried like hell to keep the tears back, but I couldn't believe how emotional that was for me and I wasn't sure if Lark felt the same way. His admission that he would forever be mine was unexpected and caused me to fall in love with him even more.

In this moment I knew I had given my heart and soul to Lark Williams and that I would love him forever unconditionally.

CHAPTER 9

Lark

I TRIED TO CALM down my breathing as I kept most of my body weight off of Azurdee. I was so caught up in the moment of us making love I said something I wasn't sure I should have admitted and it was driving me insane wondering what was running through her head. Azurdee lay under me and moved her fingertips lightly up and down my back. She had started to say something and stopped, and I knew what it was going to be.

She was going to tell me she loved me. *Could I say it back to her? Did I love her?* I knew I cared about her so much that if I ever lost her I would be forever ruined. But did I love her? I've only ever loved one person and it brought nothing but heartache.

No. I needed to protect myself from that. Guarda mi corazón siempre.

I pulled away from her some and smiled. "I didn't think anything could top our first time, *mi amor*, but I was wrong."

She nodded her head and said, "It was beautiful."

I pulled out of her and she jutted her lower lip out and pouted. I let out a chuckle and said, "Believe me, I'd love to be buried inside you all the time, but I'm starving. Let's get dinner and then go out dancing."

She looked like she was thinking about something and then she said, "Okay. But I need to shower and get ready."

I winked at her and said, "I'll shower with you and wait for you. Then we'll head to my place and I'll change."

The blush that covered her cheeks caused my dick to jump. "Okay," she whispered as I moved off her. She quickly got up and made her way through another door. I heard the shower turn on and I got up and walked into her master bathroom. It was a hell of a lot smaller than mine, but she had a huge jet tub. Her shower wasn't small, but it wasn't exactly big either. I pictured Azurdee in my shower and imagined how good it would be to fuck her in it.

I turned around and thought long and hard about what I was about to do. I walked up to the sink and splashed my face with cold water and ran my hands down my face.

I wanted this, so why was it such a fucking internal battle? I heard the shower door open and I quickly reached out for her and pulled her to me. She laughed and looked at me with that beautiful smile.

"Do you have to work at the coffee shop tomorrow?" I asked.

She began chewing on her lower lip and said, "No, I don't have to be there."

I leaned down and gently kissed her lips as I mustered up the courage and just went for it. "Pack a bag and stay with me tonight. We can spend the whole day together tomorrow."

I searched her face to see her reaction. When I saw the corners of her mouth move up in a smile, I smiled back. "You want me to stay with you at your place?"

"Yes. Please."

She nodded her head and said, "I'd love to do that."

I pushed her back into the shower and picked her up and made

100

love to her again with the hot water running down our bodies.

Those same feelings of love began bubbling back up, but I pushed them down as I whispered her name as I came. I needed to get a grip on these feelings and the sooner the better.

***

I reached across and grabbed Azurdee's hand as we drove down Congress Avenue. It wasn't lost on me how my stomach did a little stupid flip every time I touched her. I hadn't done this, held a girl's hand, since…Nikki.

I glanced over at her and she had a silly grin on her face.

"So which condos do you live in?" she asked as we crossed over the river. I took a deep breath and slowly let it out. I'd never brought a girl back to my place. Ever. One reason was I didn't want them to see that I had money, and the other was I never had the desire to share my life with anyone.

"I live at the Austonian," I said, waiting for her to make some sort of comment. Her head snapped around and she looked at me.

"Really? My parents almost bought a condo there, but ended up deciding not to when I bought my house in Wimberley."

I pulled into the parking garage and put my truck in park. I glanced at Azurdee, who just seemed to be going with the flow. I closed my eyes and got out of the truck. As Azurdee came around the back of the truck, she let out a whistle.

"Oh wow. Whose pretty yellow Suzuki bike?" she said as she fanned herself like she was hot. I turned and looked down at my bike. I slowly looked back at her and watched her as she eyed the bike.

"You like motorcycles?" I asked.

She looked up at me and her face flushed. "Well, I've actually never ridden on one before, but they are sexier than hell." She giggled and shrugged her shoulders. "At least I think they are."

My dick jumped in my pants as I had an image of Azurdee on my bike. I glanced back at the bike and then laughed as I put my arm around her and pulled her closer to me.

She turned back and looked at the bike and then looked forward. "Do you know who owns it?"

I kept walking to the elevator as I asked, "Why? Do you want to go for a ride?"

"I don't know. It seems like it would be fun."

We walked up to the elevator and Janice was standing there. *Oh great.* I'd fucked her one time against her car in the garage and ever since then she had been looking for a repeat.

She looked Azurdee up and down and then looked at me and smiled. "Your sister, Lark?"

I laughed as the elevator doors opened. I held up my card and hit the button for the fifty-second floor. Janice hit her floor, twenty-four.

"Wow. You live on one of the top floors?" Azurdee asked, and then Janice made a funny sound. I looked at her and she bolted off the elevator at her floor.

"Jesus, this elevator moves so fast," Azurdee said.

I let out a laugh and said, "Fastest ones in Texas." I took a deep breath and grabbed her hand. The elevator opened and we stepped out into the small lobby area. I turned to the right and walked into the hallway and then made another right and walked us into the open kitchen and living room area. Azurdee let out a gasp and whispered, "Oh. My. God."

She dropped my hand and walked right to the door that led to the balcony. I smiled as she said, "You can see the capitol." That would be the one thing she would notice. "Oh my gosh, and the stadium." She spun around and asked, "Can we go out there?"

"Sure we can." I walked up and unlocked the door and stepped out onto the balcony. I had two chairs and a small café table out here where I would normally drink my morning coffee.

"Lark, the view is amazing." I let out a chuckle and said, "Wait until you see the other views. My bedroom has the best view of all. It faces the south side."

She smiled and there went that beautiful red moving across her face. "Want a tour?" I asked.

She nodded her head and I held out my hand. We walked back into the condo and I stopped and said, "I wanted an open floor plan for the kitchen, dining and living room so I dedicated the north end of the unit to that. Each side has a hallway running down it and you can cross over in two different locations. One is the elevator lobby and then another cross-through further down."

She smiled and said, "Who decorated? It's breathtaking."

I smiled and said, "Me and my mother."

She dropped my hand and walked up to my leather sofa. She ran her hand along the back of it as she looked out the windows. "It's nothing but windows. The light in here is amazing."

I walked up and took her hand and led her down the hallway. "Here is a bathroom." I turned on the light and she let out a small sigh. "Lark, it's breathtaking."

I laughed and said, "It's a bathroom."

She shrugged and said, "It's a beautiful bathroom." We made our way to the next enclosed room. "The formal living room. I don't think I've ever sat in here. My mother and father like this room and my dad spends a lot of his time in here."

I watched her face as she looked around at everything. My whole condo was done in a mix of ranch style and contemporary.

"Let's keep going," I said as she followed me out of the formal living room and into a guest bedroom. "This is one of the two guest bedrooms. Each one has an en suite." She nodded her head and took a look around the room.

"This room is very contemporary in style," she said as she ran her hand along the silk bedcover. "It's beautiful. Your mother has amazing taste."

"Yeah, she does. This condo was like a blank canvas for her to try out different things."

I started to make my way out as we moved onto the next room. "Here is the game room." I let out a chuckle. "Where I spend a lot of my time when I have friends over."

I watched as Azurdee first walked up to the window and whispered something again about the view. She turned and looked at the pool table and I couldn't help but notice her glance back at me and then look away with a flushed look. *What was my girl thinking?* I wanted to know what dirty thoughts were running through her mind.

She walked up to the door that led to the guest room. "Does this go to the room next door?"

I nodded my head. "My father's idea."

She smiled and ran her fingers along the edge of the pool table. I knew exactly what I would be doing later on tonight with her when we got home.

As we walked out, I pointed across the corridor. "That is the other cut across that takes you to the west side of the condo. There is another guest room, and to the right a library and to the left my office."

She nodded her head and looked to her left. I smiled and took her hand in mine. I opened the door to my bedroom and she sucked in a breath of air.

"Oh. My. God." She walked in and spun around as she took everything in. She immediately walked up to the windows and looked out. "It's breathtaking. The view is just amazing. Look at the river. You can see it for miles." She spun around and her eyes landed on my king-size bed. When she put her finger in her mouth and gently bit down on it my pants grew a few sizes too small.

She slowly looked away and walked up to the door that led to the master bath. When she pushed the door open, she whispered something else I couldn't hear. "The shower. Oh my gosh—the shower is in the middle of the room!"

I laughed and said, "Yes, it is. I had the shower put in the middle of the room with three glass walls. The floor and the back wall are all Italian marble."

"Aren't you afraid of people seeing you in here…naked?"

I turned around and hit a button and the shades slowly began to make their descent. "Each room has shades on all the windows, but I pretty much keep them open all the time. I like the light."

She walked over to the sinks and turned around and smiled. "Your mother has beautiful taste. I think I love your bedroom and bathroom the best so far."

I smiled and felt my heart drop slightly and I had to lean against the wall since my knees felt weak. "I designed my bedroom and bathroom myself."

She snapped her head back and smiled slightly. "Oh," was all she said as she made her way over to the bathtub. "I've never seen such a deep tub before. I bet it's amazing to soak in."

I walked up behind her and placed my hands on her hips as I brushed my lips against her neck. "I bet it would be even more amazing to fuck you in it."

She quickly turned around as I pulled her body closer to mine. "Yes, please," she whispered.

I leaned down and kissed her as she laced her arms around my neck and deepened the kiss. I knew what she was wanting and I wanted it too.

I pulled away and said, "Azurdee, if I take you now, I'm going to want to take you in every single one of these rooms and we won't ever be able to go out tonight."

"I'm okay with that," she said with a crooked smile that spread across her face. I laughed as I pulled her arms from around my neck and led her back to the master bedroom. I walked up to a door and led her into my office.

She walked in and looked around. She made her way over to the bookcase and began looking at all my pictures. Most were of my family and Marine Corps buddies. She picked up the one of Skip and me when we were in Hawaii.

"Who's this?"

I swallowed hard and said, "My boss." I walked over and took the photo out of her hand and led her back out of the office. As we walked down the hall I said, "There is another guest bedroom here that pretty much looks like the one on the east side of the condo. The next room is the library."

I pushed open the door and watched her face as she walked in. "Holy shit. There are floor-to-ceiling bookshelves in here. Where are all the books?"

I looked around and shrugged. "I don't know, I'm still adding to my collection."

She walked up and pushed the ladder from one side of the room to the other. Then she turned and walked up to the leather sectional that was placed in the middle of the room and faced out to the windows.

"Sometimes I like to come in here and work and watch the sunset. It's very peaceful in this room. I think it's my second favorite room."

"Your favorite?" she asked as she tilted her head and looked at me.

"My bedroom."

We stood there and stared at each other for a few minutes before she broke the silence. "Your home is beautiful, Lark. Breathtaking, really. I can't even find the words to describe it."

I gave her a slight smile, "It's just a place to sleep and eat. Sometimes work."

She nodded her head and I knew she was wondering how many girls I had brought home. The way she was looking at the sectional I wanted to ask her what she was thinking.

"You're the first girl I've ever brought up here."

The smile that spread across her face caused me to smile. I could almost see the relief spreading across her entire body and she instantly relaxed.

"Why don't you grab a glass of wine and have a seat in here and I'll get dressed to go out."

"I'm good for now, but thank you," she said as she slowly sank down onto the sofa as her eyes began looking everywhere.

"If you change your mind, the wine cooler is in the kitchen near the end of the island."

I turned to walk out, but stopped at the door and turned to face her. I didn't know what was running through her head on how I could afford a place like this. "I got a pretty big inheritance from my grandparents, and my other grandparents set up a trust for me and Tristan."

Her mouth dropped open and her eyes filled with hurt. "Lark, you don't have to explain anything to me. It never even crossed my mind and it certainly isn't any of my business."

I nodded my head slightly and made my way to my room. I sat down on my bed and tried to control my breathing. I didn't want to be falling for her. I couldn't go through that again. The whole time she was walking around, all I wanted to do was tell her I could see her living here with me. I could see her in my future. I closed my eyes and pictured her pregnant and standing on the balcony looking out over the river.

I snapped my eyes open and stood up quickly. *What the fuck?* I ran my hands down my face and let out a frustrated moan.

Damn it, Williams. Stop dreaming this crazy-ass dream of yours and get your head out of your ass.

I decided that tonight I wasn't going to think of anything but having a good time with Azurdee. Nothing more and nothing less.

No more images of her in my bed, standing in my kitchen cooking, and certainly not of her standing on my balcony pregnant.

Recuerde guardar mi corazón.

CHAPTER 10

Azurdee

THE SECOND LARK WALKED out of the library, I fell back into the sofa. "Holy shit," I whispered. I looked around and took in the massive library. I closed my eyes and thought about his bedroom.

The beautiful sage green walls took my breath away the moment I walked in. It was so calming and not at all what I expected from Lark Williams. There was a beautiful silk comforter that was almost the exact color as the walls but with wide light cream stripes running across it. The bench that sat along one of the windows looked almost too inviting and I wanted to sit down and just take in the view.

Oh...and the balcony. Good Lord, who would ever want to leave such a beautiful room? It faced East, South, and West. The master bathroom looked like a damn spa with the marble floors and white sinks and tub. *The tub.* I let out a small whimper when I thought back to when Lark mentioned fucking me in the tub. I reached my hand down and slipped it into my skirt and then my panties. When I brushed my fingers across my clit I let out a gasp and quickly pulled my hand out.

I stood up and began pacing. "What in the hell is wrong with me? What is he doing to me?" I whispered. I heard my cell phone go off and I made my way back out to the main living area of the condo. I didn't even remember setting my purse down on the counter in the kitchen. I pulled it open and dug out my phone. I looked and saw that my mother had sent me three text messages. I knew she was wondering why I said I wouldn't be over tomorrow for lunch. I gave her no reason why I had to cancel. I wasn't ready to tell my parents about Lark. No way. No how. I tossed my phone back in my purse and decided to text her back later.

I walked up to the door that led to the balcony and made my way outside. The cool fall breeze felt amazing against my hot skin. I needed to get out and get some fresh air. All those damn dirty thoughts I had while walking around Lark's condo had my libido going insane.

I put my hands up to my cheeks and tried to steady my heartbeat as I thought about Lark and I having sex in almost every room of this place. *The kitchen island, the leather sofa in his living room…and oh God, the pool table.* That had always been a fantasy of mine—to have sex on a pool table. I let out a sigh and was about to turn around when I saw Lark's hands on both sides of my body. He placed his hands on the railing and I could practically feel the heat from his body.

"Do you like the view?"

"Yes. It's beautiful, but at the same time, it makes me feel sick when I look down."

He laughed and said, "Come on, I'm starved. I'll give you a tour of the rest of the building tomorrow."

"Where are we going to eat?" I asked as I followed him back into the condo and grabbed my purse.

He walked us to the elevator and asked, "Do you like Italian?"

I nodded my head and smiled. "Italian is probably one of my favorites."

"Then I think we should walk down to the Taverna. It's one of my favorite places to eat."

I smiled. "Sounds good."

We rode down the elevator in silence. I swear it only took like ten seconds to get from the fifty-fourth floor to the first floor. The elevator opened and as we stepped out, I almost ran into a beautiful blonde.

"Excuse me—I'm so sorry," I said as she smiled. She looked at Lark and her smile faded.

"Lark. I didn't know you lived here," she said as the smile returned to her face. But this time there was something wicked about it.

He quickly looked at me and then back at her. "What are you doing here, Sherry?"

She laughed and said, "I just bought a condo here. One of my best friends lives here and I fell in love with her place and had to have one of my own."

She looked back at me and began to eye me up and down. For some reason I instantly didn't like her. I didn't like the way Lark was so nervous and I certainly didn't like the way she was looking at him.

Lark began pulling me away from her as he started walking away. "Welcome to the neighborhood. I'll see ya around."

"Well wait, Lark, darling. Who's your friend?" she asked as she gave me a smirk.

Darling?

Lark ran his hand through his hair and said, "Azurdee, this is Sherry, a friend of mine. I've known Sherry for a few years, right before I joined the Marine Corps."

She let out the fakest laugh I'd ever heard. She held out her hand, almost like she wanted me to kiss the damn thing. I took her hand and shook it and said, "It's a pleasure to meet you. How do you and Lark know each other?"

She looked at Lark and gave him the same wicked smile as before. The way they looked at each other I could tell they shared a secret together. "Would you like to tell her the story or shall I?"

Lark gave her a dirty look and then looked at me and smiled slightly. "We met at a club one night. Sherry is a lawyer and I've used her a few times."

"More than a few," she said as she brought her finger up to her mouth.

"We were just heading to dinner, Sherry, so if you'll excuse us."

Lark pulled my hand and practically dragged me down the hallway.

"It was nice meeting you. Maybe I'll see you around, Azurdee. We can get to know each other better," Sherry called out. I turned and looked back at her and she was glaring at me.

When I turned back, I had the feeling that Lark and Sherry were more than just friends. I peeked up at Lark and he seemed pissed off. I decided not to even ask him about her. I needed to believe that what he said to me was true.

I was his and he was mine.

We walked to the restaurant in silence. The longer he remained quiet the harder it was for me to not worry about this Sherry girl.

Before we walked into the restaurant, I stopped, causing him to stop as well. He turned and looked at me and smiled. I tried to smile, but I just needed to get this over with.

"I'm not the jealous type and I realize you have a past, but the way that girl was looking at me and how nervous you were acting

112

is not sitting right with me. If there is something between the two of you, tell me now, Lark."

He went to open his mouth to talk, but then shut it again. He ran his hand through his hair again and I was quickly learning he did this when he was mad or nervous. "Sherry is just a friend. Nothing more."

I slowly nodded my head. "Have you slept with her?"

"Does it matter? Are you going to ask me that question with every single girl we run in to?"

My heart instantly sank. I knew he was right. I had no right asking and it wasn't any of my business, but by him not answering, he actually answered my question. He had slept with her and by their reaction to each other, I was going to guess they had slept together on more than one occasion.

I smiled slightly and shook my head. "I'm sorry. Let's get something to eat. I'm starving." I turned and began walking into the restaurant. I tried like hell to push this Sherry girl from my mind. I was hoping she wouldn't become an issue, but I had a feeling she was going to become more than an issue.

***

After dinner, we walked back to the condos and Lark called for a car to take us to the club. I quickly forgot about Sherry after our dinner was served. I was pretty sure I had just been hungry and cranky. Lark also seemed to snap out of it.

When we got into the car, Lark said, "Red 7, please."

I settled into Lark's side as he gently moved his fingers up and down my arm. I felt myself relaxing and had to fight to stay awake. I hadn't slept so great the night before when I was so upset about what had happened at the fundraiser the night before with Lark on the phone.

The car pulled up outside the club and we got out. I looked at the line to get in and let out a deep sigh. Lark took my hand and walked up to the bouncer.

"Lark! Dude, how are you?" the bouncer asked as he looked me up and down. I was starting to regret my decision to wear this low-cut shirt.

Lark looked back at me and then at the bouncer again. "I'm good."

The bouncer moved out of the way and we walked straight into the club. "I take it you come here often!" I shouted. Lark winked at me as we made our way over to the bar. I kept my head down after the first five guys eye-fucked the shit out of me.

I wasn't much of a club scene person but I was learning that Lark was. He was getting stopped by both men and women. One bitch threw her arms around him and kissed him with me standing right there. Lark pulled her off of him and whispered something in her ear. She looked at me and frowned before turning around and walking away.

When we finally made it to the bar, Lark ordered us both a Blue Moon. He handed one to me and smiled. I smiled back but I felt so out of place. I looked around and was shocked at all the girls openly staring at Lark. I rolled my eyes as one girl licked her lips and tried to wave at him. I practically downed my beer I was so pissed off. I guessed I had better get used to this.

I peeked up at Lark. He was talking to some guy, and it sound-ed like they knew each other. The guy looked like he was military, so maybe they both served in the Marines together.

I was totally captivated by Lark. My eyes traveled up and down his body as he stood there and talked to this guy. Lark was tall, probably six foot one, with a short military-style haircut and breathtakingly beautiful green eyes. His body was built like nothing I'd ever seen before. He was in incredible shape and my favorite part of his body was his broad chest.

I watched his lips move while he talked and I was glad it was loud in the club because I had let a small moan escape my lips. I was turned on just watching him talk. *Good God. Why does he affect me the way he does?*

I glanced at Lark's friend and he kept looking at me. I instantly felt uncomfortable. Lark was talking to another guy who had walked up. The way his friend was looking at me was like I was a bug that needed to be stepped on. My skin began crawling and I tried to give him a slight smile. He barely smiled and looked my body up and down quickly before turning his attention back to Lark.

The other guy Lark was talking to appeared to be a few years younger than Lark and this other guy. The guy who had been looking me up and down grabbed Lark's shoulder and pulled him closer and whispered something in Lark's ear. Lark pulled back quickly, looked at me and then back at the guy and said something. I was growing more and more uncomfortable.

I looked away and closed my eyes and tried to shake the uneasy feeling I had. Maybe it's because they aren't used to Lark being with someone. I felt Lark grab my hand and I was instantly calmed.

I turned and looked him in the eyes. Something about his eyes seemed…sad. I smiled and his eyes lit up and I couldn't help the feeling that swept over my body. Knowing that just a smile from me could affect him did things to my body…and heart.

Christina Aguilera's "Desnudate" began playing, and Lark's smile grew bigger and his eyes changed. He leaned down and put his lips to my ear and whispered, *"Dime tu fantasias."*

My heart began beating harder in my chest. For some reason

when he spoke Spanish to me, it turned me on so much. I motioned with my finger for him to come closer to me as I put my lips up to his ear and said, "Tell you my fantasies? I hardly think a club is the place for me to share that with you."

He pulled back and his eyes flashed with lust and I licked my lips in anticipation of what he was going to do. He pulled me closer to him as he began making his way to the dance floor. My insides were jumping all over the place and I wanted to let out a little squeal. I've been dreaming of dancing with him again after our little dance at the wedding.

Lark pulled me to him and began moving his hips against me and I immediately felt his hard-on. He was an incredible dancer and I loved how he kept my body tight against his. I was lost in his eyes as we moved to the beat of the song.

He reached up and pushed a piece of my hair back and hooked it behind my ear as his eyes moved slowly all over my face. When his eyes landed on my lips, I purposely ran my tongue along my bottom lip and watched as he closed his eyes. I smiled slightly knowing he was getting just as turned on as I was.

Before I knew what was happening the song changed and "Talk Dirty to Me" by Jason Derulo began playing. The smile that spread across Lark's face caused me to smile. He spun me around and pulled my ass up against his dick as we began dancing seductively. His hands were moving up and down my body and everywhere he touched felt like it was on fire.

I totally let myself go and danced like I'd never danced before. Lark reached around and grabbed my breast and pulled me back closer to him as he said in my ear, "You look beautiful tonight, but I don't like this shirt, *mi amor*. Too many guys are eye fucking you and it's really pissing me off."

I swallowed hard and looked around quickly. When he began kissing my neck, I let out a moan and my legs felt like jello. Lark turned me around and watching his body move was more than I could take. It was building me up and all I wanted was for him to give me my release.

I grinned as he looked at me with a look on his face that I couldn't read. He leaned down and said, "You like when I talk dirty to you, Azurdee?"

Did he really just ask me that? Do I tell him that I do and it drives me insane with lust?

"Yes," I said. His eyes grew wider as the song changed to Enrique Iglesias's "Tonight".

He pulled me to him and his eyes were filled with nothing but passion. I couldn't believe how I was grinding into him. I closed my eyes and thought of all the things I wanted him to do to me.

His hand moved down my body and he grabbed my ass and pulled me closer to him as he lifted my leg. The look in his eyes caused me to start breathing heavier. The moment I felt his hand moving up my leg I knew what he was going to do and I didn't even care we were in the middle of a group of people. I wanted him to touch me. I *needed* him to touch me.

He slowly moved his hand up and under my skirt as he slipped his fingers inside my panties and quickly pushed his fingers into me.

"Motherfucker. You're so fucking wet," he said as he closed his eyes and moved his fingers in and out of me. I buried my face into his chest and tried to hide the fact that I was enjoying this. Something about us being right out in public and Lark feeling on me had me getting so worked up and I was pretty sure I was about to have my first public orgasm.

Then I heard someone behind me shouting something and Lark pulled his fingers out and pushed my leg back down quickly. I turned around to see Lark's friend standing there. The way he was smiling gave me the creeps and I wasn't sure why.

"Mind if I cut in?" He looked directly at Lark like he was waiting to see his reaction. The song changed to "Give It to U" and Lark frowned. He pulled me to him and yelled in my ear, "Azurdee, this is Jason. I work with him."

My head snapped back to look at Lark and then at Jason. *He works with him?*

"Jason, this is my *friend*, Azurdee."

My mouth dropped open a little. *Friend? So now I'm a friend.* I instantly felt the heat move into my face and I wasn't even sure why. It wasn't like I expected him to walk around telling everyone we were boyfriend and girlfriend, but the way he stressed the word friend bothered me.

Jason held out his hand for me to take it and dance. I looked back at Lark and he took a step back. I slightly shook my head. I didn't want to dance with this guy. Lark pushed his hand through his hair and turned and walked toward the bar.

He left me. He just left me with this guy. I slowly turned and looked at Jason. His crooked smile might have caused my heart to drop before Lark had come into the picture, but now all it did was make my heart pound with fear for some reason. I took his hand and he began dancing.

Jesus. What is with these guys and how good they dance? Probably because they are at the club every weekend.

I turned back and tried to find Lark. I jumped when Jason touched my arm and pulled me closer to him. "I won't bite sweetheart, I promise."

I smiled slightly and decided to just go with it. Lark wouldn't leave me with someone he didn't trust.

He ran his hands up and down the side of my body and winked as he said, "Relax baby…just dance and have fun." *Ugh. Gag me.*

I smiled and tried to loosen up a little.

He looked in the direction to where Lark had walked and then pulled me closer to him. "How do you know Lark?" he shouted over the loud music.

I shouted back, "My best friend is married to his best friend."

He smiled and looked down at my chest. *Fuck. Why did I wear this shirt?*

"How long have you known him?"

I looked back over my shoulder for Lark. I couldn't see him anywhere. I turned back and shouted, "Almost a year."

"Y'all fucking?"

I stopped dancing and stood there. "Excuse me?" I shouted.

He started laughing, "I'm just trying to see if you're off-limits, babe."

I shook my head and turned to leave, and he grabbed my arm and pulled me back to him.

"Let go of me," I shouted. He smiled and said, "I'm sorry Azurdee, it's just most of the girls Lark is with are just fuck buddies. I didn't mean anything by it. I'm sorry."

I pulled my arm from his and said, "Whatever. I'm thirsty and just need a break from dancing."

His smile faded slightly and something in his eyes changed. "Sure. Let me walk you back to the bar. You'll never make it through the crowd alone."

He took my arm and guided me through the crowd. My eyes were darting everywhere for Lark. I started panicking when I couldn't find him. "I've got it from here, Jason. Thanks."

Lark took my other arm and the way they both looked at each other caused chills to run up and down my back. Something exchanged between the two of them and I had no idea what it was. Jason nodded his head and said, "I hope you know what the fuck you're doing."

What did he mean by that?

I looked at Lark with a confused look. He smiled and winked at me. He walked me up to the bar and ordered water for both of us. I closed my eyes and tried to make sense of everything that just happened.

When I felt Lark's hand on the small of my back, I was calmed almost instantly. Billy Currington's "Must Be Doin' Something Right" began playing and Lark leaned into my body and asked, "Will you dance with me?"

I loved to two-step and it also meant Lark would have to hold me close to him. I nodded my head and smiled. Lark reached for my hand and led me out to the dance floor. When he pulled me into his warm body I melted. I loved being in his arms. I felt safe. I felt like I was whole when he held me.

We danced in silence through most of the song. Lark kept pulling me closer and closer to him. Like he couldn't get me close enough and I felt the same way. I was ready to crawl into his body and lose myself to him.

He placed his finger on my chin and pulled my face up so that he was looking me in the eyes. I smiled and he returned the smile, but then it faded. "I'm sorry," he said.

I tilted my head and asked, "For what?"

"For letting you dance with Jason. Did he say anything to upset you?"

I shook my head and looked away. He pulled my chin back and the look in his eyes changed. "You're lying to me, Azurdee."

I swallowed hard. "It's nothing. Lark, I'm not feeling very well. Do you think we could leave?"

He nodded his head and grabbed my hand and led me to the door. The second we walked outside I took in a deep breath. I was beginning to feel like I couldn't breathe in there.

I hate clubs. I never got into the whole bar and club scene. Even in college I couldn't stand going to clubs.

Lark led me away from the entrance to the club as he pulled out his cell phone and hit a number.

"We're ready to leave," he said and then just hung up.

Not even a minute later the car from earlier pulled up and Lark was opening the car door for me. I slid inside and dropped my head back against the seat as thoughts began running through my mind.

This is my friend Azurdee.

Are you fucking him?

Is that all this was? Was that all I would ever be to Lark—his friend?

Lark took my hand in his and his thumb began moving back and forth across my hand, leaving a path of fire behind each movement. His touch did amazing things to my body and I was sure I would never get used to it.

"Are you ready to go back to the condo?" Lark asked. I lifted my head and looked at him and smiled.

"I'm sorry. I just got really tired and I've never been much of a club scene kind of girl."

He smiled and said, "Don't apologize. I'm ready to get you home and give you some of that dirty talk you like."

I felt my lower stomach clench and my eyes widened with anticipation. Lark let out a chuckle as he looked into my eyes. His smile faded and he whispered, "*Mi amor*, you bring out so many emotions in me. You have me so confused."

"Is that a bad thing or a good thing?" I whispered back.

He gently put his hand on the side of my face and pulled my lips to his as he kissed me so sweetly. He ran his tongue along my top lip and I opened my mouth to him. He let out a soft low moan as our kiss turned more passionate. Before I knew it, I was sitting in his lap and utterly lost in our kiss.

I heard the driver clear his throat and say, "Mr. Williams, we're back at the condos."

Lark pulled away and winked at me as I moved off his lap and adjusted my skirt. "Thank you so much," Lark said as he handed the driver money, opened the door, and practically pulled me out of the car.

"Good evening, Mr. Williams," the valet attendant said as he looked my body up and down and smiled at me.

I rolled my eyes and decided I was throwing this shirt away as I soon as I could.

We walked through the lobby and the young girl sitting behind the desk smiled and said, "Good evening, Mr. Williams, Ms. Emerson."

I smiled and said, "Good evening." As we kept walking, it dawned on me she knew my name.

"Wait. How did she know my name?" I asked as I looked back at the desk. Lark was now pulling me, causing me to walk faster. He let out a chuckle and said, "I told them you would be visiting me often and for them to make you a key card for the elevator. I don't have guests very often, so she probably just remembered your name."

I looked at him and the only thing I could say was, "Oh."

We stepped into the elevator and as soon as the door closed and Lark hit the button for his floor, he pushed me against the wall.

"God I want to fuck you so bad I can hardly think straight," he whispered as he moved his hand up my skirt and pushed his hand into my panties.

"Oh God," I whimpered. The elevators opened and he quickly turned me and walked us out of the elevator. He backed me right up against a table that was in the corridor. He pushed the vase off of it and I jumped when it crashed to the floor.

He lifted my skirt and quickly stripped me of my panties as he whispered, "I'm going to take you here, Azurdee, and I want to hear how good it feels for you."

My heart was slamming in my chest as he lifted me up and set my ass on the edge of the table. He quickly unbuttoned and unzipped his jeans.

My breathing became erratic as his erection sprung free.

He pulled me closer to him as he slammed his dick inside of me. I let out a small scream. It burned like a son of a bitch and Lark usually asked if I was okay but the way he relentlessly began moving in and out of me was like he couldn't fuck me fast and hard enough. I threw my head back and said, "Oh God."

"Does that feel good, baby?" Lark asked as he gripped my hips harder. "You like me fucking you hard and fast, sweetheart?"

"Oh God yes."

Then he stopped moving and quickly pulled out of me. I snapped my head up and looked at him. His eyes were filled with a look I'd never seen before. "What's wrong?" I asked as he took a few steps back and away from me. I had to shake my head to clear my vision. Were his eyes filling with…tears?

"Lark?"

"I um…I need a minute." He pulled his pants up and then walked away from me. I quickly jumped off the table and just stood there. *What just happened? Did I do or say something to him?*

I heard his bedroom door shut and I instantly felt like I wanted to cry. *He walked away from me.* He just left me here alone not knowing what in the world I just did. I reached down for my panties and quickly put them back on. I picked up my purse I must have dropped to the floor when we walked in and walked into the living room and looked around. I turned and looked down the hallway.

Should I go to his bedroom and ask him what was wrong? I decided to head over to the library. I walked in and made my way over to the sofa. I sat down and stared out at the lights. It was an amazing view and one that should have me looking at it in amazement, but all I could do was wonder what in the hell I did wrong.

I feel so tired all of a sudden. I wanted to get up and leave but I couldn't move.

I felt the tear move down my cheek as I reached up and wiped it away. There was a blanket lying on the ottoman. I reached for it and pulled it over me as I curled up on the cold leather sectional and cried myself to sleep.

CHAPTER 11

Lark

THE SECOND I REALIZED I had called Azurdee sweet-heart, I panicked. Walking away from her like that was the biggest dick move I'd ever done in my life.

I sat there on my bed and just stared out over the night sky of Austin. I couldn't believe I let all of the emotions build up like I did and then just let it go like that.

"Fuck," I whispered. I was almost positive I had to have hurt her with the way I just started fucking the shit out of her.

With running into Sherry and then Jason at the club, I was so wound up it was unreal. If Azurdee ever found out about Sherry and what I did, I knew she would leave me.

I can't lose her. I won't lose her. Not now. Not when I finally feel like a part of me is coming back to life.

I wasn't sure how long I sat there thinking before I glanced over at the clock. It was two in the morning.

Azurdee.

I jumped up and went to the first guest room. I opened the door and it was empty. I opened up the door to the game room only to find it empty. The other guest bedroom was empty as well. I walked past the library and looked through the door that was open.

The library was also empty. I headed into the living room only to find it empty and silent.

Where in the fuck was she? I began to have a feeling take over my body that hadn't been there since the day Nikki died.

Fear.

She left. She left me. I sat there and placed my head into my hands and tried to calm my breathing down.

Well, what in the hell did you expect, you dick? You pulled out of her and walked away with out so much as an explanation.

I looked to my right and saw her purse sitting on the top of the sofa. I jumped up. She wouldn't have left without her purse. I quickly made my way back to the only room that had a door open. The library. I walked in and immediately could hear the sound of her breathing. I quickly made my way around the sofa and saw her curled up under a blanket sleeping. I about dropped to my knees when I saw her. She had a tissue clutched in her hand and I knew she had been crying.

Oh God. I hurt her. The only person in this entire world I didn't want to hurt and I'd hurt her.

I got down on my knees and pushed her hair away from her face and gently kissed the corner of her lips. She slowly opened her eyes and gave me a weak smile. I tried to smile back but my heart was hurting so bad I could hardly breathe.

"I'm sorry," she whispered. I pulled back some and looked at her.

"For what?"

She slowly sat up and pulled her legs in. "I'm not sure what I did wrong, but whatever it was, I'm sorry."

I sat back and felt the tears trying to build in my eyes. *She thinks it was her?*

I slowly shook my head and pulled her down onto the floor with me. I ran my hands down the sides of her face and placed my right hand behind her neck and pulled her lips to mine. I kissed her like I was never going to kiss her again.

I pulled back slightly as she whispered, "Lark."

I stood up and helped her up. I picked her up and carried her back to my room. As I gently laid her down onto my bed, I looked into her eyes.

"Azurdee, I've never felt like this before. The feelings that I have for you are so powerful and they confuse the hell out of me. The last thing I'd ever want to do is hurt you."

She swallowed hard and said, "I don't ever want to hurt you either, Lark."

I closed my eyes and opened them again as I looked into her beautiful eyes. "I called you sweetheart. I always call girls sweetheart because using their names always made it too personal. I don't ever want you to think I'm just fucking you like some random girl I've picked up. You...you mean too much to me. You're not some random girl, Azurdee...I..."

I almost told her I loved her but I stopped myself. I knew I was quickly falling for her but I was not ready to admit that I loved her.

Her eyes moved all over my face, like she was trying to read me. "Is that why you call me *mi amor*?"

I nodded my head. "Yes," I whispered.

She got up on her knees and placed her hands on the sides of my face. She looked directly into my eyes. "I know you don't think of me like that. I see it in your eyes and I feel it in your touch. Please talk to me, Lark. I can't read what your mind is thinking. This is all new to me too, these feelings. They excite me and scare me at the same time too. I've never had anyone effect me like you do. I'm totally falling for you but I would never want to push you.

Ever. Please promise me you will always talk to me about things."

I nodded my head, but for some reason Sherry popped into my head and I felt like I needed to tell her about everything.

"I promise you I'll always talk to you," I barely said. I looked down at her lips and then back into her eyes. "I feel like I've been given a second chance and I don't want to fuck this up."

She smiled slightly. "We're both a blank canvas."

My heart began beating harder in my chest as I realized I was fighting something I couldn't control anymore.

"I feel like the only way my heart can beat normally is if we're one," I said as I placed my hands on the side of her face.

She dropped her right hand to my chest and said, "*Mi corazón.*"

I brushed my lips against hers as she let out the most beautiful moan I'd ever heard. I whispered against her lips, "*Mi corazón.*"

I could no longer fight it. I was in love with her.

She slowly began lying back as I followed her. All I wanted to do was crawl inside her body and stay there forever. "Lark, please make love to me."

My heart slammed in my chest and I buried my face in her neck so she couldn't see the tears in my eyes I was trying to control. I pushed my dick into her and listened to how she moaned.

"Please," she whispered.

I sat up and pulled my shirt up and over my head as she did the same. I moved and quickly took off my pants and tossed them to the side.

Azurdee was only in her bra and panties and I grabbed her hands and held them still. I took her wrists in one hand and pushed them over her head as I used my other hand and placed my finger lightly on her chin as I started to slowly move it down her neck, to her chest and across her breasts as she sucked in a breath of air. I was happy to see she was wearing a bra that opened in the front. One quick movement and her breasts sprung free. I pulled one nipple into my mouth and sucked it hard. She was squirming under my touch and I knew by pinning her hands above her head it would drive her crazy insane with desire.

"I need to touch you," she panted out.

I smiled as I continued to suck on her nipple. When I lightly bit down on it her hips jumped off the bed.

"Ah!" she cried out as she tried to bring her hands down but I held them firm. I slowly moved my finger down her stomach and ran it across the top of her panties.

They were a delicate lace fabric and all I wanted to do was rip them off of her, but I didn't want this to be rushed. I began slipping them off as she lifted her hips. She quickly kicked them away as I moved my body over hers. I kept her hands pinned above her head as I slowly began making my way into her body. With each movement I pushed further into her...and gave her more of my heart.

I closed my eyes and let out a moan as I felt her squeezing around my dick and pulling me in further.

I opened my eyes and her eyes locked with mine as I made love to her. No words were even needed. We spoke to each other from our hearts as I let myself fall more and more in love with her.

"Lark, I'm so close."

I let go of her hands and the moment she wrapped her arms around me she began calling out my name softly as she came.

I pushed further into her and whispered, "Azurdee...I'm forever yours."

CHAPTER 12

Lark

I opened my eyes and looked at the beautiful sunrise and smiled. I had felt Lark get up earlier. He had whispered in my ear he was going for a run and I mumbled *okay* back to him.

I stretched and smiled as I thought back to earlier this morning, when Lark had made love to me. I brought my fingertips up and gently ran them across my kiss-swollen lips.

The look in his eyes when he made love to me had my stomach going crazy. Then when he whispered he was mine forever as he came I knew I was head over heels in love with him. I put my hand up to my mouth and held back my sob.

I closed my eyes and let it soak in. *I was in love with him.* I opened my eyes and sat up as I pulled the sheet around me. I stood up and walked to the window and watched the sun move further up. I'd never seen such a beautiful sunrise. I wasn't sure if it was because I woke up more in love with Lark Williams than ever before, or if it was just a sign of what a beautiful day it was going to be.

I could feel the heat from his body before he even touched me. When he kissed my shoulder my whole body reacted. His lips moved to my neck and he said, "I love how your body reacts to me, Azurdee. It's like you were made for me."

I turned and looked up into his eyes. My eyes quickly moved down his body and I was pretty sure I let out a moan. He was wearing a dark navy T-shirt that was dampened by his sweat. His sweat pants hung off his hips in just the right way. The smell of his sweat mixed with my desire had me dropping the sheet and practically panting with need.

"Baby, I'm soaked in sweat," he said with his crooked smile that melted my heart.

"That's okay, because what I want to do will just make you sweat more," I said with the sexiest voice I could muster up.

He raised his eyebrow and tilted his head. "What's that?"

I put my right index finger in my mouth and then began running it along my lower lip.

"Jesus, Azurdee, I want you so bad," he said as he reached down and adjusted himself.

I dropped my head back and trailed my finger down my neck and then slowly looked back into his eyes as I tried to decide if I could do this.

The lust in his eyes told me I could. "I want you to finish what you started last night. I want to be fucked six ways to Sunday."

He got the same look in his eyes the first time he asked me if I was sure I wanted to be with him.

"Are you prepared for what you're asking for?" he asked as he lifted his T-shirt off and threw it to the side. I closed my eyes and nodded my head. I snapped them open and said, "The pool table first."

Lark reached down and picked me up and carried me out of the bedroom and to the game room. He pushed the door open and put me down and quickly pulled his sweats down. Then he turned me around and pushed me over the pool table.

Oh God. He's going to fuck me from behind.

He used his leg to push my right leg open more.

"I'm gonna make you scream out in nothing but pleasure, Azurdee."

I looked over my shoulder and said, "Yes…Lark."

He grabbed my hips and slammed his dick inside, causing me to call out. He waited for a second for me to get used to feeling him inside me like this.

"God…it's so deep like this," I said as he pulled out and slammed back into me. I dropped my head and let out moan after moan as he kept pulling out and pounding back into me. I could feel my build up happening quickly.

He dug into my hips harder and said, "Touch your breasts."

I moved my hand up and began touching my breasts. "Your nipple, Azurdee. Play with your nipples."

I began twisting and pulling my nipples as I became this person I'd never known I could be. "Fuck," I hissed between my teeth.

"You feel so damn good. Touch your clit, Azurdee."

I moved my hand down and lightly brushed my clit. I sucked in a breath of air and threw my head back.

"Make yourself come. Now," he said with such authority in his voice that I began coming before I even touched myself again.

"Oh God! Lark! Yes! I'm coming…oh my…oh God!" I called out as a powerful orgasm hit me fast and hard. He pulled out and turned me around and began kissing me. I reached down and began stroking his dick as he moaned into my mouth. He reached down and lifted me up again. He attempted to kick his sweats off while he held me and I couldn't help but laugh as he hopped around.

"You're going to bust your ass and my fucking will come to

an end," I said as I pouted. He set me back down and kicked off his sneakers and pulled his sweats off before picking me up and throwing me over his shoulder. As he walked down the hall he smacked my ass and I let out a scream. He walked into the kitchen and set me down onto the cold soapstone counter.

"Shit! That is cold!" I called out as he spread my legs apart and slammed into me before I even knew what was happening. The moment he began sucking on my nipples I lost it again.

"Oh God. What's happening?" I called out.

"Come on, baby…give it to me again," Lark said as he slammed so hard into me I instantly came again.

Holy shit. This orgasm was more intense than the last one. I was still throbbing when he picked me up and carried me into the library. He set me down on the very end of the leather sofa. He dropped to the floor and buried his face between my legs. I practically jumped off the sofa.

"Jesus!" I cried out. I dropped my head back and ran my hand through his hair.

"Oh shit…my mother…would be very…disappointed…in my behavior…right now," I panted between breaths. Lark pulled away and looked at me.

"Do you want me to stop?"

I quickly shook my head. "God no…I'm so close." He brought me right to the edge of my orgasm and then pulled away. He reached up and brought me down and placed his dick at the entrance to my throbbing sex.

"Don't come, Azurdee," he pushed himself into me as we both let out a moan.

What? He wants me to not come? Is that even possible?

I felt the build up and looked into his eyes. "Lark, I don't think I can…oh God…I'm going to come again and I can't…" He quickly pulled out and I cried out. "No!"

He stood up and lifted me up again. I was starting to feel weak. That was twice he denied me an orgasm.

When he walked into his office I was going insane from the throbbing sensation between my legs. He walked up and in one quick movement he pushed everything off his desk and laid me down on it as he crawled on top of me.

"Are you getting a thorough fucking?" he asked as he pushed himself into me again and began pumping me fast and hard again.

"Yes. Oh God…I'm so close. Harder! Lark, harder!"

I couldn't believe who this girl was that I'd become. I was totally letting my libido run this show and I couldn't have cared less. I'd never felt so incredible in my life.

"Fuck…there is nothing sexier than you telling me to fuck you hard," Lark hissed through his teeth.

"Lark! I'm coming! Oh God." I thrashed my head back and forth as I yelled out. I'd never had an orgasm hit me so hard. I could feel my sex squeezing him and then felt him get bigger inside of me.

"Jesus…holy shit…Azurdee…ahh!" Lark pushed into me a few more times hard and fast before he collapsed onto me. I could feel us both still pulsing and if I hadn't been so exhausted I would have been turned on again.

I closed my eyes and barely felt Lark move and then pick me up and carry me into his room. He laid me down on the bed and I opened my eyes and watched his fine naked ass walk into the bathroom. I covered my mouth and let out a giggle at my wayward thoughts. Lark just brought the naughty out in me and I liked it…a lot.

I heard the shower turn on and I sat up. This man has ruined me for all other men. No one would ever be able to hold a candle to him. When he walked out he stopped and smiled at me.

I stood up and looked down at his dick as I walked up to him. When his dick jumped I looked back into his eyes and said, "Round two." He laughed as I walked by and headed straight into the shower. I let the hot water run over my body and when I felt Larks hands on my body I smiled. He pushed me against the wall and spread my legs open with his foot. He lifted my leg and said, "Arch your back, Azurdee."

I did as he said and I let out a long moan when I felt him slide into me. "God, nothing feels better than being inside you," Lark said as he began slowly moving in and out of me.

When he grabbed my hair and pulled back, I let out a gasp. "Lark…oh God, Lark."

"You. Have. Ruined. Me," Lark said as he gripped my hips and slammed into me…over and over again. I smiled knowing I had just thought the same thing.

When he reached his hand around and began playing with my clit I lost it as I called out his name and he followed. When he pulled out of me he spun me around and slammed his lips to mine as he pushed me against the shower wall again. I thought I was lost before with his lovemaking but his kisses…his kisses took me to heaven.

When he pulled away he smiled. "Did you bring jeans?"

I smiled and nodded my head. "Good. Wear jeans and a T-shirt."

He quickly pushed away and soaped up. I stood there just staring at his body. *Could this really be happening? Could Lark really be mine?*

He rinsed off and then pulled me to him and quickly kissed me on the lips. "Take your time baby, I have a few calls to make and then we'll leave."

"Okay," I said as I reached for his soap.

I stood under the hot shower for at least fifteen minutes. My legs felt weak but I'd never felt so damn good in my life. I smiled thinking about how we had made love in so many places of his condo. Then I felt my cheeks blush. We didn't make love. We fucked.

I shook the image of Lark on top of me and turned off the shower. I reached for the towel and made a mental note to talk to Jessie about how I was feeling. Was all this sex normal? Was I craving it because it was new, or was it Lark? Was he just that... incredible?

When I walked into the bedroom Lark had my bag sitting on the bed. I headed for it and heard my cell phone ringing. I looked and my purse was sitting on the bench. Lark must have put it there for me since I didn't remember bringing it in here.

I quickly ran over to it and pulled my cell phone out to see my mother was calling. Again.

I swiped the phone and said, "Hello, Mom."

"Where in the world have you been? I called the coffee house and they said you weren't in yesterday or today. Is everything okay?"

I smiled and bit down on my lower lip. "Everything is wonderful, Mom."

"Oh. My. Lord. You've met someone."

My mouth dropped open and I stood there stunned. "How in the world did you know?"

My mom laughed and I heard the screen door open and shut. She must have walked outside.

"I hear it in your voice. Is he good?"

What? "Mom! You did not just ask me that!"

She laughed and said, "Yes I did just ask you that. Well?"

I walked over and opened up my bag and pulled out my jeans and a T-shirt. I looked for my light pink boy short panties and the white lace bra I packed. I hit speakerphone and threw my phone down on the bed.

"Mom, I'm trying to get dressed. Can I call you back?"

"No. I'm waiting…well?"

I rolled my eyes and tried to stall. "Well what, Mom?" I slipped on my panties and then my bra as I heard my mother saying something to my father about how she would be back in the house in ten minutes.

She let out a sigh and said, "This boy you've met, is he any good?"

I slipped my jeans on and my bra. "He is hardly a boy, Mom."

"Ohh…do tell. Come on, I've waited years for you to talk to me about a boyfriend."

I had to admit I was dying to talk to someone and I couldn't talk to anyone at work. I was the boss. Jessie was just back from her honeymoon and would be busy with Lauren, so in reality, I only had my mother to talk to.

Oh Jesus. I just depressed myself.

I slipped the T-shirt over my head and said, "Yes, Mom, he is very…*very* good."

She giggled and that caused me to giggle. "Jesus, Mom, this feels wrong to talk to you about this."

"I knew it. I heard it in your voice. I knew you would eventually find the boy…er…man, who would change your whole world. How long have you known him?"

And here come the questions. "It will be a year around this Christmas."

"How long have y'all been dating?"

"Um...not terribly long."

"Uh huh...I see. What does this boy do for a living?"

I paused. I had no clue what Lark did. *None.* All I knew was he flew helicopters, he had been in the Marines, and whatever it was he did, he sure didn't talk about it to anyone.

"He was in the Marines." I rolled my eyes and flopped down on the bed and hit my forehead with the palm of my hand.

"The Marines, huh? Your father will like that. What's the young man's name?"

"Lark Williams. Hey Mom, listen I hate to cut you off, but we're fixing to leave."

"Okay, darling. Will you be back at the coffee shop tomorrow?"

"Yes. I'll be there at opening and then heading over to the new place to check on things."

"All right, dear. Practice safe sex."

I shuddered and said, "Yuck, Mom...too far. You went too far!"

My mother let out a loud laugh and then said, "Bye, darling. Have fun today with Lark."

I hung up and threw myself back onto the bed. "Oh God! My mother knows I'm having sex!"

I felt the bed move and Lark was laying on me laughing. "But does she know how fucking hot the sex is?" he asked as he wiggled his eyebrows up and down. I giggled and decided I liked the playful Lark. A lot.

"I held that part back."

Lark placed both hands on the side of my face and kissed me so sweet and gentle. When he pulled back, he lifted his eyebrow and looked at me and pushed himself into me. I raised my eyebrow back and asked, "What do you feed yourself to have such stamina?"

He laughed and pushed himself off of me and then reached for my hand and pulled me up.

"Thank you for this morning. It was amazing."

I nodded my head and said, "Yes, it was."

I looked him up and down and somehow managed to keep the moan I wanted to let out buried deep down inside of me. He looked amazing. He had on Lucky jeans that fit him perfectly, a dark blue T-shirt and his cowboy boots. He looked hot as hell.

"You look…good," I said as I licked my lips. He smiled slightly and said, "You look beautiful. Come on, the day is young still and I have lots I want to do today. I have to leave town tomorrow."

My smile faded and my heart dropped. I wanted to let out a childlike *nooo* and stomp my foot and demand he not leave again. He walked up to me and lifted my chin up and brushed his lips across mine. "I don't want to leave, *mi amor*, but I have to."

I wrapped my arms around his neck and deepened the kiss. He picked me up and I wrapped my legs around him as we both kissed each other like we wouldn't see each other for days.

He pulled back and leaned his forehead against mine. "Azurdee…I hope you know how much you mean to me."

"I do. I hope you know as well," I said as he slowly slid me down his body. He grabbed my hand as I reached for my purse.

"Leave it…you won't need it. Oh wait. Grab your driver's license."

139

I reached in and took out my license and pushed it into my back pocket along with some money. My mother always told me to never go anywhere without a few dollars in your pocket.

We made our way to the elevator. I glanced at the small table and thought about last night. I chewed on my bottom lip as I tried to decide what I liked better. Lark making love to me or Lark fucking me. I looked at him and he was smiling at me, almost like he knew what I was thinking.

"I like it rough too, but I love making love to you more than anything."

My mouth parted open slightly and I was washed away with what he said. Just when I think I know him he goes off and swoons the hell out of me.

The elevator opened and we stepped inside. He swiped his card across and hit the fifty-sixth floor button.

"I'm having a key card made for you. I want you to know you can stay here anytime you want. Especially when I'm in town. I really liked waking up with you next to me."

I smiled and felt the butterflies go off in my stomach. The elevator opened and Lark motioned for me to go first. "Turn to the right." I headed to the doors and opened them. It was the gym.

"I know how much you like to workout and run so I wanted to show you the gym. The other side is the yoga and workout room."

"Wow. This is amazing." All the exercise equipment faced the windows. "Who wouldn't want to work out with this view? I swear."

Lark laughed and said, "Come on, two more floors to visit."

Lark hit the tenth floor and within seconds the door was opening and he was showing me a theater room, a game room, a spa, and the pool.

"Maybe when I get back we can barbecue down here by the pool."

I nodded my head and said, "Or my place." His smile faded for a brief second and then it was replaced by a wider smile.

"Or my ranch between Johnson City and Marble Falls. I meet with the architect in a few weeks to talk about the house."

"I forgot you owned land out that way." I looked out over the city and thought about each of our futures.

"I'd love to show it to you," he said as he took my hand in his. I knew that was huge for him. I smiled and said, "I'd love that. Maybe when you come back I can show you my new restaurant."

His smile grew wider and he said, "I'd love to see your new place."

We walked back to the elevator and made our way to the fourth floor. As we walked into the parking garage, I glanced at the yellow bike. My heart did a little drop. I wasn't sure why I thought motorcycles were sexy as hell. This one was beyond sexy. I made my way to the truck as Lark made his way to the bike. I stopped and just looked at him.

He looked at me and winked. He lifted the back seat and pulled out a helmet and walked up to me and handed it to me.

I just stood there staring at him and his drop dead gorgeous smile of his. Oh. My. Word. This is his bike. I think I just had a mini orgasm at the idea of being on that thing with him.

"You said you wanted to go for a ride, *mi amor*. You still up for it?"

I took the helmet and let out a laugh. "You're kidding. This is your bike, Lark?"

He looked back at it and said, "Yes ma'am, it is. I love the feel of being free and just going as fast as I can on her."

I snapped my head over and looked at him. I shouldn't be surprised. I'd heard Scott talk about how Lark lived life on the edge with the partying and fast living.

"Um…"

He laughed and pulled me over to the bike. "I promise not to go too fast. I have precious cargo."

I put the helmet on and my heart began pounding with excitement. Lark got on and started the motorcycle. Eminem's "Berzerk" began playing and Lark yelled, "Fuck yeah."

I wrapped my arms around him and smiled. I closed my eyes when he started going and he yelled for me to hold on. "Here we go, *mi amor*."

As we rode around Austin, something in me changed. It felt like it was a new me. I'd never done anything like this before, but with Lark, he made you want to live life to the fullest.

For lunch we went to Home Slice pizza. Then we hit Amy's for ice cream before we were back on the bike and heading to the hike-and-bike trail. We walked for a bit and then I sat and watched Lark play a quick game of sand volleyball. A group of guys he knew were playing, and though he had just come down to watch, he somehow got talked into playing. I saw Jason, Lark's friend who he said he worked with, playing. I tried not to make eye contact with him, but when I did, he politely smiled and waved. I gave him a quick wave back.

A blonde was sitting next to me and smiled at me when I sat down. We sat in silence for a few minutes as we both watched the game. I finally asked, "Is one of them yours?"

She laughed and said, "Yep." She pointed to the only other guy who looked like he might have been in the military. "That's my Ron. He's normally stationed in California, but we've been here for the last two weeks. Some kind of training."

I nodded my head and said, "Do you know what the training is for?"

She shrugged her shoulders. "Nope. Ron is a sniper in the Marines. I think Lark and Jason are training him for something."

I turned and looked at Lark. I knew he could shoot well because I'd heard Scott talk about it. *Why would Lark be training him?*

"Is Ron going out of town tomorrow?" I asked.

She shook her head. "No, I think he is in some kind of meeting all day."

I smiled at her and looked back at Lark. His eye was still really black and blue from where he fell.

I didn't take my eyes off of Lark when I asked, "Did Ron go out of town a few days back?"

"Yeah, he did. Said he had a training mission to go on. He just got back...um...the day before yesterday, I think it was. Yeah."

I turned and stuck my hand out and smiled. "I'm sorry, how rude of me. Azurdee Emerson."

She reached for my hand and said, "Lisa Kentwood."

"So Ron is active duty Marines?"

She nodded her head. "Yep. I kind of thought it was weird he was coming here to Austin for training since there is no Marine Corps base, but from the little he has told me, I guess Lark is one of the best Expert Rifleman in the Marine Corps."

My heart dropped. Lark's not in the Marines anymore.

I flashed back to the picture in Lark's office, the one with his boss. Lark was wearing a uniform and the guy had a badge on. *A CIA badge.*

I shook my head and let out a small laugh. *Geesh, Azurdee, stop overthinking.* They must have met when Lark was in the Marines.

I glanced up to see Jason staring at me as Lark talked to him off to the side. I didn't like the way he looked at me. Jason looked back at Lark and then down to his watch. He did something on his watch, nodded his head and they both turned and walked away from each other. Lark made his way back to me and grinned as he got closer.

"Ready for dinner?" he asked. I laughed and nodded my head. I looked at Lisa and said, "It was a pleasure to meet you."

She smiled and said, "You too!"

Lark was taking me out to the Salt Lick for barbecue after he bragged about how it was the best around. The whole ride there, I couldn't shake the uneasy feeling I had about Lark and his job.

Sharp shooter. Marines. Secrets.

CHAPTER 13

Lark

I PARKED THE MOTORCYCLE and Azurdee got off and handed me her helmet. She had been really quiet ever since we left Zilker Park, when I stopped to talk to Jason about our meeting at the Pentagon in two days. I wasn't sure what was up and Skip was being really silent on the whole matter.

When we got off the elevator, I followed Azurdee into the kitchen. She stopped at the bar and turned to face me. She was chewing on her lower lip, which I already knew was a nervous habit that showed she was either scared or nervous.

"Can I stay here again tonight?"

I smiled and walked up to her. "Of course you can. I was hoping you would."

She ran her hand down the side of my face and whispered, "Make love to me."

I reached down and picked her up and carried her to my room. We spent most of the night tangled in each other's arms. Azurdee fell asleep earlier after we made love the first time. I didn't want to have to say good-bye to her in the morning, so I woke her up around two in the morning and made love to her again. Once she drifted back off to sleep, I got up and began packing for my short trip to D.C. I made a call and within ten minutes I got a text that my item was waiting down in the lobby for me. I checked on Azurdee one more time before heading down there. When I walked up to the desk, Rich was working. He handed me the single red rose and said, "There ya go, Mr. Williams."

I smiled and said, "Have a good night, Rich."

"You too, sir."

Twenty minutes later, I was setting the note on my pillow and laying the rose on top of it. I wanted to kiss her good-bye but didn't want to risk her waking up. I grabbed my bag and turned to walk away, but not before I slipped the key card to my place into her purse.

One last look and I was gone.

***

After meeting with Colonel Walker, Skip, and a few other intelligence people, I made my way out of the conference room.

"Lieutenant. A word," I heard Skip say as I walked away. I closed my eyes and turned around.

"Yes, sir." I followed Skip and Jason into another conference room. I shut the door and Skip was standing there looking out the window holding a file.

He slowly turned and walked toward the table and threw the file down.

When I glanced down, I saw the word *classified* in red letters and the name…Azurdee Marie Emerson.

What in the fuck? I reached down and picked it up. When I opened it, there were pictures of Azurdee, all taken today. In one of the pictures, she was leaving my condo and getting into someone's car. There were three pictures of her in the coffee shop and one leaving the coffee shop. The last picture was of her standing outside her new restaurant space talking to what looked like the contractors.

I looked up and before I could even say anything, Skip said, "What in the fuck do you think you're doing?"

"Excuse me?"

He pointed to the pictures, and when I looked at the rest of the file it was information about Azurdee, her parents, their bank accounts, anything and everything on both her and her parents were in this file. I closed it and tossed it onto the table.

"I knew something was up with you in Venezuela. How long have you been seeing her?"

I looked at Jason. "You couldn't wait to run and tell him, huh? You fucking bastard."

I went to go after him, and Skip stepped in front of us and grabbed me.

"I asked, how long have you been seeing her?"

I pushed myself away from Skip and said, "Not long. I've known her almost a year. We were friends first."

"What are your plans with this girl, Lark? I can't afford to have you anything but one hundred percent clear-minded. A girl is going to fuck that up."

I shook my head, "I won't let it, Skip."

He let out a sigh and dropped his head back before looking at me again. "This is why I picked you. No strings. No ties. Lived life on the edge. Pussy just messes with your head, Lark. You say it won't, but pretty soon you're going to be wondering what she's doing while you're gone for days, sometimes weeks, at a time. What happens when you get hurt, how many excuses are you going to be able to give her?"

I just looked at him. "That's funny, Skip. I thought you picked me because I'm the best goddamn sniper in the country."

He just stood there and looked at me. "Sergeant Philips, will you please excuse us. Lieutenant Williams, you will refrain from saying anything else until the Sergeant has left the room."

Jason left the room and Skip glared at me. "Don't you ever call me Skip in front of another Marine or agent again—do you understand me, Lieutenant? Don't ever question my motives again either. Now I want to know why I had to have some flunky come tell me that you had a girlfriend. Why didn't you just tell me yourself?"

I pushed my hands through my hair. "Skip, I just started dating her. It's not like I'm marrying her for Christ's sake. She knows I don't talk about my job and she doesn't ask. We've been friends for awhile so I trust her with my life."

He shook his head and said, "Jesus Christ, Lark. This is going to end badly. Either for you or for her."

I looked down and then back up at him. "I won't let it. I've got this. I can handle it."

He turned and looked out the window. "The moment I even suspect it's affecting your work, I'm pulling you. You can finish out the rest of your career stationed in some remote-ass Marine Corps base."

I nodded my head. I only had six months left in active duty and I had already decided after last night I was not re-enlisting or joining the CIA. I didn't want to have to keep lying to Azurdee and sneaking away in the middle of the night to leave her.

"So let me ask you. This trip to Israel, what are you going to tell her?"

I shrugged my shoulders and said, "That I'm going out of town. That's what I've always said and no one has yet to question me."

He gave me a weak smile and said, "I'm pretty damn sure that the person who loves you and worries about you is going to start asking questions about where you're going."

Loves me? Does Azurdee love me? I knew I was falling in love with her and I was pretty sure she wanted to tell me she loved me the other night, but she didn't. I shook my head to clear my thoughts.

"Skip, I know how to block shit from my head. I won't let my relationship with Azurdee jeopardize my job."

He gave me a weak nod and said, "We'll see."

"So three weeks in Israel. Is Ricker coming with Philips?" I asked.

Skip smiled and asked, "Do you want him or you want a SEAL?"

I didn't even have to think about it. "A SEAL. Ricker always has his head up his ass."

"All right. Let's hope this mission runs smoothly. I have a feeling they're going to be expecting trouble, so it's fast in…fast out."

I nodded my head and said, "If that's all, I'm going to be heading back home."

He laughed. "No you're not, soldier. You're heading out tonight to Afghanistan. You'll meet up with your SEAL partner and then head out the next morning. Sorry buddy, there is no going home."

I nodded my head and turned to walk out the door. "Lark?"

I stopped and turned around, "Yes, sir?"

"I really hope you meant what you said earlier. I'd hate to have you or a team member get hurt because your head isn't in the game."

I nodded. "I promise, Skip. I've got this."

I opened the door and made my way outside. I got in the rental car and pulled away. Once I was off the base and a few blocks away I pulled over, got out of the car and started yelling.

"Motherfucking son of a bitch!" I put my hands on my knees and took in a few deep breaths. I stood up and began pacing. I ran my hand through my hair and tried to calm my beating heart.

"I didn't kiss her good-bye. I didn't fucking kiss her good-bye!" I yelled out. I got back into the car and by the time I got to my hotel I was calmer. I told the front desk I would be staying another night and after the clerk flirted for a bit, she finally had me booked for another night. I smiled politely and made my way to my room. I got out of my uniform and pulled on a T-shirt. I picked up my cell phone and hit Azurdee's number.

"Hello handsome. You snuck away again last night."

I smiled when I heard her voice. "Yeah, I'm not really good at saying good-bye."

There was silence for a few seconds before she said, "Thank you for the rose, and my note."

I closed my eyes and tried to picture her smelling the rose. What her face looked like while reading the note.

"I'm sorry I didn't wake you up before I left."

"It's okay. I understand. Are you still coming back tonight?"

I dropped my head back and cursed inwardly. I hated lying to her. "I thought I was, but it looks like we're heading out of town. I probably won't be back for three weeks."

"Okay," she whispered. "Lark?"

"Yeah, baby?"

She let out a sigh and said, "I'm not asking for information from you. I knew what your life was like when I stepped into this relationship. I just need to…I mean…please just tell me what you're doing is safe."

I pulled the phone away from my ear and squeezed my eyes together tightly.

I put the phone back to my ear and said, "I'll be back in three weeks, *mi amor*. I promise you."

I heard a small sob escape from her lips. "Lark, I'm falling in love with you."

I sucked in a breath of air.

"I'm not asking or expecting you to say anything back. I just wanted you to know that. I have to go. Will you call or text me when you can?"

I nodded my head even though I knew she couldn't see me. "Yes. I'll text you as much as I can and call you tomorrow before I leave."

"Okay. I'll see ya soon."

I wanted to tell her I was falling in love with her too, but it wouldn't come out.

"I'll see you soon, *mi amor*."

She hung up before I could say anything else. I tossed my phone behind me on the bed and decided to go for a run. As I got changed, my cell phone went off with a text message. I quickly grabbed it hoping it was Azurdee.

Unfortunately, it was Sherry.

Sherry: So are you up for a get together tonight?

Me: Sorry Sherry, I'm afraid our partnership is going to have to cease. I have a girlfriend now and I intend on being faithful to her.

Sherry: The brunette you were with the other night?

Me: Yes.

Sherry: I had a feeling something was going on when you kept turning me down. Well let me know when it doesn't work out. I'll be waiting.

I rolled my eyes and hit delete. I set out for my run and for the first time since Nikki, my heart longed for another person. The only question I had was would I be able to check my heart at the door when I needed to?

CHAPTER 14
Azurdee

"AZURDEE, DARLING. I SWEAR your chocolate croissants get better every time I eat them," Mrs. Hamilton said as she took the bag I was handing her. "I can't wait for the restaurant to open. I'm so excited for you. When are you planning on opening?"

I smiled and said, "I'm hoping maybe March if everything goes well. April at the latest."

"How wonderful. I'm sure I'll see you, but if not, have a wonderful Christmas."

I walked her to the door and said, "Don't forget, we will be closed for the whole week of Christmas. I'll be out of town."

"That's right. Oh dear. I'll have to pull out the old coffee pot I guess."

We both laughed and she walked out the door and then I shut it and locked it. I turned and looked at Ralph, who began laughing. I shot him a dirty look and pushed past him. If I didn't love him like a brother, he would have been fired months ago.

"My God, Dee. You practically pushed her out the door. What in the world is wrong with you this week?"

"Nothing. I'm fine," I said as I gritted my teeth. I wasn't fine. I was going crazy out of my mind. I hadn't heard from Lark in over a week. He was a week late in getting home and the thoughts running through my mind were driving me insane. I even called Scott and had him come up with some lame excuse to contact Lark's parents to make sure they hadn't heard any bad news.

"You need to get laid," Ralph said. I turned and looked at him. My mouth dropped open and I said, "Excuse me?"

He shrugged his shoulders and repeated, "You need to get laid. When is your boyfriend due back?"

How Ralph even knew I had a boyfriend was still a mystery. "How do you even know I'm dating anyone?"

He rolled his eyes as he began cleaning up. "Please. Girl, you came walking in here almost two months ago with your cheeks flushed and pep in your step. Anyone could see you'd either won the lottery or just had one hell of a night getting fucked."

I threw a rag at him and started laughing. "Oh my God! When did you start talking like that?"

It was his turn to roll his eyes at me. "Please, my partner probably has the dirtiest mouth you could ever imagine."

My mind flashed back to Lark's last phone call to me.

***

"I miss you," I whispered.

"Te extraño, mi amor."

I let out a sigh. I loved when Lark spoke to me in Spanish.

"Are you turned on?" Lark asked in a hushed voice.

"More than you could know."

"Wait till I get back. I'm going to bury myself so fucking deep inside you, you'll know I've been there for days."

"Lark." I squeezed my legs together to control the throbbing.

"God I wish I could hear you make yourself come." It sounded like he had gotten up and walked away. I bit down on my lower lip and let out a sigh.

"Can you?" I asked.

He let out a growl and said, "No. Don't fucking touch yourself either. I don't want you making yourself come until I get back. I want to hear you scream out my name."

"Okay," I barely said.

"Promise me, Azurdee."

"I promise you, I won't touch myself until you come back."

***

I was snapped out of my memory by Ralph slapping his hands together directly in my face. "Girlfriend. Where in the heck were you just now? I don't think I've ever seen that smile on your face before or seen that color on your cheeks."

I placed my hands on my cheeks. I shook my head and pushed him out of the way. "Listen, I'm exhausted. I've been here since five this morning. Do you mind if I take off?"

"Have at it, darling. Get some sleep, Dee, you look like shit."

I grumbled out a curse word and made my way to the back. Yep. If he weren't like a brother to me he'd be gone.

***

I stood in front of the mirror looking at myself. My hair was pulled up into a ponytail. I had on my favorite Victoria's Secret boyfriend sweatpants and the only reason I had them on was because of their damn name. I had taken one of Lark's T-shirts from his place before I left and had slept in it each night. I even went out and bought some of his cologne so that I could spray it on the shirt when I could no longer smell him.

Yep. I'm totally in high school again. I crawled into bed and grabbed my Kindle. I didn't even turn it on. I set it back down and grabbed my phone. Nothing. No missed calls, no text messages, no voicemails. I checked my email too. Nothing.

Lark. Please let me know you're okay.

I slipped under the covers and pulled them up around my neck. It was a cold December night and I didn't want to start a fire. I didn't even want to turn on my heater. I just wanted to bury myself under my quilt and pray that Lark was okay.

After staring at the ceiling for two hours I finally felt myself drifting off to sleep. I'd slept like shit the last week and it was catching up to me. I closed my eyes and drifted off into a deep sleep.

"*Mi amor*. Wake up."

"Hmmm…" I was dreaming of Lark. He was sitting next to me in my bed trying to wake me up but I was so tired. I just couldn't open my eyes. If only he were really here.

"Azurdee, baby, wake up."

I felt his warm lips kissing my face and I let out a soft moan. "Lark," I whispered.

Then I felt his lips on mine. I reached up and pushed my hand through his hair. *God this dream felt so real.*

"Baby wake up. I've missed you so much."

I snapped my eyes open and looked into the most beautiful green eyes ever.

"Please tell me I'm not dreaming," I said.

He smiled and said, "You really should start setting your alarm."

I sat up quickly and began crying as I threw myself into his arms. "Oh God! Oh thank you God. I was so worried when you were late and I didn't hear from you."

He ran his hand down my back and said, "I'm so sorry. I couldn't call. I wanted to call you so bad but I couldn't."

I pulled back and slammed my lips into his as I crawled out from the covers and began stripping my clothes off. My sweats came off first and then my panties. Lark pulled back and smiled. "Is that my T-shirt?"

I looked down and then back up at him as I felt the heat move across my cheeks. "I wanted to have you near me. I hope you don't mind."

He shook his head and said, "No...I don't mind at all." I reached for the T-shirt and pulled it over my head as he whispered, "Christ, you're so beautiful."

I smiled as I reached out for his shirt to take it off. My hands stopped when I saw how he was dressed. *Why is he in fatigues?*

He slowly stood up and I followed. My eyes moved up and down his body. When they landed on his dog tags I sucked in a breath of air. I looked up into his eyes and whispered, "You're still in the Marines, aren't you?"

He looked away and then looked back at me, closed his eyes and whispered, "Yes."

For the first few seconds I stood there shocked. I was so confused. There was no base here in Austin. I knew he went to the Army Reserve base a lot, but I had no idea why. I loved him unconditionally and I didn't need to know why he couldn't tell me what his job was. I had no intentions of asking him any questions about it. There was a reason he couldn't say and I knew he must have just rushed over here as soon as he got home.

I moved closer to him and reached for his shirt. I pulled it over his head, never taking my eyes from his. I glanced down at his dog tags and quickly looked away. I reached for his belt buckle and began taking it off. Lark reached down and quickly took off his boots and then his pants. He threw them to the side and pulled me to him. He lifted my chin up and when our lips touched we both let out a moan.

"Oh God. I missed you so much," he whispered as he pulled his lips back just enough to speak.

"Make love to me. Please make love to me," I said as my breathing increased. He picked me up and gently laid me down and then moved on top of me.

It wasn't lost on me that he still had his dog tags on. I opened my legs to him and when he finally pushed into me I felt like I was going to cry from the sweet relief he was providing me.

I moved my fingertips up and down his back as he slowly made love to me. He buried his face in my neck and kept repeating how much he had missed me and how sorry he was he couldn't call.

I didn't even care. All I cared about was that he was here and we were together. I felt the familiar build up and as my orgasm hit me he pushed up and looked into my eyes.

I knew what I was about to do could scare him away but I was so overcome with emotion I needed to say it.

I could feel him growing bigger inside me as he whispered, "I'm going to come."

I looked into his eyes and whispered, "I love you."

He didn't need to answer me. I saw it in his eyes. I felt it in the way his body moved with mine. He closed his eyes and quickly opened them again. I placed my hand on the side of his face and said, "I'm not looking for you to say it in return. I just wanted you to know."

"Azurdee," he whispered as he reached down and gently kissed me. He rolled off of me and pulled me to him. I loved being in his arms more than anything. I could feel the cold metal of his dog tags as I shut my eyes and fought to hold back my tears.

"Will you come home with me for Christmas?"

He barely whispered his question and my heart pounded in my chest so loudly I was sure he could hear it. *He wants me to go home with him?*

I turned around and faced him. I glanced down to his dog tags and he must have seen me, because he reached for them, took them off and set them on the side table.

"Home? Like as in your family ranch home?"

He laughed and said, "Yes. As in come and meet my father and mother."

I swallowed hard and then smiled slightly. "I'd love to."

"How many days can you take off?"

"Um…well, the coffee shop is shut down the week of Christmas and I was planning on taking a few days off the week before, but I hadn't really decided yet."

He smiled and said, "Can you take that week off, too? I'm planning on being there for two weeks. I need to decompress and nothing does it like the ranch."

I sat up and thought about it. I could leave Ralph in charge; I trusted him and I planned on making him the manager of the restaurant once it opened. This would be great practice for him.

I looked at him and smiled. "When are you leaving?"

The smile that spread across his face made my stomach drop with excitement. "Two days."

I nodded my head and said, "Okay."

He grabbed me and pulled me in for another kiss. He pulled back and said, "Come on. I want to do something." He stood up and quickly started getting dressed.

I got out of bed and looked at him and laughed. "Are we going somewhere?"

He nodded his head. "I'm going to go pack up my stuff and come back here, if that's okay? We'll leave from here and head down to the ranch."

I looked at the clock. "Lark, it's four in the morning. Can't we wait until daylight to go get your stuff?"

He shook his head and reached down for the T-shirt and handed it to me. "Put this back on and throw on something warm. I'm on the bike."

He walked up to the side table and grabbed his dog tags and put them back on and made his way out of my room. My head was spinning. *Why in the world did he want to leave now? What was the rush?*

I grabbed my cell phone and sent Ralph a text that I would be out all morning and would stop by after lunch.

I pulled the T-shirt on over my head, sans bra and then found a sweatshirt. It was abnormally warm for December so I was pretty sure I would be okay in just that and a pair of jeans.

When I walked out into my living room I looked out the French doors and saw Lark on the phone.

Who in the hell would he be talking to this early in the morning?

He walked in and smiled at me as he said, "You ready?"

I nodded my head and asked, "Should I bring my purse?"

When the left corner of his lips moved up, I knew he was up to something.

"No. You won't need it."

It didn't take me long to wish I had worn a long sleeve shirt under the sweatshirt. I buried my face behind Lark and silently said a prayer that we would not be bringing the bike back to Wimberley.

Finally Lark pulled into the parking garage and parked. I had such a chill I couldn't wait to get upstairs. I got off the bike and took my helmet off. I put it under the seat where he stored it and I stood there and just stared at Lark who was still sitting on the bike. I tilted my head and looked at him.

"What?" I asked.

"Get in my truck, back seat. You left your skirt in there. Change into it and be sure to take your panties off."

I looked at him confused. "My pink skirt? Damn. I've been looking for that skirt. You want me to change into a skirt? Why?"

"Don't ask questions. Just do it, Azurdee."

The authority in his voice had my libido hitting high and I walked around the bike and got into the back seat of the truck. Sure enough my pink skirt was right there folded up like I left it a month ago.

I pulled my shoes off and slipped off my jeans and then my panties. I slipped the skirt on and slipped my sneakers back on. I jumped out of the truck and spun around for Lark as he smiled.

"Done. Now do you want to tell me why you had me change and take off my panties?"

I watched as he unbuttoned his pants and pulled them down a bit, exposing his rock-hard erection.

Oh God.

He used his index finger to motion for me to move closer. "Climb on in front of me baby. I want to go for another ride."

My breathing became erratic at the idea of having sex, on his bike, in a public garage. I quickly looked around. People would be leaving for work soon but I didn't even care. Again my libido took over and I was finding myself climbing up and facing him. I sat myself down onto him and let out a gasp as I threw my head back.

"Fuck, you're always so damn wet and ready, aren't you?"

I snapped my head back up and nodded as I leaned down and began kissing him as I positioned my feet and began moving up and down on his dick.

"God! Lark… It's not going to…take…long."

He grabbed my hair and pulled hard, exposing my neck to him. He took his tongue and ran it along my sensitive skin as I let out a long soft moan.

"Fuck me faster, Azurdee."

"Yes," I whispered as I began moving faster. I lifted up more and slammed back down on him causing us both to suck in a breath of air.

"Lark, oh God, I'm so close."

Then I heard someone talking and I stopped. "Don't stop. Faster, Azurdee."

I began moving again. Grinding my hips into his. The idea that someone could see us did weird things to me. At first I was about to die of embarrassment, but now it was turning me on even more.

"When you come I want you to cry out how good it feels."

I looked at him. "What?"

"I want you to let everyone know how good it feels to fuck me on my bike."

I peeked over my shoulder and saw a guy walking towards his car. There was a girl walking behind him and she was looking at us. I looked away quickly and saw Lark smiling.

"I think it's turning her on to see us fucking. Harder Azurdee, faster."

I looked back at her and she was just standing there watching us. Her husband or boyfriend or whoever he was, had now stopped and was walking back over to her.

"Faster, Azurdee. Fucking ride me."

I did what he asked. It was dark enough in the parking garage that I couldn't make out the people's faces, but I was sure they could hear our bodies slapping together and our moans.

I can't believe I'm doing this. Oh God.

I lifted myself up again and slammed myself down onto Lark as he let out a loud long moan.

"Feels so fucking good." He grabbed my hips and began thrusting along with me.

"Oh no..." I whispered. The build up was growing and with the way he was hitting me inside I knew it was going to be a big orgasm.

"Tell me it feels good. Let me hear you."

I looked back over my shoulder and the couple had moved into their car. I thought I saw their window down just a bit. I looked back at Lark and said, "I'm going to come. Oh...God...ahh!"

My orgasm hit me so hard I began crying out his name.

"Ah...baby, I feel you squeezing down on me. I'm going to come."

He lifted me up and slammed me back down with such a force I cried out again as another orgasm ripped through my body.

"Oh God! Yes! Yes...I'm coming again!" I cried out as he wrapped his arms around me and released his warm cum into my body. We both sat there for a while as we tried to get our breathing under control.

"I think we might have helped someone have a good start to

their day."

I turned around and looked at the BMW and whispered, "Oh my God. Are they having sex in there?"

Lark laughed and said, "Baby, we just had sex on my bike while they watched, and you're shocked they're having sex in their car?"

I turned back and looked at Lark and giggled. I hit him on the chest and said, "What are you doing to me, Lark Williams? My parents would lock me away if they knew what I had just done."

"Did you think it was hot?"

I smiled and nodded my head.

He smiled bigger. "It made it more hot knowing we were being watched, didn't it?"

I nodded and then had a terrible thought. How many times did Lark have sex in public with other girls? How many times did he have a girl fuck him on his bike like this?

I quickly lifted myself off of him and got off the bike. I felt sick for some reason knowing that I was just another girl who fucked him on his bike.

I went to walk to the truck when he grabbed my arm. "What's wrong?"

I shook my head and tried to reel in these stupid emotions. "Nothing. I don't want to do that again."

He pulled his head back and looked at me. "What? What happened, Azurdee? Why are you so upset all of a sudden?"

I opened the back door and reached in for my jeans and panties. "I just want to get upstairs." I looked at him and said, "Please."

I began walking toward the elevator corridor. I glanced at the car and quickly turned away before I saw anything.

Lark came up behind me and pushed me against the wall after I rounded the corner.

"Talk to me, Azurdee. Tell me what in the fuck is going on in your head."

I swallowed hard. I wasn't sure I should say anything but I remembered my mother telling me not to ever let things just build up inside you. It's always best to just get it out and in the open.

"How many other girls have you fucked on your bike while people watched? I'm not some fucking whore you picked up at a club."

He stepped back and looked at me. "What? I've never treated you like that."

I wiped a tear away and whispered, "You just did."

"I thought...I thought you enjoyed what we did. You said it was hot and..."

I turned around and hit the elevator button. "That was before it hit me you've probably done this with other girls."

The elevator door opened and there was an older lady already inside. I stepped in and Lark followed. His face dropped when he looked at the older lady. I knew he wanted out of his fatigues before too many people saw him.

"Well, good morning, Mr. Williams. How are you?"

Lark smiled and said, "Good morning, Mrs. Smith."

Her floor was the floor right under Lark's. The elevator moved so fast that before I knew it, it was Lark's floor and the doors opened. I quickly walked out and tried to turn and make my way to the kitchen as fast as possible.

Lark grabbed my arm and spun me around and grabbed onto both my arms as he began walking me backwards. My heart was pounding and the look in his eyes was scaring me.

"I'll have you know I've never fucked anyone else on my bike. Ever. I've never even had a girl in my truck before you."

"Lark, let go of me. You're scaring me."

"When are you going to see that you're different for me? I know you're not some fucking whore in a club. You're my every-thing and I don't know what I'm supposed to do to prove that to you."

I felt the tears building in my eyes and I hated that I was acting so weak in front of him.

"I'm not asking you to prove anything. I'm sorry, I just…" My voice trailed off and I let out a sob. He looked down at his hands gripping my arms and he let go.

He took a few steps back and ran his hand through his hair. He shook his head and the look in his eyes about dropped me to the floor. He had tears in his eyes.

"You're my whole world, and for you to think I'd…I never want to hurt you."

He turned around and took a few steps away from me. He turned back and said, "I'm sorry I made you do something that made you feel uncomfortable. I've missed you so much and when I'm around you I can't seem to get enough of you."

I tried to say something, but when I saw him run his hands down his face and wipe his eyes it felt like someone kicked me in the stomach.

"I'm tired, Azurdee. I think I need to take a shower and get some sleep."

He turned and walked down the hall towards his bedroom.

I just stood there. *What just happened?* I walked over to the sofa and sat down. I closed my eyes and pictured us on the bike. I was shocked at myself for liking what we just did. The fact that someone saw us turned me on even more and I was trying to come to grips with that.

I took my fear out on Lark. It was easier to make it feel like it was his fault than to admit my own fears.

I looked toward his room. I stood up and took a deep breath. I knew what I had to do.

CHAPTER 15

Lark

I LET THE HOT WATER run over my face as I tried to understand what just happened. How could she think I'd treat her like all those other girls? I'm doing everything I possibly can to show her how much she means to me. *What in the fuck happened?* She'd seemed to like what we were doing. I knew it turned her on, but then something switched in her.

I'm no good for her. I made her feel dirty and used.

Maybe she was pushing me away because she found out I'm still active duty? *Fuck!*

As soon as we landed, I jumped on my bike and headed straight to her. I wasn't even thinking I was still in my uniform. *I warned her…I told her I wasn't any good for her.*

I closed my eyes and put my hands against the back of the shower. I jumped when I felt her hands touch me. The feeling that zipped through my body when she touched me caused goose bumps to come up all over my body. I turned around and she was standing there naked.

She is so damn beautiful. I don't deserve her.

"I'm sorry. I don't know why I blamed you for my own insecurities. Lark, I really enjoyed what we did…a lot. More than I want to admit."

I looked at her, confused.

She began chewing on her bottom lip. I reached up and pulled it out from her teeth.

"Talk to me Azurdee, because I'm confused as hell. I've tried so hard to show you…"

She put her finger up to my lips to stop me from talking.

"I've always been the good girl. The girl who waited to find the perfect guy to give her virginity to. The girl who was always making sure her friends got home from parties, who sat there and listened to them all talk about sex and how amazing it was. When I met you for the first time and you smiled at me, you turned something on deep inside of me. I love who I am with you, Lark, but it…it scares me that I crave your touch as much as I do. I'd never been so turned on as I was earlier. Knowing that someone was watching us…it thrilled me and I was…I was…"

"Tell me," I whispered.

"When it hit me what we had done, I panicked and I guess I let my imagination run wild when I said those things to you. You've never treated me like that. I swear to you. You've made me feel so wonderful. I feel cherished when you make love to me. I feel wanted when you look at me with lust in your eyes."

She looked down and began crying. I pulled her to me and wanted more than anything to tell her how much I loved her.

I held her for a few minutes before she looked up at me and said, "It was really hot."

I smiled and said, "Hottest damn thing I've ever done."

She grinned and said, "Me too."

I laughed and picked her up as she wrapped her legs around me.

"I can't get enough of you, *mi amor*. I rushed to your house as soon as we landed. I never wanted you to find out that I was still in the Marines."

She looked into my eyes and tilted her head. "Can I ask why you tell everyone you're not in the Marines?"

My heart slammed in my chest. "I um…I kind of work under-cover. I can't really talk about it."

She nodded her head and said, "Good enough for me. I prom-ise I won't say anything to anyone."

I pushed her against the wall and kissed her. "I love you so much," she whispered as I buried my face in her neck and closed my eyes.

Guarda mi corazón.

I wanted so badly to tell her I loved her, but I wasn't sure I was ever going to be able to tell her that.

I gently set her down and she smiled and picked up the soap and washcloth and began washing me off.

The next thing I remembered I was lying down and pulling her next to me as I fell asleep.

Right before I drifted off to sleep she whispered,

"I'll love you unconditionally, Lark Williams. Forever."

***

When I saw the house come into view I took a deep breath. Tristan had already called to tell me our mother was all over Ryn from the first moment she laid eyes on her.

"Lark? Are you okay?" Azurdee asked. I looked at her and smiled. "I am. I'm just worried my mother is going to attack you and start talking babies and shit. I don't want you to stress about what she says to you, okay?"

She threw her head back and laughed. "Please. Wait until you meet *my* parents."

I swallowed hard just thinking about meeting her father. I gripped the steering wheel harder. When she placed her hand on my arm I instantly relaxed.

"It'll be fine. Please don't worry."

I nodded and tried to smile.

"Jesus, that house is huge!" Azurdee said.

And there was my mother. Right on cue. Tristan and Ryn were walking up behind her as my mother jumped up and down clapping her hands. I wanted to just keep driving and leave.

I stopped a few feet back and put the truck in park and turned and looked at Azurdee. She was smiling as she watched my mother.

"Azurdee?"

She tilted her head as she looked at me. "I um...I haven't brought anyone here before, besides Nikki. I um...well I..."

She placed her hand on the side of my face and smiled the most beautiful smile. "Stop. It's okay and I just love that you brought me here to meet your parents. Lark, I'm not trying to push you into anything you're not ready for. Please know that."

I closed my eyes and opened them again. The look in her eyes would have dropped me to my knees if I had been standing up. "I'm scared, Azurdee. I'm so fucking scared of the feelings that I have for you."

Her lips parted open and she looked like she wanted to say something but she bit down on her lower lip and then said, "It's a shame your mother is standing there waiting for us, because I really want to crawl onto your lap and make love to you."

I looked back at my mother and sighed. "Ah fuck. This is going to be a long two weeks."

I jumped out of the truck and waved to my screaming mother. "Michael! Oh don't make me wait another second!"

I smiled and walked up to the passenger side of my truck. I opened the door and held my hand out and whispered, "Get ready for the monster."

She punched me in the stomach and said, "Stop that!"

Azurdee turned and began walking toward my mother. "Oh. My. God! You are beautiful." She placed her hands on Azurdee's face and looked her up and down. "Oh, Michael. Where did you find such a beautiful young lady?"

Azurdee's cheeks flushed and I beamed with pride. I glanced up at Tristan, who was laughing. I walked up to Ryn and gave her a kiss on the cheek and said hello. I reached for Tristan's hand to shake it. He grabbed me and pulled me into a hug and whispered, "Thank fuck you showed up. Ryn was about to kill Mom!"

I laughed and gave him a push.

Before I knew it, my mother had hooked her arm through Azurdee's and was walking into the house. "Tonight there's a dance in town. I'll introduce you to all our friends. You do two-step, right darling?"

Azurdee nodded her head and said, "Yes ma'am, I do."

"Oh good! My Michael loves to dance."

Azurdee looked over her shoulder and winked at me as she said, "Yes ma'am, he does."

"If you love that girl you will get her away from Mom, fast," Tristan said as he slapped me on the back and put his arm around Ryn's waist. Then he made his way into the house behind my mother and Azurdee.

I stood there and watched as Azurdee laughed at everything

my mother said. She immediately fit in, and I had no doubt my mother would love her.

The most overwhelming feeling moved through my body as I smiled and shook my head.

I loved her. I loved Azurdee Emerson more than the air I breathed.

CHAPTER 16

Azurdee

I HADN'T HAD THIS much fun or laughed this much in a long time. I loved Lark's parents already. Lark had made Joyce and Peter out to be terrible, but they were kindhearted and loved their two sons more than anything.

I sat at the wood table and tried to listen to Joyce and her best friend Terry talk about teaching me how to make a proper cobbler. Once Joyce found out I loved to cook and was opening my own restaurant, she was in heaven. I had made everyone French toast for dinner after Lark insisted it was the best he'd ever had.

I had been in the kitchen talking to Joyce when Lark walked in dressed in Wranglers and cowboy boots. When I looked down and saw the cowboy hat in his hands, I was almost positive I moaned. He smiled and winked at me as he made his way outside. Joyce leaned over and whispered, "I'm going to guess this is the first time you've seen my boy in his natural element."

I shook my head. I'd seen Lark in jeans and boots before but something about how he looked right now was causing my breathing to pick up and my body to ache for his touch.

"I can't believe he's mine," I whispered. I slammed my hand over my mouth and looked at Joyce. "I'm so sorry. I didn't mean to say that out loud."

She began laughing and said, "Azurdee, I've never seen my son look at another woman like he looks at you."

I dropped my hand and said, "What about Nikki?"

Her smile faded briefly before she smiled sweetly at me and said, "You know about Nikki?"

I nodded and said, "Yes."

"He loved her, Azurdee. He was devastated by her death, but the way he looks at you…" she smiled bigger and looked into my eyes. "I've never seen him so in love with someone in my life."

I sucked in a breath of air. "You think he's in love with me?"

She giggled and said, "Please. I know my son and he is head over heels in love with you, sweetheart."

I had to grab onto the counter. My heart felt like it had just dropped to my stomach and my stomach was doing some insane dance. I felt my face blushing and when Ryn walked into the kitchen, she looked at me and said, "Are you okay?" She walked up to me and whispered, "Did she say something to upset you?"

I shook my head and said, "No, not at all."

Tristan walked in behind Ryn and said, "Come on y'all, or we are going to be late. I'm ready to get my dance on."

***

I glanced over and looked at Lark talking to some guy. He was our age and I was guessing Lark knew him from high school. When Lark threw his head back and laughed, I suppressed the whimper I wanted to let out.

Everyone was so incredibly nice and they all seemed to love Lark. Although everyone here called him Michael except for Tristan, Ryn, and me. Scott had told me Lark began going by his middle name after Nikki died. I had no idea what the hidden meaning was behind why he did that and I would never ask him.

Tristan walked up to me and smiled. As I glanced up at him, I smiled back. He was just as handsome as Lark. Same height and build and almost the same smile. I'd never seen a smile like Lark's. It melted my heart and I swore I fell more in love with him every time he smiled at me.

"Care to dance with me?" He glanced at Ryn, who was sitting at the other end of the table talking to Peter. Tristan seemed to treat Ryn more like a friend. There were a few times she went to kiss him and he would just smile and turn away. Other times he kissed her with so much passion I had to look away.

I looked back up at Tristan and nodded my head as I held my hand out for him. Jason Aldean's "Even if I Wanted To Be" began playing, and we both started dancing. We didn't speak for the first minute or so. I finally pulled away some and said, "Why are you with Ryn?"

His face was shocked, but then he slowly smiled. "My brother said you were a smart one. Does it show that much?"

I smiled slightly and said, "Maybe not to everyone, but it does to me."

He tilted his head and asked, "What shows?"

I quickly looked at Ryn and then looked back at Tristan. "One thing that stands out is you love to dance and she doesn't."

He nodded and said, "True."

I continued on. "She seems like she is a safe pick for you. After talking to her, I know she is focused on her career big time. She works a lot and likes to have fun. So I'm guessing she isn't pressuring you to settle down."

He stared at me, not saying a word. "I'm guessing there might be another girl in there somewhere? Am I right?"

He closed his eyes and smiled and then opened them again. "Her name is Liberty and she is the polar opposite of Ryn."

I let out a giggle and said, "That scares you?"

He shrugged his shoulders and said, "I don't necessarily think it scares me. She just wants…more. I'm not ready for more. But I think when I am, Liberty is who I should be with. She is smart, has a good head on her shoulders and would be a good fit for me."

I nodded.

Tristan pulled back and smiled and said, "I have to tell you, Azurdee, I haven't seen my brother this happy in a very long time. You know about Nikki, right?"

I nodded my head and said, "Yes."

Tristan looked over toward Lark, who was still talking to the same guy. When he looked back at me his expression changed. "He also told me you know he is still in the Marines."

I sucked in a breath of air. "You know?"

"I'm the only other person besides you who knows. He wanted to let someone else know just in case. Well, I mean. Ah…"

Tristan must know what Lark does in the Marine Corps.

"It's okay, Tristan. I don't pressure Lark to tell me anything. I figured if he needed me to know he would tell me. It was a mistake on his part that I even found out. I had my suspicions, but I would never pressure him. I love him too much."

The smile that spread across Tristan's face caused me to smile. "What are you smiling so big about?" I asked.

"You have no idea how much my brother is in love with you, do you?"

The same feeling I had when Joyce said Lark was in love with me happened again. I gripped onto Tristan harder and looked at Lark, who was now watching Tristan and me dance. He smiled and I quickly looked back at Tristan.

"Azurdee, just be patient with him. He's guarded his heart for so long, afraid to let anyone else in for fear they would leave him like Nikki did. Her death really messed him up. He just needed to find the one person who would be able to wake up those feelings again."

I smiled slightly and whispered, "I'm not Nikki, though."

He laughed and said, "No, you are not. Nikki was Lark's safety net. She was his Ryn. Lark was planning on asking Nikki to marry him."

I momentarily stopped breathing and looked away. Panic began filling my chest and I wasn't sure why. I looked back at Tristan and gave him a confused look.

"She would have said no, and Lark knew there was no way in hell she would say yes. She was the type of girl who wanted to do things her way, was completely career driven and just wanted to have fun with no ties. When she left to go on that trip to the coast, Lark was devastated. They had planned to spend time together at our grandparents' condo in New Mexico. Nikki found out a couple friends were heading to the coast, so she dropped Lark for them. Nikki knew Lark was hurt by it and that's why she decided to come home a day earlier. She wanted to make it up to him, but she did shit like that to him all the time. Made plans and dropped them. Lark has felt guilty for her death ever since. He told me once if he hadn't made her feel guilty for leaving on that trip, maybe she would still be alive."

The song had ended and another song began playing. I shook my head and asked, "If Lark knew she wasn't the type to settle down, why was he planning on asking her to marry him if he thought she would say no?"

Tristan shrugged. "Same reason I brought Ryn home to meet

my parents and not Liberty. The idea of settling down but knowing you never really will. If I had brought Liberty to meet my parents, Liberty and my mother would have begun planning our wedding. No way in hell I'm ready for that. Ryn makes me happy. She is fun, sexy as hell, and just enjoys me for me. She could care less I have money. There is no pressure, no expectations with Ryn. I think that was how Nikki was for Lark, but deep down inside I think Lark truly wanted all of the other things, he just knew he would never get them with Nikki, even though he wanted to believe he would. I think he would have waited forever for her…or until he met someone who made him want more. You're the one who makes Lark want more, Azurdee. Don't ever think he is comparing you to Nikki. The way he looks at you—I've never seen him look at another girl that way, not even Nikki."

I shook my head and said, "I would never hurt him."

He nodded and said, "I know. That's not what I'm afraid of."

I tiled my head and asked, "What do you mean?"

"I'm afraid he is going to be the one hurting you if he doesn't open up his heart soon."

I took a step back away from Tristan and was about to ask him another question, when my whole body came to attention because Lark placed his hand on the small of my back. I quickly looked up into his eyes. He was smiling, but the smile didn't touch his eyes. He looked more concerned than anything.

"This sure looks like a serious conversation," Lark said as he slowly looked away from me and over to his brother.

Tristan smiled and when I looked at him he winked. "Azurdee is beginning to panic about her place opening soon. I was trying to let her know not to worry. Sometimes things take longer to fall into place but those are usually the best things in life. The things we have to wait longer for."

He slapped Lark on the back and began walking over to Ryn. He whispered something into her ear and she stood up and they began walking out of the dance hall.

Lark looked back at me and smiled. I smiled and tried like hell to calm my beating heart.

When Billy Currington's "Must Be Doin' Somethin' Right" began playing, Lark smiled so big it caused my stomach to drop.

"Dance with me, *mi amor*."

I nodded, and when he pulled me up against his body I instantly relaxed. The way his body moved with mine made it feel like we were one. We didn't speak at all as we danced.

Finally our silence was broken when Lark asked, "What were you and my brother talking about?"

I bit down on my lower lip. I didn't want to lie to him, but I didn't want him to think we were talking about him also. I pulled back and looked into his eyes and smiled slightly. "We talked about Ryn and Liberty. A little bit about you and me."

His jaw tightened and he attempted to smile. "What about me and you?"

"Michael, may I cut in?"

I quickly looked and saw Lark's father standing there with a smile on his face. I could tell by Lark's body language he was not happy about this, but he smiled and held out his hand for his father to take the lead.

Peter took me into his arms and we took off two-stepping. I quickly found out where Lark and Tristan got all their charm.

"I daresay you are the most beautiful girl in the room, Azurdee," Peter said with a sly smile.

"Hmm…do I detect a little bit of bribing about to head my way?" I said with a giggle. Peter threw his head back and laughed before looking at me again and saying, "Not only beautiful, but smart as well."

"Oh yeah, a bribe is coming for sure," I said as I smiled bigger. I looked across the room and saw that Lark was watching us. He had a slight smile on his face, which caused me to relax a little.

"What will it take to get you to talk my son into coming home more often? He hasn't been home in months."

I looked at Peter with a shocked look on my face. "I would figure he came home a lot. I would if this was home for me. It's beautiful here."

Peter shook his head and his eyes filled with sadness. "No, neither one of boys really come home very often. I had such dreams for them. They were both going to help me run the ranch and we would work together every day." He tilted his head and frowned. "I guess they had dreams of their own though."

I smiled slightly and said, "Lark talks so much about the ranch. I know he loves it here." I glanced back over toward Lark. He was talking to Tristan and it appeared to be a serious conversation. When Lark looked back over to me he shook his head and turned to walk out. Panic filled my body from head to toe and I wasn't sure why. *Was he leaving? Did he get called away again? Did Tristan tell him we were talking about him and Nikki?*

I stepped back and looked at Peter. "I'm sorry Peter, would you excuse me please?"

He smiled and nodded his head, "Of course, darling. I'm going to find my bride and spin her around for a bit."

I laughed and then turned and headed to where I had seen Lark go. I pushed the door open and was standing in a parking lot. I looked around and saw Lark leaning against his truck.

I took a deep breath and made my way over to him. Before I walked up to him, he began talking.

"I'm sorry everyone keeps bringing up Nikki to you."

I stopped dead in my tracks. "What?" I barely said.

He didn't bother turning around as he just kept talking. "My family seems to feel the need to keep bringing her up. I'm sorry."

I shook my head even though I knew he couldn't see me. "I'm not bothered by that. I know how much you loved her and I can't even imagine what it must have been like for you."

His head dropped and he whispered something I couldn't make out.

My heart hurt so much for him and all I wanted to do was take away his hurt. His confusion.

"Lark," I whispered. I stepped closer to him and touched his arm. He quickly turned and the way his eyes moved all over my body I knew what he was wanting. I took a step back and shook my head.

I swallowed hard and said, "If you're thinking about her, that's fine. I understand how everyone mentioning her is causing feelings to resurface, but if you think you're going to use me to forget about her…" I couldn't even finish talking. I could feel the tears burning my eyes. "I'm going back inside."

I turned and began walking to the door when Lark called out for me. "Azurdee, wait. My God, I would never…"

The doors flew open and Peter and Joyce came walking out; Peter was cursing up a storm as he was limping.

I quickly ran up to them and said, "Oh my goodness. What happened?"

Joyce rolled her eyes and said, "This old goat got a little too wild on the dance floor. He swears he's only sprained it but I swear I heard something break."

Lark came running up. "Dad, are you okay?"

Tristan was now outside with Ryn right behind him. "Damn it, Dad. You're not twenty anymore."

Peter shot Tristan a dirty look that caused both Ryn and I to chortle.

"Boys, just help me get him to the truck so we can get to the hospital."

Peter started pushing Lark away. "I'm not going to any goddamn hospital. I just sprained the damn thing."

"Dad, we're going to the hospital whether you like it or not," Lark said as he grabbed him and helped him over to their truck. "Mom, do you want me to drive?"

Joyce nodded her head and jumped into the backseat. Lark turned and looked at me. He turned back and looked at his father and pushed me away from the truck a few feet.

"I need you to follow me in my truck. Is that okay?" Lark asked.

I nodded my head and said, "Of course it's okay."

When I looked into his eyes, I couldn't believe what I saw. He was...scared.

"Lark, please don't be scared. Your Dad's going to be okay. Even if he did break his ankle, it's going to be okay."

He looked down at my lips and then back into my eyes. "I would never use you like that, Azurdee. *Ever.* Please know I'm not upset about people talking about Nikki or even my father being hurt. I'm upset that I made you think I only wanted you to forget about Nikki. I...I um...I care about you too much to ever do something like that to you. Please don't ever forget that."

My heart began beating faster as I smiled and nodded my head. "I'm sorry I thought that."

He instantly relaxed and then jumped when his mother called

out, "Michael! Come on!"

Lark leaned down and kissed me quickly against the lips before pulling back and handing me his keys.

Just a quick kiss from him caused me to lose my senses. I quickly ran over to his truck and jumped in.

The whole way to the hospital I couldn't stop thinking about everything that had happened today. All these people telling me how much Lark loved me, the look in his eyes when he was telling me he was scared I thought he wanted to use sex to forget about Nikki, the way he seemed like he wanted to tell me he loved me but he couldn't. *Motherfucker! I'm so damn confused.*

I slammed my head back against the seat as I followed Lark to the hospital. I thought back to the night of Scott and Jessie's wedding.

I'm not sure if I can be what you want me to be.

What was I wanting Lark to be? I knew I'd fallen head over heels in love with him and I was okay that he wasn't ready to say it back. *Wasn't I?* I knew I wanted to spend every waking moment with him and I was pretty sure he felt the same way about me.

Mi amor. I smiled as I thought about how Lark always called me *my love*. My smile faded as I remembered him talking in his sleep the other night and heard him repeat, "*Guarda mi corazón*" over and over again. *What did he need to guard his heart from? Me or love?*

I wanted to ask Tristan why he thought Lark would end up hurting me, and made a mental note to try and talk to him alone again. We had almost two weeks and I was pretty sure I'd be able to talk to him again.

I pulled up and followed Tristan into the parking lot and parked Lark's truck. As I made my way into the hospital, the strangest feeling came over me and I couldn't really understand what it was, but it caused my whole body to break out in goose bumps.

As I walked in, Ryn walked up to me and said, "Let's wait in the waiting room. Tristan or Lark will come get us."

I turned around and watched as Tristan, Lark, and his father all argued as their mother walked ahead of them and Lark and Tristan fought over who was going to push their dad in the wheelchair.

When I looked back at Ryn, she was smiling and I saw something in her eyes I hadn't seen yet...love.

CHAPTER 17

Lark

IT HAD BEEN A little over a week since I'd brought Azurdee home to meet my parents. As each day passed, they fell more and more in love with her. Even Tristan seemed to be falling for her…in a sister type way.

I walked into the kitchen and looked at my mother and father sitting there. My dad looked up and said, "Good morning. Did you sleep well last night?"

I gave him a smirk and said, "Yes. Yes sir, I did."

He rolled his eyes and said, "Your ass is lucky we aren't old-fashioned or you and your brother would still be sneaking off to the barn."

I laughed and grabbed a glass out of the cabinet. "Speaking of. Where is Tristan?"

"He took a few hunters out for me that were booked."

I glanced over toward my mother, who had a pissed-off look on her face. She hated it when my father booked hunts so close to Christmas Day. Hell, if he had it his way, he would be out guiding them on Christmas Day.

I walked up to the window and looked out and saw Tristan, Ryn, Azurdee, and two young guys all standing there talking.

Azurdee was dressed in jeans, boots and a tank top and the way the one fucker was looking at her was starting to piss me off.

I set my glass down and tried to settle my nerves before I walked out there and beat the shit out of the little fucker. I felt a hand on my shoulder and my body tensed up even more.

"She sure is a beautiful girl, Michael," my father said.

I turned to him and then back toward the group. I nodded my head and said, "Yes sir, she is. Inside and out."

"Sure would be a shame to let something like that slip through your hands, wouldn't it?"

I swallowed hard and remained silent.

"Did I ever tell you how I almost lost the love of my life?"

I snapped my head over and looked at him. He was staring out the window with a smile on his face.

"Are you talking about Mom?"

He looked at me and gave me a funny look and said, "Of course I'm talking about your mother."

I looked over my shoulder and my mom was standing at the sink with a smile on her face. I shook my head and said, "No, sir. I don't believe I've ever heard that story."

"It's a good story," he said as I turned and just stared at him.

"Well, are you going to tell me the story?"

He slowly turned and faced me. "Someday I'll tell ya, but just know this—if you let Azurdee go, you're going to let the love of your life slip away, son. It's okay to open your heart again, Michael. Anyone who sees the way you look at her can see how much you're in love with her. Don't let her slip away."

He grabbed his crutches and made his way out of the kitchen. I looked back at the window and watched as Azurdee laughed at something Tristan had said.

My mother walked up next to me and let out a little laugh. "Michael, just follow your heart. It will never lead you the wrong way if you truly listen to it."

I looked down at my mother and smiled. "I love you, Mom."

She returned my smile and said, "I love you too, son. Now get on out there and show that little fucker who Azurdee belongs to."

I laughed as I hugged my mother and then headed toward the door. As I pushed it open she yelled out, "Muck out the stalls in the main barn!"

"Yes, ma'am!" I yelled back.

I walked towards Azurdee and tried to keep my hands from balling up as I watched the shorter bastard put his hand on the small of Azurdee's back as they all made their way over to the jeep. I smiled when I noticed Azurdee move away from his touch.

"Heading out for a day hunt?" I asked as Tristan looked at me and gave me a look. I nodded to let him know I was okay. Azurdee spun around and smiled as she walked right into my arms. I held onto her as I looked at the bastard who couldn't seem to keep his eyes to himself.

Tristan slapped the fucker on the back, causing him to pull his eyes away from Azurdee. "Lark, this is Jonathon and Luke. They're looking to get them a nice buck. You up for a hunt?"

Azurdee pulled away and smiled as she whispered, "Good morning."

I kissed her gently on the lips and said, "Good morning, *mi amor*."

Her eyes lit up and I couldn't help but smile bigger. I knew how much she loved me calling her that and I made every attempt to use it all the time, not just when we were making love.

"I've gotta pass on this hunt, Tristan," I said as I continued to look at Azurdee. "I've got to take care of some things for Dad and Mom."

Azurdee smiled and bit down on her lower lip as I felt my pants grow a few sizes too small. I'd hardly been able to spend any time with her the last few days, what with trying to help out around the ranch since my father broke his ankle.

"Probably for the best that I take this one," Tristan said with a laugh. I looked over at him and smiled as Ryn shook her head and walked to Tristan. She reached up and kissed him and said, "Be careful. Hurry back, I'll be missing you." Tristan seemed shocked by what Ryn had just said. He smiled back at her and nodded his head. He watched as she walked back to the house. When he finally looked away he looked at me and attempted to smile. He looked back at Jonathon and Luke and clapped his hands and said, "Let's do this. Let's get us some big-ass south Texas bucks."

I helped them get all their gear into the jeep and then pulled Tristan off to the side and asked, "You want me to take them?" He pulled back and looked at me, confused.

"No dude, I got this. You took the one out yesterday. Spend some time with Azurdee today. I've got this. Tomorrow is Christmas and you know Mom is going to want us to do the whole family bullshit."

I nodded and said, "Yeah, I'm surprised Ryn hasn't fled yet."

Tristan nodded his head and looked away. "Yeah, well…let me get these guys out there before it gets too hot. We're already starting out too late."

I watched as my brother walked away and ran his hand through his hair. Yep. He was just as fucked as I was. His problem was he was falling in love with the one girl who he didn't think was the one he should be falling in love with, and my problem was I couldn't tell Azurdee I loved her.

I looked around and saw Azurdee was gone. When I walked around the corner, she was making her way down to the barn. I smiled and began jogging to catch up with her.

"Hey, where do you think you're going?" I called out as I came up behind her.

She turned and smiled and said, "To the horses."

I grabbed her and pulled her to me as I whispered against her neck, "Did Mom tell you that you had to muck out the stalls too?"

She laughed and said, "No, but I'd be more than happy to watch you do it, cowboy."

I kissed her neck and saw the goose bumps cover her body. I loved that I had such an effect on her body like I did.

I picked her up and she wrapped her legs around me as I walked her into the barn. "Fine, but I'm not taking off my shirt."

I set her down and she began laughing as she said, "Damn it. I thought I would get a free show."

I walked over and turned on the radio and picked up a rake. I watched as she sat down on a bale of hay and pulled her knees up to her chest. She smiled and motioned for me to begin. I shook my head and started off to work.

It didn't take long before I was working up a sweat. I glanced back a few times and looked over at her sitting there watching me. "You wanna help?"

She smiled as she shook her head and said, "Nope," popping the p loudly. Her smiled faded when Selena Gomez's song "Stars Dance" began playing. She slowly stood up and started walking towards me. When she walked up to me, she took the rake out of my hand and wrapped her hands around my neck and began moving her body against mine. I quickly was lost within her eyes.

I grabbed onto her body and began moving right along with her. The heat from her body and the way she was looking into my eyes had my complete attention.

What is this girl doing to me? I was totally hers, body and soul. I leaned down and brushed my lips across her neck. "Azurdee, you have no idea what you do to me," I whispered against her sensitive skin.

She dropped her head back and let out a whimper. "I do, because you do the same to me."

I kissed her along her neckline and then made my way up to her lips. I pulled her lower lip with my teeth and gently bit down on it. I felt her hands on my body as she made her way to my jeans and began unbuttoning them.

"I want you so much," I said as I pulled her tank top up and over her head. I looked at her white lace bra and moaned as her nipples hardened under my touch. I stepped back and watched as she began slipping her jeans off her body. She stood in front of me with nothing on but her panties and bra.

"Take your panties off, Azurdee, and give them to me. Keep your bra on."

She slowly slipped her panties off as she licked her lips and handed me her panties. I took them and picked her up as I carried her into the side office and shut the door.

I put her down and smiled as I said, "We're going to make love and then I'm going to do the one thing I've been dreaming about since we got here."

Her eyes lit up as she asked, "What have you been dreaming about?"

"Tying you up and fucking you in the barn."

She leaned against the wall and sucked in a quick breath of air and I quickly stripped myself of my boots and pants before I sat down on the chair. I smiled as I motioned for her to come to me. She smiled as she walked over and slowly began to sink down onto my body. The moment I felt myself slipping inside her warm body I let out a growl. Azurdee threw her head back and sighed in relief.

"Nothing feels better than you inside of me," she whispered. She snapped her head forward as she began slowly moving up and down.

I smiled and placed my hands on her hips and moved slowly in and out of her.

She smiled back at me and brought her lips to mine, but stopped just short of them and said, "I love you."

Something happened in that moment and I was overcome with such a strong emotion. I closed my eyes and got lost in her love-making. When the song "Adore You" by Miley Cyrus began playing, I looked into her eyes.

"Say it again," I whispered. At first she looked confused, and then a smile spread across her face.

She whispered to me, "I love you."

I closed my eyes. I needed to hear her say it. I needed to hear it from her lips while she made love to me.

I opened my eyes and whispered, "Say my name, too."

She moved up and down so slowly as she said, "I love you, Lark."

I shook my head and looked into her eyes. "Say my name, *mi amor.*"

She stopped, and when I saw her eyes filling with tears, I wanted to look away but I couldn't. She took a deep breath and leaned down and gently kissed me.

She pulled back slightly and her eyes moved everywhere on

my face before she embraced my eyes again. "I love you, Michael."

I wrapped my arms around her and held onto her as tight as I could. My heart was pounding in my chest so hard I was sure she could feel it. "Say it again, please," I said as my voice cracked.

She let out a sob as she said it again, "I love you, Michael. I love you so much it scares me."

I stood up as she wrapped her legs around my waist. I walked over to the small bunk that was in the office and laid her down on it. I moved onto her and slowly pushed myself back into her as she arched her back and let out a moan.

I placed my hands on the sides of her face as I slowly made love to her. I looked into her beautiful caramel eyes, now filled with tears, and I smiled as I whispered, "I love you, Azurdee. I love you so much. I'll love you forever."

Azurdee wrapped her arms around me and held onto me as she said, "I'm going to come."

I pushed myself into her harder and whispered in her ear as I came, "I'll. Love. You. Forever."

CHAPTER 18

Azurdee

I LAY WRAPPED IN Lark's arms as I silently cried. I'd never felt these emotions before in my life. There is no way to measure the love I was feeling in my heart. The moment he told me he loved me my whole world changed. There wasn't anything I wouldn't do for this man. No mountain I wouldn't climb to prove to him how much I loved him.

I closed my eyes tightly and thought back to the look in his eyes when he whispered to me that he loved me. I smiled and slowly turned to look at Lark. I could hear his breathing—slow and steady—as he lay next to me. I never wanted this moment to end.

When I heard his cell phone go off, my heart dropped. Lark jumped up and grabbed it from his pants on the floor. He frowned as he read it and then put it back into his pocket. He looked over at me and smiled that same smile that captured my heart a year ago.

"Hey," he said as he moved back over to the bed.

I slid over and said, "Hey."

He stood over me and held out his hand. When I looked down I felt the flush move across my cheeks. He was holding my panties in his hand.

"Put your hands out, *mi amor*."

My heart started pounding and I instantly felt a rush of wetness between my legs. I wasn't sure how he could turn me on so much when we had just made love not too long ago.

When Lark made love to me it was beyond beautiful, but when Lark played with me…it turned me on beyond belief. His voice would change and his eyes turned to nothing but lust and the only thing I wanted from him was to feel him inside me.

I put my hands above my head and closed my eyes. He was going to use my own panties to tie my hands together and I was beyond excited. "Lark," I barely got out as he tied my hands together and pushed them over my head.

"Don't touch me Azurdee, or I'll stop."

I shook my head, "I can't. I have to touch you."

He narrowed his eyes at me and repeated, "Don't touch me, baby, cause I really don't want to have to stop."

He pushed my legs apart and buried his face between my legs as I let out a moan. I moved my hands down and tried to run them through Lark's hair and he immediately stopped and pulled back.

No! No! No! Don't stop.

I pulled my hands back over my head and Lark chuckled. "Don't touch, baby, or I'll completely stop."

I thrashed my head from side to side. "No. Please. Lark, please!"

I hated that I turned so desperate like this, but his touch… his lips…his tongue. It did things to me that sent me into another realm. He moved his tongue slowly and gently over my clit and I could feel the build up.

Oh God. This was going to be a big one. I pulled my hands down and realized the moment I touched him what I had done. He pulled back and smiled as he stood up.

"Wait. Oh God. Shit. Fuck. Bastard hamburger!"

Lark tilted his head and laughed. "Bastard hamburger?"

I shook my head and looked at him. "What?" I was breathing like I had just run a race. Every single emotion I could possibly have was pulsing through my veins. I was confused, pissed, and horny as fuck.

Lark reached down and pulled me up as he picked me up and said, "Wrap your legs around me, Azurdee. I'm going to fuck you hard and fast."

Oh yes.

Lark walked up to the office wall and slammed me against it with such force I let out a small cry. He slammed into me so fast I didn't even have time to register anything. He quickly began fucking me so hard and fast that I wanted to beg him to slow down.

"Oh God, fuck, Azurdee. You're always so wet for me, baby."

I tried to wrap my arms around him as he pulled in and out with such force I was sure I would be sore for the rest of the day. Once I felt the build up, I dropped my head back and called out, "Yes!"

Lark thrust twice more and stopped as he let out a long moan. "Ahh…damn that felt so good."

I pulled my head up and looked at him. "What? No! No! I didn't get to come." I began moving my hips to get any kind of friction against his body that I could. Lark smiled and winked at me as he pulled out of me and gently set me down.

He took a few steps back and said, "Better get dressed and head back to the house."

My mouth dropped open and I just stood there naked. "You're…I don't get to…but…"

Lark quickly pulled his pants on and up. "I told you...don't touch."

With that he laughed and walked out the door. *Oh. My. God. He just denied me an orgasm.* I quickly located my clothing and got dressed as I plotted my revenge on Mr. Williams.

As I walked out of the barn, I was brought back to the moment Lark told me he loved me. I smiled as I made my way to the house, touching my lips gently. I would forgive him in just a few minutes for leaving me hanging.

I'll love you forever.

My heart began beating in my chest as I closed my eyes and remembered the moment like it was a second ago. When I walked up onto the front porch and saw him sitting with his mother talking, I was so overcome with emotion I fought to hold back my tears. He glanced up at me and something about his eyes was different. He seemed relaxed for the first time since I'd known him. He smiled and I couldn't help but smile back.

I quickly wiped the smile off my face and shot him a dirty look. He smiled bigger and Joyce turned and looked at me. "Why Azurdee, your face is flushed. Sweetheart, are you hot?"

I glanced at her and smiled before looking back at Lark and saying, "I am a bit hot. I'll have to go take a cold shower and... relieve myself from the heat."

Lark's smile faded and his mouth dropped open. Ryn was walking up behind me when Joyce looked at her and began saying something about dinner.

Lark stood up and I shook my head, held up my hand to stop him from walking toward me and mouthed the words, *asshole,* as he put his hand on his chest and said, "I'm wounded."

I shrugged my shoulders and turned and made my way into the house. I knew that me taking a shower right now with everyone awake would drive Lark mad. I hugged myself as I made my way upstairs. I heard Joyce telling Ryn not to worry about Tristan; he would be fine and back in a few hours. I stopped and turned around to see Ryn walking by. She looked up at me and gave me a weak smile.

I smiled back and made a note to talk to her later. I had a feeling Ryn and Tristan wanted more from each other than either of them would admit.

***

I stood in the cold shower cursing Lark. I leaned my head back and let the cool water run through my long hair. It wasn't too terribly hot out, but hot enough to make it miserable with my long hair. I reached for the soap and began quickly cleaning myself off. I hadn't had any intentions of finishing off what Lark started, but the moment I heard the bathroom door open and close quietly I knew I had to do it. I pushed my hand down between my legs and began touching myself.

"Ohh...yes...oh God..." I panted as I began moving my hand faster. I was waiting for him to tell me to push my fingers inside myself and I could almost feel the orgasm building.

I heard something drop and opened the door to find Joyce standing there shielding her eyes.

"Oh my God!" I screamed out.

"Oh goodness...Azurdee, I'm in here!" Joyce cried out.

"I know! I'm oh my God-ing that you're in here...while I'm in the shower."

I quickly grabbed a towel. "Joyce! Why are you in here?" I asked as I turned off the water.

"Well, Michael asked me to bring you this lotion. He said you would want it after your shower."

I instantly felt the anger building up in my chest. *That bastard!*

"I'm going to kill him," I whispered.

Joyce asked, "Are you covered? Can I look at you now?"

"Yes," I said as I shook my head and said, "I'm covered."

Joyce turned and gave me a weak smile. "Now I know it's none of my business, but maybe you should talk to Michael, honey. I'm sure he can…well, he can…well, I don't know if you're having sex or not, but I'm going to go with yes, and if he isn't performing to his…"

Dear God no. This is not happening. This. Is. Not. Happening.

"Joyce! *Please*. This is just weird. It's all just very weird for you to be saying what you're saying."

She nodded her head and said, "Well I think so, too. I would think if you were happy in the sex department you wouldn't need to masturbate." She tilted her head and looked up like she was thinking. "I should have Peter have a talk with Michael."

"No!" I yelled out. "Joyce, I'm very satisfied. Beyond satisfied. Lark is a very good…well…he…umm…"

I closed my eyes and wished like hell I could go back in time about ten minutes ago.

"Can we just stop this conversation, and may I please have some privacy to get dressed?"

Joyce nodded her head and said, "Of course. Well um…dinner will be ready in about forty-five minutes, so…ah…"

She looked me up and down and her cheeks blushed. "I'll just send Michael on up to um…well…help, I guess."

My mouth dropped open and I stumbled back against the wall.

I slowly slid down to the floor after she shut the bathroom door and looked up. "I'll do anything. Anything if you just give me back the last fifteen minutes or so. I swear…God. *Anything.*"

When the door opened and Lark walked in he was laughing his ass off.

I shook my head and said, "No sex for you for the rest of this trip. None."

I stood up and pushed past him and began to come up with a plan on how to not be attracted to this man.

This was never gonna work.

CHAPTER 19

Lark

I SAT ON THE SOFA opposite Azurdee and watched as she and Ryn giggled about something. This had been the perfect Christmas. Even though Azurdee was trying to stay true to her pledge not to have sex with me during the rest of our trip, I could already tell she was beginning to fold.

I glanced over and saw Tristan staring at Ryn. For someone who claimed he only wanted to have fun, he sure did look at her like I looked at Azurdee.

My father hit me on the shoulder and said, "Come on. I want to talk to you and your brother before you leave."

Azurdee snapped her head up and looked at us. "Are you leaving?" she asked in a panicked voice. I smiled and said, "We're leaving early. I thought we would go spend a few days at my parents' beach house."

The smile that spread across her face about dropped me to my knees.

My father gave Tristan a pat on the back and we both followed him into his office. He shut the door and then walked over to the window and stood there, staring out.

"Dad, is everything okay?" Tristan asked. My father stood

there for a few more seconds before he turned around and nodded his head as he took a seat in his giant leather chair.

I looked around his office. I loved it in here. I loved the smell of the leather furniture. The animals hanging on the walls and the pictures, they were everywhere. There were pictures of Tristan and I scattered through out his office. I glanced over at the one picture of me holding the antlers of my first deer. I smiled as I thought back to the day when my father and grandfather showed me how to gut and clean a deer.

My father cleared his throat and said, "The last week a few things have been brought to my attention."

Tristan and I both squirmed like two little boys who were fixin' to get into trouble.

When his eyes pierced mine and then moved over to Tristan's, I let out the breath I had been holding.

"Whatever it is, Dad, I'm sure it was Michael who did it."

I snapped my head and looked at him. "You do know the Marines trained me to kill. Right? You're aware of this information?"

Tristan rolled his eyes and my father chuckled. "Boys, settle down and listen to me."

He looked at Tristan and said, "Your intentions?"

Tristan tilted his head and said, "For?"

Now it was my father's turn to roll his eyes. "Ryn. What are your intentions with that lovely girl?"

Tristan let out a laugh and then quickly shut his mouth. "Why?"

"I see the way you look at her and it's obvious you have feelings for her."

Tristan quickly looked at me and then back at Dad. "Ryn and I are just having fun, Dad. Nothing serious. She isn't the type of girl who is looking to settle down or anything like that. She's just…

fun."

My father lifted his eyebrow in the all-knowing way of his. "Is that so?""

Tristan nodded and said, "Yep. That's so."

My father placed his hands together in a folded position and then tented his pointer fingers and rested them on his chin as he looked at me.

"Your intentions?"

My hands started to sweat and my heart began pounding. I closed my eyes and pictured Azurdee's smile when I told her I loved her.

I slowly opened my eyes and said, "I love her, Dad. I love her and see myself marrying her as soon as I get out..."

Tristan kicked me and I stopped talking. *Shit. I almost spilled out my guts a little too much.* This was why Skip said no girl-friends. They screw with your head.

"Marry her, huh? That's a pretty big commitment there, Michael. Are you sure?"

I instantly felt the heat moving through my body. *Why was my father questioning if I'm sure?*

I sat up straighter and said, "What the hell kind of question is that, sir? No disrespect, but I've never been so sure of anything in my entire life. I love her and I want to spend the rest of my life with her."

My father slowly smiled and turned slightly and opened one of his desk drawers. He pulled out two bottles and a small black jewelry box. Tristan and I both looked at each other and I shrugged my shoulders.

Tristan laughed and said, "If you want to drink to Lark's big news, Dad, we're kind of gonna need alcohol in those bottles. I mean I'm shocked, too, by his admission, but empty bottles?"

Dad just looked at Tristan as he began talking again. "I've been waiting for this moment for a few years. I had the same conversation with my old man and younger brother when I was about your age, Tristan. It was right after I met your mother. I brought her home to this very house and introduced her to your grandparents."

He smiled and shook his head as if remembering a certain memory. "I was nervous as hell about bringing your mother home to my parents. I just knew she would see the life I wanted and run as fast as she could back to Austin."

Tristan and I both looked at each other and smiled. Tristan was the one who wanted to take over the family ranch. I wanted to start a cattle ranch on the property I had bought over a year ago outside of Marble Falls. That was my dream.

I looked down and thought about Azurdee. I hadn't even thought about if that was something she would want to do. She was opening her restaurant in Wimberley. I frowned as I thought about being apart from each other.

I looked back up at my father as he continued to talk. "Lucky for me, your mother fell in love with it here and well, the rest is history."

I tilted my head and said, "Still doesn't explain the empty bottles, Dad."

My father let out a chuckle and nodded his head. "My father knew the moment he met your mother and saw the way I looked at her that she was the one I wanted to spend the rest of my life with. He waited a few days before he called me into this very office and had me sit down in the same seat you're sitting in, Michael. He asked what my intentions were with your mother. I laughed at first but when I saw he was serious, I spilled out my heart and soul to him. It was in that very moment I knew I wanted to spend the rest of my life with your mom and I would do whatever it took to make it happen."

He looked over at Tristan, who began moving around in his chair like he was very unsure of what to say or think. "Tristan, you better take a long hard look in the mirror, son, if you think for one minute that you don't have stronger feelings for Kathryn. I see the way both of you look at each other. I seriously don't think that girl is just hanging around you for a good time."

Tristan opened his mouth to talk but nothing came out. He finally looked away without saying a word.

"Michael, I've never seen you so in love."

I slowly smiled and it felt like my heart was about to lift out of my chest. "I've never felt this way before, Dad, and to be honest, it scares the hell out of me."

He chortled and said, "I'm sure it does. My advice to you both is to listen to your heart. I know you think your head will always lead you the right way, but that is wrong. It's your heart that will lead you."

He reached for a bottle and handed one to me and then set one down in front of Tristan. "With you and Azurdee heading to the beach, this is perfect timing."

I looked at him confused as I held the bottle in my hand.

"When my father handed me my bottle I thought the same thing you're both thinking. He had lost his damn mind." He let out a laugh and said, "Then he explained the journey of love to me. We all go through the journey, some easier than others. Michael, your journey has taken you down roads that I wish it hadn't. A parent wants nothing but happiness always for their child, but sometimes all you can do is sit back and watch where life takes them. Tristan, your journey has also begun, whether you want to admit it or not."

Tristan looked down at the floor and slowly shook his head.

"When you start the journey with that one person who you know you want to spend the rest of your life with, you have so many emotions going on in your heart and head. You're excited, scared, nervous, and even angry sometimes. My father passed along to me a tradition that I'm now going to pass along to you boys. The bottle."

I looked at the bottle and then looked at my father. "Dad, are we supposed to know what…the bottle…is for?"

"No, Michael. When my father saw that my journey had already started with your mother, he explained the meaning behind the 'journey of love' bottle. My father told me when he gave me my bottle to take your mother to the beach. We were both to sit in opposite rooms and write each other a letter about where we wanted our journey of love to take us. What our hopes, fears, dreams, doubts, and goals were for our relationship, or as he called it…our journey. You see boys, love is nothing more than a journey. It's a road we each venture down, not knowing how things are going to turn out. Sometimes it is filled with so much love and happiness we think this whole love thing is a piece of cake. Other times it's filled with doubt, anger, jealousy—and you will question the journey. There are going to be rough seas, boys, no matter how much in love with each other you are."

I sat there not really knowing what to say. I knew in my heart I was ready to start my journey with Azurdee. "Do you read the letters to each other?" I asked.

My father smiled. "No. After you write them, you place them together and then roll them up and put them in the bottle. Then you send your bottle out to sea."

Tristan laughed. "Why? I mean, if you're going to pour your damn heart out, why wouldn't you want the person to know what you said?"

My father looked at Tristan and shook his head. "I guess once you're ready, you'll know the answer to that question, son."

I had to admit I was a bit confused as to why you wouldn't read the letters to each other either, but I just went with it. I looked back down at the black box. "What's in the box, Dad?" I asked.

He leaned back and stared at the box. "It's your grandmother's engagement ring. She gave it to me right before she got sick. She wanted one of you boys to have it. Now, you don't have to use it if you don't want. I know things are different these days and young ladies like to pick out their own rings and such, but if you want… the ring is yours. To which ever one of y'all is wanting it."

He opened the box and I smiled the moment I saw the ring. I remember being little and spinning my grandmother's rings around on her finger. I closed my eyes and could almost smell her perfume. When I opened them again, my father was staring at me. I smiled and reached for the ring.

"I remember how much she loved this ring. She would take it off before she did anything."

Tristan let out a laugh. "Remember the one time she thought she forgot to take it off before she worked in the garden, and she had us looking for over three hours before she found it on her damn ring holder in her bathroom. Here she had taken it off and had forgotten."

I laughed and nodded my head. The oval-shaped diamond was at least a carat and had small baguettes lining the white gold band. It was simple, yet elegant.

My stomach dropped when I pictured slipping my grandmother's ring onto Azurdee's finger.

My father cleared his throat. "Now, Tristan, you're older, and per your grandmother's wishes, the ring was to either go to whoever was planning on marrying first, or to the oldest. Now you boys have to decide, who gets this ring?"

I looked over at Tristan. I knew he had feelings for Ryn and Liberty. I also knew that he thought by bringing Ryn home, he was making the safer choice, and this last week was proving his thinking wrong. The feelings he had for Ryn were stronger than he wanted to admit.

Tristan swallowed hard and then stood up. He pushed the bottle back toward our father and looked at me. "Well, I sure as hell am nowhere near ready to be making any commitment to anyone…let alone start some damn journey. I know how much you love Azurdee—I think you are the better choice for Gram's ring." I looked at my father and then back at Tristan. "Tristan, Ryn is…"

Tristan laughed and said, "A good time. That's it. That girl has no desire to settle down with anyone and that's what I like about her. We're just having a good time." He looked back at our dad and said, "Sorry Dad, I'm not quite ready for all of this right now."

He turned and walked to the door, opened it and walked out, closing it softly behind him. I slowly turned back around and looked at my father. He raised his eyebrow and said, "Honestly, I thought that whole thing was going to play out differently. I thought it would be you getting up and walking out."

I pulled my head back and looked at him with a shocked look on my face. "What? Why?"

He raised his eyebrow at me and said, "Really?"

I shrugged my shoulders and said, "She's changed me, Dad. I can't imagine my life without her in it. I mean…this past year has been nothing but hell. I couldn't stop thinking about her, dreaming about her. I would be sitting alone and she would pop into my head and I would have to force myself not to text her and ask her what she was doing." I let out a laugh and shook my head. "Then when we finally… Well, let's just say I can't get enough of her. I want to be with her all the time. When I'm gone for work she's all I can think about. She consumes my world, Dad."

He smiled and said, "Welcome to the journey of love. Hold on tight, son. Shit's about to get real."

I was totally caught off guard by my father's response. I began laughing, which caused him to laugh. Before I knew it we were both in tears as we laughed our asses off. There was a knock on the door, and when I turned around I saw my mother walking in. She had a concerned look on her face and attempted to smile but was doing a bad job of it.

My father stood up and said, "What's wrong?"

She took a deep breath and said, "Tristan just told me he was leaving early. Something about having to get home to take care of something for work. What did you say to him, Peter?"

My father let out a sigh and said, "Nothing, sweetheart. Your son is just running from love."

She nodded her head and said, "Yes, I know. I've been watching him the last three days avoid poor Ryn like she had a disease or something."

I stood up and looked down at my father. "Thanks, Dad."

My father stood up and held out his hand and said, "Just always remember…hold on, son, during both the good and the bad times. Just hold on."

I nodded and slipped the box into my pocket and reached down for the bottle. When I turned around, my mother had a tear slowly moving down her cheek.

I walked up and wiped it away before kissing her gently on the cheek.

"She loves you, Michael. I see how much you love her just by the way you look at her."

My heart began pounding again in my chest. For the first time in years I wasn't afraid to open my heart to someone.

I nodded my head and whispered, "I do, Mom. I really do love her."

CHAPTER 20

Azurdee

JOYCE GRABBED ME AND pulled me into a hug. She held me tightly as she whispered, "Have fun tonight, sweetheart."

I pulled back and smiled as I let out a giggle. "I'm sure I will." Tristan, Ryn, Lark and I were all heading to the local dance hall in town. It wasn't lost on me that Lark's mother had been walking around with the biggest smile on her face for the last day.

Lark threw his arm around me and began walking toward the door. My stomach still did that weird little dance anytime he touched me. I looked up at him and smiled as my heart plummeted in my chest.

"I really like you in a cowboy hat," I whispered as he raised his eyebrow.

"How much do you like me in it?"

For some reason, I thought back to Lark and me on his motorcycle. The flush must have shown on my face, because he put his mouth to my ear and whispered, "I'd really love to know what you're thinking about right now, *mi amor*."

"The morning on your bike in your parking garage."

He stopped dead in his tracks, stood back and tilted his head.

Then he put his arm around me again and started laughing. "My naughty little girl."

I was shocked when we walked into the dance hall and saw how packed it was. "Where do all these people live?" I asked as Tristan and Lark laughed. Ryn did a little hop and said, "Oh my God. My favorite song!" She grabbed my hand and pulled me out to the dance floor where we danced to "Blurred Lines" and laughed our asses off. I couldn't believe how many guys came up to us and attempted to dance. I was pretty sure Lark was close by making eye contact with them, because they all quickly moved away from us.

"Are you having fun?" Ryn shouted.

I nodded my head and asked, "Are you?"

Ryn smiled bigger and nodded her head. "More than I thought I would."

I began chewing on my bottom lip. I wanted to talk to her about Tristan and ask her what her true feelings were for him. I could see a difference in Tristan and I also saw how he was fighting it. I glanced over and looked at Tristan. He was texting someone and looked up toward Ryn. When I saw him walk toward the door, I knew he was going outside to talk to Liberty and I instantly got pissed. I looked back at Ryn and smiled.

I moved closer to her and yelled out. "Cowboy at ten o'clock is looking hard."

She smiled and wiggled her eyebrows up and down. "Number, please."

I tilted my head and said, "Eight, easy."

She did a little dance move and turned around quickly. She looked over and saw Lark standing alone. When I saw her face drop she looked back at me and said, "Well, since Tristan seems to be talking to Liberty again, I might as well have fun, huh?"

I stopped dancing and stood there with my mouth open. "You know about Liberty?"

She smiled weakly. "He was on the porch last night talking to her. I heard him tell her he missed her. I had a feeling he was seeing another girl as well as me, but I kind of thought him bringing me here...well..."

I shook my head and said, "Oh Ryn, I don't think..." She held up her hands and said, "It's not a big deal. I'm always the one they want to just have fun with. Excuse me Dee, I've got a cowboy to wrangle."

Ryn had been calling me Dee for the last week, and I knew she did it knowing it bugged the hell out of Lark. I watched as she walked up to the cowboy and said something in his ear.

The song changed and he scooped her into his arms as they took off two-stepping. I felt Lark's arms wrap around me as he whispered into my ear, "Dance with me."

I turned and looked into his beautiful eyes and nodded my head. "Play It Again" by Luke Bryan was playing and I knew how much Lark loved Luke Bryan.

We danced in silence for about a minute before Lark asked, "What's wrong, Azurdee?"

I glanced over and saw Ryn dancing with the cowboy. I swore I saw her wipe away a tear. I looked up into Lark's eyes and said, "Ryn knows about Liberty."

Lark's face dropped. "Did you tell her?"

I shook my head. "No! She heard Tristan talking to her last night on the porch. She heard him tell her that he missed her. Lark, my heart is breaking because I think Ryn has fallen for Tristan. I see it in the way she looks at him."

Lark looked up and found Ryn dancing. He looked around and shook his head. "The stupid bastard has been texting Liberty all day and ignoring Ryn."

"Why?" I asked.

Lark shrugged his shoulders. "Scared maybe about his feelings for Ryn. I don't know. She was supposed to just be the fun one. I don't think he counted on falling for her like he has."

I looked down and then back up at Lark. "Ryn told me she is always the one they just want to have fun with. I hate that she is hurting. I really like her."

Lark pulled me closer to him and said, "It's Tristan and Ryn's problem. Let's not get involved. I just want to feel you in my arms."

I snuggled closer into his chest and let out a sigh as we finished dancing to the song.

As the night went on, Ryn drank more and more and Tristan sat in a corner at the bar and watched Ryn dance with everyone but him. Lark and I had danced so much I was beginning to get blisters.

"Ugh, why did I wear new boots tonight?" I said as I pulled the boot off my foot and rubbed it as Ryn washed her hands in the ladies' room.

She smiled and said, "Well with the way you and Lark are cutting up the dance floor, it's no wonder you have blisters."

I smiled and said, "I love Lark in this environment. He's so happy and carefree. You can tell he just loves being in the country."

Ryn giggled and said, "Yeah, both of them are right at home here, aren't they? I think Tristan's plan is to move back home in a few years and take over the ranch for his dad."

I put my boot on and said, "Do you like the country?"

"Hell yeah. I grew up in the country. My momma still brews

her tea in the sunlight." She smiled and shook her head. "I come from a small Texas town where if you blinked when driving through, you'd miss it."

I smiled and asked, "Do you go home often?"

Her smile faded and she said, "No. I walked away from the bad memories and don't care to ever go back."

"I'm sorry," I said.

She grabbed my hand and said, "Come on...let's go dance."

As we walked out of the restroom, Ryn was approached by the same cowboy she danced with at the beginning of the night.

"Angel, dance with me again," he said as he held out his hand.

Ryn looked over toward Tristan, who was looking down at his phone.

"Sure," Ryn said as she gave me a small smile and walked away with the cowboy as Jason Aldean's song "Why" began playing. I turned and looked at Tristan and marched over to him. Lark was sitting next to him and he jumped up and took a step back when he saw me marching up.

I grabbed the cell phone out of Tristan's hand. He jumped up and yelled, "What the fuck, Azurdee?"

"She knows about Liberty, you ass. She heard you telling her how much you missed her last night on the porch."

Tristan took a step back and scanned the dance floor as he said, "What? I thought she was asleep."

I pushed the cell phone into his chest and said, "Well, she certainly has been awake all day and knows you've been texting Liberty. She is falling in love with you, Tristan, and if you don't feel the same, then take her home and let her go. Stop talking to another girl right under her nose."

He looked down at me and then looked at Lark. I could see the confusion laced all over his face. "I don't. I mean, I don't know how I feel about..." He glanced up and stopped talking. "Motherfucker."

Lark and I both turned and looked to see that the guy Ryn was talking to was moving his hand across her ass and it looked like he was about to try and kiss her.

Tristan began walking out on the dance floor and Lark grabbed him. "Dude, you've fucking ignored her all day and all night and you get pissed when another guy is giving her attention. Azurdee's right. You need to make up your mind."

Tristan looked back at the dance floor and then pushed Lark away. "I'm going home. Make sure she doesn't get drunk and leave with someone."

My mouth dropped open and I said, "Wait. You're just going to leave her here? Alone?"

Tristan looked at me and gave me a weak smile. "She's not alone."

He turned and walked away as I looked back out and saw Ryn pushing the cowboy away and saying something to him. When I looked back at Tristan, I saw he was watching what was happening. I thought for sure he would stop when he saw Ryn was pushing the guy away, or attempting to. Tristan shook his head and kept walking.

"Shit," Lark said as he made his way out to the dance floor to rescue Ryn.

Ten minutes later, we were in Lark's truck and heading back to the ranch. I heard Ryn once attempt to hold back a sob. I turned and she shook her head and looked out the window.

When we got to the ranch house Tristan's truck wasn't there. Ryn jumped out of Lark's truck and practically ran into the house. I got out and went after her as Lark called out for me.

"Give me just a couple minutes!" I called over my shoulder. By the time I got to Tristan's bedroom, Ryn was grabbing all her things and throwing them into her bag. The tears were streaming down her face. One look from me and she lost it as she sat down on the edge of the bed and buried her face in her hands.

"I knew I shouldn't have come. I knew it. I had a feeling he was seeing someone else, but I ignored it. I shouldn't have come here. I thought maybe things would be different."

I sat down next to her and put my arm around her as she dropped her head onto my shoulder. "Don't say that, Ryn. Joyce and Peter love you and I think Tristan's just scared of his feelings for you."

She let out a laugh as she wiped the tears from her face. "Azurdee, you're sweet, but let's be honest here. He's been texting another girl all day today and I'm not going to stand by like some pathetic woman who needs a man in her life."

I looked down and said, "I don't think of you that way."

Ryn stood up and grabbed a few more things and closed her suitcase. "I know you don't. I'm really glad we met. Let's keep in touch, okay?"

I stood up and hugged her. "Where are you going? How are you going to get home, Ryn?"

The tears began to build in her eyes as she dropped the suitcase and stood there. "I…I don't…I don't know."

Lark cleared his throat from behind me and I turned around to see him standing there with a slight smile on his face.

"Ryn, why don't you stay in the guest room tonight. Azurdee and I are leaving in the morning and heading to South Padre. I can take you to the airport."

Ryn swallowed hard and nodded her head. She picked up her suitcase and followed Lark to the guest room.

After getting Ryn settled in, I went back to Lark's room and began packing. When Lark walked in he wrapped his arms around me and whispered, "I want you."

I smiled and turned around. "May I ask you something?"

He moved back and ran his hand through his hair and nodded his head. "Sure you can."

"Your mom…she's been acting…different since yesterday."

The smile that spread across his face caused me to squeeze my legs together and long for his touch. I couldn't help but smile back. "Why is she acting different?"

He slowly pulled his T-shirt up and over his head. I licked my lips and just took in his upper body. When he moved his hands down and began to unbutton his pants, I put my hand up and said, "Oh no. I want you to tell me what's going on before I agree to do anything with you, Mr. Williams."

He kicked his pants away and stood in front of me in a pair of boxer briefs looking all hot and shit. My mind was beginning to go places it shouldn't, and I swear I felt dizzy.

He took a few steps toward me as he said, "I simply told my mother I loved you, *mi amor*."

My heart did that weird little dip thing and it felt like a million butterflies took off in my stomach. Hearing that from his lips again made my knees weak and left me wanting him like never before.

"Lark," I whispered. He walked up to me and began undressing me. I let myself completely go as he whispered against my skin, "I love you, Azurdee."

When I finally felt him slide into me I was completely and utterly lost to him. I would forever be lost to his voice, his touch, and his heavenly smell. Lark Williams had me, body and soul. I was sure I would never be able to breathe again without his love.

***

I rolled away from Lark to see it was five in the morning. I swore I heard a car, but the harder I listened to it the harder it was to make it out. I closed my eyes and drifted off to sleep. Dreaming of nothing but green eyes piercing mine as Lark whispered how much he loved me.

CHAPTER 21

Lark

I glanced over to see Azurdee looking at her cell phone again. "You're not going to get a signal way out here. Just wait until we get to South Padre."

She let out a sigh and tossed her phone down into her purse. "Are you not worried? I mean, she just disappeared in the middle of the night, Lark. She left and she doesn't have a car. I mean, your parents' house is in the middle of nowhere."

I reached over for her hand and pulled it to my lips. "She's a smart girl. I'm sure she is not going to do something stupid."

She dropped her head back and said, "The only good thing about this is the fact that Tristan is freaking out."

I laughed and said, "That's mean."

"He deserves it. Leaving her like that and going off and doing God knows what."

I nodded my head. "Well, my father laid into him pretty good so I'm sure he won't be doing that again."

Azurdee's phone pinged and she quickly reached for it.

"It's Ryn!" she yelled out.

"I told you she would get in touch with you," I said as I pulled into a gas station. We were only a few hours away from my parents' beach house, and I couldn't wait to get there and fuck the living shit out of Azurdee in each room and on every surface. I couldn't stop thinking about it ever since she brought up us on the bike.

"She called the cowboy! Oh. My. God. What in the hell was she thinking? He's taking her to Austin. She's driving to Austin with a complete stranger. What if he kills her?"

"He's not going to kill her," I said. "Wow, I'm shocked this guy is driving her all the way home. Ryn must be one hell of a dancer."

Azurdee hit me on the shoulder and said, "No, she asked him to drive her to a town where she could get a rental car and he offered to drive her. Oh gosh Lark, that's not very safe for her."

Azurdee typed something quickly and began biting on her thumbnail. When her phone pinged a few minutes later, she looked at her phone and said, "She sent me a picture of the guy's license. He lives in Austin and was visiting family, so he had to head back to Austin anyway. Okay, I feel better now."

I shrugged my shoulders and laughed. "Will you call and let my parents know you heard from her and that she is okay?"

She was typing away and nodded her head. "She doesn't want to worry them, so she told me I could tell them."

Azurdee called my parents and filled them in on what was happening. "Yes. I'll be sure to let her know. Yes, of course, Joyce. Thank you so much for everything."

When she hung up I looked at her and asked the one question I didn't really want to know the answer to. "How's Tristan?"

Azurdee looked at me and said, "Your mom said he had been in the barn most of the day, but I guess he was sitting there when I called. She told him Ryn got a ride home from someone she met last night. I heard him curse and your mother said he was mostly likely going to be heading home now."

I shook my head and said, "He's probably going to head straight to Ryn's."

Azurdee nodded her head and said, "I feel bad for both of them."

An hour later I pulled up to my parent's beach house gate and punched in the gate code. As the gates opened, I glanced over and looked at Azurdee. Her eyes were looking everywhere and I couldn't help but feel nervous. *What would she think about the bottle? The letters?*

I gripped the steering wheel harder and focused my thoughts on making love to her soon and tried not to worry about the rest.

We walked into the house and she immediately walked to the wall of glass and let out a gasp. "Oh my. Look at the beach. It's beautiful. Jessie told me it was breathtaking, but man oh man."

I smiled and set our luggage down. All I wanted to do was be buried so deep inside that I would forget everything else for just a bit. I didn't have the heart to tell her I had to leave as soon as we got back home. It took everything I had to talk Skip into not making me leave before Christmas.

I quickly began unzipping my pants as I walked toward her. She started to walk into the kitchen when I grabbed her and turned her around. She let out a gasp as I pulled up her skirt and in one quick move ripped her panties off.

"I need to fuck you...now," I said as I lifted her up and pushed her against the wall. When I reached down and pushed my fingers inside of her, I let out a moan as she dropped her head back against the wall.

"Do you want me, Azurdee?"

"More than you know," she whispered as she placed her hands

on my shoulders. I lifted her up and slowly filled her body with my hard dick.

"Always so ready for me," I said as I began fucking.

She made the sweetest sounds as I gave her everything I could. I couldn't get deep enough.

"I want to hear you scream out when you come," I said between breaths.

"Yes!"

"Now, Azurdee. I need you to come now!"

"I...oh God. I'm...so close."

I gritted my teeth to keep from coming as I moved in and out of her. The moment she called out my name I exploded inside of her.

I stood holding her against the wall as we both sucked in breaths of air.

"Wow. That was...unexpected," Azurdee said with a giggle. I loved how innocent she was, yet full of passion at the same time. I pulled back and looked into her eyes.

"I love you," I whispered. Her eyes lit up and the smile that spread across her face made my knees weak.

I slowly began to set her down as she placed her hand on the side of my face. "I love you too."

I closed my eyes and asked, "Why?"

"Look at me, Michael." Her saying my name caused my eyes to snap open. The moment she said my name I felt her love. I looked into her beautiful eyes and knew in this very moment that there wasn't anything I wouldn't do for her. I'd walk to the ends of the earth for her.

"I love you because when I'm with you I feel whole and I'm

filled with so much happiness I just want to stand on the tallest mountain and scream how happy I am. Your touch does things to my body that I can't even begin to put into words. I'm lost when we're not together and that scares me and excites me. I don't know any other way to explain it. My heart will always belong to you… forever."

I placed my hands on both sides of her face and gently kissed her lips. "I've never met anyone who made me feel the way you do, Azurdee. I can't seem to get enough of you."

She smiled and said, "I feel the same, Lark. My body craves your body. Now take me to the beach and make love to me in the ocean."

I laughed and nodded my head. "Your wish is my command."

She laughed. "Finally…I'm in charge, huh?"

I smacked her ass and said, "Go get your swimsuit on."

She started to walk off before stopping and turning back to me. "I didn't bring one, Lark. I didn't know we were coming to the beach."

Shit. I totally wasn't even thinking.

The idea of skinny-dipping in the ocean with her caused my dick to come to full attention again. I shrugged my shoulders and said, "Go naked then. I'll meet you down there in ten minutes." I quickly walked to the sliding glass door and opened it and walked outside.

"What? It's daylight out! Lark? Lark!" She called out as I walked over to the pool house shed, grabbed a few beach towels and began jogging down to the water with a smile plastered on my face.

I sat on the beach and leaned my head back as the warm sun hit my face. My phone buzzed and I sighed as I pulled it out.

Skip: Please tell me you are coming back tomorrow.

Me: I'm in South Padre.

Skip: ?? I thought you were with your family at the ranch.

Me: Change of plans.

Skip: Azurdee with you?

Me: Yes.

Skip: I have a really bad feeling about this, Lark. You better keep your head straight is all I'm saying. We're planning on heading out in the next few days.

Me: I'm on leave…remember?

Skip: We got a tip on Carlito Vazquez.

Fuck. He was probably the most sought after drug and arms dealer in the world. He'd been selling arms to the Middle East and we'd been searching for him for the last two years.

Me: Intel confirm it?

Skip: Would I be asking your ass to come back early if they hadn't?

Me: Fuck. I'll leave first thing in the morning.

Skip: That is the Lark I know and…well…love is such a strong word. Remember that the next time you want to whisper it in a certain girl's ear.

Me: Fuck you. I'm turning off my phone and will turn it back on tomorrow when we head back.

Skip: Plan on at least a week.

I dropped my head and shook it. I didn't want to leave her again.

I turned off my phone and pushed it into my back pocket. I looked out over the water and for the first time in the last four years, something other than the Marine Corps filled my heart. I was ready to walk away from the only thing I'd known and loved and spend the rest of my life with her.

I felt her behind me even before she said a word.

I turned and looked up at my angel. I laughed when I saw she had on one of my T-shirts, but my heart began pumping faster. Something about her in my shirt did crazy shit to me.

"God, please tell me you are naked underneath my shirt."

She bit down on her lower lip and nodded her head and dropped to her knees. "You don't mind, do you?"

I looked over her shoulder to check down the beach. I hadn't seen anyone walking by since I'd been sitting here. She must have known what I was doing, because she looked over my shoulder.

She licked her lips as she looked down at my lips. She slowly shook her head and said, "You do things to me that drive my body crazy. Do you know that?"

I slowly smiled as I reached my hand up the shirt and she let out a gasp when I touched her stomach. "Do I now?"

She nodded her head and the innocent look on her face had me falling in love with her more…if that was even possible.

"I could say the same thing. You've completely changed my life, Azurdee. You've made me re-think everything."

Her eyes widened in surprise and her mouth dropped open slightly before she smiled and leaned down to kiss me. I grabbed her and pulled her down and laid her on the sand as she let out a small cry.

"I can't believe how much I love you," I said as her eyes darkened. "We've come pretty far since that day I stood on Scott and Jessie's porch and saw the most beautiful creature ever."

"Lark," she whispered.

"Please don't ever leave me."

Her eyes filled with tears as she said, "Never."

I smiled as I slowly moved my eyes over her face, taking in every single detail. "I'm going to make love to you now, Azurdee."

She sucked in a breath of air as I stood up and quickly stripped out of my clothes. She sat up and looked up and down the beach. When she looked back at me she let out a moan and quickly stood up. I grabbed her and threw her over my shoulder as she screamed out and I took off for the water. The moment I ran in I knew I was making a mistake.

Shit! Shit!

I dropped her down into the water and she went completely under and jumped up screaming.

"Oh my God! It's freezing!"

I laughed as she began jumping up and down yelling out how cold the water was. The moment I saw her hard nipples through my T-shirt I forgot about how cold the water was and I grabbed her.

"God, Azurdee…your body is amazing."

She wrapped her legs around me and said, "Amazingly cold."

I lifted her and slowly pushed into her. The friction of the water and how cold it was made it feel ten times better.

"Why does it keep getting better?" she asked, as she held onto me tighter.

"I promise you baby, it will always be like this."

As I moved in and out of her, she buried her face into my neck and I could almost feel her squeezing down on me.

"Say my name, baby…please say my name," I said.

"Michael…oh God. I'm going to come," she whispered as she pulled back and slammed her lips to mine. It didn't take long before I was coming as well. I held onto her tightly and prayed we could just stay like this forever.

"You're leaving again, aren't you?" she said as she kept her face buried into my neck.

I swallowed hard and said, "Yes."

"Michael?"

Azurdee pulled back and looked at me with a shocked look on her face. She mouthed *who is that?*

I slowly sank further into the water to cover up her body. You could totally see right through the T-shirt she had on. Azurdee pushed away from me as I turned around and saw Lindsay.

"Lindsay?"

Lindsay smiled and nodded her head. *Fuck me.* Her family had owned the beach house next to ours since I could remember. The last time I was here we had hooked up and fucked in her hot tub…twice.

Lindsay put her finger in her mouth and said, "Wow. It's so good to see you here. You brought company this time? She up for a little bit of fun?"

Oh shit.

I looked at Azurdee as her mouth dropped open. She frowned and said, "So are we ever going to go anywhere and not run into someone you've fucked?"

The tone in her voice caught me off guard and before I could say anything she began walking out of the water. I stood there and watched her get out and walk right past Lindsay and reach down for a towel.

"Hi! I'm Lindsay. You are?"

Azurdee wrapped the towel around her and turned and looked at me without saying a word.

228

"Um...can you hand me a towel so I can get out?"

Lindsay started laughing. "Please. It's not like I haven't seen it before."

Fuck! Fuck! Son of a bitching fuck!

"Lindsay, Azurdee is my girlfriend."

Lindsay spun around and slammed her hands to her mouth. "Oh God. I'm so sorry, it's just...well, he's never had a girlfriend and...I feel like a total ass now. I'm so very sorry."

Azurdee picked up a towel and walked toward the water and threw it. She turned and began walking back up to the house. I took advantage of Lindsay walking after Azurdee as I got out of the water and ran up and collected my clothes and phone and then ran after her.

"Really, it was a few years ago and it meant nothing. Please just let me apologize," Lindsay kept saying as Azurdee ran up the stairs and into the house.

I walked up to Lindsay and said, "Hey, um...well um... yeah. I'll see you around." She grabbed my arm and asked, "She wouldn't be interested in a threesome, would she?"

My mouth dropped open and I said, "What the fuck? No. Neither she nor I would be interested in that."

I quickly turned and made my way back into the house. I shut the sliding glass door and turned to see Azurdee sitting on the sofa. She was wrapped in the towel and had her knees pulled to her chest.

"I know you have a past and I accept that, but it's just hard to share a moment like that and then have some stranger..."

Her voice cracked and I about fell to my knees. I closed my eyes and prayed to God to let me take away her pain.

I walked over to her and dropped to my knees. "I'm so sorry, *mi amor*. I wish I could shield you from everything, but I can't because I do have a past." I swallowed hard and decided to just be honest with her.

"I've been with a lot of women, and I know you know that already, but you have to believe me when I say none of it meant anything to me. You're my life. You're my everything and I would do anything right now to go back and change things…but I can't."

She let out a sob and looked at me. "I don't want you to change anything, what happened before me was before me, but I can't lie and say it doesn't hurt my heart to think about all the…all the…"

I reached up and grabbed the back of her neck and brought her lips to mine. "You are all that matters to me. I forgot about every girl I'd ever been with the moment you gave yourself to me. I swear to you, Azurdee. You're my everything. I love you and you are the only woman I've ever loved like this. I want to spend the rest of my life with you."

Her eyes widened and she whispered, "What?"

I smiled and pushed her hair back and away from her face. "That's why I brought you here."

A confused look washed over her face. "I don't understand. What are you saying, Lark?"

"Let's take a hot shower and get some dinner and I'll explain everything. Sound good?"

She seemed like she wanted to argue with me and I knew I had just dropped a bomb on her.

"I promise I'll explain everything after dinner."

She nodded and said, "Okay." I took her hand in mine and led her to the master bedroom and then into the shower where we both took a long hot shower together.

I got out of the shower first and told her to take her time while

I got dressed. I quickly dried off and got dressed. I made my way downstairs where I took the bottle out of my bag and set it down on the kitchen island.

I went and sat down in the living room and saw my jeans lying on the floor. I pulled out my phone and made one quick phone call. As I hung up I looked up and saw Azurdee coming down the stairs.

She was dressed in a navy blue strapless dress that hugged her body in all the right places but was free and flowing right around her knees. She had a white sweater on and her hair was pulled up with a few curls hanging down. My eyes moved down her perfect legs to see she was wearing a pair of black wedge shoes. My breath caught in my throat as I said, "Wow. You look beautiful."

She stopped at the bottom of the stairs and spun around and said, "I wasn't sure where we were going for dinner, so I dressed kind of in the middle."

I walked up to her and reached out for her hands. I stood back and looked her body up and down and smiled.

"You hungry?" I asked.

She quickly nodded her head and said, "Starved. All that sex worked up my appetite."

I laughed and said, "Oh, there is plenty more of that after dessert."

"Well, we better bring home leftovers then," she said with a wink as we made our way out to my truck.

I opened the door for her, shut it, and said a quick prayer that I didn't fuck this evening up.

CHAPTER 22

Azurdee

LARK AND I WALKED along the beach after dinner and I could tell he had something on his mind. There was also the elephant in the room that neither one of us wanted to bring up again. I took a deep breath and just asked.

"When do you have to leave?"

He gripped my hand tighter and said, "We have to head back to Austin tomorrow."

My heart sunk and I could feel the tears building in my eyes. I hated that I was so emotional around him. "I thought you were on leave?"

"I have to go back for…something."

I nodded my head. I knew getting into this relationship with him meant that there was the big secret of his job. The fact that he told me he was still in the Marines, coupled with the lifestyle he led had me piecing things together. It was almost like he was a secret agent type person. Living a life that he wasn't really living. I was a part of that pretend life and I wasn't so sure how I felt about that.

"Will I ever get to meet your boss?" I asked.

Lark let out a chuckle and said, "Skip?" He shrugged his

shoulders and said, "Maybe."

I nodded my head and asked, "Is Jason or Paul going with you?"

Lark stopped and looked at me. "Why?"

I shook my head and said, "I don't know…I'm just trying to make small talk about your job and since I only know bits and pieces of it…"

"Can we change the subject?" he asked as he looked out into the black sea of water.

"Of course we can."

We walked a bit longer in silence when we stopped and Lark turned and looked at me. "My father talked to me on Christmas night about something."

I smiled and nodded my head. I remembered when he asked to talk to both Lark and Tristan. After that conversation was when Tristan became really distant with Ryn and Lark's mother smiled at me like she knew a secret.

I nodded my head and said, "I remember."

He smiled and shook his head. "My father and mother both knew the moment they saw us together that I loved you. Me on the other hand, I was nothing but scared and unprepared for falling in love with you."

He looked down and then back up at me. "I think I fell in love with you the moment I saw you. Something happened and I fought like hell for almost a year to push it away. I'd find myself just sitting there thinking about you. I wondered what you were doing. If you were happy, sad, lonely. I prayed like hell you weren't dating anyone."

I grinned as he smiled at me. "I've lived my life on the edge for so many years, Azurdee. Not caring if I died or not because I thought I didn't have anything, or anyone, to live for. Then I met you and everything changed. It was like I was a blank page waiting for you to write our future together on it."

I swallowed hard and wiped away the tear that was making its way down my cheek.

"You think about our future?" I asked.

He smiled and nodded his head. "Yes. Do you?"

I felt my cheeks heat up as I nodded my head. "Probably more than I should," I said.

He took my hand in his and said, "Let's go back to the house. I have to tell you about the journey."

I looked at him confused. "What journey?"

He laughed and said, "That was my response, too."

We walked into the house and Lark led me into the kitchen. Each time we walked into the beach house I couldn't help but smile. It was decorated in a beach theme but was also a tad on the fancy side. I could easily see this house sitting on the shore of Nantucket. It was not decorated like Lark's parents' ranch house at all. The whites and light blues made it completely relaxing. I fell in love with it the moment we walked in.

Lark motioned for me to sit down on the stool at the kitchen island. I glanced down and saw a bottle with a cork in it sitting on the island.

Lark sat down across from me. "My father asked me what my intentions were with you."

I swallowed hard. "I would think that would be my father asking that question." Lark smiled and nodded his head. I knew he was nervous about meeting my parents. It looked like he was going to get out of meeting them again, depending on how long he would be out of town for.

"Do you want to know what my answer was?"

I got that weird feeling in my chest again where it feels like my heart is just dropping to the ground. *Did I want to know what he said? No! Yes! No! Yes!*

I nodded my head and took a deep breath.

"I told him I wanted to marry you someday."

I let out a gasp as Lark looked intently into my eyes.

"I want to see you walking toward me dressed in a beautiful white gown. I want a future with you, Azurdee. I want to wake up every morning and feel you in my arms. I want to fall asleep with you whispering that you love me. I want…"

He took a deep breath and gave me a smile. "I want to have kids with you. I keep dreaming of touching your stomach when it's swollen with our child. I want to give you everything you want. I want to support you in your dreams, hold you when you hurt, make you laugh when you're sad, and make love to you every day. I want to start our journey of love."

I covered my mouth and began crying. Lark placed his hand on the side of my face as I dropped my hands from my mouth. "I've never had anyone say such amazing things to me before."

He looked down and reached for the bottle. "My father told me that his dad had talked to him about something called the journey of love. My father told me that when I was ready to start my journey, I needed to talk to you about it. There is this tradition in my family that starts this journey."

I nodded my head and said, "What is it?"

"My father brought my mother to the beach when he knew she was the one he wanted to spend the rest of his life with, when he knew he was ready to start his journey of love. They both were in separate rooms and wrote each other a letter about their hopes, dreams, doubts, and goals for their love. They put the letters in the bottle and they put it in the ocean. The idea is that each journey is different. It's filled with calm seas and rough seas but together you can weather anything."

He laughed and shook his head as if remembering something. "I was confused after I walked out of that room about the whole bottle thing, but it just all clicked. All of it made sense when I was telling you."

He looked into my eyes and I realized I was holding my breath. His beautiful green eyes were filled with nothing but pure love.

"I want to share this journey with you and only you, Azurdee. I love you."

I smiled and wiped the tears from my eyes. "I love you too. Fate has already stepped in…you're who I'm meant to be with, Lark. I knew it the moment you first touched me."

He stood up and walked around the island and grabbed me and pulled me up. He looked into my eyes and whispered, "You're mine."

I nodded my head and said, "Always."

He picked me up and began walking toward the stairs. I looked back at the bottle and said, "I thought we were going to write our letters."

As he took the stairs two at a time, still carrying me, he said, "After I make love to you."

***

I stared down at the piece of paper and looked at my shaking hand. I closed my eyes tightly and thought back to just an hour ago when Lark made such sweet love to me. I placed my hand on my neck and could almost feel the warmth of his breath on my skin as he whispered how much he loved me.

I opened my eyes and smiled. I reached for my phone and sent him a text message:

Me: Are you done?

Lark: No. Are you?

Me: No. I have a question. Are we reading each other's letters?

Lark: Nope.

Me: K.

Lark: Does that make a difference?

Me: I don't think so. For some reason I'm really nervous.

Lark: Me too!

I laughed when I read his last text. My big tough Marine. I couldn't imagine him nervous about anything.

Me: You're nervous? That turns me on.

Lark: Oh yeah? How turned on are you?

Me: Let me check...yep, pretty turned on.

Lark: Fuck.

I hugged myself as I let out a chuckle. I could just picture him now adjusting his hardening dick. I let out a breath and tried to contain my uncontrollable urge to go find him.

Lark: Are you touching yourself?

Me: Are you?

Lark: Yes.

Oh. My. God.

Me: Then so am I.

Lark: Tell me what you feel like.

I slipped my hand under my dress and down into my panties as I pushed my fingers inside. I let out a moan and dropped my head back as I moved my fingers in and out.

My phone pinged and I looked at the text.

Lark: I'm waiting, mi amor.

Me: I'm wet. Very wet.

Lark: Taste yourself.

My stomach dropped and I set my phone down and pulled my hand from my panties. I bit down on my lower lip and sighed how it turned me on when he talked dirty like that to me. I wanted nothing more than to put my fingers in my mouth and do what he said.

My phone pinged and I glanced down at it.

Lark: Touch yourself again, Azurdee.

I pushed my fingers down into my panties again and began finger fucking myself.

I closed my eyes and imagined Lark's lips down there.

My phone pinged again and I opened my eyes to read his message.

Lark: I'm imagining my cock deep inside you. It feels so good.

Oh God. How does he do this to me? One minute he is so utterly romantic and the next...

Lark: Are you getting close to coming baby?

Me: Yes.

Lark: Tell me how it feels.

Trying to type with one hand while my other hand was bringing me so close to an orgasm proved harder than I thought. I carried on though, breathing hard.

Me: I feel myself getting wetter. The sound is turning me on.

Lark: I'm so close. Fuck yourself harder and faster.

Just seeing his words caused me to move my hand faster and I could feel the build up growing stronger.

Me: I'm coming!

I let out a scream as one of the most intense orgasms ripped through my body. I heard the door open and before I knew what was happening I was on the desk getting my panties ripped off of me and Lark was moving in and out of me.

The next orgasm hit me even harder as I screamed out, "Oh God! Yes! Oh God, I'm coming again. Yes!"

I looked at Lark as he grunted and moaned. He pulled out and slammed back into me so hard I let out another scream.

I was so lost in what he was doing to me I hardly noticed him pulling me off the desk and turning me around.

"Put your hands on the desk. I'm going to take you from behind."

I put my hands on the desk and Lark pushed back into me. He grabbed onto my hips and fucked me hard. I could feel another orgasm building. When he reached up and grabbed a fistful of hair I began calling out his name as he called out mine.

"God…Azurdee…I'm coming. Feels so fucking good."

When he finally dropped on me we were both panting like we had run a marathon.

"Holy shit," he said between breaths.

I attempted to breath, but was panting. I turned and looked at him and smiled. "That was…kind of…hot."

He pushed himself up and looked at me as he raised his eyebrow. "Kind of?"

"Okay, it was hot as hell."

He stood up and pulled up his pants and winked at me as he leaned over and kissed me quickly.

"Stop bugging me. I'm trying to write a letter here," he turned and walked out of the room and shut the door. I got off the desk and began looking for my panties. I was so worked up when he walked into the room I didn't even remember him taking them off.

I looked around and saw them and my piece of paper on the floor behind the desk. I smiled as I reached for both. I slipped my panties back on and sat back down in the chair and put my blank piece of paper in front of me.

I heard my phone ping and started looking for it. After crawling around on the floor I finally found it under the chair across the room. I expected to see a text from Lark, but it was from my mother:

Mom: So, how was it meeting his family? Were they nice? Did they treat you well?

I rolled my eyes. I didn't really want to get into this now with her.

Me: Hey Mom. Christmas with the Williams family was amazing. Lark was amazing as he always is and he is so excited to meet y'all. He's been called out of town with work though and we are cutting our trip short. Heading home tomorrow. We might not make it there for the New Year's Eve party.

Mom: No! Oh no, we were really looking forward to meeting the man who has swept my daughter off her feet.

Me: Soon, Mom. I'm sorry I missed Christmas and now New Year's Eve.

Mom: How is the restaurant coming along?

Me: Good. A few setbacks but I think we will be back on schedule after the new year. I'm meeting with Dan in a few days.

Mom: Good. Do you have time to chat? Can I call?

Shit.

Me: Wish I could Mom, but I kind of have to run. In the middle of a family tradition.

Mom: How fun! Okay well enjoy yourself, sweetheart.

Me: Trust me Mom, I am!

Mom: See you soon, Azurdee. Love you.

Me: See ya soon, Mom. Love you back.

I put my phone down on the desk and picked up the pen. I closed my eyes and thought about Lark. I thought about the first time he made love to me. The first time he called me *mi amor*. The first time I heard him say in his sleep he needed to guard his heart. An overwhelming feeling rushed over me and I began to write.

Dear Lark,

The first moment I ever saw you, something happened to me that I have yet to understand. A feeling washed over my body that I'd never experienced before in my life. Then you touched me. I remember thinking this could be it. I'd waited so long for someone to have that effect on me. The wait for you was agonizing. Each time I saw you, my feelings grew stronger. It went from thinking this could be it, to thinking I'm falling for a man who has never even kissed me.

Then you kissed me. The world totally disappeared and it was just you and me. Finally. Everything changed in that very moment and I knew I would forever be yours and all my lonely nights would be over.

When I think of our future, I think of us sitting on the porch at your ranch. I see my stomach growing bigger with our child. I see the two of us, running around chasing a little girl who you will be way too protective of. I see you making love to me when we are old and gray.

To think it all started with a smile..then a touch..a kiss. When you kiss me now I feel how much you love me. How much you care about me. How much you've missed me when you're gone. You make me feel so cherished. I want everything with you. I want to fight, make up, laugh, cry, disagree, and most of all make love to only you. I want nothing more than to spend the rest of my life with you.

I can't think of anyone else I'd rather go on this journey with than you. If you're ready..I'm ready. I love you Michael. I love you more than you will ever know.

Always yours,
Azurdee

I read through the letter and decided to not change a thing. I wrote from my heart and that was important to me. I got up and walked over to the copy machine that was sitting on the other desk and made two copies. I knew we weren't supposed to read each other's letter but something told me I needed to do this. I made the copies and folded one in half and walked over to all the books. I looked to see if my favorite book was here. I smiled when I saw Jane Austen's *Pride and Prejudice.* I opened up the book to chapter three and tucked my letter in there. I closed it and smiled as I placed the book back onto the shelf. My phone went off and I quickly folded up the other letter and slipped it into the small pocket of my dress.

I picked up my phone and smiled.

Lark: Done! Did I win?

Me: Nope. I've been done for a few minutes.

Lark: What? Well what have you been doing?

Me: Reading my all time favorite book ever.

Lark: Winnie the Pooh?

Me: Haha. Jane Austen's Pride and Prejudice, if you must know.

Lark: Classic. Come find me. I may or may not be naked.

I laughed as I made my way out of the library in search of Lark.

After searching for fifteen minutes, I gave up and sat down at the kitchen island and stared at the bottle. I heard the sliding glass door open and Lark walked in with a smile.

I tilted my head and said, "Well hell. I didn't think to look outside."

He laughed and said, "Nope. Good thing I wasn't really naked though. The old man next door came over to say hi."

I held up my letter. He smiled and held up his finger. "Give me two minutes."

I nodded my head and got up and headed to the refrigerator and took a beer out as I looked for something to snack on. I glanced around the kitchen and took in the beach décor. I grabbed a handful of grapes and made my way back to the bar and waited.

I let out a smile when Lark wrapped his arms around me and then placed his letter on top of mine.

"You ready?" he whispered against my neck, causing goose bumps to pop out all over my body.

I nodded and he reached for both letters and put them together and handed them to me. My hand was shaking as I took them and began rolling them up. I slid them into the bottle and Lark set glue down onto the counter. He must have gotten some when he came in.

I bit down on my lower lip as I watched him put glue onto the cork and push it into the bottle. Then he put a bead of glue around the outside of the bottle and cork.

"It's marine glue, so I'm thinking it's leak-proof or my father's boat is in a heap of trouble."

I laughed as I watched him put just a little bit more glue on. He grabbed my hand and we made our way out the sliding glass door and headed down to the beach.

As we got closer to the water I could hear the seagulls. The salty ocean air made me smile as Lark squeezed my hand harder. We slipped our shoes off and made our way into the chilly waters of the Gulf of Mexico. I looked at Lark and said, "What if it washes back in?"

He looked out to the seas and then at me. "Shit. Should we take the boat out?"

"Will the glue hold up on the boat?"

Lark laughed and said, "The rip tides are so strong here. I can't tell you how many times we got pulled out on our boards and my mother freaked. One good toss and I think we're good."

I nodded my head and smiled. "Ready?"

"I've never been more ready for anything in my life," he said as he placed his hand on the side of my face and gently rubbed his thumb back and forth.

I nodded and he dropped his hand and took a step back as he reached back and then gave the bottle a good throw. I couldn't believe how far he threw it out there. I did a little jump when it landed in the water. Lark slipped his arm around my waist and we stood there for I don't how long, just staring out to the ocean in silence.

When Lark finally talked I jumped. "I'm sorry baby, I didn't mean to scare you." I shook my head and turned to face him.

"I love you," I said as the sound of the waves crashed onto the shoreline.

He smiled and said, "I love you, too."

I crinkled up my nose and said, "I'm kind of hungry. I didn't eat very much at dinner. Nerves I guess."

Lark let out a sigh and said, "My oh-so-romantic girl." He tapped my nose and laughed. "I know a great place where we can go and sit and grab something light, maybe a glass or two of wine."

The rest of the evening was spent in a wonderful seafood restaurant where we drank a bottle of wine, talked about the restaurant, me possibly moving some things over to Lark's place and him doing the same. Lark mentioned wanting to wait a bit more before we talked about getting engaged, which I agreed on. Even though we had known each other a year, we were really just starting this relationship. We talked about everything—except Lark's job.

The restaurant had a small outdoor patio and Lark stood up and asked me to dance as "Come a Little Closer" by Dierks Bentley began playing.

The way he was holding me, I knew he was beginning to say good-bye. My heart began breaking knowing that we would be leaving to head back home first thing tomorrow morning. I held onto him tighter as we danced in silence.

When the song ended he looked down at me and said, "Let's go. I want to make love to you all night."

***

I rolled over to see the clock read five in the morning. I moved my hand to find an empty spot next to me. I sat up quickly expecting to see a rose sitting on the pillow. I let out the breath I was holding when I didn't see one. I got up out of bed and made my way downstairs. I stopped on the landing when I heard Lark talking in a hushed voice.

"I told you, I've got it together. No, she isn't a distraction and I can handle it. Have I ever not finished a mission or put any other soldiers' lives in danger?"

My heart started pounding. I took a step back. I knew I shouldn't be eavesdropping, but I was frozen.

"Yes sir, I know. No sir, I won't."

His voice was so cold and distant it reminded me of the guarded Lark from a year ago.

"It's never interfered with my job before, Skip, so why are you making it a big deal? I'll fuck whomever I want to fuck."

I put my hand over my mouth. For him to say that after what we shared the last couple of days hurt. I knew he was upset and didn't mean it the way it was coming out. I decided I was making it worse on myself to stand here and listen.

"The flight plan to South America is set. Yes."

I froze. South America?

"I've been watching the videos. Carlito Vazquez doesn't travel anywhere without a large security detail."

Who was Carlito Vazquez? Lark's voice sounded odd.

"Skip, don't worry. I only need one shot to take the guy out. Just let me do my job."

Oh God. Oh God no. I quickly turned and made my way back up to the master bedroom and crawled into bed. I was shaking from head to toe.

Lark's a...sniper? Is this what he does in the Marines? Kills people?

I heard him walking down the hall, and I closed my eyes tightly. I couldn't face him right now. I needed to let this sink in and try to decide if I was going to talk to him about it.

When I felt him sit down on the bed, I held my breath. He let out a sigh and I could picture him running his hands down his face.

My heart was beating so loudly I was sure he could hear it. Then he talked.

"I hate doing this," he whispered as he lay down and wrapped his arms around me. I slowly let out the breath I was holding, but I stayed perfectly still.

He hated doing what? Leaving? His job? Keeping this life a secret? I had so many questions I wanted answered, but I also remembered when we first started this relationship he warned me. I promised myself I wouldn't ever push him for answers, but news of all of this was weakening my resolve.

I closed my eyes and after picturing Lark doing his job over and over in my mind, I finally fell asleep.

CHAPTER 23

Lark

After heading to my apartment and changing out of my uniform, I made my way down to my bike. I couldn't stop thinking about this latest mission. We had no luck in finding our target and the stress was beginning to take its toll on Skip. I knew Azurdee was meeting the contractor at the restaurant around two. One quick look at my watch and I high-tailed it out of the parking garage and made my way to Wimberley.

I pulled up next to a BMW. I saw Azurdee's new Toyota 4-Runner parked near the front of the restaurant. I put my helmet down on my bike and made my way over to the front entrance.

I walked in and smiled as I looked at how much work had been done. All the natural wood just screamed out Azurdee. One look to my right and I saw the kitchen. I walked over and looked and shook my head. "Hell of a lot bigger than the coffee shop."

I looked around and called out, "Azurdee?"

A young guy came walking out and smiled at me. "You must be Lark."

He reached out his hand and I extended mine. "Yes sir, I am."

"The name is Ralph. I work for Dee."

Shit. Not another person who called her Dee. I tilted my head and asked, "Dee?"

He laughed, "Azurdee. I shortened it 'cause I'm lazy."

I looked him up and down. He was built, but not as big as me. He was preppy, but a good-looking guy for sure.

"Stop eyeing me, Lark. I'm gay."

I instantly relaxed and I could tell Ralph knew by the smile on his face.

"But that asshole out there. He won't stop asking her out." Ralph pointed behind me. I turned and looked at the sea of glass that faced the back outdoor patio. The creek was right below; Azurdee had gone on and on about the views and she was right. It was beautiful.

"Really?" I asked as I started to walk to the door that led outside.

"Yep. Pushy fucker."

I smiled and made a note that Ralph was for sure on my side and one of the good guys. "Thanks for the heads up, Ralph. Looks like I'm gonna have to show him she's mine."

Ralph laughed and said, "I'm just glad you're back. She needs to be laid. She's been a moody bitch."

I snapped my head to look at him but he had turned and started back to the door he came out of.

I let out a laugh. Ralph isn't afraid to speak his mind.

I opened the sliding door and made my way out. Azurdee was talking to the asshole and began laughing as she shook her head. Her laugh instantly moved through my body and brought my dick to attention. When I saw him place his hand on her arm, I could see her body tense up.

"*Mi amor*," I said as I moved closer. The ass dropped his hand as Azurdee looked over at me. The smile that spread across her face was one I always wanted to see on her face when I'd been gone for so long.

She practically ran into my arms. When she slammed her body against mine, she whispered, "I was so worried."

I looked at the fucker was who now glaring at me and gave him a slight smile. "You never have to worry, *mi amor*. I'll always come back to you."

She pulled back and wiped a tear away. I was confused as to why she was so emotional.

She cleared her throat and said, "I'm so sorry. Dan, this is my boyfriend, Lark Williams. Lark, this is Dan Jons. He's the contractor."

I held out my hand and when he shook it, I might have squeezed harder than I should have.

I looked back down at Azurdee and asked, "Are you about done? A week away from you is too much to stand. I need to hold you…soon."

Her face blushed and she nodded her head as she looked at Dan. "Is there anything else we need to talk about?"

He shook his head and said, "Nah, I think we covered everything. I think we're looking at another month, month and a half if we run into anymore problems."

Azurdee did a little jump and clapped her hands. "Perfect. You can reach me on my cell if you need anything."

He nodded his head and began walking back into the restaurant as I watched him retreating away.

Fucker.

I turned to look at Azurdee and she slammed her body back into mine and pulled my lips down to hers. She kissed me like she hadn't seen me in years. When she finally pulled back I let out a laugh. "You missed me, I take it?"

She closed her eyes and said, "More than you know. Please take me home. I need to be with you. I need to know I'm not dreaming."

"I'm on my bike. I'll follow you."

She nodded her head. "No, we can pick my car up later. Let's go." She walked back into the restaurant and I followed. She grabbed her purse and yelled out, "Ralph, I'm out of here."

Ralph called out, "Thank God! I was about to do the deed myself. Get it girl."

Azurdee laughed as I shook my head. *Bastard is lucky he's gay.*

We walked up to my bike and she turned and winked at me as her cheeks were covered in a beautiful rose color. I smiled knowing what she was thinking about. I got on the bike and handed her a helmet. "You want another round?"

She got on behind me and said, "Not now. I just want to go home."

We spent the rest of the afternoon making love. A quick trip to grab pizza for dinner, and we were back at her house and I was making love to her in the bathtub. I couldn't get enough of her. Azurdee woke me up with soft kisses around nine in the morning. "I made you breakfast. Your favorite, French toast. I need to go get my car."

I nodded and got myself up and dressed. After eating breakfast we made our way back to the restaurant. We pulled up and Azurdee asked if I wanted to take a tour of the place. I nodded. "Of course I do."

When we walked in she leaned over a counter and hit a button and music started playing. As we walked around the restaurant she pointed out everything. From where the extra linens would be kept to where the flour was going to be stored. I could hear the excitement in her voice and I was surprised at how it filled my own heart with happiness.

"Give me two seconds to run to the restroom and then we can leave."

I nodded my head and walked to the middle of the restaurant and sat down on a chair that was in the middle of the room. When "Give It 2 U" began playing, I couldn't help but smile.

"Damn girl. You got some Robin Thicke playing. What must the workers think?" I called out.

I felt her hands move down my chest as she put her lips on my neck. "Do you want me to give it to you?"

I dropped my head back and looked up at her. "Oh baby…I always want you to give it to me."

She smiled and walked around me and stood in front of me. She began dancing as she started to take off her shoes and then her pants. I watched as she moved her hands up and down her body and moved to the beat of the song. I quickly unzipped my pants and pulled them down.

She was biting down on her lips as she straddled me.

"Are you ready for my cock?" I asked as she sucked in a breath of air.

She slowly slid her hand down and touched herself. She began panting faster as I grabbed my dick and began stroking it. Her eyes widened as she watched me. "Does it turn you on to watch me play with myself?" I asked her as she looked into my eyes. She nodded her head and I said, "Tell me."

She moved closer to me as she looked down at my hand still stroking my dick. "It turns me on to watch you play with yourself."

I dropped my hand and grabbed her hips. The song changed

and "Not Myself Tonight" by Christina Aguilera began playing. "You certainly have good taste in music, baby."

I held her right above me. She was practically pushing herself against me.

"Fuck me, Azurdee. Fast and hard."

I brought her down and filled her body in one quick movement.

"God yes!" she cried out as she began moving up and down faster. "Feels…so…good."

The little sounds she was making were pushing me over the edge and I had to fight like hell not to come.

"Yeah…so close," she called out as her moans echoed throughout the restaurant. I loved seeing her like this. I knew there was a side of her that liked our rough play and it turned me on so much. She was the perfect mixture of naughty and nice.

"Faster," I said as I grabbed her hips and she rode the fuck out of me.

"God. Yes. Lark. I'm going to come. Oh God….Oh God!" She began screaming out my name like never before. She dropped her head back and called out, "Yes!" She snapped her head forward and smiled as she slowed down and moved against me. She was driving me crazy.

"Azurdee," I whispered as I felt my own orgasm begin to build.

It didn't take me long to let out my own cries of pleasure when one of the most intense orgasms of my life ripped through my body. When her lips pressed against mine I held her tightly and poured myself into her. I could almost feel the love moving between us.

When she finally stopped moving, we were able to catch our breath. "Jesus Christ, Azurdee. You are going to drive me over the edge one of these days."

"That felt amazing."

Then I heard someone clear their throat. "I would hope so. I heard you calling out his name from the damn parking lot."

Azurdee snapped her head up and screamed. "Ralph! Get out of here! Now!"

I closed my eyes and cursed myself for letting her fuck me here. A dark parking lot was one thing, but not the restaurant where anyone could walk in at any time.

"Hey, it's not like I've never seen a va-jay-jay before. Hold your horses, I'm heading to the back office. Better hurry though. Danny boy is not too far behind me."

I pushed her off of me and reached down for her pants and tried to help her put them on.

She pushed my hands away and said, "Jesus, you're making it harder to get them on. Just let me do it, please."

I pulled up my zipper and reached down for her sandals and handed them to her as she zipped up her pants. She slipped on her sandals and then attempted to fix her hair.

I smiled and pulled her to me. "You look beautiful with your just-fucked glow on your face."

She blushed and the door to the restaurant opened. She quickly turned away and walked to the front again and reached under the counter and stopped the music. Dan said, "Good morning. I didn't expect to see you here this morning. Would you like to grab breakfast?"

That motherfucker. He obviously didn't see me standing in the middle of the damn restaurant. Looks like I didn't make myself very clear yesterday.

"Oh...um...well I..." Azurdee was still flustered from Ralph.

I walked up to her and grabbed her hand.

I gritted my teeth together and decided to put his ass straight. "She just had breakfast—a good hard fucking in her new restaurant. I'd appreciate it if you'd stop asking my girlfriend out or we'll be finding another contractor."

Dan's mouth dropped open and he was shocked as shit. I felt triumphant…until I looked at Azurdee, who was giving me a dirty look.

"I'm ready to leave now," she said through gritted teeth.

She turned and made her way outside. Once she walked outside I walked up to Dan and got right in his face.

"She's mine. I suggest if you want to keep your hands from being broken you stop asking her out. Do we understand each other?"

He nodded his head and turned away from me and headed to the kitchen area.

I took a deep breath and made my way outside. Azurdee was leaning against her car and when I walked up she pushed me and then punched me in the arm.

She yelled out, "What in the fuck was that about?"

"What?"

She placed her hands on her hips and said, "What? What! You just told him we fucked in there, Lark! You just told him we fucked and then you threatened to fire him! Do you know what it took for me to get him in the first place?"

I felt the anger build inside my body. "No Azurdee, tell me what it took for you to get him. Maybe a promise of some sort. He sure seems fixated on going out with you."

Her mouth dropped open. "How dare you. I can't even believe you would say that."

I closed my eyes and shook my head. "I'm sorry. I didn't mean that. I'm just angry that he asked you out after I made it clear yesterday that we were together."

She slowly shook her head and said, "Lark, I can handle myself. I've had guys come onto me before and I've been able to deal with it just fine."

"You're mine now, Azurdee."

"That doesn't give you the right to go off and tell someone working for me that we just fucked. Or to say you're going to fire him. Lark, this is my business. You have to trust me like I trust you with yours."

I ran my hand through my hair and nodded. I knew she was right. "I'm sorry. This jealousy thing is all new to me. I guess I didn't handle that well."

"Ya think?"

I walked up to her and wrapped my arms around her and pulled her closer to me. "I promise not to act like a total ass next time."

She looked at me as she raised her eyebrow. "I trust you. You have to trust me."

"I do trust you. I just don't trust all the fuckers out there who want in your pants."

She smiled and said, "Well, what's inside these pants only belongs to you, so don't worry."

I nodded and said, "You want to go back to my place and pack up a few things and go camping for a few days?"

The smile that spread across her face told me she had already forgiven me and all was good again.

"Camping? Yes!"

We took Azurdee's 4-Runner back to her house and made our way into Austin. We spent the next three days doing nothing but enjoying the beautiful mild winter days, hiking, making love, running along the trails, grilling fish we caught in the river, and making love some more. I never wanted this to end. The moment my cell went off, I saw it on her face. The worry and concern appeared again. The whole way back to Austin I could feel the tension coming from her body.

I stood outside her door and leaned down to kiss her. She held up her hand and said, "Just promise me that whatever it is that you do, there is not a risk of you being…killed."

I looked at her and shook my head. "I can't promise you that, Azurdee. I'm in the Marines. We sometimes go into active war zones. I can't make that kind of promise to you, baby. I'm sorry."

Her eyes filled with tears. "Then promise me you'll come back to me."

I leaned down and brushed my lips across hers. I could taste her tears and it broke my heart.

"I promise you," I whispered as I kissed her. She wrapped her arms around my neck and held onto me tighter. "I love you," she whispered.

"I love you too," I said as she opened the door and walked into her house.

I quickly walked to my truck and got inside. I pulled out my phone and hit Jerry's number.

"Lark. It's about damn time you got back in touch with me. You said you needed this and then dropped off the face of the planet for days."

"Just tell me what you found out."

"The moment I found out this was personal and not for a mission I should have stopped."

I let out a long sigh. "Jerry, knock it the fuck off. You've used CIA shit to spy on your own damn wife."

"I don't know what you're talking about."

"The information, Jerry."

"He took over his father's construction company shortly after high school. No college degree, married with two kids."

I sat up straighter as I pulled out of Azurdee's driveway. "What? The fucker is married? Is he separated maybe?"

I heard him moving some papers around and then heard typing on the computer. "Um…nope. He is for sure married. Just posted a Facebook picture of him and his wife from last weekend at some party they went to."

I shook my head. "What in the fuck is wrong with people?"

"His wife is probably a bad fuck."

"Thanks, Jerry. I owe you one."

"Just remember that next time it takes me longer to pull up real intel."

"Deal." I hung up and tossed my phone in the passenger seat.

"Fucker's married."

I got home and began packing up my bag. My phone went off and I pulled it out of my back pocket.

Azurdee: How in the world did you get the rose in here?

Me: I have my ways!

Azurdee: Why do you leave them? The roses?

Me: I want you to know how much I love you. How hard it is for me to leave you each time. It's my way of leaving behind a piece of me with you. Roses remind me of you.

Azurdee: I love them. More than you will ever know. Please be careful.

Me: I will. Gotta go. I love you.

Azurdee: I love you, too.

I grabbed my bag and hit Skip's number. When he answered, I asked, "We find him?"

The second he said yes, I had a terrible feeling I might be breaking my promise to Azurdee.

CHAPTER 24

Azurdee

I WALKED AROUND TO each table and asked the customers how everything was. It was Valentine's Day and my restaurant "The Leaning Tree" was finally open. It was just a preview night but it was packed.

I walked up to a couple and smiled as I asked, "How are you enjoying your meal?"

The girl raised her eyebrows and said, "Oh, it's so good. The chicken and grits are to die for."

The guy nodded and said, "The smoked pork chop is wonderful."

I smiled and said, "Thank you so much. I'm so glad you enjoyed them. Be sure to try the ancho dark chocolate terrine. It's one of my specialties and a favorite dessert among the staff."

I turned and walked up to the next table and was shocked to see Dan sitting there. He was trying not to look at me. "Dan. I'm so glad you were able to make it."

The blonde sitting across from him was smiling with the biggest smile on her face and she looked so familiar. "I practically had to beg him to bring me tonight. The moment I found out he had the job for this place I went crazy. I went to your coffee shop almost every single day and was so sad when you closed it."

Then it clicked. "Yes. I knew I recognized you from somewhere." She smiled and looked at Dan.

"How do you know each other?" I asked.

Her smile faded briefly. "Well, we're married."

I was sure the shocked look on my face was going to be the cause of an interesting ride home this evening for Dan.

I smiled and said, "Well please, enjoy whatever you would like on the menu. It's on the house."

I quickly turned and walked away and headed into the kitchen. I pulled Ralph by the shirt and said, "Talk. Now."

When we walked into my office I shut the door, or rather slammed the door. "Oh. My. God. Dan's married and he and his wife are eating here tonight!"

"I know! Lark already told me he was married."

My mouth dropped open as I looked at him. "When?"

Ralph shrugged his shoulders and said, "I don't remember. Last time he was here maybe? Speaking of. Why isn't he here?"

My heart dropped. How did Lark know Dan was married and why did he feel the need to tell Ralph and not me?

"Azurdee? Where is Lark?"

I shook my head and said, "Working. He got called out of town."

Ralph's face fell and he said, "I'm sorry, honey. I'm sure if he could be here he would."

I gave him a weak smile and nodded my head. We made our way back out into the restaurant and I plastered on my fake-ass smile and prayed I'd make it through the rest of the night.

***

"So, how is the restaurant doing?" Jessie asked as she placed Lauren down in the portable crib in my living room.

I smiled weakly. "Good."

She turned and looked at me. "Just good? You don't seem very happy. Azurdee, this is your dream come true, honey. You should be bouncing off the walls."

I smiled and nodded my head. "I am honestly. It's been open over a month now and it's doing wonderful. I've actually had to hire two new people."

Jessie jumped up and down and pretended to clap her hands. "That's wonderful! I bet Lark is so proud of you."

My smile faded and my heart dropped. Lark had been gone for over a week. He was leaving more and more and each time he came back, he grew more and more distant about his job. Something was weighing heavy on his mind. I knew I should be used to this since he had been gone almost all of the last two months except a few days here and there.

Jessie sat down and looked at me. "Azurdee, is everything okay with you and Lark?"

I smiled weakly and said, "Yes. I mean, no. I mean, yes it is, but things aren't okay with me. God Jessie, I knew getting into this that his job was top secret but…I kind of overheard him talking about something and ever since I heard it, I can't push it out of my mind. I would worry about him before, but now. God, now I find myself not able to sleep. And this trip…I haven't even heard from him once. He at least checks in with me, but this time…it's like radio silence."

She got up and moved over to sit next to me. She took her hands into mine and said, "You knew that his job was probably a little…dangerous. You even said yourself he had a few scars from where it looked like he had been shot. Why haven't you talked to him about it?"

I fell back against the sofa and let out a sigh. "'Cause if he found out I was eavesdropping, he would be pissed. He's given so much of himself to me, Jess. More than I could have ever thought he would. I feel like if I push him…I'll push him away."

She shook her head and said, "No. I think you're afraid he'll tell you. You're afraid to know the truth, honey."

I rolled my eyes at Jessie. I wasn't afraid of knowing the truth. *Was I?*

I sat up and looked at her. "Oh my God. You're right. I am afraid of knowing the truth." I glanced around and looked back at her and said, "I'm scared shitless, to be honest."

"Scared your feelings for him will change?"

I shook my head and said, "Never. My love for him is too strong. There is nothing he could say or do to make me not love him."

She smiled and said, "There you go. If it bothers you that much, talk to him."

I leaned over and pulled her into a hug. "God I miss you. I hate that you live so far from me."

She hugged me back and said, "I know." She leaned back onto the sofa and said, "Man. This whole mom thing is crazy."

I laughed and stood up and made my way into the kitchen. "Root beer?"

She sat up and gave me a wicked smile. "Ice cream?"

I pulled my head back and gave her a what-the-hell look. "Do you not know me at all?" I pulled out the Bluebell ice cream and smiled as I held it up.

We spent the rest of the afternoon shopping for clothes for

Lauren and making plans for her baptism. Scott's parents insisted on a party to celebrate their granddaughter being baptized, and Scott wasn't about to turn down a free party.

We sat at Starbucks and laughed our asses off as we planned the menu and decided the best place for the party was at Jessie and Scott's house.

When my phone buzzed I pulled it out and smiled. I looked up at Jessie and said, "It's Lark."

Lark: Sorry, mi amor. First chance to text you. Will be leaving tomorrow.

Me: It's okay! I'm glad you're okay. I can't wait to see you! Let me know when you're home.

Lark: Will do. Gotta go, baby. I love you.

Me: Love you too!

Jessie smiled and winked as she said, "Victoria's Secret?"

I nodded my head and said, "Hell yeah."

CHAPTER 25

Lark

I PUSHED MY PHONE into my pocket and gritted my teeth as the medic cleaned out the bullet wound. I looked down and rolled my eyes when I saw the gunshot wound on my left side.

Fuck! I can't believe I fucked up like I did.

The door flew open and Skip walked in. "Get the fuck out of here."

The medic stood up and said, "Sir, he's bleeding pretty bad still and I haven't finished stitching him up."

Skip pointed to the door and said, "You can finish in ten minutes. He's been out for three days with the bullet wound. Another ten minutes isn't going to kill him."

The medic nodded and walked out. I took a deep breath and braced myself.

He turned away from me and pushed his hands through his hair. "Sergeant Philips said you tried getting information from Vazquez's brother after he shot you, then you argued with Philips about interrogating him and the fucker got away while the two of you fought to see who had the most testosterone. Are you fucking nuts, Lark?"

I shook my head. "It was my mistake. I was tired and shot. I wasn't thinking clearly."

Skip just stood there staring at me. "You lasted three fucking days out there with a gunshot wound, you're trained for that shit so I don't buy that. Philips thinks you arguing with him has to do with the fact that he called you out on the girl. You had no idea your fucking informant was the target's own brother. How in the hell did that happen, Lark? You should have felt something was off."

I placed the cloth over my side to keep the bleeding down. I looked up at him and said, "I don't fucking know, Skip. It was your intelligence that gave me Vazquez's brother's name in the first place. Didn't they do a run on him before you threw him in with me?"

Skip began pacing back and forth. "I think it was a set up. They knew we were coming for Vazquez and somehow got his brother planted in with you. They just didn't plan on you actually killing Vazquez. They underestimated you."

My stomach dropped and I instantly felt sick. "What do you mean, a set up?"

He stopped walking and said, "A set up, Lark. Someone tipped off Vazquez. He planted his own brother in with us. The only problem was you stripped the brother of his gun and had another man with you. They were planning on you being alone. The brother was going to let you get close enough to where they could take you in."

I stood up. "Wait a minute. You just said you *thought* it was a set up, and now you're talking like it was a set up. Which one is it, Skip?"

He sat down and let out a deep breath. "It was a set up. Intel busted a house not far from the border. The last known place Vazquez was. It appears you've already taken out two of his best men. Somehow it got back to Vazquez that it was a Marine sniper. I guess one night you were in a bar and were talking Spanish and it drew attention to Vazquez's brother. He began following you. Saw you come back to the base. Your last hit when Ricker was with you, well, I guess he got drunk in a bar and made some comment about being a sniper for the US Marine Corps. Vazquez's brother began pumping him for information. Ricker admitted last night he mentioned your name."

I sat down and whispered, "Motherfucker." I looked at Skip. "Is that why you pulled him?"

He nodded his head. "When in the fuck were you planning on telling me I was compromised?"

He looked up at me and for the first time since I'd known Skip I saw regret in his eyes. "Command wasn't sure you had been. They wanted to be sure."

"So was this a set up on both sides?" I asked.

"No. Fuck no, Williams. I'd never do that to you. We didn't find out about the house until after y'all humped in. Then we couldn't get radio contact with you to warn you about the brother. The only thing we could hope for was you to do what you're good at. I wasn't planning on your ass getting shot though."

I sat there staring down at the floor. "What was in the house?"

His face dropped and he stood up and turned away from me.

"Skip?"

He stood there for a few minutes before he reached into his pocket and pulled out a few photos. When he handed them to me and I looked at them I would have dropped to the ground if I had been standing up.

"Oh my God. *No.*"

I was staring down at a picture of Azurdee and me eating dinner at a restaurant in Austin. The next photo was of Azurdee walking into her house. The next photo was of me running on Town Lake. I dropped the photos and reached for my phone.

Skip reached for my phone and pulled it out of my hands. "What are you going to do? Call her up and say, 'Hey honey I just killed one of the most sought-after drug lords in the world, got shot by his brother who I let get away, and now you're in danger?' It's not going to work that way, Lark."

I swallowed hard. "How's it supposed to work then, Skip?"

He sat down and put his hands on his face and then raked them down as he let out a moan. "Listen. I know you love her. I saw your discharge paperwork come across my desk as well as the decline letter for the CIA position. I get that you want out and want a normal life with this girl."

"But…"

He shook his head. "Lark, you've got to make it look like she is nothing, like she isn't an asset to them. If they think she's just another one of your fuck buddies, they'll most likely move on and just target you."

"I have to tell her."

"No. If they come after her and she knows anything, they'll either kill her or use her to get to you."

My heart started pounding in my chest. I knew what he was saying was true but it didn't make me feel any better. "Well fuck. Neither one of those are good, so why not just tell her?"

Skip stood there staring at me with his cigar hanging from his mouth. His eyes narrowed. "Does she have any idea of what you do?"

I shook my head. "No. I mean she knows I'm still in the Marines. She doesn't know what I do."

He nodded his head as his face tightened more. I knew he didn't like the idea of Azurdee knowing I was still in the Marines. "Good. The less she knows the better. You need to come up with some reason you're leaving her."

I instantly felt sick. "I can't hurt her, Skip. I promised her. I promised."

"Lark, if you love this girl…you have to let her go, at least until we can track down the fuckers who are after you. Once we get them and you do your job and finish the bastards off, you can tell her the truth."

My stomach dropped and I felt sick. I didn't let my emotions show at all to Skip. "What if it takes too long? What if she won't take me back?"

"If she loves you anything like how you love her…she will." Skip stood up and walked to the door and opened it. He called for the medic to come back in and finish up.

"We leave tomorrow morning at daybreak. You have twenty-four hours to break it off with her. We'll make sure she has a tag at all times. If anything looks suspicious…well…we'll take care of it. The main thing you have to do is stay away from her. No contact whatsoever after the twenty-four hours is up." He slowly turned and looked at me. "I'm sorry, Lark. I really am."

***

I stood outside my door and took a deep breath in. I knew Azurdee was at my place because I sent her a text saying I was coming home tonight and wanted to see her. Plus the tag we had on her informed she arrived earlier this evening. I opened the door and made my way into the kitchen. I placed my keys and phone down and walked to the refrigerator and grabbed a beer. I opened it and downed it in practically one drink. I grabbed another one and drank it just as fast.

I reached for my phone and sent Scott a message:

Me: Don't ask me why, but Azurdee is going to need Jessie. Make an excuse to come into town today.

I placed my phone back down onto the counter and slowly made my way back to my bedroom as I downed my second beer.

I opened the door and was instantly hit with her smell. The tears building in my eyes caused me to almost turn around and leave. Maybe if I just disappeared from her life that would be better.

She rolled over and made a noise. When I set the beer down on the side table she sat up quickly. She rubbed her eyes and whispered, "Lark?"

"Yeah, it's me, *mi amor*."

She jumped out of bed and ran to me. When she slammed into my body I cried out in pain and she jumped back.

"What's wrong?" she asked as she turned on the side lamp. The moment I saw her beautiful face, I knew I wasn't going to be able to do this. I loved her so much and the thought of hurting her about destroyed me. When she smiled at me it hit me hard…the idea of putting her life in danger destroyed me even more.

I shook my head and said, "Nothing. I missed you so much, baby."

She smiled bigger and pulled my T-shirt over her head and stood before me naked. "Show me how much you missed me."

One more time. I needed to make love to her one more time. I needed her to feel my love.

I reached over and turned off the light and began taking off my clothes.

"Get back on the bed, Azurdee. Get on your hands and knees."

She shook her head. "No. I don't want to be fucked, Lark. I

want you to make love to me."

I closed my eyes and almost begged her to just let me have her from behind. If I was behind her she wouldn't see the gunshot wound on my side.

"Please," she whispered as she lay down on the bed. I quickly stripped out of my clothes and crawled on top of her. I pushed her hands above her head and said, "Hold onto the bed. Don't touch me."

She bit down on her lip and did as I said. I began teasing her wet entrance with my tip and I about came on the spot when I felt how wet she was.

I pushed into her and we both let out a moan. "I missed you so much, Azurdee."

"I've missed you too."

I began making love to her slowly. She kept her hands above her head and as she began softly calling out my name she wrapped her legs around me and then wrapped her arms around me.

The pain shot through me like I was getting hit with the bullet all over again. I closed my eyes tightly as she rode out her orgasm. I wasn't sure how I was able to do it, but I came right after she did.

She held onto me and I finally had to push her legs away. She sat up quickly and looked at me. She looked down at my left side and then quickly moved to turn on the light.

"Azurdee, no." I reached for her, but it was too late. The light was on and she had her hands up to her mouth. When her eyes met mine they were filling with tears.

She jumped up and grabbed my T-shirt and put it back on. "You're hurt. You're bleeding."

I shook my head and said, "Its okay, baby. It's gonna be okay."

"What? What happened?"

I stood up and walked into the bathroom. *Fuck, I needed to take something for the pain.* I stood there and took in a few deep breaths to control the pain.

She walked in behind me and whispered, "You've been shot."

I didn't turn to look at her as I said, "It's all a part of the job."

She remained silent for a few seconds before she said, "Please tell me what happened. Tell me what's going on. Lark, this is killing me not knowing."

I opened the cabinet and looked for some pain pills. I had some in my jacket pocket but my jacket was in the kitchen.

I grabbed some Advil and swallowed four of them.

"You know I can't tell you, Azurdee."

"Bullshit. This whole top-secret shit is getting old. I have the right to know how in the hell you got shot."

I closed my eyes. This was it. This was my out.

I turned to face her. "No you don't. It's none of your business and I told you in the beginning I wasn't going to be able to give you what you wanted."

She looked at me confused. "What? You give me everything I've ever wanted. Lark, I'm just trying to understand what is happening here. Please tell me what you're doing? What do you do? For Christ's sake, you're standing here in front of me bleeding from a gunshot wound!"

I let out a gruff laugh. "You'd leave me if you ever knew what I did, Azurdee."

She looked at me and dropped her mouth open. "Am I getting a little too close to the truth? Is that why you're pushing me away? I won't let you. I take the bad with the good, Lark. I love you and I've always told you I will love you unconditionally."

I walked past her and said, "I'm not telling you, Azurdee, so either you drop it or you leave."

I died when I heard the sob escape her lips. "What?"

I closed my eyes tightly and got ready to do the one thing I promised myself I would never do to her. I got ready to destroy her love for me.

I spun around and yelled out, "What do you want from me? I've given you everything that I can. I told you I couldn't give you my complete self. I told you my job was not open for talking about, yet you stand here and push and push. I'm sick of this shit. I'm done. This was all a mistake and I should have known I couldn't do this."

I stopped and waited for her to say something back. She stood there for a few seconds before she tried to talk. Her voice cracked and my heart broke in two. She slowly shook her head and said, "Why are you pushing me away? If you don't want to tell me…you don't have to tell me…but please…please don't push me away."

I closed my eyes and said, "I can't do it anymore. It's too hard."

She put her hand up to her mouth and asked, "What's too hard?"

"You…you're expecting too much from me, and I'm not sure I'm ready to give you all of me."

She slowly started to sink down to the floor as she began crying. I went to reach out for her but I saw Vazquez's brother's face as I faced him after I killed his brother, and the pictures of her flooded my mind.

"But…you said…you said you loved me. Our letters…the bottle…our journey. What about you telling me you loved me?"

I closed my eyes and turned away from her before she could see my tears.

"I slept with someone before I left on this last mission."

She let out a gasp and whispered, "What?"

God please forgive me.

"I saw Sherry in the elevator before I left. She started coming on to me and we ended up fucking in the elevator. I just couldn't stop myself."

I felt her brush past me. When I heard her crying harder I wanted to immediately tell her I was lying, but all I could see was the pictures of her. They consumed my mind.

She quickly pulled on a pair of pants and grabbed her cell phone. She walked to the door and turned to look at me as she attempted to settle down.

"Here I thought I saw what was really on the inside." She shook her head. "I see what you're doing and I don't know why you're pushing me away." She let out a sob and wiped the tears from her face. "I've loved you from the very beginning and will always love you. I'll love you for the rest of my life, Michael Williams. You'll never begin to know how you just destroyed my whole world."

She pulled open the door and walked out. I started to go after her. I walked out into the hall and heard her doing something in the kitchen. When I heard glass breaking I began walking faster.

As I turned on the light I saw a vase smashed on the floor. It had been filled with red roses. I heard the elevator shut and I stood there and listened as the only girl I'd ever loved...and would ever love...disappeared from my life.

I stood there frozen in place. I hadn't felt this numb since Nikki's death. No...I'd never in my life felt this numb. Azurdee was my entire life. I'd have given my last breath for her love.

I walked over and picked up my phone and typed out a message:

Me: It's done.

Skip: You just saved her life.

Me: I hope so, because I feel like I just destroyed both of our lives. I have nothing left to fight for.

Skip: Yes you do. To kill the bastards who are out to kill you. Get them and you can tell her the truth.

I reached for another beer as I made my way back to my room. I sent out one more text to the man we had tagging her before I downed two pain pills and another beer:

Me: I want daily reports. Where she is and who she's been with. Every night at twenty-one hundred hours.

Intel1: Yes sir.

As soon as my head hit the pillow I could smell her. I wasn't sure how long I tossed and turned. When I finally couldn't keep my eyes open another minute, I drifted off into a dream. A dream of Azurdee walking along a trail with her hand on her swollen stomach.

CHAPTER 26

Azurdee

I WALKED OUT OF the elevator still dazed, confused, hurt, and angry. I wasn't even paying attention when I ran right into someone.

"Excuse me," I barely said as I tried to hold back my sobs.

"Azurdee?"

I stopped in my tracks and turned to see Sherry standing there.

Her smiled dropped and she said, "What's wrong? Are you okay? Is Lark okay?"

My heart began slamming in my chest so hard it felt like I was having a hard time breathing.

"Azurdee...sweetheart. Come on." She put her arm around me and quickly ushered me into the elevator.

Oh God. I'm with the woman who Lark cheated on me with. Oh God. Can't breathe.

The elevator doors opened and we stepped into a small hallway. She guided me around a corner and quickly opened her door. The next thing I knew I was on her sofa and she was kneeling in front of me.

"Breathe...honey, breathe. You have to calm down."

I shook my head and attempted to take deep breaths. I felt like I was in a haze. Nothing made sense right now. I put my hand on my chest and whispered, "Can't breathe."

"You're having an anxiety attack. Darling, just close your eyes and focus on calming down."

I did what she said. I was almost afraid to close my eyes for fear of picturing Lark and Sherry together in the elevator.

When I began getting my breathing under control, Sherry stood up and walked over to a mini bar. She opened a bottle of wine and poured two glasses. She walked back over and sat down on her coffee table and handed me the glass.

"Now, when you're ready, tell me what happened."

I took a sip of the wine. I took a deep breath in and closed my eyes.

"He pushed me away."

"Fuck," Sherry whispered.

I snapped my eyes open and looked at her.

She shook her head slowly and said, "He got scared. Maybe things were getting too real for him?"

I wasn't sure why I did it but I just blurted out what I was thinking. "He said he fucked you when he left to go out of town. In the elevator. He said he couldn't control himself any longer."

Sherry stood up and I swore I almost saw steam coming from her ears. "That little fucking bastard. I can't believe he brought me into this."

She began pacing back and forth. She turned and looked at me. "When did he leave?"

I shrugged my shoulders. I couldn't even think straight.

She began laughing. "I just got home last night from a four-week vacation in France."

My stomach dropped. "He lied?"

She nodded her head. "Of course he lied. Think about it. What better way to push you away than say he cheated on you? Trust me sweetheart when I say this, that boy is head over heels in love with you and I've known him for a long time. I would bet my career that he hasn't even glanced in the direction of another woman since you came into the picture."

I took another sip of the wine. Then I downed it.

"Want another glass?" Sherry asked.

I nodded and said, "Please."

I sat there and racked my brain trying to think if that was what Lark was doing. Was he pushing me away because things were getting too real for him?

I shook my head. No. The letters. The bottle. Our Journey.

I looked up at Sherry as she handed me another glass of wine. "No, he is pushing me away because of something different. I think he's...I think he's trying to protect me from something. Or someone."

Sherry raised her eyebrow and tilted her head. "Like who?"

I needed to be careful what I said to her. "Gah...I don't know. Maybe I'm making excuses for him. Maybe he just isn't the one girl kind of guy." I felt the tears building in my eyes again. If he truly loved me though...he would want to protect me. He would want me near him to keep me safe. Maybe he cheated on me with someone else and just said Sherry.

I took in a deep breath and let it out slowly. I stood up and smiled at Sherry. "Thank you so much for being so kind. I really appreciate it. I think I better get home."

Sherry walked me to the door and placed her hand on my

shoulder. "Please know that I'm here for you if you ever need anything."

I smiled but it was weird knowing that she and Lark had a past together. "I appreciate that. I just think I need to get some sleep."

I walked into the elevator and made my way to my car. Lark had gotten another spot for me to park and I held my breath the entire way there. I was sure he would be standing there. When I walked around the corner and didn't see him I began crying again.

I drove the whole way home crying my eyes out and trying to understand how a person goes from telling you they love you to telling you they don't.

By the time my head hit the pillow, I was completely out of tears. I just needed to sleep. I needed to sleep and thought that maybe I would wake up and it would all have been just a bad dream.

***

"Azurdee? Azurdee?" I saw Jessie snapping her fingers in front of my face, but I was totally lost in another world as I sat on the sofa. A world where Lark never hurt me. A world where he never let me walk out of his life like I never meant a thing to him.

I smiled weakly and said, "Sorry. I was just thinking."

Jessie smiled and tilted her head. "Have you heard from him at all?"

I shook my head. "Has Scott?"

She frowned and said, "I don't think so. If Scott's talked to him, he hasn't told me."

"I can't believe it's been a month already. He hasn't called, texted, nothing. I just sit here every day expecting him to come to his senses but maybe...maybe he never really loved me in the first place."

Jessie grabbed my hands and got down on the floor in front of me as she looked up into my eyes. "Bullshit. I saw the way he looked at you. Everyone saw it. Have you talked to Tristan?"

I shook my head. "No. Ryn's called me though. She and I are actually going out tonight. She is insisting we are going out to drink and party the Williams boys out of our system." I quickly wiped the tear from my face and said, "I don't want to forget him. I love him, Jess. I love him so much and something just doesn't feel right. The way he looked at me. It was like he was pushing me away for a reason and he didn't want to do it."

Jessie let out a sigh and said, "You're going out? Where?"

I rolled my eyes. "The Red 7. Ryn has been bugging me for two weeks."

Jessie sat down next to me and let out a laugh. "Does she know you are so not a club kind of girl?"

I smiled weakly. "Yes. But she said she wants to see my ass grinding on some serious dick tonight."

I looked at Jessie and we both busted out laughing. We laughed so hard I had tears coming from my eyes. I wasn't even sure why we thought that was so funny. I needed that laugh. It was almost therapeutic in a way.

Jessie had stayed for a few hours and I knew what she was doing. I felt like I was being babysat. She had been calling me every single day since the breakup, and I knew it must have been because Lark told Scott.

After I walked Jessie out to her car and made plans to meet for lunch the next week, I turned and slowly made my way back into the house. I was tempted to text Ryn and tell her I wasn't up for going out, but she had been so excited and honestly I was so sick of trying to figure out what happened with me and Lark that I needed a night out. Maybe I would even get drunk.

As I walked up to Ryn's door my stomach felt sick. I wasn't really in the mood for this, but maybe this would get my mind off of Lark. Ryn opened her door and looked me up and down. "Holy hell. Look at you."

I held my hands up and smiled.

"Jesus. I'm going to have to fight you for men tonight," she said as I laughed and looked down at my satin cocktail dress. It was covered in beaded crystals with a high round collar. It opened in the back and went so far down I was pretty sure my ass would be showing if it went any lower. The dress was gold with silver accents on it.

"You like it? I actually bought it for Joyce and Peter's anniversary party but…"

She held up her hand and said, "No talk of the Williams boys or their adorable parents who I fell in love with. That just makes me hate Tristan even more."

I chuckled as I walked into her apartment and looked around. It was the first time I had been here. It was decorated exactly like I had pictured it would look like. Very simple with just small touches of the outside brought in. No bright colors. All neutral and soft colors.

I turned and looked at her. Ryn was breathtaking. She must have been about five-four. Beautiful wavy brown hair, and the bluest of blue eyes. She was wearing a light blue cocktail dress that emphasized her eyes even more. Her hair was pulled up, with pieces of hair pulled down to frame her beautiful face. She grabbed her clutch purse and put a scarf over her shoulders and gave me a wink.

"Let's go party."

The second we walked into the club I felt the headache coming on. The music was moving through my body and I instantly thought of Lark. I was wishing Ryn had picked another club to come to, but she knew the manager and from what I could gather they might have had something going on. She waved and pointed as she shouted to me. "There's Dodge. Come on, I want to introduce you. He's gonna shit his pants when he lays his eyes on you."

I grabbed her arm and pulled her to me. "I thought you were dating him." She shook her head.

"He was my rebound fuck. That's what you need and trust me…he is worth it."

I stopped and dropped my mouth open. "What?" I screamed out.

She wrapped her arm around my waist and said, "Don't be all innocent. Trust me—the rebound fuck is important. It has to be good. You need something to push Lark out of your head."

"Did it push Tristan out of yours?" She stopped and looked at me. Then she shrugged and said, "Maybe you're right. Maybe I'm not ready to give up my rebound fuck."

"Oh. My. God," I shouted as she threw her head back and laughed.

As we made our way over to Dodge, or who Ryn was now affectionately calling RFB, I was taken by how handsome he was. The way his eyes moved up and down my body made my stomach dip a little. I liked the way he was taking his time looking my body over from head to toe. He smiled and that was it. My heart began to race and I leaned over and said, "Too late. RFB is mine tonight." Ryn wiggled her eyebrows up and down and winked at me.

"He's got a big dick too!" she shouted and the girl standing next to us looked at us.

I glanced back at Dodge. He had piercing blue eyes that almost appeared to look right into my soul. Almost as if he knew what he needed to do for me to forget everything else but how he was admiring my body.

I licked my lips as I looked up at his blonde messy hair. Both of his ears were pierced with a small diamond stud in each one and for some reason it turned me on even more.

"Dodge, this is my friend Azurdee. She needs to be shown a good time tonight. Can you take her under your wing, please?"

Dodge smiled and nodded his head as he held his hand out. I placed my hand in his and he started to walk out to the dance floor.

I was hoping to God that my right hand wasn't sweating like my left one was. I turned back and looked at Ryn who was giving me a thumbs-up as another guy was whispering something in her ear.

Usher's "Hot Tottie" began playing as Dodge smiled and pulled me close to him, but not too close. The way his body moved was quickly beginning to make my body react in a way I was not too sure about. Was I just that desperate to forget about Lark?

As the song finished, he pulled me closer and put his lips to my neck right under my ear. "That dress should be illegal. I'm going to have to take my job serious tonight."

I pulled back slightly and smiled. When he pushed one of my curls behind my ear I let out a giggle. His touch didn't affect me the way Lark's did, but it certainly caused my libido to come to attention.

We walked back to the bar and Dodge pulled out a stool for me at the end of the bar and walked around to the other side. "What will you be having tonight, Azurdee?"

The way he smiled at me caused me to suck in a breath of air. For the first time in a month, I actually felt alive. Maybe Ryn was right. Maybe I needed my own RFB.

"Bud Light."

He smiled that big bright smile and said, "A simple girl. I think I'm ready to marry you already."

I laughed and shook my head. "No, not what I'm looking for."

His eyes darkened as he handed me the beer and shouted over the song that was now playing.

"What are you looking for?"

I bit down on my lower lip and smiled slightly. "To forget about him."

His eyes moved down to my lips as he licked his own lips and said, "I'm your guy then."

The rest of the night Dodge showered me with attention…and drinks. I wasn't drunk, but I was well on my way to feeling pretty damn good. The whole night I felt like someone had been watching me. For a moment I panicked thinking Lark could be here, but I knew he was at his parents' party. Even though it was in Austin somewhere, I knew he wouldn't be going out tonight. It was the main reason Ryn and I picked tonight to go out. Zero risk of running into the Williams boys.

Dodge pulled me out to the dance floor and we began dancing to "Don't You Wanna Stay." I instantly buried my face into his chest. Jason Aldean was one of Lark's favorite singers.

"Azurdee, I don't really get the feeling that you're the kind of girl who just goes home with guys."

I pulled back and looked at him. The alcohol was begging to settle in and I was feeling tipsy.

"I'm not but…"

He smiled so sweetly at me as he placed his hand on the side of my face. "How about if I take down your number. We can take this slow."

I was relieved and then pissed. "Do you not want me?" I asked, surprising myself at how bold I was being.

His eyes lit up and he pulled me into him. I felt how much he wanted me and I was instantly turned on. *I needed this. I needed to forget about Lark for just one night.*

"Baby, you have no idea how much I want you. You're the most beautiful woman I've ever laid eyes on and whoever he was…he didn't deserve you if he let you go."

I swallowed and reached both my hands up and around his neck. "Please…"

He quickly grabbed my hand and began walking through the crowd. My stomach was in knots and I prepared myself to have sex with another person besides Lark.

Dodge walked up to the bar and shouted, "Lisa, I'll be in my office."

She nodded her head and kept talking to a customer sitting at the bar. I looked around for Ryn. She was sitting at a table and our eyes met. She smiled and nodded her head. *Oh my God. She knows what we're about to do.*

Dodge walked down a hallway and the further we walked the more the music faded. He stopped at an office that was marked *Dodge, General Manager.*

He opened the door and led me in. Once he shut it, I couldn't hear the music.

"Talk about soundproof. So if I wanted to scream…I could?"

He smiled and said, "Only if you're screaming in pleasure."

I felt a tug in my lower stomach as I walked over to the desk and leaned against it.

Dodge walked up to me and used his hands to push my dress all the way up. I let out a gasp as he let out a moan.

He stared down at my silver lace panties and said, "At any moment you want to stop…" He looked into my eyes. "We'll stop."

I nodded my head and whispered, "Okay."

He began to unzip his pants and push them down. When his dick sprung free I just stared at it.

I want this.

He placed his hand on my thigh and I jumped. "I'm going to touch you, Azurdee."

I nodded my head and as he moved his hand further up, my heart began beating harder in my chest.

He slipped his finger along my panties and my mouth parted slightly open. It felt good to be touched.

I need this.

He reached his hands around and I lifted up as he slipped my panties off. He pushed them down to where they pooled at my ankles. I kicked them off and sucked in a breath of air when he pushed my legs apart. Exposing me to him.

"Fuck, I bet you taste amazing."

*Oh God…*I closed my eyes and all I saw was Lark, so I snapped them open and said, "Touch me."

He slowly moved his hand along my inner thigh. He reached behind me and pulled my ass to the edge of the desk.

He slipped two fingers in and I let out a long moan as he moved in and out of me slowly. "You're so wet."

I have to do this.

He pushed another finger inside me as he buried his face in my neck. "So. Damn. Tight. How do you want this?"

"What do you mean?"

"Do you want to play nice or do you want me to fuck him out of your mind?"

He reached for a condom and began to roll it on.

I can't do this.

He looked at me and stopped putting the condom on. He took a step back and pulled it off and then reached down for his pants. I looked at him confused as hell.

I shook my head and asked, "What's wrong? Why are you stopping? I just need…I just need a minute…"

He zipped up his pants and leaned down and picked up my panties and began slipping them back on and pulling them up as he helped me stand up and push my dress back down.

He closed his eyes and said, "Azurdee, I've never wanted anyone so badly in my life, but this just doesn't feel right."

"What? What do you mean? Did I do something wrong?"

He smiled and placed his finger on my chin and lifted my eyes to his.

"Baby, as much as you think you want this. I can see it in your eyes—you don't."

I felt the tears building as he leaned over and grabbed something off his desk. He took a step back and handed me his business card.

"I really like you and I'd really like to see you again. Maybe dinner? Take things slowly?"

I took the card and smiled as I began to chew on my bottom lip. He reached up and pulled it from my teeth and then leaned down and kissed me. It wasn't the most dramatic kiss but it was enough to leave me possibly wanting more.

There was a loud knock on the door that caused both of us to jump.

"Shall I call y'all a cab?"

I nodded and said, "Please."

He turned to head to the door, but before opening it I said, "Hey Dodge?"

He turned around. "Yeah?"

I smiled and said, "Thank you."

He smiled back and I had to admit it: my knees went weak.

He opened the door and another guy was standing there. "Sorry Dodge, but some guy out here is flashing around some sort of badge saying he needs to talk to you."

Dodge stepped to the side and I walked out and headed down the hallway. When I popped out and made my way over toward Ryn, she frowned. I shook my head no and she smiled slightly. I sat down and she yelled across the table.

"Too soon?"

I shrugged and looked away. The moment my eyes met his I sucked in a breath of air. Dodge walked up and leaned down and yelled. "I called a cab."

Ryn sat up straight and said, "Wait! We're leaving?"

I glanced behind Lark and saw Tristan. I snapped my head at Ryn and yelled. "They're here!"

She narrowed her eyes at me confused as she said, "Who?"

I just looked at her and her eyes widened. "No!"

"Yes."

We both turned and saw Lark and Tristan standing there, staring at both of us. We both turned and looked at each other and said at the same time, "We're leaving."

Dodge took a step back and said, "I don't think the cab is here yet."

I looked over his shoulder and saw Lark talking to some

bleached blonde. He was smiling, but kept glancing over our way. Tristan was with a girl and I was guessing it was Liberty.

Ryn grabbed my arm and put her lips up to my ear. "Oh God, Dee. Do you think that's Liberty?"

I nodded my head and shouted toward Dodge. "Will you walk us outside?"

He smiled and said, "Sure."

I pointed to cut across the dance floor. He looked confused but then recognition crossed over his face. "He's here?"

I mouthed *yes.*

As we made our way across the dance floor and down the other side of the club, Ryn and I both started looking behind us. The second the fresh air hit my face I let out the breath I had been holding. Dodge held up his hand and a taxi pulled up. Ryn immediately jumped in. I turned to face Dodge and said, "Thank you again for being so understanding."

He smiled and winked. "Dinner though, right?" I laughed and said yes. He leaned down and kissed me gently on the cheek and turned and headed back into the club. I went to turn and get into the cab when someone bumped into me and knocked my clutch out of my hand and to the ground. He kept walking as I called out. "Excuse you, asshole." I bent down and went to reach for my purse when another hand grabbed it.

I stood up and came face to face with Lark.

CHAPTER 27

Lark

My heart was pounding so hard in my chest it felt like it would pound right out. The way she looked at me almost had me in tears. I wanted to ask who the fucker was she went into the back with. They hadn't been gone long enough for anything to have happened, but my mind was going crazy with thoughts.

"Azurdee," I whispered.

She turned and looked at the cab and then back at me. "What… I thought your parents' party was tonight?"

I gave her a weak smile. "It was. Tristan and I left early. Nothing but a bunch of old people sitting around telling stories."

She didn't smile and my heart broke even more.

"Is that Liberty?"

I looked at Ryn sitting in the cab, then back at Azurdee, and slowly nodded my head. "Yeah."

"Must be nice to just brush someone aside and go about your life with no thought to the person left behind hurting."

I swallowed hard. "Who was the guy you were with?"

She looked shocked and her mouth opened a little before she

tightened her jaw and said, "He's a friend of Ryn's. The manager here."

I nodded my head and said, "You went back to his office. What for?"

She squared off her shoulders and said, "That's none of your business. You made that choice when you let me walk away from you." She turned and headed to the taxi before turning back and walking up to me. She took her finger and began poking me in the chest.

"You're a liar, Lark. You never fucked Sherry because she was in France. She wasn't even in town when you left town. You lied to me."

I pushed my hand through my hair and said, "Listen, Azurdee, I just need…"

"Need what, Lark? Space? Freedom? A good fuck from a strange random girl?"

"No. I haven't been with anyone since before our first night together. There was never anyone else, Azurdee. I'm so sorry I lied to you. I just need some time."

She laughed and shook her head. "Did you ever even love me?"

I stood there shocked by her question. I looked around. Anyone could be watching us or listening to us.

When I saw the tear slide down her face I took a step toward her as she took a step back.

She slowly shook her head and whispered, "I hate you."

She turned and got into the taxi, as I stood there frozen. I watched as her taxi drove off. I shook my head and felt my phone go off in my pocket. I took it out and was hoping like hell it would be Azurdee.

I read the message and said, "Fuck." I made my way back into the club and started looking for Tristan. When I walked up to him, he looked pissed.

"Where is Liberty?"

He looked behind him and said, "Bathroom. Who do you think the fucker was who had his hands all over Ryn?"

I let out a gruff laugh and said, "Are you fucking kidding me? You're upset because Ryn was at a club, with another guy?"

"You can't tell me you weren't pissed off watching Azurdee walk to the back with some guy."

I tightened my jaw and said, "I'm going home. Are you staying?"

He shook his head. "Liberty has a headache."

I laughed and said, "Have fun with that."

He shot me a dirty look and said, "I've tried calling her. She won't return my calls."

"Who? Ryn?"

He nodded and looked toward the restrooms. "I'm so fucking confused. Ryn was supposed to be the girl I had fun with. The one I wasn't going to have to worry about feelings and shit. I should have brought Liberty home at Christmas. I can at least deal with her."

I let out a chuckle. "Yeah, 'cause she makes you so happy."

He snapped his head over and said, "She does, in her own little way."

"Keep telling yourself that, Tristan. I'm leaving. You taking a cab or what?"

He let out a sigh and said, "Nah, just go on. I'll wait for Liberty and just stay at her place tonight."

I shook my head. "I'll talk to you tomorrow."

"Later."

As I walked out of the club and to my truck my heart grew heavy and the feeling that I was being followed grew even heavier. I stopped and pulled out my cell phone and hit Skip's number before turning and seeing someone leaning against a building.

"Lark, what's going on?"

I began walking again as I asked, "Any new leads?"

"No. None. It's like Vazquez's brother vanished into thin air. We have gotten a few informants to talk though. Looks like there is talk of something going down to where he might be present."

I closed my eyes and said, "Azurdee?"

"They haven't been able to tell if she's being followed. Right now we don't think so."

I opened my eyes and looked to see that the guy who was leaning against the wall was now walking behind me texting someone.

"Well, that's a negative for myself at the moment."

"Fuck. You carrying?"

"Hell yeah I am," I said as I reached and felt the pistol tucked into my holster.

"Check in when you get home. Looks like we might be heading out in a few days."

I nodded my head and said, "Right. Got to go—at my truck and I'm just ready to get the hell home."

"Lark, she's gonna be safe. You did the right thing."

I took a deep breath and let it out. "I know I did. I just wish keeping her safe wasn't breaking her heart and making her hate me in the process."

***

I stood down and looked at the report. Azurdee had been out with this Dodge guy twice in the last two weeks. I stripped out of my uniform and changed into jeans and a T-shirt. I started to make my way out to my bike when I turned and punched the wall.

"Motherfucker!" I cried out as my fist slammed into the wall.

"You know you need your hand to do your job, right?" Jason said from behind me.

I glanced over and said, "Fuck off, Philips."

He lifted his hands and said, "Hey. I'm not the one who has a crazy guy after me trying to kill me. I just thought you'd want to make sure your shooting hand wasn't damaged when we got the call."

I shook my head, "The call. What call? They have no idea where this guy is. He was right there with us, Jason. Right there and I fucking let him get away."

He walked up to me and put his hand on my shoulder. "Dude, neither one of us knew it was a setup. Let's just be glad we got out of there alive. We're gonna get him next time. I promise you."

I nodded my head and said, "Yeah. I know we'll get him. Doesn't help that I've pushed the woman I love away to keep her safe and she is moving on without me."

Jason looked away and then looked back at me. "We'll get him, Lark. If it helps any, I'm really sorry for running to Skip about Azurdee."

I smiled and said, "Yeah, I know you are and I know we will. I got to get going."

Jason smiled and said, "Club tonight?"

"Nah, I can't. Heading out to Mason. I'm going to be the god-parent to my best friend's little girl. I didn't think we would be back in time to make it, so I'm going to head on out."

Jason laughed and said, "Are they sure you're the best pick?"

I chuckled and said, "I asked them the same thing."

I decided to take my bike to Mason. I needed to feel the wind and just let it go. There was nothing better than going down a country road on a fast-ass bike.

I pulled into Scott and Jessie's gate and hit the buzzer. "Hello?"

I smiled when I heard Jessie's voice. "Hey beautiful. Want to buzz me in?"

"Lark?"

My smile faded when she seemed surprised it was me. "Yeah. This is the right weekend, right? Lauren's being baptized tomorrow, right?"

"Umm, yes! Yes!" she said as she covered up the phone and said something to someone.

As the gate opened, it hit me. Azurdee would probably be here. I sat there for a few seconds as I looked up and down the road to see if there were any cars. As fast as I was driving, if anyone was following me, I would have lost them miles ago.

I started to make my way down the driveway. I let out the breath I was holding when I didn't see Azurdee's car. I parked my bike and turned to see Jessie and Scott walking out. Jessie looked pissed.

"Hey y'all."

Scott shook his head slightly and gave me a warning look, but it was too late. Jessie walked up and slapped the shit out of me. I closed my eyes and then slowly opened them.

"That was for what you did to my best friend, you asshole." She turned and looked at Scott. "Do something about this, because Azurdee will be here later. I don't want him here when she gets here."

"Hey, wait a minute. What's going on between Azurdee and me has nothing to do with either one of our friendships with y'all. This has been planned for a few months now and I have every intention of being there for Lauren's baptism."

Jessie closed her eyes and dropped her head back and then looked at me. "God, Lark, I'm so sorry. I don't know what came over me. It's just I saw you and that day came flooding back, and all I could see was Azurdee on the sofa crying and her world falling apart."

I swallowed hard and went to say something, but nothing would come out. Scott and Jessie both stood there and stared at me. I ran my hand through my hair and whispered, "Fuck."

"I'm still in the Marine Corps. I'm a sniper, but I'm working under the CIA right now. My job is to go and kill people and we don't really make it known that's what I do. I do what the military doesn't want anyone to know. The CIA has been trying to recruit me ever since they found out I'm not re-enlisting with the corps. Azurdee found out I was still in the Marines when I came back from a mission and was still dressed in my uniform. She has no idea what I do, and if she ever found out I'm afraid she would hate me. I killed one of the most sought after drug lords a few months back. The only problem was it was a setup. They were after me. Now his brother is after me, and they had pictures of Azurdee, and I had to break up with her to protect her. I love her more than anything. She's my life. No one fucks with my life."

When I finally took a breath and stopped talking, Scott and Jessie were just standing there staring at me. Jessie had her hand over her mouth and Scott looked confused as hell. I closed my eyes and realized what I had just done. I let a moment of weakness touch the lives of two people I cared about. I totally just put their lives and Lauren's in danger.

"Son of a bitch. I'm sorry y'all. I should never have told y'all that. It 's just…I'm just. Fuck, everything is just so messed up right now. You can't repeat what I just spit out."

"I thought…you said you were discharged. What is Skip in all of this?" Scott asked.

"Senior level CIA agent. Or as I like to call him, my boss."

Scott shook his head. "That house in Belize. How does he afford it, or does the CIA pay that well?"

I made a face and said, "Well…that house is actually mine. Well, my family's house anyway."

Scott and Jessie said at the same time, "Yours?"

I nodded my head.

"But…they knew who Skip was and…they let us go…and you said communications, you piece of shit," Scott said as he turned and started pacing.

"Scott, I paid them to let us get through and told them to act like it was because of my boss."

Jessie's mouth dropped. "Are you selling drugs?"

I laughed and said, "No. I already told you I'm not doing anything illegal and for the record, Skip has a degree in communications."

Jessie walked up to me and said, "Okay, I'm going to have to ask. How in the hell do you have a multi-million dollar condo in Austin, a house in Belize and God knows what else, when you're just in the Marines?"

I glanced over to Scott. He frowned. "I never told Jessie about your grandparents. Then again, I never really knew how rich you were, dude."

I looked back at Jessie. "My grandparents were very wealthy. Oil wells in Texas. When they passed away, they left everything

297

to my brother and me. My parents are also pretty well off, not like my grandparents by any means, but the house in Belize was their house."

"Holy shit. This explains so much," Jessie whispered.

"It definitely explains some things, that's for sure," Scott said.

My phone pinged and I pulled it out to see I had a text message from Jerry.

Jerry: Sorry it took me so long. Dodge isn't the guy's real name. Sent you all the info in an email.

Me: Thanks. Owe you.

"I mean, now I know how you were able to look up all that information so fast and the connections you have."

I gave him a weak smile as I said, "I do have connections, but not all of them are military. Most are CIA."

Jessie looked at Scott and then me, "Wait. You said the CIA is trying to bring you on with them, so does that mean your time in the Marines is almost up?"

I nodded my head.

"Why didn't you just tell Azurdee all of this?"

"I can't. You can't either. Why I just spilled my guts out I have no idea, but you cannot repeat anything to anyone. The less Azurdee knows, the better. I need this crazy lunatic to think that Azurdee was just another girl and no one important to me. If they think she can be used to get to me they will take her, and God knows what they would do. You cannot tell her anything."

Scott walked backwards and when he hit the steps he sat down. "Holy shit. Lark. This is some…this is…"

"Heavy shit?" I asked as I walked over and sat down next to him.

I looked at Jessie and said, "I wasn't even thinking about Azurdee being here because I kept thinking I was going to miss it."

She put her hands up to her mouth again and said, "She asked if you would be here. When Scott said you were out of town I told her no. She said…she said she was bringing someone."

I stood up quickly and tried to settle down my instantly beating heart. "Who? Dodge?"

Jessie gave me a funny look. "Dodge? Who is Dodge?"

"You don't know about Dodge? The guy she has gone out with a few times?"

She shook her head. "No. She hasn't mentioned him at all, but she also didn't say who was coming with her. Oh Lark! I'm so sorry."

I grabbed onto the railing and slowly sat back down. I was so pissed off I wanted to hit something. I looked over at Scott and he jumped up.

"Yeah. I've seen that look before. Come on, before you want to take your anger out on me. Let's go shoot."

Jessie stood in front of Scott and said, "What? Azurdee is coming soon and possibly with a guy, and you want to give Lark, a trained killer, a gun? Are you insane, Scott?"

I couldn't help it. I started laughing. "She does have a point. You know what a good shot I am."

The door opened and Scott's mom called out. "Azurdee is on her way down the drive!"

I looked at Scott and Jessie and we all said "Oh shit" at the same time.

Scott grabbed me to walk away but it was too late. She was already in sight and Jessie stood in front of me. "Whoever it is, you have to promise me, you will neither hurt nor kill anyone in the next 24 hours."

I gritted my teeth and nodded my head. Jessie turned and began waving as Azurdee parked the car. When an older woman began getting out of the passenger seat, Jessie said, "Thank you God. It's Azurdee's mom."

I leaned down and whispered, "I promise not to kill Azurdee's mother."

Jessie snapped her head around and glared at me. "Not funny, Lark Williams."

Azurdee was smiling until she glanced up and saw me. Her smile faded and then was replaced by a fake smile.

"Mrs. Emerson! What a surprise! Azurdee said she was bringing someone, but didn't say it was her mom."

Azurdee smiled bigger and said, "Mom, this is Scott Reynolds."

Scott walked up and shook her hand and then kissed the back of it, making her blush.

Azurdee looked at me and I smiled and mouthed *hello.*

Mrs. Emerson turned and looked at me and I smiled. We both stood there waiting for Azurdee to introduce us. I finally took the lead.

"Mrs. Emerson, it is a pleasure to finally meet you. I'm Lark Williams."

Her mother's smile faded for one quick second before returning. "Mr. Williams. It's nice to finally meet you."

"Lark is Lauren's godfather," Azurdee said. It was like she had to explain my reason for being there.

"Oh. Very lovely. Jessie, I'm parched. Tea?"

Jessie gave a nervous laugh and said, "Yes! My mother in law just made some. Let's head on in."

Azurdee and I managed to avoid each other for the rest of Friday and most of Saturday. I walked around Scott and Jessie's backyard carrying Lauren in my arms. I hadn't seen Azurdee since she went inside with her mother and a few other ladies. Lauren laughed and I looked down at her and smiled. She was nine months old now and the cutest damn thing ever. She was so happy all the time, and when I was around her it just made me realize the life I wanted with Azurdee. As we walked up to each person, I said, "My god-daughter, Lauren. Isn't she going to be a heartbreaker?"

When Florida Georgia Line's song "This is How We Roll" began playing, I walked to the dance floor and began dancing with Lauren. As I bounced her around, she began laughing out loud, which caused me to laugh out loud. It was the first time in two months I felt a moment of happiness. Scott walked up and tried to take my sweet angel out of my arms and I turned away from him. He walked around me and I spun away again. This time Lauren really started laughing so Scott and I made a game out of it.

I finally gave up my girl and handed her to Scott. As he began walking to the house with her, I glanced over and saw Azurdee standing there watching me. My heart dropped just as fast as my smile did when I saw the look on her face. She looked…sad. I smiled, and she returned my smile, but it didn't touch her eyes. She turned and walked away.

"Lark, are you up for another dance with a pretty girl?"

I turned to see one of Jessie's friends standing there. I gave her a polite smile and said, "Maybe in a bit." When I turned back around, Azurdee was gone. *Shit.*

The party was beginning to wind down and I still hadn't seen Azurdee. I walked over to Jessie and when she saw me she smiled. "Hey. Looks like you might have stolen another girl's heart. You know what this means, don't you?"

I laughed and said, "No, what does it mean?"

"You need to come visit your new girl more often," she said with a wink.

I nodded my head as I said, "That sounds like a plan." I glanced around again and asked, "Have you seen Azurdee?"

She looked around and said, "No. Come to think of it, I haven't seen her in about thirty minutes. Right before Lauren went down for a nap."

Jessie's friend Ari walked by and said, "She's down at the main barn. Alone, so if you want to talk to her you better get your ass down there, cowboy."

I shook my head and laughed. There was something about that girl. Ari's husband Jeff was a lucky son of a bitch, that was for sure.

I looked back at Jessie, "Do you need help with anything?"

She smiled softly and said, "No. Go talk to her. And Lark, think about telling her the truth. If anyone can keep her safe, it's you."

I felt a sharp pain in my chest as I looked down and said, "I wish that was true."

I made my way down to the barn. When I walked in I saw her in a stall brushing a horse. She was humming and I instantly wanted to take her in my arms.

When I walked closer, I cleared my throat and said, "Hey." She looked up and the sadness in her eyes caused my heart to feel like a knife just pierced through it.

She was never going to forgive me. In that very moment, I felt it hit me like a rock wall.

I'd lost the only woman I'd ever loved.

CHAPTER 28

Azurdee

I found myself struggling to breathe as I watched Lark dancing with Lauren. The smile on his face was painful and I began dreaming that he was dancing with our daughter.

Then reality hit me. He didn't want me. He didn't want the same things I wanted, which was a future with him. A family. A life together.

When he looked at me and smiled, I tried so hard to smile back. My heart was breaking all over again.

I need to get away from him. I can't take this pain.

I walked into the barn feeling so tired and so small. Everyone was happy and celebrating, and all I could do was think how I had finally started to feel human again when I had to see him. All the hurt and anger came flooding back.

I didn't see him walk into the barn, but I felt him. Any time he entered a room, I could feel his energy move through the air and straight to my body.

"Hey."

I glanced up at him and it felt like I'd died a million deaths when I looked into his eyes. I turned away and went back to brushing the horse.

When I didn't answer him, he walked into the stall and picked up another brush and walked to the other side of the horse.

"Did Scott get a new horse?" he asked.

I shrugged my shoulders. "I don't know when they got Biscuit."

Another minute or so went by and I couldn't take it any longer. I took a step away from the horse and walked out of the stall. I felt him behind me. I quickly turned and looked at him.

"Why did you come down here?" I asked.

He stared at me and whispered, "I...I just wanted to be near you. I wanted to hear your voice."

I looked at him, confused. I shook my head. "I can't do this." I let a sob escape and I immediately saw the pain in his eyes.

My voice cracked as I whispered, "If you don't want me, you have to let me go."

Lark's eyes narrowed as they searched my face before he looked into my eyes. "No. I never said I didn't want you."

"You did when you let me walk away from you. When you pushed me away from you. I never asked you for anything. I would have done anything for you, Lark. Gone anywhere for you. I'd have given up my dream to be with you."

If I hadn't known better I would swear he was tearing up.

"Just when I start feeling like I can breathe again, there you are. You show up just to remind me all over again of the pain. Then you have the nerve to tell me you just wanted to be near me."

He stood there and said nothing. I could see the pain in his eyes and I was so confused.

"I love you, Michael. Please tell me how you feel about me. Please just tell me why you're doing this to me."

He looked down and then outside the barn like he was waiting for someone to walk in. When he looked back at me, he went to talk but then stopped himself.

"Say something to me! Tell me something! Anything!" I shouted as he jumped.

"Azurdee, I can't give you what you want. Not yet anyway."

I felt the tears begin to fall and my heart was completely shattered.

"When? When do you think you're going to be able to, Lark? I love you and if you don't feel the same…"

He began shaking his head. Then his cell phone went off and he pulled it out and looked at it. His eyes got big and he looked at me.

"I am…I have to go. Azurdee, please. Let me talk to you when I get back. Please."

I shook my head. "Tell me right now. Do you love me or not?"

He didn't say a word, and in that moment his silence told me everything I needed to know.

"I'm sorry that we don't want the same things, but I have to say good-bye to you now. I'm officially giving up us, Lark."

I turned and walked away from the one man I loved more than life itself.

Lark called out after me, "Azurdee! Wait! Please let me just talk to you when I get back. *Please.*"

I picked up my pace and as soon as I rounded the corner of the barn, I took off running as fast as I could. I had no idea where I was going. I just needed to get as far away as possible.

***

I walked into my house and immediately walked to my bedroom

and changed into a pair of comfy sweats. I walked up to my drawer and pulled it open. Lark's T-shirt was sitting right on top. I'd put it there two months ago and hadn't touched it.

I grabbed it and pulled it over my head and made my way to the kitchen. I opened the freezer and pulled out my new boyfriend: Ben and Jerry's Cherry Garcia.

I flopped down on the sofa and started digging in. My mind traveled back to every look and every word that Lark said to me earlier. I shook my head. I had been thinking about it all on the drive home. Jessie had begged me to stay with them tonight but I needed to be alone to think.

He looked so sad…almost devastated. I swore at one point he wanted to tell me something but couldn't. I let out a deep sigh and went to take a bite of my ice cream.

Carlito Vazquez.

The name just popped into my head and I remembered the conversation Lark had that I overheard. I sat up and put my ice cream on the coffee table as I got up and made my way over to my laptop. I sat down and pulled up Google. When I typed in the name, the first return caused me to gasp.

"Most-wanted drug cartel leader Carlito Vazquez was killed by single gunshot wound to the head by a sniper on March 18. United States government denies any involvement."

"Oh. My. God."

I began clicking on all the links and reading. They all said the same thing and it all started to click.

Lark. Marines. Missions. Sniper. Gunshot wounds.

I picked up the phone and called Scott and Jessie's number. When no one answered, I ran and grabbed my cell phone.

I quickly pulled up my last text from Lark and began texting him. I knew he would still probably be traveling to wherever he was going.

Me: I heard you one night on the phone talking about a Carlito Vazquez. Tell me who he is.

I stared at my phone and waited for his response. About a minute later my phone pinged.

Lark: Please, Azurdee. Leave it alone.

Me: I want to know who he is. Right after that conversation you came back with a gunshot wound and I just found out this Vazquez guy was shot. By a sniper. That's when you pushed me away.

Lark: Please. Stop. I'll talk to you when I get back.

Me: No! I'm tired of you pushing me away. I want answers. You're a sniper in the Marines, aren't you? That's why you leave. Your missions…that's what you do.

Lark: I'm turning off my phone. I'll talk to you when I get back.

Me: No! Don't turn off your phone. Lark, please. I deserve to know.

I sat there and stared at my phone. Nothing. I jumped up and headed into the bedroom. I walked in and came to a halt. I slowly brought my hand up and covered my mouth.

A red rose. There was a red rose sitting on the pillow where Lark used to sleep. There was a piece of paper under the rose.

How did I not see that when I first walked in?

I began to send him another text.

Me: When did you leave the rose?

Lark: Before I left earlier. Please stop texting me. I'll talk to you in a few days when I get back.

My stomach dipped at the idea that Lark was here. In my house. In my bedroom. *Why didn't I just leave before him?* I would have been home and would have been able to talk to him.

I walked over and picked up the rose and smelled it like I did every time before when he left one.

I picked up the letter, opened it and began reading it. Two sentences in I realized what it was, and I began crying as I sat down on the bed.

"Oh shit. I'm gonna need more ice cream."

I walked into the living room and picked up my melted ice cream. I headed to the kitchen to get a rag to clean up the melted mess.

After cleaning it up, I called Ralph. "I need ice cream. A lot of ice cream."

"What do you think I am? Your bitch? I worked all day managing *your* restaurant while you played in the country."

I let out a sigh and said, "You can totally have tomorrow off. I'll take care of the restaurant all day."

He let out a chuckle. "Are you going to close it up by yourself? Meg isn't going to be there tomorrow."

"Yes. It's my damn restaurant and I know how to close it up by myself."

"Fine. Cherry Garcia?"

I smiled and said, "You may be getting a raise soon."

"I'd be happy if you just got some action soon and stopped being such a bitch."

"Hurry! I'm going to need it."

I hung up and sat down on the sofa. I pulled the blanket over me and grabbed one of the pillows. I opened up the letter and took a deep breath as I began reading it.

My Dearest Azurdee,

I never thought in my wildest imagination I would even feel the way I've felt since I've been with you. Each moment with you causes me to fall more and more in love with you. The only person I want to kiss is you. The only person I want to make love to for the rest of my life is you.

There is nothing I wouldn't do for you. Nothing I wouldn't give to you. I want to give you everything Azurdee. Not just material things. I want to give you my love, happiness, contentment...all the things you deserve. I want to protect you from everything that could possibly hurt you. I'd lay my life down to protect you. I want to be your rescuer just like you've been mine, mi amor.

The day we met, fate looked down upon destiny. I knew it the moment you smiled at me. The moment you touched me. We were meant to be together and I want you to always remember that. Please never doubt it or forget it.

Sometimes I think this is all too good to be real. It's like I'm the sand in an hourglass and I'm falling deeper and deeper in love you with, yet I'm so scared my sand will run out.

Every breath I now take is taken with new meaning I can't wait to start our life together. I can't wait to wake up next to you every single day for the rest of my life. To see your beautiful face first thing every morning I imagine would be some of the most beautiful moments of my life.

You've bewitched me, Azurdee. You've made me want to be a different man. You've taught me how to love again. You've showed me there is so much more to life. I can't imagine a life without you in it now.

I'll love you always. I'll always be faithful to you. I'll always protect you.

I've never been so ready in my life to start a new journey. I'm so blessed I'm starting that journey with you.

My love to you always and forever,

Michael

I could barely see the words through my tears as I read the letter again, and again, and again. I folded it up and held it to my chest as I sat on the sofa and cried. When I heard my doorbell ring, I flew up and ran to the door. I opened it and said, "It's about damn time! I've been…"

I stopped talking when I saw a gentleman standing there smiling at me.

"Azurdee Emerson?"

I nodded my head. "Yes. May I help you?"

"May I come in?"

I planted my foot in front of the door and smiled while I said, "No. I don't think so. May I ask who you are?"

He turned and looked at the car that was pulling up. When I looked and saw it was Ralph I almost broke down crying again.

"Lark has a message for you."

I sucked in a breath of air. "What?"

He took a step closer as he said, "I'd feel more comfortable if we were able to talk to you in private."

I frantically began looking around.

"We?"

Ralph got out of his car and when I saw Mark getting out too, I let out the breath I was holding.

"What's going on?" Ralph said as he walked up. The guy standing at my door smiled and said, "It's a personal matter. I'm going to have to ask you to leave."

I shook my head and Ralph took another step closer to the guy. "I believe the lady doesn't know who you are and is not comfortable with you approaching her."

My phone beeped and I realized it was stuck in my sweats. I pulled it out and saw a text from Lark.

Lark: Baby listen to me. If anyone tells you that I sent them or they work with me, they are lying. Try to get away from them as quickly as possible.

Me: Okay.

Lark: I'll text you when I get service again.

Me: Okay.

Lark: I hope you read the letter.

Me: I did.

Lark: I meant every word I wrote. I still mean it. I swear to you.

I looked up at everyone staring at me texting. "My mother. She is having some weird pains. I'm sorry, Mr…?"

I waited for him to give me his name.

"I can see now is not a good time to talk to you, Ms. Emerson. I'll come back tomorrow morning."

I nodded my head and said, "Fine."

When he turned and walked away, I thought I was going to fall to the ground. Mark grabbed my arm and led me into the house and I sat down on the sofa.

I could no longer hold back my tears, and I typed my last text to Lark.

Me: I believe you. Someone just stopped by and wouldn't leave his name but said he had a message from you. Lark, please hurry home. Please be careful.

I sat there for a few seconds and waited. Nothing. A good three minutes went by and still nothing. Ralph shoved a bowl in my face and said, "Here. You ask and I deliver. Now, who in the hell was Mr. Creepy?"

I shook my head as I ate my ice cream. I handed the letter over to Ralph and he read it while Mark sat down next to me and I curled up to his side. He worked out at least three hours a day and looked like a Greek god. I had to say one thing about Ralph; he had great taste in guys. Every guy he had ever been with was built and good-looking.

Ralph looked up at me and smiled. "I knew he still loved you."

I shook my head. "He wrote that before we broke up. It was the letter we each wrote."

"The ones you put in the bottles?"

I slowly nodded my head. "He left it here for me tonight before he left."

Ralph smiled and said, "Dee, he wouldn't have left this letter if the things he wrote in it were not still true."

"I know. I think he pushed me away because…" I stopped talking when I realized I couldn't share with them what Lark did.

"Because of what?"

I shook my head and stood up. "Will y'all stay with me tonight? That guy kind of freaked me out."

Ralph stood up and said, "I'm one step ahead of you, darling." He looked over at Mark and asked, "Would you mind getting the bag?"

Mark smiled and said, "Sure." He stood up and kissed me on top of the head and said, "Don't worry. Everything is going to work out."

I nodded and watched him walk out the door. I glanced over to Ralph and said, "I have the strangest feeling something bad is about to happen and I can't shake it."

He laughed and said, "Nonsense. Your hunk of a boyfriend, or ex, soon-to-be not ex, is going to come back, give you some much needed nooky and all will be right in the world again."

I tried to smile but the feeling I had in my stomach wouldn't go away. It seemed to be getting worse.

CHAPTER 29

Lark

I CLOSED MY EYES and began slowly falling asleep. I needed to get just a few minutes of sleep. We got here a few hours ago and humped up the side of this damn mountain and I was more mentally exhausted than anything.

After what only seemed like thirty seconds, someone was bumping my foot. I opened my eyes and looked at the Navy SEAL who was signaling movement. I slowly turned and crawled over to the lookout. Jason was already there glassing the location.

When I got up next to him, he signaled that four guys had just arrived and our target was identified as one of the four. I smiled and felt an instant relief wash over my body. Finally we would get this fucker. *As long as no one screwed up.*

I took the binoculars and spotted Jose Vazquez, Carlito's brother, and the fucker who tried to kill me once before. I slowly gave the binoculars back to Jason and made my way back over to the SEAL team. Their job was to take out the camp after the main target had been taken out.

"You guys ready?" I whispered.

"Yes sir, we are more than ready. We'll await your signal."

I nodded and pointed to two and told them to head over behind a set of trees. The other two I had flank us on the opposite side. No one was to shoot until I took the first shot and gave the signal that the target was down.

We moved into position and waited. I had no idea if they would be in the house for five minutes, or five hours. I bunkered down in my spot as I put my ear buds in and pulled up "Gotta Be Tonight" by Lifehouse. I never did a shot without that song playing.

As I sat there I thought back to two weeks ago when I went to my parents' beach house and found Azurdee's letter.

***

I hung up the phone with my mother and let out a sigh. I wanted to come to the beach house to get away from everything and all it did was make me think of Azurdee. I couldn't get it out of my mind, the time we spent here.

I walked into the library and smiled when I looked over at the desk. My smiled faded when I remembered the look in her eyes when she walked out of my condo that night. I let out a long breath and made my way over to the books. I slowly started walking as I read the titles. When I saw Pride and Prejudice, Azurdee's favorite book, I reached for it and pulled it out. I walked over to the chair and sat down as I opened the book. My hands started shaking and I wasn't sure why. I began reading and quickly got lost in the story. When I opened it up to chapter three, there was a folded piece of paper.

I took it out and began to read it. The first few words and I knew it was Azurdee's letter to me. She must have made a copy and stuck it in the book. I continued to read as I fought to hold back the tears in my eyes as I read the words she had written down. Words from her heart. When I finished the letter, I folded it up and placed it back where she put it.

I wasn't sure how long I sat there just staring off into space.

Memories of Azurdee flooded my mind and I fought like hell to keep from calling her and telling her how much I loved her.

I closed the book and got up and put it back where I found it. I turned and made my way to the bedroom and crawled into bed. For the first time in my life, I felt like I wanted to cry.

***

The loud noise pulled me out of my thoughts and I quickly looked around. I looked over to Jason and he gave the all clear.

Fuck. My nerves are on edge. I pushed Azurdee out of my mind and focused on the mission.

Another two hours passed as we sat there and did what we were good at: Waiting. I looked at each set of teams and then over to Jason. I slowly raised my hand and signaled to make sure he didn't need a rest. When he said he was okay, I turned back around and closed my eyes. I quickly opened them again. The only thing I saw when I closed my damn eyes was her smile and the pain in her eyes when she ran out of the barn.

I thought back to the night we went for a drive in the ranch jeep.

***

I pulled up to the old shed and parked the jeep. I looked over at Azurdee and when she smiled I instantly smiled back at her. "You want to go for a walk? The night is beautiful and it's a nice cool evening."

She nodded her head and jumped out of the jeep and met me in front of it. I grabbed her hand and we slowly started walking.

"So how do you like my family?"

She laughed and said, "I love them. They're funny. I can see how much they love you and Tristan. Your mom cracks me up. I'm going to have to cook one of her recipes and put on a daily special and take a picture."

We walked for a bit in silence. Azurdee stopped and looked at me. "Dance with me."

I laughed and said, "There's no music."

She shrugged and said, "Do we need music?"

"I need music to dance."

She laughed and pulled my hand and began walking back to the jeep. "Does the jeep have FM stereo? Please say it does."

I chortled and said, "Yes ma'am, it does."

She jumped into the jeep and turned it on and then turned on the radio. The moment "Best Night Ever" by Gloriana began playing she let out a small scream and jumped out and ran into my arms.

I laughed and spun her around and then began dancing with her. "I take it you like this song."

She laughed as she nodded her head. "It makes me think of that first night I made you dinner. Then our first night together."

I pulled her closer to me. "That day changed my life."

"Which one?" she whispered.

"Both."

She pulled back and gave me the sweetest smile ever. I leaned down and gently kissed her soft sweet lips.

I pulled back a bit and said, "I'm thinking we make this the best night ever too."

She bit down on her lower lip and nodded her head in that innocent way that turns me on even more. I picked her up and she wrapped her legs around me as I walked her over to the jeep and set her down on the hood.

And it was indeed the best night ever.

***

I jumped when I felt my phone vibrate in my pocket. *Fuck! I was sure I turned it off.* I quickly pulled it out.

We had been sitting here all night and well into the morning. I saw Scott's text message scroll across my screen. I looked over to Jason who was looking through the binoculars.

I opened up the text message:

Lark. As soon as you get this call me ASAP. Azurdee's restaurant caught fire. Her car is still there. They think she may still be inside.

I just stared at the text message for a couple of minutes trying to make sense out of it. My heart dropped to my stomach and I leaned over and began throwing up. I tried like hell to stay quiet. One of the SEAL team members looked at me and signaled to see if I was okay. I held up my thumb and wiped my mouth off.

I got a drink from my canteen and hit reply:

Me: When? When did this happen? Is the fire going on right now? Maybe she got out the back? I can't come home, I'm on a mission. Keep me updated.

I hit send and prayed to God I would keep the signal long enough to get it out. When it popped up that the message delivered my hands started shaking as I turned off my phone.

Azurdee. Please God. Please don't take her from me too.

I needed to get to Azurdee. I needed to get home. I was just about to reach for the radio to call an abort on the mission when Jason gave the signal sound. I quickly got into position and tried to calm my shaking hands. I turned on my iPod and took a deep breath and cleared my mind of everything. I looked and saw Jose walking out. They were laughing and high-fiving each other.

The fire. It wasn't an accident.

I focused my scope in and put my target right on that fucker's head.

"This is for you, Azurdee," I whispered as I pulled the trigger.

The moment he slumped to the ground, I yelled out the signal and gunshots rang out all around me. I checked through my scope to make sure Jose was down. I aimed one more time and shot again for good measure.

Jason held up his fist and called out "All down!" We jumped up and grabbed our stuff and began humping out. We got a few miles out and Jason called in our location and estimated time to the extraction location. I walked up to him and grabbed the radio from him.

"Skip. Is Azurdee okay? There was a fire."

"How in the fuck did you know?"

"I forgot to turn off my phone. I got a text."

"What?" he yelled out.

"Skip!"

"Our guy saw her walk in, only he never saw her come out. He said he heard a car door shut and looked up to see a car pulling away. He grabbed the plates and they are being run now. He decided to follow the car. He got about a mile away when he heard a loud explosion. He looked in his mirror and saw flames shooting in the sky in the direction of the restaurant. He turned around and went back to find the restaurant up in flames."

"Did he see who got in or out of the car?"

Silence.

"Fucking hell, Skip, don't do this to me."

He let out a sigh. "He said he fell asleep, so the car door was someone getting in and then they drove off. We're thinking they planted the bomb and then gave themselves plenty of time to get away before it exploded."

"Did she get out?"

"Lark, let's just get y'all off the goddamn mountain."

"Did. She. Get. Out?"

He let out a sigh and said, "They just got the fire under control. Her car is still there though."

I stopped and tried to keep my legs from giving out on me. "No," I whispered.

"Lark, we don't know anything yet. Let's just get you off that mountain. Get your ass to the extraction location and by the time you get back we'll have more information."

"Oh my God. She can't leave me. She can't leave me," I cried out.

CHAPTER 30

Azurdee

"I can't believe we get to hang out. It's about time," Ryn said with a wink.

"I know." I chuckled to myself when I thought about Ralph. He had no idea I had planned on closing down the restaurant today. He never paid attention to what our website said, or the door for that matter. It wasn't a planned closing but the regulars were aware we changed the schedule up sometimes.

We heard a loud bang and Ryn jumped. "Shit. What in the hell was that?"

I shrugged my shoulders. "Not sure, but damn it was loud. Hey, we have to go to the Wimberley glass blowers. It's a bit outside of town, but I think they have the pendants you're looking for."

Ryn looked at me and raised her eyebrow. "Really? Don't get my hopes up, Azurdee. You know how I've been searching for the perfect pendant lamp."

I laughed as we continued to drive through Wimberley. When we pulled up to the Wimberley Glass House, I let out a little squeal. I knew Ryn was going to flip when she saw this place. It was just the type of place she had been looking for.

When we walked in, I watched her face. I smiled knowing I had hit a home run.

"Oh, Azurdee. This place is amazing."

I nodded and said, "I know, isn't it?"

We walked around a bit and we were even lucky enough to see a demonstration of glass blowing. Ryn finally picked out the pendants she wanted.

We were walking out when her cell phone rang. "Ugh. It's Tristan. What the fuck does he want? He hasn't called in a few months."

She hit ignore and sent it to voicemail. As we walked outside her phone rang again. She hit ignore again and rolled her eyes. We got in the car and before she put it in park a text message came through. She sighed as she opened it up.

She looked at me and said in a scared voice, "He said it's an emergency."

My heart began pounding in my chest so loud I could hear it in my ears.

"Lark," I whispered.

Ryn hit Tristan's number.

"What's wrong?" Ryn asked.

She looked at me and gave me a weak smile. "Why do you want to know where I am? Listen, I don't have time to…"

"Yes, I'm in Wimberley. How did you know that?"

Her mouth dropped open and she began shaking her head. "Wait. Tristan. Slow down. Azurdee is with me. Yes! She is sitting right here next to me. What do you mean there was an explosion?"

I started wringing my hands together. I was wishing she would just put it on speakerphone.

Her face turned white as a ghost as she handed me the phone.

"Hello? Tristan! Is Lark okay? What's going on?"

"Azurdee! Oh my God." I heard him muffle the phone and then yell, "She's okay! I'm talking to her. She isn't in the restaurant. She's with Ryn. She's okay."

"Tristan. What in the hell is going on?"

"Azurdee, I don't know how to tell you this but…your restaurant. There was some kind of explosion and it…there was a fire. Honey, I'm so sorry but it is a total loss," Tristan said in a worried voice.

I swallowed hard and looked at Ryn who had tears streaming down her face. "Oh my God. If we hadn't left, we would have been…"

"What? What did you say, Azurdee?" Tristan asked.

I shook my head. "We're on our way." I hung up and Ryn and I just stared at each other.

"The explosion we heard, Ryn. That was the restaurant. That must have been like three minutes after we left. We could…we might have been…" I put my hand over my mouth and jumped out of her car. I felt like I was going to throw up. I closed my eyes and thought about the strange man who came to the house last night.

Once my stomach settled I turned and numbly got back into the car.

We pulled up and I let out a small cry. My entire restaurant was gone. Ryn parked the car and we both got out. Tristan and Ralph both came running over. Ralph grabbed me and began saying. "You bitch. You tricked me into thinking I had the day off!" I couldn't help it, I started laughing. Only he could make a joke at a time like this. Ralph pulled back and said, "Dee, we thought you were in there. Your car was still here. Then when this guy said he saw a car driving off and gave the plates to the police and it pulled up as Ryn's car, we had a bit of hope."

I looked over at Ryn and Tristan was hugging her. She gave me a confused look as he kept repeating: "Thank God you're both okay." She finally pushed him away and said, "What are you doing here?"

"Lark. He sent me a text to come check everything out."

My heart skipped a beat when he mentioned Lark. "Is he okay?" I asked.

He nodded his head and said, "He said he was on his way back. He's really upset. He's been trying to call you."

I put both my hands over my face and tried to calm myself down. I dropped my hands and looked at what was once was my dream.

"I left my cell phone in my office. Ryn called and said she was here and I just quickly got up and left. If I hadn't left though..."

Tristan walked up to me and pulled me into a hug and I lost it. I hadn't cried this hard since the night Lark and I broke up.

"It's okay, sweetheart. Shh. I promise it's okay."

Ralph put his hand on my back and said, "We'll start over, Dee. It can be even better, honey."

I knew they were trying to make me feel better but it wasn't working. The only thing that would make me feel better was if it were Lark holding me in his arms.

***

I hung up the phone and let out a long, drawn-out sigh. I had to practically beg Jessie to just stay in Mason. There was nothing she could do. It was looking more and more like arson, and I kept thinking of the creepy guy who had stopped by my house the night before. I told the police about him and they said they would look into it.

Meanwhile there was a CIA agent who was parked outside my house. He claimed at first the local police called him in but I knew it had to have had something to do with Lark. When he pulled me to the side and mentioned Skip and Lark and that he was the one who reported the tags, it all made sense.

My eyes were so tired and I just needed to sleep. I wasn't even sure what time it was. All I knew was it was late at night and I was exhausted. I was drained emotionally. My entire world was now gone.

No Lark. No restaurant. Nothing.

I crawled into bed and got settled in for what I hoped was at least a few hours of sleep. Within minutes I was fast asleep.

I woke up and sat up quickly. My breathing was erratic and I had to concentrate on getting it under control. Ever since that first panic attack when I saw Sherry, I'd been having them more and more.

"Fuck. Just one night. I just ask for one good night of sleep." I lay down and grabbed the other pillow and felt something. I jumped up thinking it was a giant bug. I stood on the bed and looked down.

It took a few seconds for my eyes to focus. *Was that a...rose?* I reached down and picked it up. I smelled it and immediately began crying as I jumped off the bed and ran out of my room. When I ran into the living room I practically ran into the coffee table. I let out a gasp and cried harder when I saw him sleeping on the sofa. He was still dressed in his uniform.

I moved around the coffee table and sat down on it and watched him sleep. His phone was sitting on the coffee table and it went off. I looked down and saw it was a message from Skip. I picked it up and slid it to open the message:

Skip: Your last mission was a success. All subjects have been taken out. The offer for the job is still open, you know.

I looked at Lark and whispered, "Last mission?"

I set his phone down and got down on my knees. He looked so beautiful but so very tired. Even in a deep sleep I could tell he was exhausted.

I bent down and lightly brushed my lips against his. He moved slightly and I whispered, "I love you, Michael."

He lifted his hand and put it behind my neck and pulled my lips to his. We both let out a moan as we opened our mouths and kissed. What started out as a small kiss quickly turned passionate as Lark began to sit up...never breaking our kiss once. I crawled onto his lap and began running my hands through his hair.

God I missed this. I missed him. His touch. His smell. His taste. Everything about him made me lose all control.

When we finally broke the kiss, we were both panting. Lark placed his hands on each side of my face and looked into my eyes.

"I love you. I love you so damn much. I had to do what I did to keep you safe and if all that pain and hurt had been for nothing and you died in that explosion I would never have forgiven myself. I never wanted to hurt you. *Ever.* I promise you I will never hurt you again. Please believe me. You're my whole life. You're the reason I live each day."

I sucked in a breath of air and then slammed my lips to his. We both frantically began taking our clothes off. I'd never moved so fast in my life to get undressed. I stood up so he could take his pants off. I let out a sigh when I saw him.

He sat back down and I crawled back on him. He grabbed my hips and began moving me just enough to where he was barely going inside of me. He moved me back and slipped his fingers inside me as I whimpered.

"Lark, please."

He ran his lips along my jaw and down my neck and back to my ear where he whispered, "You're so wet, *mi amor*. I've missed you."

I couldn't believe how much I needed him. "Yes. I've missed you. I need you so much."

He placed his hands on my hips and guided me to my sweet relief. I dropped my head back as he filled my body. I knew it wasn't going to be long. I was already feeling the build up. I began moving up and down faster as he moved along with me. I snapped my head forward and our eyes met.

"I'm going to come," I panted.

He wrapped his arms around me as we both gently whispered each other's names.

***

As I lay in my bed wrapped in Lark's arms, I couldn't help but think of how close I came to dying today. I could hear Lark breathing slow and steady. After we had made love we came in here and he told me everything. My heart ended up hurting even more knowing how painful it was for him to push me away to protect me.

I asked him about the text I read from Skip and he confirmed to me he wasn't going to be in the Marines much longer, and how the CIA wanted him, but he turned down the job offer. When he asked me if I hated him for what his job was, I ended up crawling back on top of him and we made love again. I knew he was exhausted. The moment he came he about fell asleep.

I ran my fingers lightly up and down his arm and smiled. *This feels perfect.* All we needed was each other. Nothing else. Just us.

Lark had mentioned rebuilding the restaurant, but knowing

that he was getting out of the Marines and soon wouldn't be taking off all the time, I knew exactly what I was going to do.

We were finally together again. There was no way I was ever going to let him go.

CHAPTER 31

Lark

I sat on the hay bale and watched the horse Scott was brushing. It had been two months since Azurdee's restaurant burned down. I was now officially discharged and was working on building our house on the ranch I had bought right between Johnson City and Marble Falls. The CIA had been out to the ranch I don't know how many times trying to recruit me, and each time I would ask them to please stop coming out.

Scott stopped brushing the horse and turned to look at me. "Are you even listening to me?"

I smiled and nodded my head. "Sorry. I was thinking."

He smiled and said, "Is it weird not being in the service anymore? No more always on call and being all secret and shit?"

I laughed and said, "Yeah, it's a little weird."

He nodded and said, "Pretty soon when you get your place up and running, you will be wishing for downtime."

I agreed and said, "I still don't know if I want cattle or hunting."

"Do both," Scott said as he began brushing the horse again.

I sat back and thought about it. "Both. I wonder if I could make that work?"

"Sure you can. It will be hard work, especially if you bring in the game and really get some good bucks on there. You could do guided like your parents. Maybe Azurdee would even do like your mom and cook for them. You could charge more if you do the same set up as your parents."

I nodded and said, "Yeah, but I'm not sure if she is going to rebuild in Wimberley or not."

Scott looked at me funny and then looked back at the horse and smiled slightly.

I got up and ran my hand through my hair and whispered, "Shit."

"Lark, something is bugging you. Dude, just spit it the hell out. I can't take your suffering anymore. It's rubbing off on me."

I stopped pacing and reached into my pocket and walked up to Scott. I handed him the ring box.

He smiled when he took it and opened it.

"Holy shit, dude. That is one nice diamond. You do this by yourself?" Scott asked with a laugh.

I rolled my eyes and snatched the box out of his hand. "It was my grandmother's ring."

Scott shook his head and asked, "When are you asking her?"

"This weekend."

Scott stopped and looked at me. "What? Here? Do you have a plan?"

I just looked at him. "Yes, I have a plan. Azurdee doesn't need anything grand and fancy. I've got this. Don't worry pretty boy. It's covered. Don't forget, I'm still not pussy-whipped like the rest of you."

Scott nodded his head and looked at me with a cocky grin. "Dude, you keep filling your head with that shit. You are now a member of the pussy-whipped boys club. Just embrace it. The perks are fantastic."

I laughed and slapped him on the back. "I'm going to find Azurdee. "

He called out from behind me, "You're going to be watching Twilight soon! Or sitting there listening to a book."

I put up my hand and waved it. As I rounded the corner of the barn I laughed. No way in hell I was going to admit I had watched Twilight with Azurdee a few weeks ago. I made her swear to secrecy not to tell a soul. I may or may not have threatened her as well.

I walked into the kitchen and smiled when I saw my girl standing at the stove trying to reach up to the microwave. I leaned back and watched her as those first moments of being with her in this very kitchen flooded my mind.

"Fucker. I hate you! Stupid microwave."

I smiled and said a silent prayer thanking God she was mine. I cleared my throat and walked up to her. "Would you like some help with that?"

"No. I don't know why they made this damn thing so high."

I leaned against her as I reached up and took out the bowl. I set it on the counter and then turned her to face me.

"No, you're just short."

She smiled and began chewing on her lower lip.

"Seems like yesterday, not a year and a half ago."

I nodded my head and said, "It was a moment ago."

I leaned down and sucked her bottom lip between my lips and gently bit down. She reached her hands up and laced them around my neck as we deepened our kiss.

"Get a room," Jessie said as she walked into the kitchen.

I pulled back and wiggled my eyebrows up and down as Azurdee laughed and shook her head.

"Don't make plans for this evening. I made us dinner plans," I said as I smacked her ass and walked out of the kitchen, then headed up to the room we were staying in. When I walked down the hall, I peeked into Lauren's room. I walked in and stood over her crib.

I gazed down at the only other girl who had changed my life. This precious little girl changed me forever the moment I held her in my arms. I couldn't even imagine what it would feel like to hold my own child someday.

I moved and sat down on the small bench and watched her sleep. The small little sounds she made had my heart soaring.

I glanced over to the door when I saw it open. Jessie smiled and walked in. She peeked at Lauren and then sat down next to me on the bench.

"What are you doing in here?" she whispered.

I smiled and shrugged. "I don't know. I guess she just captured my heart and I wanted to watch her sleep. I love watching Azurdee sleep. Even when her mouth hangs open and she drools and then snores really loud. Sexiest thing ever."

Jessie giggled and hit my leg. "You're going to ask her to marry you, aren't you?"

I snapped my head and looked at her. "Scott tell you?"

She smiled bigger and said, "No. I can tell by the nervous way you're acting."

Shit.

I dropped my head and asked, "Do you think she knows?"

"Nope. She's clueless."

I grinned and said, "Good."

"Do you need help?"

I looked at her and said, "I just need you to keep her busy right before sunset. I'm having someone come in and set up a picnic in your front yard. I'm going to ask her at sunset."

She pulled her head back and asked, "Why in the hell are you asking her to marry you in our front yard?"

"It's where we first met. It's where I knew I would love her for the rest of my life. I just didn't know I loved her then."

I saw the tears build up in Jessie's eyes. "Wow. Lark Williams. Romantic." She shook her head as she stood up. "Never thought I'd see the day." She leaned down and kissed my cheek as she reached for my hand and led me out of Lauren's room.

The rest of the afternoon was spent with me checking my pocket every five minutes to make sure the ring was still there. Looking at the time on my phone and trying to act normal so Azurdee wouldn't pick up on anything.

I looked at Jessie and winked.

She stood up and said, "Azurdee, how would you feel about going with me for a walk? I'd love to get out of this house for a bit. What do you say?"

Azurdee stood up and handed Lauren to Scott. "Just you and me?"

Jessie smiled and nodded her head. "Yes! Girl time!"

When they walked out the back door, I ran to the buzzer and waited.

"You know, a watched gate buzzer takes longer to go off than if you just walk away."

I looked at Scott and said, "Fuck off dick. I'm sure you were just as nervous."

He shook his head and said, "Nope."

I made a mental note to ask Jessie.

The buzzer went off and I fumbled to hit answer.

"Yes! I'm here!"

"Hello, this is Hill Country Catering. Mr. Williams?"

"Yes. Come on up." I hit the button to open the gate. I turned and looked at Scott and smiled. I clapped my hands and said, "Let's do this!"

Scott started laughing and said, "I never thought I would see the day." Scott's mom walked up and took Lauren and laughed.

Thirty minutes later, me, Scott, Francis from Mason Florist, and Linda from Hill Country Catering all stood back and looked at our creation. A small table with two chairs had been set up under the giant elm tree in front of the house. Francis had hung lanterns down from the tree branches so that at sunset we would still have light. She also had one lantern set in the middle of the table with red rose petals spread on the table.

"Will she like it?" I asked as I looked over at Scott. He smiled and nodded his head.

"Dude, she is going to love it and be totally surprised."

Linda let out a chuckle and said, "Mr. Williams, it looks perfect. We will be over in the trailer. Once you come out, just give us a wave when you are ready for us to start bringing out the food."

I nodded my head and watched as Linda walked to the trailer. I looked at Scott and said, "Hell, I hope she can cook and Azurdee likes the food."

Francis smiled and said, "I'll be leaving now. Thank you so much, Mr. Williams."

I shook her hand and said, "Thank you! Let me walk you to your van."

As I walked back toward the front door, it opened and Jessie stepped outside and attempted at least four times to whistle.

"What in the hell are you doing?" I asked as Scott walked up to her and kissed her as he laughed.

"I was giving you a signal. You know, whistling. I told Azurdee to go change for dinner. Are you ready?"

I nodded and Jessie turned as we followed her into the house. We walked into the living room and Jessie looked over my shoulder and smiled. When I turned around, Azurdee was standing there in a pale pink sundress and cowboy boots.

"I'm ready. Are we all going out to eat?" she asked as she looked between the three of us.

Jessie grinned and said, "Nope. This is just dinner for two. Scott, Lauren and I are leaving and heading to his parents' house and spending the night there."

I looked at Scott and he winked and nodded his head. "The house is y'all's tonight."

I walked up to Azurdee and kissed her on the forehead as I took her hands and led her to the front door.

"Where are we going?" she asked with a confused look on her face.

I looked at her and said, "Dinner."

She laughed and said, "On the front porch?"

I glanced at her and said, "Kind of. Close your eyes, *mi amor.*"

She tilted her head and gave me a questioning look as she closed her eyes. I opened the front door and guided her out the door, down the steps and to the side of the table.

"Can I open my eyes?" she asked with a giggle.

"Not yet," I whispered as I pulled the ring box out of my pocket.

I knelt down on my knee and took a deep breath as I opened the box.

I slowly let out the breath I was holding and tried to talk, but my voice cracked. I cleared my throat and said a quick prayer.

"Open your eyes, *mi amor*."

She opened her eyes and then looked down. She threw her hands up to her mouth and instantly started to cry.

"I'm really hoping that you don't think I'm moving too fast. Something hit me the other night though. Do you want to know what it was?"

She nodded her head as tears flowed down her beautiful face. "I can't ever live this life without you in it. It's been over a year since I stood here and laid my eyes on the most beautiful woman ever. I felt something that day that scared me. Then you smiled at me and I knew in my heart I was going to love you for the rest of my life."

She wiped her tears away as she whispered, "Lark."

"You took me exactly how I was, faults and all. You never once judged my life or me. You made me feel worthy of your love. Your unconditional love brought me out of the darkness and into a light I never dreamed could be so amazing. You taught me how to open my heart again, Azurdee. You are the only person I want to give my heart to. The only person I want to spend the rest of my life with. You're my whole world...my entire life."

She dropped to her knees and looked into my eyes like she was looking into my soul.

"Azurdee, will you please go on this journey with me? Will you spend the rest of your life with me?"

She began nodding her head as the most beautiful smile spread across her face.

"Will you marry me, Azurdee?"

"Yes. Yes. Yes. Yes!"

She threw herself into my arms as we wrapped our arms around each other. I held her as she cried and I fought like hell not to be a pansy ass and cry. Scott and Jessie had already left so no chance of him seeing me if I did let a tear…or two…slip.

"Lark, I love you so much. I can't wait to start my journey as Mrs. Michael Williams."

And there are the tears. Shit. There goes my man card.

CHAPTER 32

Azurdee

THE MOMENT I OPENED my eyes and saw Lark on his knee, my heart began pounding and my stomach had been doing a complete circus act.

Lark stood up and gently lifted me up with him. He took the ring out of the ring box and took my left hand as he slipped the ring onto my finger. I looked down at the most breathtaking ring I'd ever seen. It was an oval diamond framed by round diamonds. Ribbons of diamonds overlapped to form the band, which was white gold.

I sucked in a breath of air and said, "Oh Lark…it's beautiful."

His whole body seemed to relax as he asked, "You like it?"

I looked into his eyes and smiled. "Like it? I absolutely love it!"

"It was my grandmother's ring."

"Oh my! Oh…Lark…this is just…" I shook my head and attempted to hold back more tears.

Lark glanced over his shoulder and gave a thumbs-up, and that is when I noticed the small white table. I looked up and saw the lanterns and let out a small gasp.

"Lark. Oh my gosh. When did you do all of this?"

He let out a chuckle and said, "When Jessie and you went for a walk."

I raised my eyebrow and said, "Sneaky."

"I've had extensive training in the area of sneaky."

He sat down across from me and a young lady walked over and poured us each a glass of champagne. She gave me a sweet smile and said, "Congratulations."

I felt the heat move up my face as I quickly looked over at Lark and back at her. "Thank you so much."

"Did he surprise you?"

I grinned and said, "Yes. Very much so."

She took a step back and said, "Your salads will be out momentarily followed by dinner. My name is Linda, so if you need anything just be sure to ask."

When she turned and walked away I looked back at Lark. "You couldn't have picked a more romantic way to do this."

He grinned from ear to ear and said, "Well, I kind of borrowed Scott's idea when he asked Jessie. I just knew I wanted to ask you in the same spot I first saw you. The same spot I knew my life would never be the same again."

"Lark…I love you so much."

Lark reached for my hand and said, "I love you too, Azurdee. I never thought I could ever be as happy as I am right now."

I looked away for a quick second. I needed to tell him about my decision for the restaurant.

I looked back into his beautiful green eyes and my heart just melted on the spot. *I wonder how long he will have such an effect on my emotions like this.*

"I made a decision about the restaurant. I've wanted to talk to you about it. I already talked to my parents and let them know my decision."

I saw him tense up and I knew he had been worried I would be rebuilding in Wimberley. There was no way I could run a restaurant and have him be almost two hours from me.

"Oh yeah? What's the decision?" he asked, trying to seem casual.

I took in a deep breath and slowly let it out. "I'm not rebuilding."

His body didn't relax and he tilted his head and looked at me.

"But, that's your dream. You were so happy, baby. Why would you walk away like that?"

I smiled and said, "I have a new dream now. Living on a ranch near Marble Falls, Texas, with the most amazing man who I love more than life itself. I've been tossing around a few ideas and looking into a few things in Marble Falls. I'm not given up my dream forever. I'm taking a break."

"Azurdee, are you sure about this? We could make it work if you wanted to rebuild in Wimberley. I don't want you to walk away from your dreams because of me."

I shook my head and said, "I saw how much your mother loved helping your father on their ranch. I talked to her about it last Christmas. I want that life with you. Lark, my dreams now involve you. Maybe one or two little Larks at some point in the future."

The way his eyes lit up when I mentioned babies had my stomach drop like I was on a rollercoaster.

He slowly shook his head and said, "I don't deserve you."

"Do we have to eat?"

He pulled his head back in surprise and asked, "What? Aren't you hungry?"

I bit down on my lower lip and said, "What I'm hungry for Linda can't give me."

The left corner of his mouth rose a bit with that damn sexy smile of his. I could see it in his eyes and my body instantly craved his touch.

"Are you sure you want to play? Now?" he asked in that tone of voice that took control and demanded my body's attention.

The feeling in the pit of my stomach grew stronger and I slowly nodded my head.

Linda walked up and set our salads down. Neither one of us broke our eye contact with each other. Finally Lark pulled his eyes away and looked up at her.

"Linda, we're going to have to pass on dinner."

When I peeked up at her she looked confused. "I'm sorry. What do you mean?"

Lark stood up and held his hand out for me as Linda took a step back.

"I mean y'all enjoy the meal. It's on me. Right now there is something else that is requiring my attention."

I felt my cheeks flush as I looked away and let Lark lead me back to the house. Before walking through the door I glanced back at Linda, who had the goofiest smile on her face.

"Lark! She knows what we are going to do," I said as we walked through the door. The door no sooner shut before he pushed me against it and pinned my hands above my head. I loved when he took control like this and I was instantly wet and panting with need.

"Tell me what you want, *mi amor*. Is this a time to make love, or a time to fuck?"

My mouth dropped open as I looked down at his beautiful lips.

I wanted them on my body. I wanted him to take me right here and I didn't care who knew, who saw, or who heard us.

"My body craves your touch like it's a drug. I need to feel your lips on my body. I need to feel you inside me," I whispered.

I swear his eyes lit up even more. He reached his hand up and under my dress as he found his way to my desire. When he pushed my panties to the side and slipped his fingers in he let out a moan.

"I love you baby, and I want to make this special, but right now, I need to fuck you. Hard."

I dropped my head back against the door and whispered, "Yes."

He ripped my panties off and then unzipped his pants as he pushed them down. I watched as his own need was revealed.

He picked me up and a few seconds later I got the relief my body longed for. "Oh God. Yes!" I said as he moved in and out of me easing my desire one thrust at a time.

"Lark…"

"Talk to me," he said between pants.

"Feels…so…good."

He pushed me more into the door and reached up and grabbed my hair and pulled my head back, exposing my neck to him. The moment his lips touched my skin I exploded.

"Yes! Yes! Lark, harder."

He gave me just what I asked for and I began calling out his name as a powerful orgasm ripped through my body.

"God, you drive me crazy, baby. I can't hold off, Azurdee. Baby, I'm coming."

I held onto him as he rode out his own orgasm, massaging mine into almost another one. He pulled out of me and set me down as he reached down for my ripped panties. He wiped between my legs and then picked me up and carried me upstairs and to the bathroom.

My body was still attempting to recover from the powerful orgasm as he set me down on the bench at the end of the bed. He walked into the bathroom and turned on the shower.

He walked back up to me and began getting undressed. Every time I saw his scars I wanted to cry. We were both safe now. No one would ever harm us again and I knew Lark would always keep us safe.

I stood up and turned around as he unzipped my dress and let it fall to the floor and pool at my feet. I turned around and faced him.

He placed both hands on each side of my face and gently moved his thumbs across my face. "As much as I love doing what we just did, my favorite thing is making love to you slow and gentle. I feel like when we make love, we're one."

I nodded my head. "I love you, Lark."

He reached down and gently kissed me. When he pulled back slightly he whispered against my lips, "You will forever be the love of my life."

My heart felt like it was floating in my chest and I wanted to cry out I was so happy. He reached down and picked me up and carried me into the shower where we cleaned each other's bodies off before he slowly made love to me with the hot water pouring over us.

Best. Day. Of. My. Life.

CHAPTER 33
Lark

I slowly got out of the bed, slipped on a pair of pants and a T-shirt, grabbed my cell and headed downstairs. I walked into the kitchen and turned on the light and reached into the refrigerator and pulled out a bottled water.

I made my way over to the back door and headed out to the back porch. I sat down and inhaled a deep breath of fresh air and then released it. I closed my eyes and saw Azurdee's beautiful caramel eyes looking into mine as I made love to her.

"How did I get so damn lucky?" I whispered as I smiled and shook my head. I pulled out my cell phone and started a text message to my mother.

Me: She said yes.

Mom: I never had a doubt in my mind.

Me: Mom, I've never felt so happy in my life. I love her so much it scares me.

Mom: Welcome to love. It's one hell of a journey.

I smiled and in that very moment I knew what my wedding present to Azurdee was going to be.

Me: But what a beautiful journey it will be.

Mom: I raised you right.

Me: It's late. Why are you up?

Mom: I could ask the same thing.

Me: I asked first.

I shook my head. I was two fucking steps away from my man card being revoked.

Mom: I got up to get a drink and saw your text come through. Go back to sleep son. Hug and kiss that beautiful future daughter-in-law of mine. Sleep well and call me tomorrow. I want to hear all about when you asked her to marry you.

Me: Okay, will do, Mom. Night. I love you, Mom.

Mom: I love you too, Michael.

I finished my water and stood up. I looked out into the dark pasture and smiled. I had no idea where the future would take Azurdee and me, but I knew one thing. I loved her and I would go to the ends of the earth for her.

I made my way back up to the bedroom and when I walked in Azurdee was standing at the window looking out into the night. She was completely naked and the sight of her caused my knees to wobble.

I walked up behind her and placed my hands on her breasts and began massaging them. She dropped her head back and I began kissing her neck. "I love you, *mi amor.*"

"I love you too. So very much."

I moved my hands along her body as she completely relaxed into me.

"Your touch calms me so much. I'll never be able to explain what your touch does to me. What it has done since the first moment you touched me."

I wrapped my arms around her and took in a deep breath as I took in her heavenly scent.

"Those few months we were apart, I felt like a part of me couldn't breathe right. I couldn't think right, if that makes any sense," I said as I moved my lips against her neck.

"Lark, can I ask you a question?" Her voice turned serious and I held her tighter.

"Of course you can."

She took in a breath and slowly let it out. "Will you miss it? Will you miss the Marines and the CIA. I worry you will miss the…" She shook her head and continued speaking. "The thrill of your job? That's the only word I can think of."

I turned her body around and placed my hands on both sides of her face.

My eyes moved across her beautiful face. "Azurdee, I've changed. You changed me and it was for the better. What I want from life now is time with you. I want to start a cattle company, I want to build up the ranch to where I'm doing guided hunts like my father, and I want you to be a major part in all of that. I'm not looking back. I'm only looking forward to a peaceful quiet life with the woman I love."

Her eyes filled with tears and she said, "So no more buildings blowing up and people trying to kill you?"

I slowly shook my head. "No more, baby. I have officially turned in my man card and give my entire life to you."

She laughed and said, "No! Don't turn in your man card. I kind of like that side of you."

I raised my eyebrow at her. "What side?"

She bit down on her lower lip and her eyes filled with passion. "The side that takes control. I love when you make love to me but when…when you…" She looked down and I saw her cheeks flush.

"Talk to me."

She slowly looked up at me and smiled. "When you take control of sex. It turns me on even more and sometimes I feel like I can't get you deep enough inside of me. It's like a drug."

I raised my mouth in a smirk and said, "You have no idea how much I want to tie your ass up and bury myself inside of you."

Her eyes lit up and she whispered, "Yes."

I took her hands in mine and led her over to the bed. "Lay down, Azurdee."

Her breathing picked up as I watched her chest heave up and down. I loved how turned on I could make her just by speaking to her.

She lay down on the bed and I moved my eyes over her body. I couldn't wait to ask her how long she wanted to wait before we could start trying for a baby.

I pulled my eyes from her body and looked around. Her robe caught my eye and I grinned. I walked over and pulled the belt out from it and walked back over to her.

"Put your hands up over your head, Azurdee."

Her whole body shivered as she quickly did as I asked. I tied her hands to the bed frame and used my knee to push her legs apart.

"Lark…" she whispered.

I leaned down and took her nipple into my mouth as I moved my hand down between her legs. I slipped three fingers inside her and moaned when I felt how wet she was.

Always so ready.

When my thumb touched her clit she jumped. "I want to touch

your body," she whispered as I smiled. I knew how much she loved touching me and I knew that her not being able to touch me would drive her more over the edge.

I looked up at her and she had her eyes closed while she chewed on her lower lip. I moved my lips up to her neck and then to her mouth. I sucked her lower lip into my mouth and then pulled back some. I ran my tongue along her lips as she pulled on the robe and let out a moan.

"Azurdee…"

She snapped her eyes open and looked into my eyes. "Michael."

"I'm going to make you come now, baby," I said as her eyes filled with need.

"Please."

I quickly pulled my fingers out and moved down and buried my face between her legs. The moment my tongue moved across her clit she let out a gasp. I teased her clit and knew I was driving her insane. She began lifting her hips up and I smiled knowing how turned on she was.

"God…please…I can't take it. I need to come," she begged.

I moved both my hands up to her breasts and began playing with her nipples as I continued to barely touch her clit with my tongue.

She began thrashing her head back and forth. "I can't take it. Oh God. Michael…please!"

I loved hearing her say my name with so much passion in her voice. I began sucking on her clit as I pushed three fingers inside of her. I immediately felt her pussy squeezing down on my fingers and I knew she was close.

"Good God…ahh!" she cried out as I sucked harder and then

flicked my tongue along her clit.

"Shit! Yes! I'm going to come. Oh…don't stop please! I'm coming! I'm coming! Oh…God…"

She began calling out my name and thrashing her head from side to side.

As she started to come down from her orgasm I slowed down and pulled my fingers out of her and moved them to her ass. She bucked when she felt me slide my finger across her ass before I slipped my finger in as my tongue assaulted her clit again.

"Holy fucking shit!" she screamed out as I felt another orgasm hit her again.

"Oh God! Oh God! What's happening? Lark!" I was so fucking turned on I was about to come myself. "I. Can't. Take. It. Anymore. Ahh! Yes!"

I pulled my finger from her ass and quickly moved and lifted her hips and pushed my dick into her. One or two pumps was all it was going to take and I would come I was so fucking turned on.

"Yes! Oh God yes! Fuck me harder!" she cried out as I slammed into her.

"Azurdee…baby, I'm going to come."

She wrapped her legs around me and began moving in perfect rhythm with me. Nothing felt better than being with her like this.

I called out her name as I poured myself into her body.

I reached up and untied her hands and she wrapped her arms around my body. Her legs were still wrapped around me as my dick twitched and jumped inside her. I was breathing so heavy as I tried to come down from one of the most amazing orgasms of my life.

She was gasping for air as she barely said, "Don't pull out yet."

I wasn't sure how long we laid wrapped up in each other. We were one and there was nothing like it in the world.

I heard a sniffle and I pulled back to see her crying. My heart dropped instantly.

"Did I hurt you? I'm so sorry I did that, I should have asked. I'm so sorry."

She smiled and shook her head. "No…everything we just did was amazing. I loved every second of it and you didn't hurt me. I'm just so happy. I never want this moment to end. I love you inside of me. I love your warmth, your smell, and your touch. God…I feel so complete when we are together."

I slowly began moving in and out of her again as I said, "I feel the same way, *mi amor*. I feel the same way." I couldn't believe my dick was growing hard again. I placed my elbows down on the bed as I took her face in my hands. She smiled as I began making love to her. I leaned down and kissed her. I poured nothing but love into the kiss and was so overcome with emotion I wanted to shout how much I loved her from the tallest mountain in the world.

I'd never in my life experienced such feelings. We kissed each other the entire time I made love to her. When we both pulled away from each other and looked into each other's eyes it was like we were looking into our souls.

"Michael. I'm coming."

I pushed my lips to hers again as we both came together. *Together.* Everything in this life from now on I wanted to do together.

I slowly pulled out of her and moved to the side as she pushed her body into mine and we both settled in to fall asleep. Right before I fell asleep, Azurdee whispered, "I love the way you want me. The way you love me."

I pulled her closer to me and whispered back, "You've got my heart, *mi amor*. I'll want you and love you forever."

"Mmm…" she said as her breathing slowed and she fell asleep. I closed my eyes tightly and when I opened them I felt a tear slide down my face.

I smiled and whispered, "I'll love you forever."

CHAPTER 34
Azurdee

Five Months Later

"HOW ARE YOU DOING?" my mother asked from behind me.

I gradually turned around and smiled at her. "I'm not going to lie. I'm nervous as hell. My hands won't stop sweating. Hell, my body won't stop sweating. I feel sick to my stomach and all I really want to do is see him."

She laughed and nodded her head. "You're doing great then!"

I looked at her confused. "Huh? Mom, am I suppose to be freaking out like this? I've been so calm the last five months planning this wedding. I mean, we've built a house, planned a wedding and started Lark's cattle business. Why is this freaking me out? I want it more than anything, so why…why am I terrified out of my wits?"

She walked up to me and took my hands in hers. "Sit down, darling."

We both sat down and I took a long breath.

"Do you love him?"

"Yes! Mom, I love him so much I can hardly stand to be away

from him." I looked around and then back at my mother. "Oh God! Is that even healthy? Should I need him so much? Should I be sitting here before my wedding thinking about how I just want to be in his arms? Is it healthy to want someone so much?"

She let out a giggle and said, "My goodness. I'm having déjà vu right now!"

I pulled back and looked at her confused.

She took a small breath and let it out. "When I married your father, I felt the same exact way. I remember telling my mother I felt like I was addicted to him."

I put my hand up to my mouth and said, "Yes!"

She chuckled again and said, "What you are feeling, honey, is true love. A love like this doesn't come along to everyone. Embrace it. Shelter it. Nurture it, and never take it for granted."

I nodded my head and wiped the tears from my face. My mother reached up and wiped a tear away as she said, "Marriage takes work. Even the strongest of loves need to be taken care of."

A sob escaped my mouth and I said, "I love him so much, Mom. I just want to make him happy."

She tilted her head and grinned from ear to ear. "Your father and I just left Lark."

I sat up straighter and asked, "You did? How is he? How did he look?"

She giggled and said, "Yes, we did. He was nervous just like you, but when he saw your father I'm pretty sure I saw that Marine's hands start shaking."

I laughed and shook my head.

She winked and said, "He looked very handsome, but then again he always looks handsome."

"Yeah he does," I said as I wiggled my eyebrows up and down.

She got up and rolled her eyes. "You have got it bad, my dear."

I stood up and hugged her. "Thank you, Mom."

The door opened and Jessie, Ryn, and Stephanie, the wedding planner, came walking in.

Jessie smiled and said, "We need to start getting you ready."

My mom kissed me on the cheek and said, "I'll be back in a bit."

I nodded my head and fought to hold back my tears. When she walked out, I looked over at Jessie. "How is he?"

She laughed and said, "Well, considering Scott is going on and on about a man card or something and Lark just keeps telling him to fuck off...I think he is doing good."

I grinned and asked, "Do you think we can change our minds and just elope?"

Jessie put her finger to her chin and looked up as she said, "Umm...no. Too late for that, my dear. Sit down so I can do your hair. We are running out of time."

I let out a sigh and sat down. I had asked everyone to give me a few minutes to myself and that's when they sent my mother in.

I watched as Jessie worked her magic with my long brown hair. She had pulled it up and piled it on top of my head loosely. I had a few curls hanging down to frame my face.

"The key here is hairspray," Jessie said as I busted out laughing.

Stephanie looked at us with a questioning look. "What is so funny?"

Jessie shrugged and said, "Inside joke."

Next came the makeup. Ryn was doing my makeup. When Lark and I talked about our wedding, we knew we wanted two things: keep it small and have the wedding at the beach where our journey to love officially began.

I wanted my makeup to look as natural as possible, but I told Ryn smoky eyes were a must. I knew it would bring out the light brown in my eyes and Lark always talked about how much he loved my eyes.

Ryn turned me around and said, "If you cry, don't worry. I used waterproof mascara."

I grinned as I turned and looked into the mirror. I let out a gasp and gently touched the side of my face. "Ryn. I look…"

Ryn, Jessie and Stephanie all whispered, "Beautiful."

I turned around and looked at her. "I love you." I held back the sob I almost let out as she pulled me up and into a hug. I pulled back and looked at Jessie and Ryn. "I love you both so much. Thank you for being here."

The music began playing and I looked at Stephanie and said, "Oh God."

She smiled sweetly at me and said, "Deep breaths. You're marrying the love of your life."

I nodded my head and followed her over to the dress that was hanging up.

I felt my heart drop when Stephanie unzipped the bag. "Oh wow. It's just as beautiful as it was the first time I saw it," Jessie said.

Jessie, Ryn and I had gone to Houston for the dress. I had seen a Galia Lahav dress in a bridal magazine and had set my sights on finding it. I knew the moment I tried it on it was the perfect dress. It softly embraced my curves with the French lace corset top and the draped silk netting exposed my legs from mid-thigh down. The lace appliques and pearl embellishments added the perfect touch. It was perfect for a beach wedding.

I opened my robe and dropped it on the floor and Jessie attempted to whistle. "Hot damn girl. Look at you in that sexy-ass corset! Lark is going to fall over."

I wrinkled my nose and giggled. I had bought a practically see-through corset that jacked my breasts almost up to my chin. I knew Jessie was right. Lark was going to be so over stimulated tonight and just the thought made me wet. I closed my eyes and turned my wayward thoughts to something else.

When we carefully put the dress on and got the silk netting to fall just perfect, I turned and looked at myself in the mirror.

I let out a gasp and shook my head. "I look like a princess."

"You are a princess."

I turned to see my father standing there. "Daddy," I whispered.

He walked up to me and took the veil from Jessie and motioned for me to turn around as he placed the veil on my head. Jessie handed him a few pins to pin it in my hair.

"I figured if I had to lift it up I should be able to put it on."

I smiled and watched in the mirror as my father smoothed out my veil.

I turned and looked up into his eyes. "I love him, Daddy."

He nodded and said, "I know you do, princess. I know he loves you too. His eyes light up at just the mention of your name. I know he will love you and take care of you, but I need you to remember something."

I nodded and waited for him to talk. He seemed to be struggling not to cry and I was doing the same.

He placed his hands on the side of my face and grinned slightly. "No one…will ever love you…the way I do."

"Oh Daddy."

He leaned down and gently kissed me on the nose through the veil. "Are you ready?"

I nodded my head and said, "Never more ready." I had instantly relaxed. I was no longer nervous. I was now excited to see the love of my life.

I slipped on my shoes and put my hand on my father's arm as we made our way to Lark.

Lark and I both decided it was only going to be family and our closet friends. I had asked both Jessie and Ryn to be in the wedding since Lark couldn't pick Scott or Tristan as best man so he picked them both. Jessie was my matron of honor and Ryn was my maid of honor.

I couldn't help but notice the way Tristan couldn't keep his eyes off of Ryn for the last three days. At the rehearsal last night and dinner, he kept trying to not look at her, but he did a shitty job of doing it.

Before Ryn walked down the aisle, she turned back and looked at me. I was standing around the corner so I couldn't see anyone yet.

She smiled weakly and said, "Damn Williams brothers." She sniffled and said, "Stupid good-looking bastards."

I laughed and gave her a thumbs-up. I knew it was hard for her to see Tristan, but I was so relieved when he showed up alone. I told Lark if Tristan brought Liberty, I would kick him so hard in the balls he wouldn't be able to use his dick for a year. I'm pretty sure Lark passed that along because not only did Tristan show up alone, he made it known he and Liberty were just an off-and-on couple for right now. Lark pointed out he had said it loud enough for Ryn to hear.

"You ready, princess?"

My father's voice pulled me out of my thoughts and I nodded my head. "Ready." Stephanie handed me the bouquet of red roses. I smiled as I looked at the roses. Jessie and Ryn also had a smaller bouquet of red roses. The decorations for the wedding I kept simple. I wanted a white arch at the end of the massive deck that faced out to the ocean. It was covered in red and white roses. The tables had white linens, silver plastic plates and flatware and a simple red candle in sand sitting among red rose petals in the middle of each table. It was elegant...yet simple.

When the wedding march began, I took a deep breath and we began walking. I had to walk around the pool and for the last month I had dreamt the same damn dream each night. I was walking with my father and slipped and fell into the pool. I would wake up sweating and calling out *no* every single time I dreamed that stupid dream.

As we walked along the pool, I watched where I was going very carefully. "Honey, you have to breathe or you will pass out, and then you really will fall in the pool," my father whispered. I let out the breath I was holding and began taking in deep breaths.

As we rounded the pool I finally looked up and saw Lark. My mouth dropped open as he stood there in black pants, a white shirt, a black silk vest, and matching black tie. My heart began beating so fast and so loud I was sure everyone could hear it.

"Take in some air, angel," my father whispered.

I sucked in a breath of air. I hadn't even noticed I was holding my breath. As I moved closer to him his smile grew bigger and bigger. His eyes looked up and down my body and I was on fire from head to toe. How he could turn me on while I walked with my father I had no idea. I licked my lips and he arched his eyebrow.

My father walked us up and stopped in front of Lark. He raised my veil and leaned in and gently kissed me on the cheek. He was about to place my hand in Lark's hand and the way he was looking at Lark made me giggle.

My father reached out for Lark's hand and said, "You may have been in the Marines…but I can still break you like a twig if you hurt her."

Lark's smile faded and he swallowed hard as he said, "Yes, sir."

He placed my hand in Lark's and his voice cracked as he said, "Take care of my baby girl."

Lark nodded his head and said, "Yes, sir. Forever and always."

We stood before our family and friends as Pastor Nickels began talking. Lark and I decided that instead of saying our own vows, we would read the letters we wrote to each other. I barely made it through reading my letter, and when Lark had to stop three times during his letter, Scott would lean over and say something about his man card.

When it finally came time for Pastor Nickels to announce husband and wife, I was longing for Lark's touch. The way he kept smiling at me and rubbing his thumbs across the top of my hands, and wiping the tears away from his face…it all played with every single emotion. My heart was bursting with so much happiness and love I just wanted to scream out how happy I was.

"You may kiss the bride," Pastor Nickels said with a smile.

Lark placed his hands on my face and used his thumb to wipe away a tear. "You are breathtaking. You are officially mine," he whispered.

I whispered back, "I've always been yours."

He leaned down and kissed me so sweetly. I slid my hand behind his neck and deepened our kiss. We were so lost in our kiss, it took Tristan stepping up to us and saying, "Our parents are watching y'all. I'm pretty sure her daddy is ready to kill you."

Lark pulled back and laughed. "I love you."

"I love you too."

CHAPTER 35

Lark

I SAT BACK AND watched Azurdee move around talking to everyone. If I didn't get her alone soon, I was going to sneak her off somewhere and make love to her. The moment she looked me up and down and licked her lips when she walked down the aisle, I'd been fighting a hard-on. Her wedding dress was driving me crazy. The fact that I could see her legs through the damn thing was bad enough, but I had to threaten my own cousin's life for looking at them too long.

"How many different ways have you come up with to take her away from the reception?" Scott said as he sat down and handed me a beer.

I chortled and said, "I lost count after twenty."

Scott threw his head back and laughed. "Sounds like me. I couldn't wait to get Jessie alone. This isn't even the best part."

Tristan walked up and sat down as he hit both Scott and I on the backs. He tossed back his bottle and took a long drink of beer. "Slow down, big brother."

He rolled his eyes and said, "I can't seem to drink enough these days."

I looked at him with a questioning look as he shook his head.

I glanced back at Scott and asked, "What do you mean this isn't even the best part?"

He winked and said, "You think the dress knocks you out. Wait until you see what's under it. Jessie about had me acting like a crazed man. I just wanted to rip it off her body."

Tristan laughed. "I heard what's under the dress is almost as important as the dress itself."

Selena Gomez's "Stars Dance" started playing. I looked over toward Azurdee and she looked at me and raised her eyebrows and gave me a sexy-ass grin. I couldn't help but think of that day in the barn when I told her I loved her.

"What's next?" I asked as I looked at Scott.

"Let's see, you've cut the cake. Now you just have to do the dance."

"Then we can go?"

Tristan laughed and said, "Jesus, do you have a helicopter waiting for you two?"

I snapped my head and looked at him. I tilted my head and wanted to ask how he knew. I'd called Skip and asked him for a favor. I was taking Azurdee to Skip's house right outside of Cancun. I didn't want to take her to Belize. Not when I'd had so many one-night stands in that damn house.

"Jesus Christ. Are you kidding me, dude?" He shook his head and ran his hand through his hair. "I fucking knew when you took those flying lessons I should have taken them with you. You're killing me here. Some day when I get married, Azurdee will tell my wife 'I got flown in a helicopter to my honeymoon' and then what am I going to do?"

I gave him a snarky smile and said, "Hire me to fly y'all somewhere."

He stood up and said, "Fuck you, asshole."

Scott and I both started laughing as I stood up and made my way over to the DJ. Azurdee had pretty much taken care of all the plans for the wedding, so when I asked if I could pick out our wedding song and surprise her with it, she said of course.

I walked back over toward where Azurdee was standing talking to her mom and my mom.

"Ladies and gentlemen. It is now time for the bride and groom to dance."

Azurdee looked around and the second our eyes met she gave me that smile that melted my heart, made me weak in the knees, and still caused my stomach to do some weird flipping action that I would never truly be able to explain.

She walked up to me and I took her in my arms. "Finally," she said as we made our way to the dance floor.

I placed my finger on her chin and lifted her eyes to mine. "After this, we're leaving. I want to see what's under this amazing dress you're wearing."

She gave me the sexiest smile and said, "Not much."

"Oh Christ."

"Ladies and gentlemen. Mr. and Mrs. Michael Williams."

Before the song started I said, "I loved you the first moment I saw you, Azurdee." I shook my head and said, "I pray to God I'm not dreaming right now."

Brad Paisley's "Then" began playing, and Azurdee instantly began tearing up. When the chorus began, I pulled her to me tighter and put my lips to her ear and began singing to her. I could feel her crying in my arms, so I held her tighter.

As I sung the song to her she kept grabbing my shirt in her hand. When the song ended we just stood there. I knew she was crying still, so I gave her a few seconds before I pulled away from her. I smiled as I wiped her tears away with my thumbs and gently brushed my lips across her lips.

Katy Perry's "Dark Horse" started and Azurdee and I both looked at each other. She bit down on her lip and then said, "What a perfect song to start off our journey."

I gave her the sexiest smile I could and began dancing with her. "Just remember, our parents are here," she said as she raised her eyebrow up.

I laughed as I pulled her to me so she could feel my hard-on. "I want you," I whispered.

She let out a small moan and said, "Give it to me."

Her eyes darkened and my heartbeat picked up. I slowly shook my head and took a few steps away from her. "Say good-bye to your parents. I'll meet you in the kitchen in two minutes."

She made a little squeak sound and turned and walked toward her parents as I turned and walked to mine. I couldn't help but laugh at the irony of it all. The first time that damn song played I was in control and now…she was the one in control and I was ready to do or give her anything she wanted.

Ten minutes later we were in my truck and making our way to where the helicopter was. When we pulled up, Azurdee sat there, frozen.

"We're…flying…in a…helicopter?" She turned and stared at me.

Oh shit. I hadn't even thought she might be afraid of flying in a helicopter.

I looked back at it and then back at her. "Umm…yeah. Shit, I didn't even think to ask if you would be okay with it."

She jumped out of the truck as I got out and walked over to

her. She looked at it and then turned to me. "Are you flying it?"

"I was gonna, but…" She put her finger up to my lips and said, "Stop talking. I'm so incredibly turned on right now you have no idea."

Now it was me who wanted to make the little girly sound. I quickly kissed her on the lips and grabbed our suitcase out of the back of the truck. I had told Azurdee where we were going and to pack light because I intended on having her naked most of the time. We both packed all our stuff in one suitcase.

I grabbed her hand and we made our way over to the helicopter. I saw Jason standing there and I smiled. "What in the hell?" I said as I walked up to him.

"Azurdee, it's a pleasure seeing you again."

Azurdee smiled and said, "Yes, it is. Things going well with you?"

Jason nodded and said, "Yes ma'am."

He looked back at me and said, "When Skip said you called in a favor I told him I had to be the one to deliver this to you. I'll take your truck back to your parents beach house, and I believe your brother Tristan will be here to pick you back up in two weeks."

I nodded and said, "Sounds good. Thanks so much, Jason."

As I got Azurdee all buckled in and secure, I looked down and saw her gripping the seat so hard her knuckles were turning white.

I handed her the headphones and gave her a thumbs-up as she gave me a weak smile. I headed over and got in and put my headphones on. I looked at her and said, "Baby, are you afraid of flying?"

She let out a nervous chuckle and said, "Not in planes. In a helicopter, with my husband flying it? Yes. I'm nervous."

I got the goofiest grin on my face and my heart felt like it was soaring. She looked at me and said, "What?"

"Say that again?"

She made a funny face and asked, "Which part?"

"The part where you called me your husband."

She smiled and bit down on her lower lip. "I said I was nervous that my husband is fixin' to fly us in a helicopter."

I reached for her hand and kissed the back of it. "You know I would never put your life in danger, right? I'll always protect you, *mi amor*."

She nodded her head and said, "I know. I'm totally okay. I'm just ready to get out of this dress."

"Is what you're wearing under the dress going to steal my breath away like your wedding dress did?"

She looked away and shrugged. "Most likely. Especially since you can see through it."

"Oh hell. Let's go. Now."

She laughed and I went through all the preflight protocol. Before long we were on our way and Azurdee was talking up a storm. She was excited, exhausted or nervous as hell. I was betting on the last.

As we landed on the helipad, I looked at Azurdee. She let out the breath she was holding and looked at me and gave me thumbs-up…again. It must have been the twentieth one she gave me since I took off. I laughed and shut down the helicopter. I'd never been to Skip's place here, but from the looks of it, it was pretty nice.

I grabbed the suitcase and then her hand as we made our way to the house. A young lady came out and introduced herself to us.

"Hello, Mr. and Mrs. Williams. My name is Maria. Mr. Martin asked me to make sure that you were well taken care of for the next two weeks. I'm at your complete disposal."

Azurdee and I both shook her hand. Azurdee said, "Oh my gosh, it is beautiful here." The house faced out to the Gulf of Mexico and I had to admit the view was breathtaking.

We made our way into the house and Maria showed us around as she asked her husband Jose to take our suitcase to the master bedroom.

"Now any meals you would like for me to cook, just let me know ahead of time so that I can prepare them for you. Jose will also be stopping by if you need anything. We live in a small cottage just on the other side of the property, but just push this button and it will call my *casa*."

Azurdee and I both nodded our heads. When she finally showed us to the master bedroom Azurdee collapsed onto the bed. I turned and looked at Maria and said, "I'm pretty positive we won't be needing anything tonight. Maybe breakfast in the morning?"

Azurdee popped up and looked at me with her mouth hanging open. Maria nodded and smiled slightly as she excused herself and shut the door behind her. Azurdee waited a few seconds before standing up and saying, "Lark! That was so rude. You practically told her to get out."

I began taking my tie, vest and shoes off. I wanted out of these damn clothes and I wanted her out of that dress even more. Azurdee looked at me and raised her eyebrows as she watched me undress.

"You in a rush for something, Mr. Williams?"

"Yes I am, Mrs. Williams. I'm in a rush to see what's under that dress."

I stripped completely down to my boxer briefs as she stood there and watched me. "Your turn now, baby. Turn around."

She turned around and looked over her shoulder at me. I carefully unbuttoned her dress and ran my fingers down her exposed back. Her body shivered and I couldn't help but smile knowing my touch still evoked such a reaction from her.

She turned around and took a few steps back. She was holding up her dress as she asked, "Are you ready?"

I licked my lips and nodded my head. She let the dress fall and my eyes took in every square inch of her beautiful body.

Her corset was lace and I could see completely through it. Her breasts were pushed up so far and the way her hard nipples were poking through the soft fabric instantly had my dick throbbing.

"Holy shit. I'm the luckiest son of a bitch on earth."

She giggled as she stepped out of the dress that was pooled on the floor and asked, "Do you like it?"

My eyes moved down her body to the garter, the thigh highs, and her high heel shoes.

"Turn around," I said as I moved my finger in a circle.

She turned slowly, and that's when I saw she had a thong on.

"My God…what your body does to me."

Her cheeks flushed and it was all I could do to hold back.

"Azurdee, right now I want you so much, but you have to tell me how you want this. Baby, I'll take it slow or I'll go fast and hard."

She looked slightly away and then looked back at me as she slowly began slipping her thong off. She took her finger and placed it in her mouth as she dragged it down her bottom lip to her chest and then to her nipple.

"Honestly? I want to be fucked by my husband."

I dropped my boxers so fast I almost tripped getting them off. I moved to her, but she put up her hand to stop me.

"Wait. At some point during this honeymoon I want to tie you up and have my wicked way with you. And maybe you could do what you did before…that one time."

Jesus H. Christ. I just died and went to heaven.

"Baby, I will do whatever you want."

She dropped her hand and I quickly walked up to her and picked her up as she wrapped her legs around me. I walked her up against the wall and pushed my dick inside her. She let out a small whimper and then began riding me like she couldn't get enough.

"Faster!" she cried out. When she dropped her head back and began calling out my name, I grabbed her and walked over to the bed. I put her down and pulled out as I flipped her over and took her from behind.

"Fuck…you look so goddamn amazing in this."

"Harder, Lark. Harder!"

I grabbed her hips and began to thrust into her deeper and harder.

"Yes! I want more. Give me more!" she cried out. I reached up and grabbed a handful of her hair and pushed in hard and deep. When I felt her squeeze down on my dick and start calling out my name, I poured myself into her as I called out her name with each thrust.

I pulled out and she dropped to the bed as I dropped next to her.

She panted for air as she said, "My. God. Sex. With. You. Is. Amazing."

I shook my head and said, "It's only…because I'm with… you."

We laid there for a good ten minutes before she stood up and began taking off her shoes. I sat up and moved to the edge of the bed where she placed her foot in between my legs. I unclipped the garter belt and slowly began taking off her stockings. She took her one foot down and put the other up as she reached up and pulled out a few pins and her beautiful hair fell down on top of her shoulders.

She turned around and I stood up and began taking off the corset. When I unbuttoned the last button, she let out a breath of air and said, "Thank God."

She spun around and looked at me. "I'm starved. Do you think there is anything in the kitchen to make something?"

I walked over to our suitcase and opened it up. I pulled out two T-shirts and threw her one. "Keep your panties off, though."

She blushed as she slipped the T-shirt on. It fell to the middle of her thighs and it was probably sexier than the damn corset she just took off. I slipped my boxer briefs on and she put her hand on her hips as she tilted her head and said, "Hey. How come you get to wear underwear and I can't?"

I shrugged and took her hand in mine as we made our way down to the kitchen. I sat down at the bar as Azurdee began looking around. She let out a giggle and said, "French toast?"

I did a fist pump and said, "Yes! Perfect first meal as husband and wife."

She nodded and said, "I agree."

I watched as my beautiful wife began whipping out French toast almost the exact same way as the first day I met her. I watched her every move and thanked God for the blessings in my life at least five times as I watched her cook.

She set two plates down in front of us and we both ate in silence. Azurdee only ate half of her French toast while I finished off mine and the rest of hers. I loved her cooking so damn much.

I threw my napkin down on the plate and smiled as I said, "Done! Woman, get me a beer now!"

Azurdee laughed as she rolled her eyes.

"What were you thinking about? While we were eating, I mean?" she asked as she ran her fingers along the edge of the T-shirt.

I shrugged and said, "Us. How much I love you. How much I love your cooking." I said as I wiggled my eyebrows up and down. "How much I want to make love to you on this kitchen island."

She placed her finger in her mouth and her eyes turned almost black with desire. I gave her a look and said, "Why, Mrs. Williams, would you like for me to take you on the island?"

She nodded her head and said, "Very much so." I took the two plates and put them in the sink and then turned around and picked her up and set her down on the island.

"Move back baby, and spread your legs open."

"Oh God, Lark."

We ended up making love on the island and then in the living room where I took her from behind as she leaned over the leather sofa. Then on the stairs and finally in the shower where we both collapsed to the floor and just sat there with the hot water running on us.

"I think you have officially worn me out," I said as I pulled her closer to me.

"I'm so tired I just want to sleep in the shower," she said with a yawn.

I got up and turned off the shower. I reached down and pulled her up. We stepped out of the giant shower and I wrapped a towel around me as I dried her off. I picked her up and carried her into the bedroom. I pulled the sheets back and gently laid her down on the bed and covered her up. I sat down on the bed and ran my hand down along her face.

"If I haven't told you, you looked beautiful today."

She smiled and said, "Mmm…you have. Like a million times."

"I wish I could rewind this whole day and relive it again."

She opened her eyes and said, "Me too."

I leaned down and kissed her gently on the lips and said, "I haven't given you my wedding present yet. We have to be home for you to see it."

She barely smiled. "Mmm. Okay."

I smiled to myself knowing how happy she would be. Ralph had told me Azurdee had been looking shortly after the fire into buying a coffee shop that was for sale in Marble Falls I bought it and was planning on surprising her when we got back home. I couldn't wait to see her face when I pulled up and she saw the new sign.

"Go to sleep, baby. Rest up. We have ten more days of this."

"Mmm…can we just stay in the bedroom the whole time?" she said as she closed her eyes again.

I let out a chuckle and said, "If that's what you want, baby, that's what we'll do."

She shook her head slightly and said, "No. I'd like to see the beach at least once."

I ran my hand through her hair and whispered, "Thank you."

She snapped her eyes open and looked at me. She sat up and asked, "For what?"

I swallowed hard and said, "For always loving me. For making me feel like I deserved your love. For accepting me for who I was and never judging me."

"Lark…I will love you forever. Our love is and will always be a lasting love."

I kissed her gently on the lips and began pushing her back down until she was lying down again.

I stood up and stripped my towel off and crawled into the bed and next to my wife. I'd never felt so much love from one person in my life.

"Azurdee...I love you so much."

I slowly pulled her up against my body and wrapped my arms around her.

"I love you too, Michael."

I listened as her breathing got deeper and slower. When I closed my eyes and began drifting off to sleep I dreamed of a brunette with shoulder-length hair walking along the beach with her hands resting on her swollen belly. I walked up to her and when she turned around she smiled the biggest smile I'd ever seen. My knees about buckled and my stomach did that weird little flip it does when she smiles at me like that.

She looked down and then back up into my eyes and said, "We've been waiting for you."

I smiled and placed my hands on Azurdee's stomach. "You don't have to wait anymore, *mi amor*. I'm here."

EPILOGUE

Azurdee

One Year Later

I WALKED ALONG THE beach and tried my best to listen to Joyce go on and on about how excited everyone was.

I would say the occasional "Oh I know." Or "I'm so excited, too." Every now and then I'd have to throw in an "Aww… that is so sweet," when she would talk about something someone in the family was making for the baby.

I placed my hand on my stomach and felt my little angel. She was super active today and I was pretty sure it was because daddy woke mommy up this morning with a good hard fu…

"Azurdee? Darling, are you listening to me?"

I stopped and looked at Joyce and said, "I'm sorry. I was lost in thought. I was thinking about this morning."

"What about this morning?" she asked.

Nice Azurdee. What are you going to tell her now? Oh you know Joyce, I was thinking how your son had me on my hands and knees and fucked the hell out of my almost nine-month pregnant self.

"There is my favorite girl," Lark said from behind me. I turned and smiled as I saw Lark walking toward me. He stopped dead in his tracks and looked at me with the strangest look. I tilted my head and asked, "Are you okay?"

He walked up to me and ran his hands through my hair. I had Joyce cut it for me this morning in preparation for the baby. It fell just below my shoulders now.

"Your hair," he whispered. He placed his hand on my stomach and looked into my eyes.

"Do you not like it shorter? I just had to get it cut—your mom did it for me earlier."

The corner of his mouth lifted in that oh so sexy way of his as a smile spread across his face.

He shook his head and said, "I love it. It just…it reminds me of a dream I had about you…twice."

I made a goofy face and said, "Oh. You dreamed I cut my hair?"

He smiled and nodded his head.

He put both hands on my stomach and dropped to his knees in the sand. "*¿Cómo está mi niña?*"

I ran my hands through his hair as he talked to our daughter. I loved his hair a bit longer. He had grown it out a bit after he got out of the Corps. It wasn't too long, but it was long enough to where I could run my fingers through it and grab it as we made love.

Lark stood up and placed his hand behind my neck and pulled my lips to his. I was still shocked at how passionately he would kiss me in front of people, especially his parents.

"How do you feel?" he asked against my lips.

I nodded and said, "Good. She's kicking a lot today. She's been very active since this morning." If I hadn't known any better I would say my husband just blushed.

Joyce clapped her hands and said, "Okay, your father and I are leaving in a bit, so you two are going to be okay, right?"

Lark rolled his eyes and said, "Yes, Mom. We're heading back today too. With Azurdee getting so close to her due date we are going to hunker down."

Joyce grinned from ear to ear and I could see the excitement in her eyes. "Your father and I will plan on coming up after the baby is born. I want y'all to settle in first before we come bursting in and intruding."

Lark nodded his head and said, "If only the other grandparents thought that way."

I hit him in the stomach and said, "Stop it."

We all headed back to the beach house, where we said our good-byes to Joyce and Peter and began loading up the new Toyota Sequoia we had bought.

"How many kids are we planning on having again? " I said as Lark helped me into the passenger seat. He shrugged and said, "I would think no more than two."

I nodded my head. "So tell me why we needed this tank?"

He looked at me like I was stupid as he answered, "It's safe." He shut the door and made his way to the driver's side. For the next thirty minutes I had to hear all about the safety features of our new car...again. I finally put my head back and slowly drifted off to sleep.

*** *

One Month Later

My eyes snapped open when I heard Akayla start crying. I went to get up, but Lark reached for my arm and pulled me back. He leaned over and kissed me as he whispered, "Rest, *mi amor*. I've got this."

I fell back and let out a sigh. "Thank you." Lark had been so amazing with the baby. She was almost a week old and the apple of his eye. I giggled as I thought about Scott and Jessie coming over and Lark not wanting to give Akayla to Scott. I'd never seen Scott look so mad in my life.

I closed my eyes and attempted to go back to sleep, but I could hear Lark talking to the baby. I got out of bed and quietly made my way to the kitchen. I stopped around the corner and listened to him talking to her.

"There are so many things I'm going to teach you. One is how to shoot a gun."

I rolled my eyes and smiled as I shook my head.

"Then I'm going to teach you how to hunt. Your mommy will have to teach you how to cook it all though, 'cause daddy is no good at that kind of stuff."

He got quiet and I peeked around the corner. He was walking while he fed her, and he had stopped to look at a picture. The picture was of he and I when we first started building this house.

"I have so many wishes for you my sweet little angel, but one of my biggest wishes is that you find a love like your mommy and daddy share. I love her so much and sometimes I'll watch her, and she doesn't know I'm watching her, and my heart just overflows with love. I mean it just pours over. She's the most amazing woman I've ever met. Every morning when she wakes up and smiles at me I have to pinch myself to make sure I'm not dreaming."

I put my hand up to my mouth and tried to hold back my tears.

"I want that kind of love for you. Now I know that no man could ever possibly love you as much as I do. And we will have to make it known to all boys who even have an interest in you that

I'm a trained killer. And a damn good shot."

I giggled and shook my head.

"Akayla, my sweet little angel. I never thought I would be able to love someone like I love your mother. And when I let her into my heart I couldn't imagine there would be room for another until your mommy showed me her pregnancy test and told me I was going to be a daddy. I didn't even have to see or hear you to know that I loved you so much."

When I heard his voice crack I walked into the living room and he turned to look at me. I could never sneak up on him. I wasn't sure if it was his military or CIA training or if he just felt my presence when I walked into a room, but sneaking up on him was nearly impossible.

I walked up to him and looked down at our baby. I kissed her on the forehead and then kissed him.

"I love you, Lark. I love you so much."

His eyes filled with tears and it was the second time since I'd known him that I saw a tear slip from his eyes. I reached up and wiped it away.

"Thank you," he whispered.

"For what?" I asked.

"For loving me. Believing in me and standing by me, and every crazy idea I've had and you've supported. Thank you for this beautiful and precious gift in my arms."

I ran my finger along her cheek and said, "You had a hand in that last one."

He chuckled and looked down at our daughter who stopped drinking and stared into his eyes. The way they were looking at each other caused a shiver to run through my body.

"I'm going to make the same promise to you that I made your

mommy. I promise to always protect you and love you."

He pulled his eyes away from Akayla and looked me in the eyes as another tear traveled down his cheek and he whispered, "Unconditionally."

Undeniable LOVE

A JOURNEY OF love NOVEL

Tristan

I HAD BEEN SITTING on the beach for the last hour just staring out at the black ocean. I tipped the beer bottle back and drank the last of my beer.

"Well hell. Looks like I have to go back," I said as I got up and brushed the sand off my pants. I turned and looked back at the house. Lark and Azurdee had left two hours ago for their honeymoon and I couldn't take watching Ryn another second.

I sucked in a deep breath of salty air and slowly let it out. My phone went off and I pulled it out of my pocket. I sighed when I saw it was Liberty.

Liberty: Just letting you know I'm thinking about you. If you want me to join you I'll come down. Just text me back and I'll be there.

Me: I think I just need some time to think, Liberty. We need this time apart.

Liberty: I didn't mean to push you. I'm always pushing you, I know. I just really wanted to see your parents and would have loved to have seen the wedding but I understand you have your reasons for going alone. Things haven't been so great with us lately. I'll work on that. Promise.

Me: We'll talk when I get back to Austin.

Liberty: Okay. I love you, Tristan.

I let out a sigh and shook my head. I've never told Liberty I loved her. I wasn't sure anymore how I felt about her. All she had been doing is pushing an engagement ever since she found out Lark and Azurdee were getting married. When I thought of my future I didn't see Liberty. I only saw…Ryn. That scared the piss out of me.

I turned my phone to silent and shoved it into my pocket. I started heading back to the house and began putting on my game face. The one I'd been wearing for the last ten months. The one where everyone thought I was happy, but deep down inside I was the unhappiest I'd ever been in my life.

I walked up the stairs to the deck and the first person I saw was Ryn. She was leaning against the railing with her head back and her eyes closed. There was no one else out here.

She looked tired. I smiled when I thought about what I had overheard earlier when Mom and Jessie were talking. Ryn had taken a two-week vacation and was renting a condo on the beach just two houses down from here. I already began planning ways to 'run into her' while we were both here.

She hadn't talked to me in over ten months. No matter how many times I called and left her messages begging her to call me, she never would.

Her cell phone rang and she quickly answered it. I walked around to the other side of the deck and sat down to where she couldn't see me.

"Hey Dodge. Are you on your way? Yes. I thought I could, but

I can't. I need you."

Dodge? Who the fuck is Dodge?

She laughed at something he said and then she let out a sigh. "Well, considering I still need my RFB, I'd say yes…it's been a sucky last three days.

I peeked around the corner and saw her smiling. She reached her hand up and began playing with her nipple.

What the fuck?

"That sounds like heaven. Yes. I'm going to need it a lot. I don't know, you'd think after all this time you'd have been able to fuck him out of my head and heart. Maybe you're not as good as you think you are?"

My mouth dropped open and I quickly turned back and stared out in the night sky.

She laughed again and said, "I'm still at the wedding. Yes. It was hard to see him. I don't know. Maybe, I've thought about that. Yes. I realize I only use you for sex to forget about Tristan but maybe I'm falling for you and just want your company. You ever think of that?"

My heart started beating faster and I wanted to pound this ass-hole's head in.

She let out a sigh and said, "Okay. I'll see you then. Oh trust me. I'll be waiting and I will most certainly be ready for you. Yes naked. Hey Dodge? Hurry please. I need to be fucked in a bad way. Bye."

She let out a sigh and then I swore I heard her crying. I slowly stood up. She was looking out toward the ocean. Her shoulders were moving up and down and when I saw her wipe away her tears, my knees about buckled out from underneath me.

I started making my way toward her. I didn't want to walk up on her crying, so I cleared my throat and asked, "May I join you?"

She quickly wiped her tears away and looked the other way.

"It's your house," she whispered.

"How have you been, Ryn?"

She turned and looked at me. If looks could kill I'd be laying on the floor right now.

"You've ignored me for three days and *now* you ask how I've been?"

I shrugged my shoulders and said, "I wasn't sure you wanted to talk to me."

She let out a small laugh. "Usually people attempt to talk to a person before they make that assumption."

"Well, considering I've been calling you for months, and you ignore my calls..."

She took a step back and shook her head. "You're seeing... another...girl."

"It's not like that. We are kind of off and on. I mean...I'm not seeing her right now."

She rolled her eyes and then looked into my eyes. "Do you have any idea how much you hurt me?"

I swallowed and said, "I just thought...I wasn't planning on..." I looked away and then back into her eyes. "I thought you just wanted to have fun, Ryn. Then you started acting different and I started having these feelings and... I was confused."

She shook her head. "The only thing that confused you is why you brought the wrong girl to meet mom and dad."

She turned and began walking into the house. I wanted to call out for her but I couldn't. My heart felt like it was squeezing in my chest as I stood there and listened to her retreating footsteps.

I turned and stared out at the dark ocean again.

That's what my heart felt like.

A dark deep sea of…darkness.

Thank You

I'd like to thank God for the amazing blessings in my life. There are so many people I'd love to thank, but just know you are all in my heart.

Darrin Elliott ~ I love you. You inspire me daily. You keep my life in focus and always believe in me. You let me bitch and you share me with so many people. You are my forever.

Lauren Elliott ~ I love that you read a book in a day. My heart is bursting with joy! I'm sorry you cried, but it was a good book huh?! I love you so much. You are the light that shines every day in my world. Now clean your damn room please!

Heather Davenport ~ Thank you! Thank you! Thank you! It will never be enough, but know how much I truly appreciate all that you do for me. Love you girl.

Kristin Mayer ~ You truly keep me sane and your overly chipper Voxer's in the morning really do make me smile. Okay, I'll say it. So do the damn little icons you send. Love ya girl!!

Jovana Shirley ~ What can I say? I'd be lost without you. Your kick-ass formatting is like no other. Thank you for putting up with me and my last-minute ideas! You're the best.

Kelly's Most Wanted ~ Thank you for sharing my stuff y'all. You'll never know what it truly means to me. BIG HUGS!

My HIPAA girls ~ Y'all are the true driving force behind pimping me out. Thank you from the bottom of my heart for being there for me always and doing what you do. I count myself lucky to have you has friends.

My beta readers – Jemma, JoJo, Heather, Kristin, and Nikki ~ Wow. Just wow. The fact that y'all take the time out of your busy world to help me with each one of these books blows my mind away. THANK YOU! Love each of y'all to the moon and back.

Shannon Cain ~ Your pictures bring to life what is in my head. Not many people can do that. Your talent is beyond words and you have a gift. Thank you for being a part of this journey with me.

My readers/friends ~ Every day you move me beyond words. Your posts, emails, and messages mean more to me than you will ever know. I'm so glad I get to share these crazy voices in my head with y'all. They scream to be heard and sometimes I feel like I can't write them down fast enough. I not only do this for my love of writing, but y'all as well. Thank you for allowing me to share my stories with you. I hope our relationship continues for a very, very, VERY….long time!

OTHER BOOKS BY KELLY ELLIOTT

Coming Soon

Blind Love (Book five in the Cowboys and Angels Series) coming July 2018

Blind Love (Book five in the Cowboys and Angels series) coming July 2018

This Love (Book six in the Cowboys and Angels series) coming October 2018

Seduced (Book one in the Austin Singles Series)

Delicate Promises (Standalone book) coming fall 2018

Guarded Hearts (Historical) coming 2018

Standalones

The Journey Home

Finding Forever (Co-written with Kristin Mayer)

Who We Were (Available on audio book)

The Playbook (Available on audio book)

Made for You (Available on audio)

Wanted Series

Wanted

Saved

Faithful

Believe

Cherished

A Forever Love

The Wanted Short Stories

All They Wanted

Entire series available on audio book except Believe, The Wanted Short Stories and All They Wanted

Love Wanted in Texas Series

Spin-off series to the WANTED Series

Without You

Saving You

Holding You

Finding You

Chasing You

Loving You

Entire series available on audio book

Please note Loving You combines the last book of the Broken and Love Wanted in Texas series.

Broken Series

Broken

Broken Dreams

Broken Promises

Broken Love

Book 1-3 available on audio book

The Journey of Love Series

Unconditional Love

Undeniable Love

Unforgettable Love

Entire series available on audio book

With Me Series

Stay With Me

Only With Me

Entire series on audiobook

Speed Series

Ignite

Adrenaline

Boston Love Series

(Available on audio book)

Searching for Harmony
Fighting for Love

YA Novels written under the pen name Ella Bordeaux

Beautiful

Forever Beautiful

Historical

Finding Forever by Kelly Elliott and Kristin Mayer (formally Predestined Hearts)

Guarded Hearts – Coming 2018

For upcoming books and more information about Kelly Elliott, please visit her website at www.kellyelliottauthor.com

For exclusive releases and giveaways signup for Kelly's newsletter at www.kellyelliottauthor.com/newsletter

PLAYLIST

"The One" by Static Cycle – Lark and Azurdee make love for the first time.

"Can't Stay Away" by Kris Allen – Lark after telling Azurdee she was everything he wanted.

"Gotta Be Tonight" by Lifehouse – Lark's song when shooting.

"My Weakness" by Kris Allen – Lark and Azurdee after have playful sex.

"Never Say Never" by The Fray – Lark and Azurdee making love in her house after he comes home from his first mission away from her.

"Desnudate" By Christina Aguilera – Lark and Azurdee dancing in the club.

"Talk Dirty To Me" by Jason Derulo – Lark and Azurdee dancing at Red 7.

"Tonight (I'm Fuckin' You) by Enrique Iglesias – Lark and Azurdee dancing at the Red 7.

"Give it 2 U" by Robin Thicke – Azurdee dancing with Jason at Red 7.

"Must be Doin' Something Right" by Billy Currington – Lark dancing with Azurdee at Red 7.

"Blank Page" by Christina Aguilera – Lark and Azurdee after he panics about calling her sweetheart.

"Story of My Life" by Static Cycle – Lark making love to Azurdee after he realizes he is in love with her.

"Berzerk" by Eminem – Lark taking Azurdee out on his bike for the day.

"Monster" by Kris Allen – Lark thinking he is no good for Azurdee.

"Even if I Wanted To" by Jason Aldean – Tristan and Azurdee dancing at the barn dance.

"Must Be Doin' Something Right" by Billy Currington – Lark and Azurdee dancing at the dance hall.

"Lookin' For That Girl" by Tim McGraw – Lark in the kitchen when his dad tells him not to let Azurdee go.

"Stars Dance" by Selena Gomez – Aazurdee dancing for Lark in the barn.

"Adore You" by Miley Cyrus – Lark and Azurdee in the barn making love and Lark tells Azurdee he loves her.

"Blurred Line" by Robin Thicke – Azurdee and Ryn dancing in the dance hall.

"Play It Again" by Luke Bryan – Lark and Azurdee dancing at the dance all and talking about Ryn.

"Why" by Jason Aldean – Ryn dancing with the cowboy while Lark jumps on Tristan for how he is treating Ryn.

"Best Night Ever" by Gloriana – Lark and Azurdee dancing on the ranch in front of the jeep.

"When You Kiss Me" by Shania Twain – Azurdee writing her letter to Lark.

"Come A Little Closer" by Lark and Azurdee dancing at the restaurant in South Padre.

"Give It 2 U" by Robin Thicke – Lark and Azurdee in her restaurant having sex in the chair.

"Not Myself Tonight" by Christina Aguilera – Lark and Azurdee in her restaurant having sex.

"Hot Tottie" by Usher – Azurdee dancing with Dodge at Red 7.

"Don't You Wanna Stay" by Jason Aldean – Azurdee dancing with Dodge and thinking about Lark.

"Leave You Alone" by Kris Allen – Lark and Azurdee outside Red 7 after Azurdee sees Lark in the club and leaves.

"This Is How We Roll" by Florida Georgia Line – Lark dancing with Lauren at Scott and Jessie's house.

"It Only Hurts When I'm Breathing" by Shania Twain – Azurdee watching Lark with Laruen at the baptism party at Scott and Jessie's.

"Say Something" by A Great Big World and Christina Aguilera – Azurdee and Lark in the barn when she tells him she has given up on them.

"From This Moment" by Shania Twain – Azurdee reading Larks letter in her house.

"Out Alive" by Kris Allen – Lark trying to get back to Azurdee after he finds out about the explosion.

"Unconditionally" by Katy Perry – Lark asking Azurdee to marry him.

"You've Got A Way" by Shania Twain – Lark and Azurdee making love and Lark cries.

"Stars Dance" by Selena Gomez – Lark at the wedding when he thinks back to when he told Azurdee he loved her.

"Dark Horse" by Katy Perry – Lark thinking how things have changed since their first dance together.

"Then" by Brad Paisley – Lark and Azurdee's wedding song.

"Hold On" by Colbie Caillet – Lark and Azurdee leaving for their honeymoon.

"Rewind" by Rascal Flatts – Lark and Azurdee's honeymoon night.